Queen Lucia

BOOKS BY E. F. BENSON

Poland
Poland and Mittel Europa
David Blaize
David Blaize and the Blue Door
David of Kings
Rex
Mother
Mapp and Lucia
Secret Lives
Travail of Gold
Lucia's Progress
Trouble for Lucia
Lucia in London
Miss Mapp (and the Male Impersonator)

E. F. Benson

Queen Lucia

Foreword by
Micheál Mac Liammóir

HEINEMANN : LONDON

William Heinemann Ltd
10 Upper Grosvenor Street, London W1X 9PA

LONDON   MELBOURNE   TORONTO
JOHANNESBURG   AUCKLAND

First published in Great Britain
1920 by Hutchinson & Co
This edition 1970

Reprinted 1976, 1986

Foreword © Micheál Mac Liammóir 1970

SBN 434 06505 6

Printed in Great Britain by
Redwood Burn Limited, Trowbridge, Wiltshire

Foreword by
Micheál Mac Liammóir

In these books, what may at first appear as a mere reportage of trivia, darkling with malice and wit as in some eighteenth-century comedy, a chronicle of the goings-on in two small and superb English country towns, swiftly reveals itself as something much more. The success of the first solo portraits of Miss Elizabeth Mapp of Tilling and of Mrs. Emmeline Lucas of Riseholme encouraged their creator to bring, at some time or another, the two ladies together—a terrifying moment for everyone—and these abstract and brief chronicles of their time, which happened to begin, as far as we are concerned, in the early years of the nineteen-twenties, grew gradually into an epic.

The delicate, deadly storms that ensue are, of course, inevitable when two such personalities are brought face to face. Molière, Goldoni, Congreve, Sheridan and Wilde have created a no more triumphantly trivial tyrant and snob than Mrs. Lucas, later in her radiant career to become Mrs. Georgie Pillson but remaining always Lucia to her friends. Wagner has given us no more ferocious Walküre, Shakespeare himself no more adamant Goneril, than Miss Elizabeth Mapp, later in her inexorable fashion to become Mrs. Benjamin Mapp-Flint, but remaining always Elizabeth to her friend Diva Plaistow, and Mapp to her tormentor Irene Coles, the painter, a gifted young lady who affects breeches and close-cropped hair, smokes a pipe, and is known to Mapp as Quaint Irene.

The portrait gallery may be limited in range; it is superlative in quality. We catch glimpses of Mapp herself at many exquisite and unexpected moments as she shops and spies and prowls and pries about the pleasant town where she has reigned so long. She is described on one occasion, when her brain is seething with the foulest schemes, as buying " six pennyworth of parsnips, deep in thought ", and we can see her vividly as she does it. Habitually, at other people's luncheon or dinner parties, she tastes a dish, shudders a little, and " hides the rest of the revolting concoction under her knife and fork ". Sometimes, however, the food is so delicious that she finds it impossible to be " good for her hostess " and hastily gobbles it up with a wry face. As if following the advice of Lady Macbeth, she manages to look like the innocent flower; a large, jocund lady with " dimpled, well nourished cheeks " and an enormous smile—rather, as Lucia pensively remarks, like the grin of a handsome hyena—and she seldom forgets, when others are present, to kiss the sweet roses in her garden as " they would scold her if she did not say good-night ".

Her lovely Queen Anne house, known as Mallards, is the social (and somewhat dubiously cultural) centre of Tilling until the advent of Lucia: " That sweet woman ", as Elizabeth calls her for the first day or two of her interminable invasion. Speedily, however, the adjective is omitted, and before long Lucia becomes known to Mapp as She. " If you meant Diva or Evie or Quaint Irene," Mr. Benson explains, " you said so. But She was Lucia."

And She, with her lofty superiority, her famous trill of silvery laughter " beginning on A flat ", her music, her Dante, her duchesses, her Italian, her psychic powers, her callisthenics, her financial speculations, her bicycle riding and her all the rest of it, swiftly proves herself an insufferable rival; and the war that rages between the two Queens and their rather fickle allies is the main background to the fantastically intricate stratagems and spoils you will find in the pages of these chronicles.

At last She actually becomes Mayor of Tilling, and with super-subtle diplomacy chooses her rival as Mayoress. " Poor Worship! I tremble to think of the mess she would have made of things by this time without me to guide her," the Mayoress confides to Diva, who immediately tells everyone, and then the dogs of war are let slip indeed. Yet, although hostilities are endless, the two ladies are seldom out of each other's sight, and frequently in each other's houses.

" Quite a nice little house-warming, dear," Elizabeth remarks to her friend Diva on the day after Lucia has given it, " and to be sure the house needed it, for I was half-frozen in the dining-room, and I strongly suspect that chicken cream of being rabbit."

Mr. E. F. Benson, who has written what I imagine to be the most penetrating historical studies in the English language of such oddly contrasted figures as Alcibiades and Charlotte Brontë (what would Miss Brontë have said to that, I wonder?), was also the author of a score or so of distinguished and diverting novels, of some superbly terrifying ghost tales, and the creator, in 1894, of the nimble-tongued, illustrious Dodo. Yet he gave no hint until the dawn of the nineteen-twenties of the merciless dissecting knife he uses so unnervingly in these inimitably English portraits of the busy, shallow, shamelessly respectable, ecstatically inquisitive schemers and plotters, who, in spite of their age—Quaint Irene is the only prominent character in the book who is not well past forty and often fifty—flutter and bustle with such zest through the pages. Everyone seems to have attained a smouldering maturity, unless one accepts the world-famous soprano, Olga Braceley, as being young; and she, although any mention of her years is chivalrously avoided by the author, can hardly be regarded as a girl. For has she not for countless seasons been taking the world, as she takes Mr. Benson and us, by storm with her beauty, her even good temper, her generosity—such a contrast to Elizabeth—her maquillage, her free and easy ways, and her extraordinary power of singing it would seem every great rôle in every sort of opera, from " Elektra " to " Donna-Elvira ", from " Isolde " to " Madam Butterfly "? She is the only ideal figure in the book, as poor Georgie Pillson is the only other good-natured one. Georgie is not ideal, but he is nice: he collects bibelots and dusts them himself, does little water-colours and charming embroidery and becomes, in time, a devoted second husband—in name only, for his attitude to his wife is more that of an affectionate sister than a suitor—to Lucia. Apart, indeed, from Olga and Georgie, these studies form a tapestry of early-twentieth-century Candours and Backbites and Snakes. The only character who has the elements even of common honesty is the downright Diva, who actually says, as a rule, what she thinks, and whose face, when for a moment she is not being truthful, invariably turns " a rich crimson ". All the rest are swept here and there by the frolic winds of sheer villainy, and for those readers, mostly feminine, who whisper " misogynist " as they read, it would be well to remind themselves that Mr. Benson is quite as remorseless about members of his own sex. One has only to think of Major Benjamin Flint with his secret boozing

and his appalling lies about tiger-shooting in India; of
dear Georgie with his *petit point* and his lamentable
schemings; of the Padre from Birmingham with his
Highland accent, his sedulous running with hare and
hounds; of Algernon Wyse with his monumental
snobbery and ghastly good taste, to understand that the
author is singularly free of sexual prejudice, and that if
we grow indignant as we laugh at these flutterpates, and
laugh again as we attempt to reject them as caricatures
of man and womankind alike, it may be because we
recognize somewhere in ourselves the awful truth of the
portraiture.

* * *

Elizabeth Mapp, at some moment of more than
usually palsied fury, fell one evening into a doze by the
fire and " had a pleasant dream that Dr. Dobbie had just
popped in to tell her that Lucia had developed unmistakable symptoms of leprosy ".

I myself, as I read and reread those studies of men and
women who had become as real to me—as they have
become real to many—as any friend or acquaintance,
was growing a little restive under the stream of inevitable
victories for Lucia. Luciaphil as I was, I yet had my
secret admiration too for the fell Elizabeth (at certain
moments one prefers Wagner to Mozart); and my
partner Hilton Edwards and I persuaded a number of
actors and actresses in our Gate Theatre in Dublin to
join their names to ours in sending a round robin to the
author demanding some ultimate triumph, however
trivial, for Mayoress Mapp-Flint. The letter was written
and many names were signed, but before the invitations
to various possible sympathisers in England and America
to join in the cause were ready for the post, the news
came through of the death of E. F. Benson.

I had never met him and knew but few of his friends,

yet I was deeply saddened, and one night I dreamed of
him. It was, in my dream, a summer morning in
Tilling. There were the grass-grown cobbles, the hilly
streets with their Elizabethan, Queen Anne and Georgian
houses, the gentle breeze from the English Channel, the
crooked chimneys and irregular corners, the trees
throwing cool shadows here and there; and then I
seemed to be in the High Street among groups of Tilling's
leading characters. And to them Elizabeth Mapp-Flint
herself appeared suddenly in great agitation, her shopping basket in her hand; darting across the street to Diva
who was coming out of Twistevant's shop, she whispered
something in Diva's ear. Major Benjy, unusually silent,
stood at his wife's side.

" No!" said Diva and whirled away with a sudden
curious dragging gait to tell what she had heard.

The groups drew closer together as the news went
round. The Wyses' great lumbering Royce came to a
standstill.

" No!" said Susan Wyse as, looking out of the window,
she received the information. " Oh, Algernon!" she
cried and turned to her husband to whisper in his ear
what had happened. Algernon said no word but sat
staring in front of him.

" No!" said Quaint Irene when she had heard.
" You're lying, Mapp. As usual."

" No, Quaint One!" Elizabeth said in a voice that
dwindled oddly. " It is all too true."

" No!" said the Padre and Wee Wifie together. They
turned to look at each other with stricken faces.

At last, Elizabeth, who was feeling cold in spite of the
genial morning, caught sight of Lucia and Georgie on
their bicycles. " Lucia," she whispered—the words
came with difficulty from her mouth—" have you
heard?"

And she told them. Without comment. They dismounted silently.

" No! " said Georgie at last and said no more.

" Not Mr. Benson? " Lucia murmured after a pause.

She propped her bicycle against the curbstone. She was horribly pale.

" Oh, Georgie! " she said at last. " Oh, Elizabeth! What is going to *happen* to all of us? "

And in my dream, the Comedians of Tilling stood, phantomlike under the morning sun, motionless as stone, smitten by immortality.

QUEEN LUCIA

CHAPTER I

THOUGH the sun was hot on this July morning, Mrs.
Lucas preferred to cover the half-mile that lay between
the station and her house on her own feet, and sent
on her maid and her luggage in the fly that her husband had ordered to meet her. After those four hours
in the train a short walk would be pleasant; but,
though she veiled it from her conscious mind, another
motive, subconsciously entertained, prompted her
action. It would, of course, be universally known
to all her friends in Riseholme that she was arriving
to-day by the 12.26, and at that hour the village street
would be sure to be full of them, and they would see
the fly with luggage draw up at the door of The Hurst,
and nobody except her maid would get out.

That would be an interesting thing for them : it
would cause one of those little thrills of pleasant
excitement and conjecture which daily supplied
Riseholme with its emotional bread. They would
all wonder what had happened to her, whether
she had been taken ill at the very last moment before
leaving town, and with her well-known fortitude and
consideration for the feelings of others, had sent her

maid on to assure her husband that he need not be
anxious. That would clearly be Mrs. Quantock's
suggestion, for Mrs. Quantock's mind, devoted as it
was now to the study of Christian Science, and the
determination to deny the existence of pain, disease
and death as regards herself, was always full of the
gloomiest views as regards her friends, and on the
slightest excuse, conjectured that they, poor blind
things, were suffering from false claims. Indeed, given
that the fly had already arrived at The Hurst, and that
its arrival had at this moment been seen by or
reported to Daisy Quantock, the chances were vastly
in favour of that lady's having already started in to
give her absent treatment. Very likely Georgie
Pillson had also seen the anticlimax of the fly's arrival,
but he would hazard a much more probable though
erroneous solution of her absence. He would certainly
guess that she had sent her maid with her luggage on
to the station to take her place for her, while she herself, oblivious of the passage of time, was spending her
last half-hour in contemplation of the Italian masterpieces at the National Gallery, or the Greek bronzes
at the British Museum. Certainly she would not be at
the Royal Academy, for the culture of Riseholme, led
by herself, rejected as valueless all artistic efforts later
than the death of Sir Joshua Reynolds, and a great
deal of what went before. . . . Her husband, on the
other hand, with his firm grasp of the obvious, would
be disappointingly capable, even before her maid confirmed his conjecture, of concluding that she had merely
walked from the station.

The motive, then, that made her send her cab on,
though subconsciously generated, soon penetrated
into her consciousness, and these guesses at what
other people would think when they saw it arrive

without her, sprang from the dramatic instincts that
formed so large a part of her mentality, and made her
always take, as by right divine, the leading part in
the histrionic entertainments with which the cultured
of Riseholme beguiled, or rather strenuously occupied,
such moments that could be spared from their studies
of art and literature, and their social engagements.
Indeed, she did not usually stop at taking the leading
part, but, if possible, doubled another character with
it, as well as being stage-manager and adapter, if not
designer of scenery. Whatever she did (and really
she did an incredible deal), she did it with all the might
of her dramatic perceptions—did it, in fact, with such
earnestness that she had not time to have an eye to
the gallery at all : she simply contemplated herself
and her own strenuousness. When she played the
piano, as she frequently did, reserving an hour for
practice every day, she cared not in the smallest degree
for what anybody who passed down the road outside
her house might be thinking of the roulades that poured
from her open window : she was simply Emmeline
Lucas, absorbed in glorious Bach, or dainty Scarlatti,
or noble Beethoven. The latter, perhaps, was her
favourite composer, and many were the evenings
when, with lights quenched, and only the soft
effulgence of the moon pouring in through the un-
curtained windows, she sat with her profile, cameo-
like (or liker perhaps to the head on a postage-stamp),
against the dark-oak walls of her music-room, and
entranced herself and her listeners, if there were
people to dinner, with the exquisite pathos of the
first movements of the " Moonlight Sonata." Devo-
tedly as she worshipped the Master, whose picture
hung above her Steinway Grand, she could never bring
herself to believe that the two succeeding movements

were on the same astounding level as the first, and, besides, they " went " very much faster. But she had seriously thought, as she came down in the train to-day, and planned her fresh activities at home, of trying to master them, so that she could get through their intricacies with tolerable accuracy. Until then, she would assuredly stop at the end of the first movement, in these moonlit séances, and say that the other two were more like morning and afternoon. Then with a sigh she would softly shut the piano-lid, and perhaps wiping a little genuine moisture from her eyes, would turn on the electric light, and taking up a book from the table, in which a paper-knife marked the extent of her penetration, say : " Georgie, you must really promise me to read this life of Antonio Caporelli the moment I have finished it. I never understood the rise of the Venetian School before. I can smell the salt tide creeping up over the lagoon, and see the campanile of dear Torcello."

And Georgie would put down the tambour on which he was working his copy drawn from a design on an Italian cope and sigh too.

" You are too wonderful ! " he would say. " How do you find time for everything ? "

She rejoined with the apophthegm that made the rounds of Riseholme next day :

" My dear, it is just busy people who have time for everything."

It might be thought that even such activities as have been here indicated would be enough to occupy anyone so busily that she would positively not have time for more, but such was far from being the case with Mrs. Lucas. Just as the painter Rubens amused himself with being Ambassador to the Court of St.

James's (a sufficient career in itself for most busy men), so Mrs. Lucas amused herself, in the intervals of her pursuit of Art for Art's sake, with being not only an ambassador but a monarch. Riseholme might perhaps, according to the crude materialism of maps, be included in the kingdom of Great Britain, but in a more real and inward sense it formed a complete kingdom of its own, and its queen was undoubtedly Mrs. Lucas, who ruled it with a secure autocracy pleasant to contemplate at a time when thrones were toppling, and imperial crowns whirling like dead leaves down the autumn winds. The ruler of Riseholme, happier than he of Russia, had no need to fear the heady poison of Bolshevism, for there was not in the whole of that vat, which seethed so pleasantly with culture, one bubble of revolutionary ferment. Here there was neither poverty nor discontent nor muttered menace of any upheaval. Mrs. Lucas, busy and serene, worked harder than any of her subjects, and exercised a control that was both popular and autocratic.

Something of the consciousness of her sovereignty was in her mind, as she turned the last hot corner of the road and came in sight of the village street that constituted her kingdom. Indeed, it belonged to her, as treasure-trove belongs to the Crown, for it was she who had been the first to begin the transformation of this remote Elizabethan village into the palace of culture that was now reared on the spot where ten years ago an agricultural population had led their bovine and unilluminated lives in these grey stone or brick-and-timber cottages. Before that, while her husband amassed a fortune, respectable in amount as in origin, at the Bar, she had merely held up a small but unwavering lamp of culture in Onslow Gardens. But both

her ambition and his had been to bask and be busy under
artistic skies when the materialistic needs were provided for by sound investments. So when there were
sufficient thousands of pounds in firm securities,
she had easily persuaded him to buy three of these
cottages that stood together in a low two-storied
block, and had, by judicious removal of partition
walls, transmuted them into a most comfortable
dwelling, subsequently adding on a new wing running
out at right-angles at the back, which was, if anything, a shade more blatantly Elizabethan than the
stem on to which it was grafted, for here was situated
the famous smoking-parlour, with rushes on the
floor, a dresser ranged with pewter tankards, and
leaded lattice-windows of glass so antique that it was
practically impossible to see out of them. It had a
huge open fireplace framed in oak beams, with a seat
on each side of the iron-backed hearth within the
chimney, and an iron spit hung over the middle of
the fire. Here, though in the rest of the house she
had, for the sake of convenience, allowed the installa-
tion of electric light, there was no such concession
made, and sconces on the walls held dim iron lamps,
so that only those of the most acute vision were able
to read. Even to them reading was difficult, for the
book-stand on the table contained nothing but a
few crabbed black-letter volumes dating from not
later than the early seventeenth century, and you had
to be in a fanatically Elizabethan frame of mind to
be at ease there. But Mrs. Lucas often spent rare
leisure moments there, playing on the virginal that
stood in the window, or kippering herself in the smoke
of the wood-fire as with streaming eyes she deci-
phered an Elzevir Horace, rather late for inclusion
under the rule, but an undoubted bargain.

The house stood at that end of the village which was nearest the station ; and thus, when the panorama of her kingdom opened before her, she had but a few steps further to go. A yew-hedge, bought entire from a neighbouring farm, and transplanted with solid lumps of earth and indignant snails around its roots, separated the small oblong of garden from the road, and cast monstrous shadows of the shapes into which it was cut, across the little lawn inside. Here, as was only right and proper, there was not a flower to be found save such as were mentioned in the plays of Shakespeare : indeed, it was called Shakespeare's garden, and the bed that ran below the windows of the dining-room was Ophelia's border, for it consisted solely of those flowers which that distraught maiden distributed to her friends when she should have been in a lunatic asylum. Mrs. Lucas often reflected how lucky it was that such institutions were unknown in Elizabeth's day. Pansies, naturally, formed the chief decoration (though there were some very flourishing plants of rue), and Mrs. Lucas always wore a little bunch of them when in flower, to inspire her thoughts, and found them wonderfully efficacious. Round the sundial, which was set in the middle of one of the squares of grass between which a path of broken paving-stones led to the front-door, was a circular border, now, in July, sadly vacant, for it harboured only the spring flowers enumerated by Perdita. But the first day every year when Perdita's border put forth its earliest blossom was a delicious anniversary, and the news of it spread like wildfire through Mrs. Lucas's kingdom, and her subjects were very joyful, and came to salute the violet or daffodil, or whatever it was.

The three cottages dexterously transformed into

The Hurst, presented a charmingly irregular and
picturesque front. Two were of the grey stone of the
district, and the middle one, to the door of which led
the paved path, of brick and timber. Latticed windows with stout mullions gave illumination to the room
within, and to the original windows certain new lights
had been added ; these could be detected by the
observant eye, for they had a markedly older appearance than the rest. The front-door, similarly, seemed
amazingly antique, the fact being that the one which
Mrs. Lucas had found there was too dilapidated to
be of the slightest service in keeping out wind and
wet. She had therefore caused to be constructed an
even older one made from oak planks in a dismantled
barn, and had it studded with large iron nails of
antique pattern fashioned by the village blacksmith.
He had arranged some of them to look as if they
spelled A.D. 1603. Over the door hung an inn-sign,
and into the space where once the sign had swung was
now inserted a lantern, in which was ensconced, well
hidden from view by its patinated glass sides, an
electric light. This was one of the necessary con-
cessions to modern convenience, for no lamp nurtured
on oil would pierce those genuinely opaque panes,
and illuminate the path to the gate. Better to have
an electric light than cause your guests to take a header
into Perdita's border. By the side of this fortress-door
hung a heavy iron bell-pull, ending in a mermaid.
When Mrs. Lucas had that first installed, it was a
bell-pull in the sense that an extremely athletic man
could, if he used both hands and planted his feet firmly,
cause it to act, and a huge bronze bell swung in the
servants' passage, and eventually gave tongue (if the
athlete continued pulling) with vibrations so sonorous
that the whitewash from the ceiling fell down in

flakes. She had therefore made another concession to the frailty of the present generation and the inconvenience of having whitewash falling into cold dishes on their way to the dining-room, and now at the back of the mermaid's tail was a little bone button, coloured black and practically invisible, and thus the bell-pull had been converted into an electric bell-push. In this way visitors could make their advent known without violent exertion, the mermaid lost no visible whit of her Elizabethan virginity, and the spirit of Shakespeare wandering in his garden would not notice any anachronism.

Though Mrs. Lucas's parents had bestowed the name of Emmeline on her, it was not to be wondered at that she was always known among the more intimate of her subjects as Lucia, pronounced, of course, in the Italian mode (*la Lucia*, the wife of Lucas), and it was as *Lucia mia* that her husband hailed her as he met her at the door of The Hurst. He had been watching for her arrival through the panes of the parlour while he meditated upon one of the little prose-poems which formed so delectable a contribution to the culture of Riseholme ; for though, as has been hinted, he had in practical life a firm grasp of the obvious, there were windows in his soul which looked out on to vague and ethereal prospects which so far from being obvious were only dimly intelligible. In form these odes were cast in the loose rhythm of Walt Whitman, but their smooth suavity and their contents bore no resemblance whatever to the productions of that barbaric bard, for no one thought of Walt Whitman as anything but a crude, rude American. Already a couple of volumes of these prose-poems had been published, not of course in the hard, business-like establishments of London, but at " Ye Sign of Ye

Daffodil," on the village green, where type was set
up by hand, and very little, but that of the best, was
printed. The press had only been recently started
at Mr. Lucas's expense. But it had put forth a
reprint of Shakespeare's sonnets already, as well as
his own poems. They were printed in blunt type on
thick yellowish paper, the edges of which seemed as if
they had been cut by the forefinger of an impatient
reader, so ragged and irregular were they, and they
were bound in vellum. The titles of these two slim
flowers of poetry, " Flotsam " and " Jetsam," were
printed on the outside in black-letter type, and the
covers were further adorned with a sort of embossed
seal, and with antique-looking tapes, so that you
could tie it all up with two bows when you had
finished with Mr. Lucas's " Flotsam " for the time
being, and turned to " Jetsam."

To-day the prose-poem on " Loneliness " had not
been getting on very well, and Philip Lucas was glad
to hear the click of the garden-gate, which showed
that his loneliness was over for the present, and,
looking up, he saw his wife's figure waveringly presented to his eyes through the twisted and knotty
glass of the parlour window, which had taken so long
to collect, but which now completely replaced the
plain, commonplace, unrefracting stuff which was
there before. He jumped up with an alacrity remarkable in so solid and well-furnished a person, and had
thrown open the nail-studded front-door long before
Lucia had traversed the path of broken paving-stones,
for she had lingered at Perdita's border.

" *Lucia mia !* " he exclaimed. " *Ben arrivata !*
So you walked from the station."

" *Si, Peppino, mio caro,*" she said. " *Sta bene ?* "

He kissed her, and relapsed into Shakespeare's

tongue, for their Italian, though firm and perfect as
far as it went, could not be considered as going far,
and was useless for conversational purposes, unless
they merely wanted to greet each other, or to know
the time. But it was interesting to talk Italian,
however little way it went.

" *Molto bene*," said he, " and it's delightful to
have you home again. And how was London ? "
he asked, in the sort of tone in which he might have
inquired after the health of a poor relation who was
not likely to recover.

She smiled rather sadly.

" Terrifically busy about nothing," she said. " All
this fortnight I have scarcely had a moment to myself.
Lunches, dinners, parties of all kinds : I could not go
to half the gatherings I was bidden to. Dear South
Kensington ! "

" *Carissima*, when London does manage to catch
you, it is no wonder they all make the most of you,"
said he. " You mustn't blame them for that."

" No, dear, I don't. Everyone was tremendously
kind and hospitable : they all did their best. If I
blame anyone, I blame myself. But I think this
Riseholme life with its finish and its exquisiteness
spoils one for other places. London is like a railway-
junction : it has no true life of its own. There is no
delicacy, no appreciation of fine shades. Indivi-
dualism has no existence there : everyone gabbles
together, gabbles and gobbles. If there is a concert
in a private house—you know my views about music,
and the impossibility of hearing music at all, if you
are stuck in the middle of a row of people—even then
the moment it is over you are whisked away to supper.
There is always a crowd ; there is always food ; you
cannot be alone, and it is only in loneliness, as

Goethe says, that perceptions put forth their flowers. No one in London has time to listen : they are all thinking about who is there and who isn't there, and what is the next thing. The exquisite present, as you put it in one of your poems, has no existence there : it is always the feverish future."

"Delicious phrase ! I should have stolen that gem for my poor poem if you had discovered it before."

She was too much used to this incense to do more than sniff it in unconsciously, and she went on with her tremendous indictment.

" It isn't that I find fault with London for being so busy," she said with strict impartiality, " for if being busy was a crime, I am sure there are few of us here who would 'scape hanging. But take my life here, or yours for that matter—well, mine if you like. Often and often I am alone from breakfast till lunch-time, but in those hours I get through more that is worth doing than London gets through all day and night. I have an hour at my music, not looking about and wondering who my neighbours are, but learning, studying, drinking in divine melody. Then I have my letters to write, and you know what that means, and I still have time for an hour's reading, so that when you come to tell me lunch is ready, you will find that I have been wandering through Venetian churches, or sitting in that little dark room at Weimar, or was it Leipzig ? How would those same hours have passed in London ? Sitting perhaps for half an hour in the Park, with dearest Aggie pointing out to me with thrills of breathless excitement a woman who was in the divorce court, or a coronetted bankrupt. Then she would drag me off to some terrible private view full of the same people all staring and gabbling

at each other, or looking at pictures that made poor
me gasp and shudder. No, I am thankful to be back
at my own sweet Riseholme again. I can work and
think here."

She looked round the panelled entrance-hall with
a glow of warm content at being at home again that
quite eclipsed the mere physical heat produced by
her walk from the station. Wherever her eyes fell,
those sharp, dark eyes that resembled buttons covered
with shiny American cloth, they saw nothing that
jarred, as so much in London jarred. There were
bright brass jugs on the window-sill, a bowl of pot-
pourri on the black table in the centre, an oak settee
by the open fireplace, a couple of Persian rugs on the
polished floor. The room had its quaintnesses too,
such as she had alluded to in her memorable essay
read before the Riseholme Literary Society, called
" Humour in Furniture," and a brass milk-can served
as a receptacle for sticks and umbrellas. Equally
quaint was the dish of highly realistic stone fruit
that stood beside the potpourri, and the furry Japanese
spider in a silk web over the window. Such was
the fearful verisimilitude of this that Lucia's new
housemaid had once fled from her duties in the early
morning, to seek the assistance of the gardener in
killing it. The dish of stone fruit had scored a similar
success, for once she had said to Georgie Pillson :
" Ah, my gardener has sent in some early apples and
pears—won't you take one home with you ? " It
was not till the weight of the pear (he swiftly selected
the largest) betrayed the joke that he had any notion
that they were not real ones. But then Georgie had
had his revenge, for waiting his opportunity he had
inserted a real pear among those stony specimens,
and again passing through with Lucia, he had picked

it out, and with lips drawn back had snapped at it
with all the force of his jaws. For the moment
she had felt quite faint at the thought of his teeth
crashing into fragments. . . . These humorous touches
were altered from time to time ; the spider, for instance,
might be taken down and replaced by a china canary
in a Chippendale cage, and the selection of the entrance-
hall for those whimsicalities was intentional, for guests
found something to smile at, as they took off their
cloaks and entered the drawing-room with a topic
on their lips, something light, something amusing
about what they had seen. For the gong similarly
was sometimes substituted a set of bells that had
once decked the collar of the leading horse in a wag-
goner's team somewhere in Flanders : in fact, when
Lucia was at home there was often a new little quaint-
ness for quite a sequence of days, and she had held
out hopes to the Literary Society that perhaps some
day, when she was not so rushed, she would jot down
material for a sequel to her essay, or write another
covering a rather larger field on " Gambits of Conversation derived from Furniture."

On the table there was a pile of letters waiting for
Mrs. Lucas, for yesterday's posts had not been for-
warded her for fear of their missing her (London
postmen were probably very careless and untrust-
worthy), and she gave a little cry of dismay as she
saw them.

"But I shall be very naughty," she said, " and
not look at one of them till after lunch. Take them
away, *caro*, and promise me to lock them up till then,
and not give me them, however much I beg. Then I
will get into the saddle again, such a dear saddle, too,
and tackle them. I shall have a stroll in the garden
till the bell rings. What is it that Nietzsche says about

the necessity to *Mediterranize* yourself every now and then ? I must *Riseholme* myself."

Peppino remembered the quotation, which had occurred in a review of some work of that celebrated author, where Lucia had also seen it, and went back, with the force of contrast to aid him, to his prose-poem of " Loneliness," while his wife went through the smoking-parlour into the garden, in order to soak herself once more in the cultured atmosphere. In this garden behind the house there was no attempt to construct a Shakespearian plot, for, as she so rightly observed, Shakespeare, who loved flowers so well, would wish her to enjoy every conceivable horti-cultural treasure. But furniture played a prominent part in the place, and there were statues and sun-dials and stone seats scattered about with almost too profuse a hand. Mottoes also were in great evidence, and while a sundial reminded you that *Tempus fugit,* an enticing resting-place somewhat bewilderingly bade you " Bide a wee." But then, again, the rustic seat in the pleached alley of labur-nums had carved on its back, " Much have I travelled in the realms of gold," so that meditating on Keats, you could bide a wee with a clear conscience. Indeed, so copious was the wealth of familiar and stimulating quotations, that one of her subjects had once said that a stroll in Lucia's garden was not only to enjoy her lovely flowers, but to spend a simultaneous half-hour with the best authors.

There was a dovecote of course, but since the cats always killed the doves, Mrs. Lucas had put up round the desecrated home several pigeons of Copenhagen china, which were both immortal as regards cats and also carried on the suggestion of humour in furniture. The humour had attained the highest point of felicity

when Peppino concealed a mechanical nightingale
in a bush, which sang " Jug-jug " in the most realistic
manner when you pulled a string. Georgie had not
yet seen the Copenhagen pigeons, and, being rather
short-sighted, thought they were real. Then, oh,
then, Peppino pulled the string, and for quite a long
time Georgie listened entranced to their melodious
cooings. That served him out for his " trap " about
the real pear introduced among the stone specimens.
For in spite of the rarefied atmosphere of culture at
Riseholme, Riseholme knew how to *desipere in loco*,
and its strenuous culture was often refreshed by these
light refined touches.

Mrs. Lucas walked quickly and decisively up and
down the paths as she waited for the summons to
lunch ; the activity of her mind reacted on her body,
making her brisk in movement. On each side of her
forehead were hard, neat undulations of black hair,
that concealed the tops of her ears. She had laid
aside her London hat, and carried a red cotton Conta-
dina's umbrella, which threw a rosy glow on the
oval of her thin face, with its colourless complexion.
She bore the weight of her forty years extremely
lightly, and but for the droop of skin at the corners of
her tight and compressed mouth, she might have
passed as a much younger woman. Her face was
otherwise unlined, and bore no trace of the ravages
of emotional living, which both ages and softens.
Certainly there was nothing soft about her, and very
little of the signs of age, and it would have been
reasonable to conjecture that twenty years later she
would look but little older than she did to-day.
Such emotions as she was victim of were the sterile
and ageless ecstasies of art ; such desires as beset
her were not connected with her affections, but her

ambitions. Dynasty she had none, for she was child-
less, and thus her ambitions were limited to the per-
manence and security of her own throne as Queen of
Riseholme. She really asked nothing more of life
than the continuance of such harvests as she had so
plenteously reaped for those last ten years. As long
as she directed the life of Riseholme, took the lead in
its culture and entertainment, was the undisputed
fountain-head of all its inspirations, and from time
to time refreshed her memory as to the utter inferiority
of London, she wanted nothing more. But to secure
that she dedicated all that she had of ease, leisure
and income. Being practically indefatigable, the loss
of ease and leisure troubled her but little, and being
in extremely comfortable circumstances, the question
of money did not trouble her. She might easily look
forward to enjoying an unchanging middle-aged
activity, while generations of youth withered round
her, and no star, remotely rising, had as yet threatened
to dim her unrivalled effulgence. Though essentially
autocratic, her subjects were allowed and even
encouraged to develop their own minds on their own
lines, provided always that those lines met at the
junction where she was station-master. With regard
to religion, finally, it may be briefly said that she
believed in God in much the same way as she believed
in Australia, for she had no doubts whatever as to
the existence of either, and she went to church on
Sunday in much the same spirit as she would look at a
kangaroo in the Zoological Gardens, for kangaroos
came from Australia.

A low wall separated the far end of her garden from
the meadow outside ; beyond that lay the stream
which flowed into the Avon, and it often seemed
wonderful to her that the water which wimpled by

would (unless a cow happened to drink it) soon be
stealing along past the church at Stratford where
Shakespeare lay. Peppino had written a very moving
little prose-poem about it, for she had royally presented him with the idea, and had suggested a beautiful analogy between the earthly dew that refreshed
the flowers, and was drawn up by the fire of the sun,
and Thought, the spiritual dew, that refreshed the
mind, and thereafter, rather vaguely, was drawn up
into the Full-orbed Soul of the World. . . .

At that moment her eye was attracted by an
apparition on the road which lay adjacent to the
further side of the happy stream which flowed into the
Avon. There was no mistaking the identity of the
stout figure of Mrs. Quantock, with its short steps and
its gesticulations, but why, in the name of wonder,
should that Christian Scientist be walking with the
draped and turbaned figure of a man with a tropical
complexion and a black beard ? His robe of saffron-
yellow, with a violently green girdle, was hitched
up for ease in walking, and unless he had chocolate-
coloured stockings on, Mrs. Lucas saw human legs
of the same shade. Next moment that debatable
point was set at rest, for she caught sight of short
pink socks in red slippers. . . . Even as she looked,
Mrs. Quantock saw her (for owing to Christian Science
she had recaptured the quick vision of youth), and
waggled her hand and kissed it, and evidently called
her companion's attention, for next moment he was
salaaming to her in some stately Oriental manner.
There was nothing to be done for the moment except
to return these salutations, as she could not yell an
aside to Mrs. Quantock, screaming out " Who is
that Indian ? " for if Mrs. Quantock heard, that
Indian would hear too ; but as soon as she could

she turned back towards the house again, and when
once the lilac-bushes were between her and the road
she walked with more than her usual speed, in order
to learn with the shortest possible delay from Peppino
who this fresh subject of hers could be. She knew
there were some Indian princes in London : perhaps
it was one of them, in which case it would be necessary
to read up Benares or Delhi in the Encyclopædia
without loss of time.

CHAPTER II

As she traversed the smoking-parlour the cheerful
sounds that had once tinkled from the collar of a
Flemish horse chimed through the house, and simultaneously she became aware that there would be
macaroni au gratin for lunch, which was very dear
and remembering of Peppino. But before setting
fork to her piled-up plate, she had to question him,
for her mental craving for information was far keener
than her appetite for food.

" *Caro*, who is an Indian," she asked, " whom I
saw just now with Daisy Quantock? They were
walking on the other side of *il piccolo Avono*."

Peppino had already begun his macaroni and must
pause to shovel the outlying strings of it into his
mouth. But the haste with which he did so was
sufficient guarantee for his eagerness to reply as soon
as it was humanly possible to do so.

" Indian, my dear? " he asked with the greatest
interest.

" Yes ; turban and burnous and calves and
slippers," she said rather impatiently, for what was
the good of Peppino having remained in Riseholme,
if he could not give her precise and certain information on local news when she returned? His prose-
poems were all very well, but as prince-consort he
had other duties of state which must not be neglected
for the calls of Art.

This slight asperity on her part seemed to sharpen his wits.

" Really, I don't know for certain, Lucia," he said, " for I have not set eyes on him.   But putting two and two together, I might make a guess."

" Two and two make four," she said, with that irony for which she was feared and famous.   " Now for your guess.   I hope it is equally accurate."

" Well, as I told you in one of my letters," said he, " Mrs. Quantock showed signs of being a little off with Christian Science.   She had a cold, and though she recited the ' True Statement of Being ' just as frequently as before, her cold got no better.   But when I saw her on Tuesday last, unless it was Wednesday— no, it couldn't have been Wednesday, so it must have been Tuesday——"

" Whenever it was then," interrupted his wife, brilliantly summing up his indecision.

" Yes, whenever it was, as you say, on that occasion Mrs. Quantock was very full of some Indian philosophy which made you quite well at once. What did she call it, now ?   Yoga ! Yes, that was it ! "

" And then ? " asked Lucia.

" Well, it appears you must have a teacher in Yoga, or else you may injure yourself.   You have to breathe deeply and say ' Om '——"

" Say what ? "

" ' Om.'   I understood the ejaculation to be ' Om.' And there are very curious physical exercises : you have to hold your ear with one hand and your toes with the other, and you may strain yourself unless you do it properly.   That was the general gist of it."

" And shall we come to the Indian soon ? " said Lucia.

" *Carissima*, you have come to him already.   I

suggest that Mrs. Quantock has applied for a teacher and got him. *Ecco !* "

Mrs. Lucas wore a heavily corrugated forehead at this news. Peppino had a wonderful *flair* in explaining unusual circumstances in the life of Riseholme, and his conjectures were generally correct. But if he was right in this instance, it struck Lucia as being a very irregular thing that anyone should have imported a mystical Indian into Riseholme without consulting her. It is true ·that she had been away, but still there was the medium of the post.

" *Ecco*, indeed ! " she said. " It puts me in rather a difficult position, for I must send out the invitations to my garden-party to-day, and I really don't know whether I ought to be officially aware of this man's existence or not. I can't write to Daisy Quantock and say ' Pray bring your black friend Om,' or whatever his name proves to be, and on the other hand, if he is the sort of person whom one would be sorry to miss, I should not like to have passed over him."

" After all, my dear, you have only been back in Riseholme half an hour," said her husband. " It would have been difficult for Mrs. Quantock to have told you yet."

Her face cleared.

" Perhaps Daisy has written to me about him," she said. " I may find a full account of it all when I open my letters."

" Depend upon it you will. She would hardly have been so wanting in proper feeling as not to have told you. I think, too, that her visitor must only have just arrived, or I should have been sure to see him about somewhere."

She rose.

" Well, we will see," she said. " Now I shall be

very busy all afternoon, but by tea-time I shall be ready to see anyone who calls. Give me my letters, *caro*, and I will find out if Daisy has written to me."

She turned them over as she went to her room, and there among them was a bulky envelope addressed in Mrs. Quantock's great sprawling hand, which looked at first sight so large and legible, but on closer examination turned out to be so baffling. You had to hold it at some distance off to make anything out of it, and look at it in an abstracted and general manner much as you would look at a view. Treated thus, scattered words began to leap into being, and when you had got a sufficiency of these, like glimpses of the country seen by flashes of lightning, you could hope to get a collective idea of it all. This procedure led to the most promising results as Mrs. Lucas sat with the sheets at arm's length, occasionally altering the range to try the effect of a different focus. " Benares " blinked at her, also " Brahmin " ; also " highest caste," " extraordinary sanctity " and " Guru." And when the meaning of the latter was ascertained from the article on " Yoga " in her Encyclopædia, she progressed very swiftly towards a complete comprehension of the letter.

The letter, when fully pieced together, was certainly enough to rivet her whole attention, and make her leave unopened the rest of her correspondence, for such a prelude to adventure had seldom sounded in Riseholme. It appeared, even as her husband had told her at lunch, that Mrs. Quantock found her cold too obstinate for all the precepts of Mrs. Eddy ; the " True Statement of Being," however often repeated, only seemed to inflame it further, and one day, when confined to the house, she had taken a book " quite at random " from the shelves in her library, under, she supposed, the influence of some interior compulsion. This then was clearly a " leading."

Mrs. Lucas paused a moment as she pieced together these first sentences. She seemed to remember that Mrs. Quantock had experienced a similar leading when first she took up Christian Science. That day it was a leading from the sight of a new church off Sloane Street ; Mrs. Quantock had entered (she scarcely knew why), and had found herself in a Testimony Meeting, where witness after witness declared the miraculous healings they had experienced. One had had a cough, another cancer, another a fractured bone, but all had been cured by the blessed truths conveyed in the Gospel according to Mrs. Eddy. However, Lucia's memories on this subject were not to the point now : she burned to arrive at the story of the new leading.

Well, the book that Mrs. Quantock had taken down in obedience to the last leading proved to be a little hand-book of Oriental Philosophies, and it opened all of its own accord at a chapter called " Yoga." Instantly she perceived, as by the unclosing of an inward eye, that Yoga was what she wanted, and she instantly wrote to the address from which the book was issued, asking for any guidance on the subject. She had read in " Oriental Philosophies " that for the successful practice of Yoga it was necessary to have a teacher, and did they know of any teacher who could give her instruction ? A wonderful answer came to that, for two days afterwards her maid came to her and said that an Indian gentleman would like to see her. He was ushered in, and with a profound obeisance, said : " Beloved lady : I am the teacher you asked for : I am your Guru. Peace be to this house ! Om ! "

Mrs. Lucas had by this time got her view of Mrs. Quantock's letter into perfect focus, and she read on without missing a word :

" Is it not wonderful, dearest Lucia," it ran, " that my desire for light should have been so instantly answered ? And yet my Guru tells me that it always happens so. I was sent to him, and he was sent to me, just like that ! He had been expecting some call when my letter asking for guidance came, and he started at once because he knew he was sent. Fancy ! I don't even know his name, and his religion forbids him to tell it me. He is just my Guru, my guide, and he is going to be with me as long as he knows I need him to show me the True Path. He has the spare bedroom and the little room adjoining, where he meditates and does Prana and Pranayama, which is breathing. If you persevere in them under instruction, you have perfect health and youth, and my cold is gone already. He is a Brahmin of the very highest caste ; indeed, caste means nothing to him any longer, just as a Baronet and an Honourable must seem about the same thing to the King. He comes from Benares, where he used to meditate all day by the Ganges, and I can see for myself that he is a person of the most extraordinary sanctity. But he can meditate just as well in my little room, for he says he was never in any house that had such a wonderful atmosphere. He has no money at all, which is so beautiful of him, and looked so pained and disappointed when I asked him if I might not give him some. He doesn't even know how he got here from London ; he doesn't think he came by train ; so perhaps he was wafted here in some astral manner. He looked so bewildered, too, when I said the word

' money,' and evidently he had to think what it was,
because it is so long since it has meant anything to
him. So if he wants anything, I have told him to go
into any shop and ask that it shall be put down to me.
He has often been without food or sleep for days
together when he is meditating. Just think !

" Shall I bring him to see you, or will you come
here ? He wants to meet you, because he feels you
have a beautiful soul, and may help him on the Way,
as well as his helping you. I am helping him too, he
says, which seems more wonderful than I can believe.
Send me a line as soon as you get back. *Addio !*

" Your own
" DAISY."

The voluminous sheets which had taken so long
in reading rustled as Mrs. Lucas folded them up.
She felt that she had to make a swift decision that
called into play all her mental powers. On the one
hand, it was " up to her " to return a frigid reply,
conveying, without making any bones about the
matter, that she had no interest in nameless Gurus
who might or might not be Brahmins from Benares,
and presented themselves at poor Daisy's door in a
penniless condition without clear knowledge whether
they had come by train or not. In favour of such
prudent measures was the truly Athenian character of
Daisy's mind, for she was always inquiring into
" some new thing," which was the secret of life when
first discovered, and got speedily relegated to the
dust-heap. But against such a course was the undoubted fact that Daisy did occasionally get hold of
somebody who subsequently proved to be of interest,
and Lucia would never forget to her dying day the
advent in Riseholme of a mean little Scotch attorney,

in whom Daisy had discovered a wonderful mentality.
Lucia had refused to extend her queenly hospitality
to him, or to recognize his existence in any way during
the fortnight when he stayed with Daisy, and she was
naturally very much annoyed to find him in a
prominent position in the Government not many
years later. Indeed, she had snubbed him so
markedly on his first appearance at Riseholme that
he had refused on subsequent visits to come to her
house at all, though he several times visited Mrs.
Quantock again, and told her all sorts of political
secrets (so she said), which she would not divulge
for anything in the world. There must never be a
repetition of so fatal an error.

Another thing inclined the wavering balance. She
distinctly wanted at her court some fresh element
which should make Riseholme know that she was in
residence again. August would soon be here with
its languor and absence of stimulus, when it was
really rather difficult in the drowsy, windless weather
to keep the flag of culture flying strongly from her
palace. The Guru had already said that he felt
sure she had a beautiful soul, and—— The outline
of the scheme flashed upon her. She would have
Yoga evenings in the hot August weather, at which,
as the heat of the day abated, graceful groups should
assemble among the mottoes in the garden and listen
to high talk on spiritual subjects. They would adjourn
to delicious moonlit suppers in the pergola, or, if the
moon was indisposed—she could not be expected
to regulate the affairs of the moon as well as of Riseholme—there would be dim séances and sandwiches
in the smoking-parlour. The humorous furniture
should be put in cupboards, and as they drifted
towards the front hall again, when the clocks struck

an unexpectedly late hour, little whispered colloquies
of "How wonderful he was to-night," would be
heard, and there would be far-away looks and sighs,
and the notings down of the titles of books that
conducted the pilgrim on the Way. Perhaps, as they
softly assembled for departure, a little music would
be suggested to round off the evening, and she saw
herself putting down the soft pedal, as people rustled
into their places, for the first movement of the "Moonlight Sonata." Then at the end there would be
silence, and she would get up with a sigh, and someone
would say, "Lucia *mia!*" and somebody else,
"Heavenly music," and perhaps the Guru would
say, "Beloved lady," as he had *apparently* said to
poor Daisy Quantock. Flowers, music, addresses from
the Guru, soft partings, sense of refreshment. . . .
. . . With the memory of the Scotch attorney in her
mind, it seemed clearly wiser to annex rather than
to repudiate the Guru.

She seized a pen and drew the topmost of a pile of
postcards towards her, on which was printed her name
and address.

"Too wonderful," she wrote. "Pray bring him
yourself to my little garden-party on Friday. There
will be only a few. Let me know if he wants a quiet
room ready for him."

All this had taken time, and she had but scribbled
a dozen postcards to friends, bidding them come to
her garden-party on Friday, when tea was announced.
These invitations had the mystic word "Titum"
written at the bottom left-hand corner, which conveyed to the enlightened recipient what sort of party
it was to be, and denoted the standard of dress. For

one of Lucia's quaint ideas was to divide dresses into
three classes : " Hitum," " Titum " and " Scrub."
Hitum was your very best dress, the smartest and
newest of all, and when " Hitum " was written on a card
of invitation, it implied that the party was a very
resplendent one. " Titum " similarly indicated a
moderately smart party, and conveyed the kind of
dress that would be suitable ; while for picnics
" Scrub " was a sufficient guidance. Those terms
applied to men's dress as well, and as regards evening
parties, a dinner-party Hitum would indicate a
white tie and a tail coat ; a dinner-party Titum
a black tie and a short coat, and a dinner Scrub
would mean morning clothes.

With tea was announced also the advent of Georgie
Pillson, who was her gentleman-in-waiting, her A.D.C.,
her devoted subordinate. In order to save subsequent disappointment, it may be at once stated
that there never had been, was, or ever would
be, the smallest approach to a flirtation between
them. Neither of them, she with her forty respectable years, and he with his blameless forty-five
years, had ever flirted with anybody at all. But it
was one of the polite and pleasant fictions of Riseholme that Georgie was passionately attached to
her, and that it was for her sake that he had settled
in Riseholme now some seven years ago, and that
for her sake he remained still unmarried. She never,
to do her justice, had affirmed anything of the sort,
but it is a fact that sometimes when Georgie's name
came up in conversation, her eyes wore that " far-
away " look that only the masterpieces of Art could
otherwise call up, and she would sigh and murmur,
" Dear Georgie ! " and change the subject, with the
tact that characterized her. In fact, their mutual

relations were among the most Beautiful things of
Riseholme, and hardly less beautiful was Peppino's
attitude towards it all. That large-hearted man
trusted them both, and his trust was not misplaced.
Georgie was in and out of the house all day, chiefly
in ; and not only did scandal never rear its hissing
head, but it had positively not a head to hiss with
or a foot to stand on. On his side again, Georgie had
never said that he was in love with her (nor would
it have been true if he had), but by his complete
silence on the subject, coupled with his constancy,
he seemed to admit the truth of this bloodless idyll.
They talked and walked and read the masterpieces
of literature and played duets on the piano together.
Sometimes (for he was the more brilliant performer,
though, as he said " terribly lazy about practising,"
for which she scolded him) he would gently slap the
back of her hand if she played a wrong note, and
say, " Naughty ! " And she would reply in baby
language, " Me vewy sowwy ! 'Oo naughty, too,
to hurt Lucia ! " That was the utmost extent of
their carnal familiarities, and with bright eyes fixed
on the music, they would break into peals of girlish
laughter, until the beauty of the music sobered them
again.

Georgie (he was. Georgie or Mr. Georgie, never
Pillson, for the whole of Riseholme) was not an
obtrusively masculine sort of person. Such mas-
culinity as he was possessed of was boyish rather
than adult, and the most important ingredients in
his nature were feminine. He had, in common
with the rest of Riseholme, strong artistic tastes,
and, in addition to playing the piano, made charming
little water-colour sketches, many of which he framed
at his own expense and gave to friends, with slightly

sentimental titles neatly printed in gilt letters on the mount. " Golden Autumn Woodland," " Bleak December," " Yellow Daffodils," " Roses of Summer," were perhaps his most notable series, and these he had given to Lucia on the occasion of four successive birthdays. He did portraits as well in pastel : those were of two types, elderly ladies in lace caps, with a row of pearls, and boys in cricket shirts, with their sleeves rolled up. He was not very good at eyes, so his sitters always were looking down, but he was excellent at smiles, and the old ladies smiled patiently and sweetly, and the boys gaily. His finest accomplishment was needle-work, and his house was full of the trophies of his skill : wool-work curtains, petit-point chair-seats and silk embroideries framed and glazed. Next to Lucia he was the hardest-worked inhabitant of Riseholme, but not being so strong as the Queen, he had often to go away for little rests by the sea-side. Travelling by train fussed him a good deal, for he might not be able to get a corner-seat, or somebody with a pipe or a baby might get into his carriage, or the porter might be rough with his luggage, so he usually went in his car to some neighbouring watering-place where they knew him. Dicky, his handsome young chauffeur, drove him, and by Dicky's side sat Foljambe, his very pretty parlour-maid, who valetted him. If Dicky took the wrong turn, his master called " Naughty boy " through the tube, and Foljambe smiled respectfully. For the month of August, his two plain, strapping sisters (Hermione and Ursula, alas !) always came to stay with him. They liked pigs and dogs, and otter-hunting and mutton-chops, and were rather a discordant element in Riseholme. But Georgie had a kind heart, and never even debated whether he should ask Hermy and Ursy or not, though he had to do a great deal of tidying up after they had gone.

There was always a touch between the meetings of these two when either of them had been away from Riseholme that very prettily concealed the depth of Georgie's supposed devotion, and when she came out into the garden where her *cavaliere* and her husband were waiting for their tea under the pergola, Georgie jumped up very nimbly and took a few chassée-ing steps towards her, with both hands outstretched in welcome. She caught at his humour, made him a curtsey, and next moment they were treading a little improvised minuet together with hands held high, and pointed toes. Georgie had very small feet, and it was a really elegant toe that he pointed, encased in cloth-topped boots. He had on a suit of fresh white flannels, and over his shoulders, for fear of the evening air being chilly after that hot day, he had a little cape of a military cut, like those in which young ladies at music-halls enact the part of colonels. He had a straw hat on, with a blue riband, a pink shirt and a red tie, rather loose and billowy. His face was pink and round, with blue eyes, a short nose and very red lips. An almost complete absence of eyebrow was made up for by a firm little brown moustache clipped very short, and brushed upwards at its extremities. Contrary to expectation, he was quite tall, and fitted very neatly into his clothes.

The dance came to an end with a low curtsey on Lucia's part, an obeisance hat in hand from Georgie (this exposure showing a crop of hair grown on one side of his head, and brushed smoothly over the top until it joined the hair on the other side), and a clapping of the hands from Peppino.

" *Bravo, bravo,*" he cried from the tea-table.
" Capital ! "

Mrs. Lucas blew him a kiss in acknowledgment
of this compliment, and smiled on her partner.
" *Amico !* " she said. " It is nice to see you again.
How goes it ? "

" *Va bene,*" said Georgie, to show he could talk
Italian too. " *Va* very *bene* now that you've come
back."

" Georgie ! Now tell me all the news. We'll have
a good gossip."

Georgie's face beamed with a " solemn gladness " at
the word, like a drunkard's when brandy is mentioned.

" Where shall we begin ? " he said. " Such a lot
to tell you. I think we must begin with a great bit
of news. Something really mysterious."

Lucia smiled inwardly. She felt that she knew
for dead certain what the mysterious news was, and
also that she knew far more about it than Georgie.
This superiority she completely concealed. Nobody
could have guessed it.

" *Presto, presto,*" she said. " You excite me."

" Yesterday morning I was in Rush's," said Georgie,
" seeing about some *crème de menthe,* which ought to
have been sent the day before—Rush is very negligent
sometimes—and I was just saying a sharp word about
it, when suddenly I saw that Rush was not attending
at all, but was looking at something behind my back,
and so I looked round. Guess ! "

" Don't be tantalizing, *amico,*" said she. " How
can I guess ? A pink elephant with blue spots ! "

" No, guess again ! "

" A red Indian in full war paint ? "

" Certainly not ! Guess again," said Georgie, with
a little sigh of relief. (It would have been awful if

she had guessed.) At this moment Peppino suddenly became aware that Lucia had guessed, and was up to some game.

"Give me your hand, Georgie," she said, "and look at me. I'm going to read your thoughts. Think of what you saw when you turned round."

She took his hand and pressed it to her forehead, closing her eyes.

"But I do seem to see an Indian," she said. "Ah, not Red Indian, other Indian. And—and he has slippers on and brown stockings—no, not brown stockings : it's legs. And there's a beard and a turban."

She gave a sigh.

"That's all I can see," she said.

"My dear, you're marvellous," said he. "You're quite right."

A slight bubbling sound came from Peppino, and Georgie began to suspect.

"I believe you've seen him," he said. "How tarsome you are. . ."

When they had all laughed a great deal, and Georgie had been assured that Lucia really, word of honour, had no idea what happened next, the narrative was resumed.

"So there stood the Indian, bowing and salaaming most politely, and when Rush had promised me he would send my *crème de menthe* that very morning, I just looked through a wine-list for a moment, and the Indian with quantities more bows came up to the counter, and said : 'If you will have the great goodness to give me a little brandy-bottle.' So Rush gave it him, and instead of paying for it, what do you think he said ? Guess ! "

Mrs. Lucas rose with the air of Lady Macbeth, and pointed her finger at Georgie.

" He said, ' Put it down to Mrs. Quantock's account,' " she hissed.

Of course the explanation came now, and Lucia told the two men the contents of Mrs. Quantock's letter. With that her cards were on the table, and though the fact of the Brahmin from Benares was news to Georgie, he had got many interesting things to tell her, for his house adjoined Mrs. Quantock's, and there were plenty of things which Mrs. Quantock had not mentioned in her letter, so that Georgie was soon in the position of informant again. His windows overlooked Mrs. Quantock's garden, and since he could not keep his eyes shut all day, it followed that the happenings there were quite common property. Indeed, that was a general rule in Riseholme : anyone in an adjoining house could say, " What an exciting game of lawn-tennis you had this afternoon ! " having followed it from his bedroom. That was part of the charm : it was as if all Riseholme was a happy family with common interests and pursuits, and neighbours talked over the garden walls to each other. What happened in the house was a more private matter, and Mrs. Quantock, for instance, would never look from the rising ground at the end of her garden into Georgie's dining-room, or, if she did, she would never tell anyone how many places were laid at table on that particular day when she had asked if he could give her lunch, and he had replied that, with great regret, his table was full. But nobody could help seeing into gardens from back windows : the " view " belonged to everybody.

Georgie had had wonderful views.

" That very day," he said, " soon after lunch I was looking for a letter I thought I had left in my bedroom, and happening to glance out, I saw the Indian sitting

under Mrs. Quantock's pear tree. He was swaying
a little backwards and forwards."

"The brandy!" said Lucia excitedly. "He has
his meals in his own room."

"No, *amica*, it was not the brandy. In fact, I
don't suppose the brandy had gone to Mrs. Quantock's house, for he did not take it from Rush's, but
asked that it should be sent——" He paused a
moment—"Or did he take it away? I declare I can't
remember. But anyhow, when he swayed backwards and forwards, he wasn't drunk, if you mean
that, for presently he stood on one leg, and crooked
the other behind it, and remained there with his hands
up, as if he was praying, for quite a long time, without swaying at all. So he couldn't have been tipsy.
And then he sat down again, and took off his slippers,
and held his toes with one hand, while his legs were
quite straight out, and put his left hand round
behind his head, and grasped his right ear with it.
I tried to do it on my bedroom floor, but I couldn't
get near it. . . . Then he sat up again, and called,
' *Chela! Chela!* ' and Mrs. Quantock came running out."

"Why did he say ' *Chela* '?" asked Lucia.

"I wondered too. But I knew I had some clue
to it, so I looked through some books by Rudyard
Kipling, and found that ' Chela ' meant ' Disciple '.
What you told us just now about ' Guru ' being
' teacher,' seems to piece the whole thing together."

"And what did Daisy do?" asked Mrs. Lucas
breathlessly.

"She sat down too, and put her legs out straight
in front of her, like the Guru, and tried to hold the
toe of her shoe in her fingers, and naturally she couldn't
get within yards of it. I got nearer than she did.
And he said, ' Beloved lady, not too far at first.' "

" So you could hear, too ? " said Lucia.

" Naturally, for my window was open, and as you know, Mrs. Quantock's pear-tree is quite close to the house. And then he told her to stop up one nostril with her finger and inhale through the other, and then hold her breath while he counted six. Then she breathed it all out again, and started with the other side. She repeated that several times, and he was very much pleased with her. Then she said : ' It is quite wonderful : I feel so light and vigorous.' "

" It would be very wonderful indeed if dear Daisy felt light," remarked Lucia. " What next ? "

" Then they sat and swayed backwards and forwards again, and muttered something that sounded like ' Pom.' "

" That would be ' Om ' ; and then ? "

" I couldn't wait any longer, for I had some letters to write."

She smiled at him.

" I shall give you another cup of tea to reward you for your report," she said. " It has all been most interesting. Tell me again about the breathing in and holding your breath."

Georgie did so, and illustrated in his own person what had happened. Next moment Lucia was imitating him, and Peppino came round in order to get a better view of what Georgie was doing. Then they all sat, inhaling through one nostril, holding their breath, and then expelling it again.

" Very interesting," said Lucia at the end. " Upon my word, it does give one a sort of feeling of vigour and lightness. I wonder if there is something in it."

CHAPTER III

THOUGH The Hurst was, as befitted its *châtelaine*, the most Elizabethanly complete abode in Riseholme, the rest of the village, in its due degrees, fell very little short of perfection. It had but its one street, some half-mile in length, but that street was a gem of mediæval domestic architecture. For the most part the houses that lined it were blocks of contiguous cottages, which had been converted, either singly or by twos and threes, into dwellings containing the comforts demanded by the twentieth century, but externally they preserved the antiquity which, though it might be restored or even added on to, presented a truly Elizabethan appearance There were, of course, accretions, such as old inn signs above front-doors, and old bell-pulls at their sides, but the doors were uniformly of inconveniently low stature, roofs were of stone slabs or old brick, in which a surprisingly abundant crop of antirrhinums and stone-crops had anchored itself, and there was hardly a garden that did not contain a path of old paving-stones, a mulberry tree and some yews cut into shape.

Nothing in the place was more blatantly mediæval than the village-green, across which Georgie took his tripping steps after leaving the presence of his Queen. Round it stood a row of great elms, and in its centre was the ducking-pond, according to Riseholme tradition, though perhaps in less classical villages it might have passed merely for a duck-pond. But in Riseholme it would have been rank heresy to have dreamed, even in the most pessimistic moments, of its being anything but a ducking-pond. Close by it stood a pair of stocks, about which there was no doubt whatever, for Mr. Lucas had purchased them from a neighbouring iconoclastic village, where they were on the point of being broken up, and, after having them repaired, had presented them to the village-green, and chosen their site close to the ducking-pond. Round the green were grouped the shops of the village, slightly apart from the residential street, and at the far end of it was that undoubtedly Elizabethan hostelry, the "Ambermere Arms," full to over-flowing of ancient tables and Bible-boxes, and fire-dogs, and fire-backs, and bottles, and chests and settles. These were purchased in large quantities by the American tourists who swarmed there during the summer months, at a high profit to the nimble pro-prietor, who thereupon purchased fresh antiquities to take their places. The "Ambermere Arms," in fact, was the antique furniture shop of the place, and did a thriving trade, for it was much more interesting to buy objects out of a real old Elizabethan inn, than out of a shop.

Georgie had put his smart military cape over his arm for his walk, and at intervals applied his slim fore-finger to one nostril, while he breathed in through the other, continuing the practice which he had observed going on in Mrs. Quantock's garden. Though it made him a little dizzy, it certainly produced a sort of lightness, but soon he remembered the letter from Mrs. Quantock, which the Queen had quoted from, warning her that these exercises ought to be taken under instruction, and so he desisted. He was going to

deliver the Queen's answer at Mrs. Quantock's house,
and with a view to possibly meeting the Guru, and
being introduced to him, he said over to himself,
" Guru, Guru, Guru," instead of doing deep breathing, in order to accustom himself to the unusual
syllables.

It would, of course, have been very strange and
un-Riseholmelike to have gone to a friend's door, even
though the errand was so impersonal a one as leaving
somebody else's note, without inquiring whether
the friend was in, and being instantly admitted if
she was, and as a matter of fact, Georgie caught a
glimpse, when the knocker was answered (Mrs.
Quantock did not have a bell at all), through the
open door of the hall, of Mrs. Quantock standing in
the middle of the lawn on one leg. Naturally, therefore, he ran out into the garden without any further
formality. She looked like a little round fat stork,
whose legs had not grown, but who preserved the
habits of her kind.

" Dear lady, I've brought a note for you," he
said. " It's from Lucia."

The other leg went down, and she turned on him
the wide, firm smile that she had learned in the
vanished days of Christian Science.

" Om," said Mrs. Quantock, expelling the remainder
of her breath. " Thank you, my dear Georgie. It's
extraordinary what Yoga has done for me already.
Cold quite gone. If ever you feel out of sorts, or
depressed or cross, you can cure yourself at once. I've
got a visitor staying with me."

" Have you indeed ? " asked Georgie, without
alluding to the thrilling excitements which had
trodden so closely on each other's heels since yesterday
morning, when he had seen the Guru in Rush's shop.

" Yes ; and as you've just come from dear Lucia's, perhaps she may have said something to you about him, for I wrote to her. He's a Guru of extraordinary sanctity from Benares, and he's teaching me the Way. You shall see him, too, unless he's meditating. I will call to him ; if he's meditating he won't hear me, so we shan't be interrupting him. He wouldn't hear a railway accident if he was meditating."

She turned round towards the house.

" Guru, dear ! " she called.

There was a moment's pause, and the Indian's face appeared at a window.

" Beloved lady ! " he said.

" Guru, dear, I want to introduce a friend of mine to you," she said. " This is Mr. Pillson, and when you know him a little better you will call him Georgie."

" Beloved lady, I know him very well indeed. I see into his clear, white soul. Peace be unto you, my friend."

" Isn't he marvellous ! Fancy ! " said Mrs. Quantock, in an aside.

Georgie raised his hat very politely.

" How do you do ? " he said. (After his quiet practice he would have said, " How do you do, Guru ? " but it rhymed in a ridiculous manner, and his red lips could not frame the word.)

" I am always well," said the Guru. " I am always young and well because I follow the Way."

" Sixty at least he tells me," said Mrs. Quantock, in a hissing aside, probably audible across the Channel, " and he thinks more, but the years make no difference to him. He is like a boy. Call him ' Guru.' "

" Guru——" began Georgie.

" Yes, my friend."

" I am very glad you are well," said Georgie wildly. He was greatly impressed, but much embarrassed. Also it was so hard to talk to a second-storey window with any sense of ease, especially when you had to address a total stranger of extraordinary sanctity from Benares.

Mrs. Quantock came to the assistance of his embarrassment.

" Guru dear, are you coming down to see us ? " she asked.

" Beloved lady, no," said the level voice. " It is laid on me to wait here. It is the time of calm and prayer, when it is good to be alone. I will come down when the Guides bid me. But teach our dear friend what I have taught you. Surely before long I will grasp his earthly hand, but not now. Peace ! Peace and light ! "

" Have you got some Guides as well ? " asked Georgie, when the Guru disappeared from the window. " And are they Indians too ? "

" Oh, those are his spiritual guides," said Mrs. Quantock. " He sees them and talks to them, but they are not in the body."

She gave a happy sigh.

" I never have felt anything like it," she said. " He has brought such an atmosphere into the house that even Robert feels it, and doesn't mind being turned out of his dressing-room. There, he has shut the window. Isn't it all marvellous ? "

Georgie had not seen anything particularly marvellous yet, except the phenomenon of Mrs. Quantock standing on one leg in the middle of the lawn, but presumably her emotion communicated itself to him by the subtle infection of the spirit.

" And what does he do ? " he asked.

" My dear, it is not what he does, but what he
is," said she. " Why, even my little bald account
of him to Lucia has made her ask him to her garden-
party. Of course, I can't tell whether he will go or
not. He seems so very much—how shall I say it ?
—so very much sent to me. But I shall, of course,
ask him whether he will come. Trances and meditation all day ! And in the intervals such serenity
and sweetness. You know, for instance, how tiresome Robert is about his food. Well, last night the
mutton, I am bound to say, was a little underdone,
and Robert was beginning to throw it about the
plate in the way he has. Well, my Guru got up,
and just said, ' Show me the way to kitchen '—he
leaves out little words sometimes, because they don't
matter—and I took him down, and he said, ' Peace ! '
He told me to leave him there, and in ten minutes he
was up again with a little plate of curry and rice and
what had been underdone mutton, and you never ate
anything so good. Robert had most of it, gobbling
it up, and I had the rest, and my Guru was so pleased
at seeing Robert pleased. He said Robert had a pure
white soul, just like you, only I wasn't to tell him,
because for him the Way ordained that he must find
it out for himself. And to-day, before lunch again,
he went down to the kitchen, and my cook told
me he only took a pinch of pepper and a tomato
and a little bit of mutton fat, and a sardine and a
bit of cheese, and a scraping of gentleman's relish, and
a little nutmeg, and he brought up a dish that you
never saw equalled. Delicious ! I shouldn't a bit
wonder if Robert began breathing exercises soon.
There is one that makes you lean and young, and
strengthens the liver."

This sounded very entrancing.

" Can't you teach me that ? " asked Georgie eagerly. He had been rather disturbed about his increasing plumpness for a year past, and about his increasing age for longer than that. As for his liver he always had to be careful, and was often a little pale after a party.

She shook her head.

" You cannot practise it except under tuition from an expert," she said.

Georgie rapidly considered what Hermy's and Ursy's comments would be, if, when they arrived to-morrow, he was found doing exercises under the tuition of a Guru. Hermy, when she was not otter-hunting, could be very sarcastic, and he had a clear month of Hermy in front of him, without any otter-hunting, which, so she had informed him, was not possible in August. This was mysterious to Georgie, because it did not seem likely that all otters died in August, or turned into something else like caterpillars. If Hermy was here in October, she would otter-hunt all morning, and snore all afternoon, and be in the best of tempers, but the August visit required more careful handling. Yet the prospect of being lean and young, and internally controlled was wonderfully tempting.

" But couldn't he be my Guru as well ? " he asked.

Quite suddenly, as by some demoniac possession, a desire that had been only intermittently in Mrs. Quantock's consciousness took full possession of her ; a red revolutionary insurgence hoisted its banners. Why, with this stupendous novelty in the shape of a Guru, shouldn't she lead and direct Riseholme instead of Lucia ? She had long wondered why darling Lucia should be queen of Riseholme, and had, by momentary illumination, seen herself, thus equipped, as far more capable of exercising supremacy. After all, everybody in Riseholme knew Lucia's old tunes by now, and were in their secret consciousnesses quite aware that she did not play the second and third movements of the Moonlight Sonata simply because they " went faster," however much she might cloak the omission by saying that they resembled eleven o'clock in the morning or three o'clock in the afternoon. And Mrs. Quantock had often suspected that she did not read one quarter of the books she talked about, and that she got up subjects in the Encyclopædia in order to make a brave show that covered essential ignorance. Certainly she spent a good deal of money over entertaining, but Robert had lately made twenty times what darling Lucia spent annually, over Roumanian oils. As for her acting, had she not completely forgotten her words as Lady Macbeth in the middle of the sleep-walking scene ?

But here was Lucia, as proved by her note and the mission A.D.C., wildly interested in her Guru. Mrs. Quantock conjectured that Lucia's plan was to launch the Guru at her August parties, as her own discovery. He would be a novelty, and it would be Lucia who gave Om-parties, and breathing-parties, and standing-on-one-leg-parties, while she herself, Daisy Quantock, would be bidden to these as a humble guest, and Lucia would get all the credit, and, as likely as not, invite the discoverer, the inventress, just now and then. Mrs. Quantock's Guru would become Lucia's Guru, and all Riseholme would flock hungrily for light and leading to The Hurst. She had written to Lucia in all sincerity, hoping that she would extend the hospitality of her garden-parties to the Guru, but now the very warmth of Lucia's reply caused her to suspect this ulterior motive. She had been too precipitate, too rash, " too ill-advised, too sudden," as Lucia would say. She ought to have known that Lucia, with her August parties coming on, would have jumped at a Guru, and withheld him for her own parties, taking the wind out of Lucia's arrogant sails. Lucia had already suborned Georgie to leave this note and begin to filch the Guru away. Mrs. Quantock saw it all now, and clearly this was not to be borne. Before she answered, she steeled herself with the triumph she had once scored in the matter of the Scotch attorney.

" Dear Georgie," she said, " no one would be more delighted than I if my Guru consented to take you as a pupil. But you can't tell what he will do ; as he said to me to-day, apropos of myself : ' I cannot come unless I be sent.' Was not that wonderful ? He knew at once he had been sent to me."

By this time Georgie was quite determined to have the Guru. The measure of his determination may be gauged from the fact that he forgot all about Lucia's garden-party.

" But he called me his friend," he said. " He told me I had a clear white soul."

" Yes ; but that is his attitude towards everybody," said Mrs. Quantock. " His religion makes it impossible for him to think ill of anybody."

" But he didn't say that to Rush," cried Georgie, " when he asked for some brandy, to be put down to you."

Mrs. Quantock's expression changed for a moment, but that moment was too short for Georgie to notice it. Her face instantly cleared again.

" Naturally he cannot go about saying that sort of thing," she observed. " Common people—he is of the highest caste—would not understand him."

Georgie made the direct appeal.

" Please ask him to teach me," he said.

For a moment Mrs. Quantock did not answer, but cocked her head sideways in the direction of the pear tree, where a thrush was singing. It fluted but a couple of repeated phrases, and then was silent again.

Mrs. Quantock gave a gasp and a smile to the pear tree.

" Thank you, little brother," she said.

She turned to Georgie again.

" That comes out of St. Francis," she said, " but Yoga embraces all that is true in every religion. Well, I will ask my Guru whether he will take you as a pupil, but I can't answer for what he will say."

" What does he—what does he charge for his lessons ? " asked Georgie.

The Christian-Science smile illuminated her face again.

" The word ' money ' never passes his lips," she said. " I don't think he really knows what it means. He proposed to sit on the village green with a beggar's bowl, but of course I would not permit that ; for the present I just give him all he wants. No doubt when he goes away—which I hope will not be for many weeks yet, though no one can tell when he has another call— I shall slip something suitably generous into his hand, but I don't think about that. Must you be going ? Good-night, dear Georgie ! Peace ! Om ! "

His last backward glance as he went out of the front-door revealed her standing on one leg again, just as he had seen her first. He remembered a print of a fakir at Benares, standing in just that attitude ; and if the stream that flowed into the Avon could be construed into the Ganges, and the garden into the burning-ghaut, and the swooping swallows into the kites, and the neat parlour-maid who showed him out into a Brahmin, and the Chinese gong that was so prominent an object in the hall into a piece of Benares brass-ware, he could almost have fancied himself as standing on the brink of the sacred river. The marigolds in the garden required no transmutation. . . . Georgie had quite " to pull himself together," as he stepped round Mrs. Quantock's mulberry tree, and ten paces later round his own, before he could recapture his normal evening mood on those occasions when he was going to dine alone. Usually these evenings were very pleasant and much occupied, for they did not occur very often in the whirl of Riseholme life, and it was not more than once a week that he spent a solitary evening, and even then, if he got tired of his own company, there were half a dozen houses, easy of access, where after throwing on his military cloak, he could spend a post-prandial hour. But oftener than not when these occasions occurred, he would be quite busy at home, dusting a little china, and rearranging ornaments on his shelves, and, after putting his rings and handkerchief in the candle-bracket of his piano, spending a serious hour (with the soft-pedal down, for fear of irritating Robert) in reading his share of such duets as he would be likely to be called upon to play with his Queen during the next day or two. Though he read music much better than she did, he used to " go over " his part alone first, and let it be understood that he had not seen it before. But then he was sure that she had done precisely the same, so they started fair. Such things whiled away very pleasantly the hours till eleven, when he went to bed, and it was seldom that he had to put out Patience-cards to tide him over the slow minutes.

But every now and then—and to-night was one of the " nows "—there occurred evenings when he never went out to dinner, even if he was asked, because he "was busy indoors." They occurred about once a month, these evenings when he was " busy indoors," and even an invitation from his Queen would not interrupt them. A faint suspicion of what Georgie was " busy indoors " about had long ago become public property in Riseholme, but though none of Georgie's friends talked about the nature of his engagements to anyone else, everybody else knew. His business indoors, in fact, was a perfect secret, simply because everybody was quite aware what it was.

June had been a very busy time, not " indoors," but with other engagements, and as Georgie went up to his bedroom, having been told by Foljambe that the hair-dresser was waiting for him, and had been waiting " this last ten minutes," he glanced at his hair in the Cromwellian mirror that hung on the stairs, and was quite conscious that it was time he submitted himself to Mr. Holroyd's ministrations. There was certainly an undergrowth of grey hair visible beneath his chestnut crop, that should have been attended to at least a fortnight ago. Also there was a certain added thinness in the locks that crossed his head. Mr. Holroyd had alluded to that before, and had suggested a certain remedy, not in the least inconvenient, unless Georgie purposed to be athletic, without a cap, in a high wind, and even then not necessarily so. But as he had no intention of being athletic anywhere, with or without a cap, he determined as he went up the stairs that he would follow Mr. Holroyd's advice. Mr. Holroyd's procedure, even without this added formula, entailed sitting " till it dried," and after that he would have dinner, and then Mr. Holroyd would begin again. He was a very clever person with regard to the face and the hands and the feet. Georgie had been conscious of walking a little lamely lately ; he had been even more conscious of the need of hot wet towels on his face and the " tap-tap " of Mr. Holroyd's fingers, and stretchings of Mr. Holroyd's thumb across rather slack surfaces of cheek and chin. In the interval between the hair and the face, Mr. Holroyd should have a good dinner downstairs with Foljambe and the cook. And to-morrow morning, when he met Hermy and Ursy, Georgie would be just as spick and span and young as ever, if not more so.

Georgie (happy innocent !) was completely unaware that the whole of Riseholme knew that the smooth chestnut locks which covered the top of his head were trained like the tendrils of a grape-vine from their roots, and flowed like a river over a bare bed, and consequently when Mr. Holroyd explained the proposed innovation, a little central wig, the edges of which would mingle in the most natural manner with his own hair, it seemed to Georgie that nobody would know the difference. In addition he would be spared those risky moments when he had to take off his hat to a friend in a high wind, for there was always the danger of his hair blowing away from the top of his head, and hanging down, like the tresses of a Rhine-maiden, over one shoulder. So Mr. Holroyd was commissioned to put that little affair in hand at once, and when the greyness had been attended to, Georgie sat down to dinner while " it " dried. After that came hot towels and tappings on his face, and other ministrations, and when about half-past ten he came downstairs again for a short practice at the bass part of Beethoven's Fifth Symphony, ingeniously arranged for two performers on the piano, he looked with sincere satisfaction at his rosy face in the Cromwellian mirror, and his shoes felt quite comfortable again, and his nails

shone like pink stars as his hands dashed wildly about
the piano in the quicker passages. But all the time
the thought of the Guru next door, under whose tuition
he might be able to regain his youth without recourse
to those expensive subterfuges (for the price of the
undetectable *toupet* astonished him), sang in his head
with a melody more haunting than Beethoven's.
What he would have liked best of all would have been
to have the Guru all to himself, so that he should
remain perpetually young, while all the rest of Riseholme (including Hermy and Ursy) grew old. Then,
indeed, he would be king of the place, instead of
serving the interests of its queen.

He rose with a little sigh, and after adjusting the
strip of flannel over the keys, shut his piano, and busied
himself for a little with a soft duster over his cabinet
of *bibelots*, which not even Foljambe was allowed to
touch. It was generally understood that he had
inherited them (though the inheritance had chiefly
passed to him through the medium of curiosity shops),
and there were several pieces of considerable value
among them. There was a gold Louis XVI. snuff-
box, a miniature by Karl Huth, a silver toy porringer
of the time of Queen Anne, a piece of Bow china, and
an enamelled cigarette case by Fabergé. But to-night
his handling of them was not so dainty and delicate
as usual, and he actually dropped the porringer on the
floor as he was dusting it, for his mind still occupied
itself with the Guru and the practices that led to
permanent youth. How quick Lucia had been to
snap him up for her garden-party! Yet perhaps she
would not get him, for he might say he was not sent.
But surely he would be sent to Georgie, whom he
knew, the moment he set eyes on him, to have a clear
white soul. . . .

The clock struck eleven, and, as usual on warm nights, Georgie opened the glass door into his garden, and drew in a breath of the night air. The sky was thickly peppered with pretty stars, which Georgie, after his busy, interesting day, enjoyed looking at, though, if he had had the arrangement of them, he would certainly have put them in more definite patterns. Among them was a very red planet, and Georgie, with recollections of his classical education, easily remembered that Mars, the God of War, was symbolized in the heavens by a red star. Could that mean anything to peaceful Riseholme? Were internal warfare, revolutionary movements, possible in so serene a realm?

CHAPTER IV

PINK, irascible Robert, prone to throw his food about his plate, if it did not commend itself to him, felt in an extremely good-natured mood that same night after dinner, for the Guru had again made a visit to the kitchen, with the result that instead of a slab of pale dead codfish being put before him after he had eaten some tepid soup, there appeared a delicious little fish-curry. The Guru had behaved with great tact : he had seen the storm gathering on poor Robert's face, as he sipped the cool effete concoction, and put down his spoon again with a splash in his soup-plate, and thereupon had bowed and smiled and scurried away to the kitchen to intercept the next abomination. Then, returning with the little curry, he explained that it was entirely for Robert, since those who sought after the Way did not indulge in hot sharp foods, and so he had gobbled it up to the very last morsel.

In consequence when the Guru salaamed very humbly, and said that with gracious permission of beloved lady and kind master he would go and meditate in his room, and had shambled away in his red slippers, the discussion which Robert had felt himself obliged to open with his wife, on the subject of having an unknown Indian staying with them for an indefinite period, was opened in a much more amicable key than it would have been on a slice of codfish.

" Well now, about this Golliwog—I should say Guru,
my dear," he began, " what's going to happen ? "

Daisy Quantock drew in her breath sharply and
winced at this irreverence, but quickly remembered
that she must always be sending out messages of love
north, east, south and west. She sent a rather
spiky one in the direction of her husband, who was
sitting due east, so that it probably got to him at
once, and smiled the particular hard, firm smile
which was an heirloom inherited from her last rule of
life.

" No one knows," she said brightly. " Even the
Guides can't tell where and when a Guru may be
called."

" Then do you propose he should stop here till he's
called somewhere else ? "

She continued smiling.

" I don't propose anything," she said. " It's not
in my hands."

Under the calming influence of the fish-curry,
Robert remained still placid.

" He's a first-rate cook, anyhow," he said. " Can't
you engage him as that ? Call to the kitchen, you
know."

" Darling ! " said Mrs. Quantock, sending out more
love. But she had a quick temper, and indeed the
two were outpoured together, like hot and cold taps
turned on in a bath. The pellucid stream of love
served to keep her temper moderately cool.

" Well, ask him," suggested Mr. Quantock; " as
you say, you never can tell where a Guru may be called.
Give him forty pounds a year and beer money——"

" Beer ! " began Mrs. Quantock, when she suddenly
remembered Georgie's story about Rush and the Guru
and the brandy-bottle, and stopped.

" Yes, dear, I said ' beer,' " remarked Robert a little irritably, " and in any case I insist that you dismiss your present cook. You only took her because she was a Christian Scientist, and you've left that little sheep-fold now. You used to talk about false claims, I remember. Well, her claim to be a cook is the falsest I ever heard of. I'd sooner take my chance with an itinerant organ-grinder. But that fish-curry to-night, and that other thing last night, that's what I mean by good eating."

The thought even of good food always calmed Robert's savage breast ; it blew upon him as the wind on an Æolian harp hung in the trees, evoking faint, sweet sounds.

" I'm sure, my dear," he said, " that I will be willing to fall in with any pleasant arrangement about your Guru, but it really isn't unreasonable in me to ask what sort of arrangement you propose. I haven't a word to say against him, especially when he goes to the kitchen ; I only want to know if he is going to stop here a night or two or a year or two. Talk to him about it to-morrow, with my love. I wonder if he can make bisque soup."

Daisy Quantock carried quite a quantity of material for reflection upstairs with her, when she went to bed, pausing a moment opposite the Guru's door, from inside of which came sounds of breathing so deep that it sounded almost like snoring, but she seemed to detect a timbre of spirituality about it which convinced her that he was holding high communion with the Guides. It was round him that her thoughts centred, he the tree through the branches of which they scampered chattering.

Her first and main interest in him was sheer Guru-ism, for she was one of those intensely happy people

who pass through life in ecstatic pursuit of some idea
which those who do not share it call a fad. Well
might poor Robert remember the devastation of his
home when Daisy, after the perusal of a little pamphlet
which she picked up on a book-stall called " The Uric
Acid Monthly," came to the shattering conclusion that
her buxom frame consisted almost entirely of waste-
products which must be eliminated. For a greedy
man the situation was frankly intolerable, for when he
continued his ordinary diet (this was before the
cursed advent of the Christian Science cook) she kept
pointing to his well-furnished plate, and told him that
every atom of that beef or mutton and potatoes turned
from the moment he swallowed it into chromagens and
toxins, and that his apparent appetite was merely the
result of fermentation.   For herself, her platter was an
abominable mess of cheese and proteid-powder, and
apples and salad-oil, while round her, like saucers of
specimen seeds, were ranged little piles of nuts and
pine-kernels, which supplied body-building material,
and which she weighed out with scrupulous accuracy,
in accordance with the directions of " The Uric Acid
Monthly." Tea and coffee were taboo, since they
flooded the blood with poisons, and the kitchen boiler
rumbled day and night to supply the rivers of boiling
water with which (taken in sips) she inundated her
system.   Strange gaunt females used to come down
from London, with small parcels full of tough food
that tasted of travelling-bags, and contained so much
nutrition that quite a few pounds of it would furnish
the daily rations of an army.   Luckily even her iron
constitution could not stand the strain of such ideal
living for long, and her growing anæmia threatened to
undermine a constitution seriously impaired by the
precepts of perfect health.   A course of beef-steaks

and other substantial viands loaded with uric acid restored her to her former vigour.

Thus reinforced, she plunged with the same energy as she had devoted to repelling uric acid into the embraces of Christian Science. The inhumanity of that sect towards both herself and others took complete possession of her, and when her husband complained on a bitter January morning that his smoking-room was like an ice-house, because the housemaid had forgotten to light the fire, she had no touch of pity for him, since she knew that there was no such thing as cold or heat or pain, and therefore you could not feel cold. But now, since, according to the new creed, such things as uric acid, chromagens and purins had no existence, she could safely indulge in decent viands again. But her unhappy husband was not a real gainer in this respect, for while he ate, she brightly discoursed to him on the new creed, and asked him to recite with her the "True Statement of Being." And on the top of that she dismissed the admirable cook, and engaged the miscreant from whom he suffered still, though Christian Science, which had allowed her cold to make so long a false claim on her, had followed the Uric-Acid fad into the limbo of her discarded beliefs.

But now once more she had temporarily discovered the secret of life in the teachings of her Guru, and it was, as has been mentioned, sheer Guruism that constituted the main attraction of the new creed. That then being taken for granted, she turned her mind to certain side-issues, which to a true Riseholmeite were of entrancing interest. She felt a strong suspicion that Lucia contemplated annexing her Guru altogether, for otherwise she would not have returned so enthusiastic a response to her note, nor have sent Georgie to

deliver it and to profess the same violent interest in the
Guru. What, then, was the correctly diabolical policy
to pursue ? Should Daisy Quantock refuse to take
him to Mrs. Lucas altogether, with a message of regret
that he did not feel himself sent ? If she did this,
did she feel herself strong enough to throw down the
gauntlet (in the shape of the Guru) and, using him as
the attraction, challenge darling Lucia to mortal combat, in order to decide who should be the leader of
all that was advanced and cultured in Riseholme
society ? Still following that ramification of this policy,
should she bribe Georgie over to her own revolutionary
camp, by promising him instruction from the Guru ?
Or following a less daring line, should she take darling
Lucia and Georgie into the charmed circle, and while
retaining her own right of treasure trove, yet share it
with them in some inner ring, dispensing the Guru
to them, if they were good, in small doses ?

Mrs. Quantock's mind resembled in its workings the
manœuvres of a moth distracted by the glory of several
bright lights. It dashed at one, got slightly singed, and
forgetting all about that. turned its attention to the
second, and the third, taking headers into each in
turn, without deciding which, on the whole, was the
most enchanting of those luminaries. So, in order to
curb the exuberance of these frenzied excursions, she
got a half-sheet of paper, and noted down the alter-
natives that she must choose from.

(i.) Shall I keep him entirely to myself ?

(ii.) Shall I run him for all he is worth, and leave
out L. ?

(iii.) Shall I get G. on my side ?

(iv.) Shall I give L. and G. bits ?

She paused a moment, and then, remembering that
he had voluntarily helped her very pretty housemaid

to make the beds that morning, saying that his business (like the Prince of Wales's) was to serve, she added :

(v.) Shall I ask him to be my cook ?

For a few seconds the brightness of her eager interest was dimmed as the unworthy suspicion occurred to her that perhaps the prettiness of her housemaid had something to do with his usefulness in the bedroom, but she instantly dismissed it. There was the bottle of brandy, too, which he had ordered from Rush's— where she had begged him to order anything he wanted and cause it to be put down to her account, she had not actually contemplated brandy. . . . Then, remembering that one of the most necessary conditions for progress in Yoga was that the disciple should have complete confidence in the Guru, she chased that also out of her mind. But still, even when the lines of all possible policies were written down, she could come to no decision, and putting her paper by her bed, resolved to sleep over it. The rhythmical sounds of hallowed breathing came steadily from next door, and she murmured " Om, Om," in time with them.

The hours of the morning between breakfast and lunch were the times which the inhabitants of Riseholme chiefly devoted to spying on each other. They went about from shop to shop on household businesses, occasionally making purchases which they carried away with them in little paper parcels with convenient loops of string, but the real object of those excursions was to see what everybody else was doing, and learn what fresh interests had sprung up like mushrooms during the night. Georgie would be matching silks at the draper's, and very naturally he would carry them from the obscurity of the interior to the door, in order to be certain about the shades, and keep an eye on the comings and goings in the street, and very naturally Mr. Lucas, on his way to the market-gardener's to inquire whether he had yet received the bulbs from Holland, would tell him that Lucia had received the piano-arrangement of the Mozart trio. Georgie, for his part, would mention that Hermy and Ursy were expected that evening, and Peppino, enriched by this item, would " toddle on," as his phrase went, to meet and exchange confidences with the next spy. He had noticed incidentally that Georgie carried a small oblong box with hard corners, which, perfectly correctly, he conjectured to be cigarettes for Hermy and Ursy, since Georgie never smoked.

" Well, I must be toddling on," he said, after identifying Georgie's box of cigarettes, and being rather puzzled by a bulge in Georgie's pocket. " You'll be looking in some time this morning, perhaps ? "

Georgie had not been quite sure that he would (for he was very busy, owing to the arrival of his sisters, and the necessity of going to Mr. Holroyd's, in order that that artist might accurately match the shade of his hair with a view to the expensive *toupet*), but the mention of the arrival of the Mozart trio decided him. He intended anyhow before he went home for lunch to stroll past The Hurst, and see if he did not hear—to adopt a mixed metaphor—the sound of the diligent practice of that classical morsel going on inside. Probably the soft pedal would be down, but he had marvellously acute hearing, and he would be very much surprised if he did not hear the recognisable chords, and even more surprised if, when they came to practise the piece together, Lucia did not give him to understand that she was reading it for the first time. He had already got a copy, and had practised his part

last night, but then he was in the superior position of
not having a husband who could inadvertently " tell
on him." Meantime it was of the first importance to
get that particular shade of purple that had none of
that " tarsome " magenta-tint in it. Meantime, also,
it was of even greater importance to observe the movements of Riseholme.

Just opposite was the village green, and as nobody
was quite close to him, Georgie put on his wire-rimmed
spectacles, which he could whisk off in a moment.
It was they which formed that bulge in his pocket
which Peppino had noticed, but the fact of his using
spectacles at all was a secret that would have to be
profoundly kept for several years yet. But as there
was no one at all near him, he stealthily adjusted them
on his small straight nose. The morning train from
town had evidently come in, for there was a bustle of
cabs about the door of the Ambermere Arms, and
a thing that thrilled him to the marrow was the fact
that Lady Ambermere's motor was undoubtedly among
them. That must surely mean that Lady Ambermere
herself was here, for when poor thin Miss Lyall, her
companion, came in to Riseholme to do shopping, or
transact such business as the majestic life at The Hall
required, she always came on foot, or, in very inclement
weather, in a small two-wheeled cart like a hip-bath.
At this moment, steeped in conjecture, who should
appear, walking stiffly, with her nose in the air, as if
suspecting, and not choosing to verify, some faint
unpleasant odour, but Lady Ambermere herself,
coming from the direction of The Hurst. . . . Clearly
she must have got there after Peppino had left, or he
would surely have mentioned the fact that Lady Ambermere had been at The Hurst, if she *had* been at The
Hurst. It is true that she was only coming from the

direction of The Hurst, but Georgie practised, though
he was not aware of, Darwin's proposition, that in
order to observe usefully you must have a theory.
Georgie's theory was that Lady Ambermere had been
at The Hurst just for a minute or two, and hastily
put his spectacles in his pocket. With the precision
of a trained mind, he also formed the theory that some
business had brought Lady Ambermere into Riseholme,
and that taking advantage of her presence there, she
had probably returned a verbal answer to Lucia's
invitation to her garden-party, which she would have
received by the first post this morning. He was
quite ready to put his theory to the test when Lady
Ambermere had arrived at the suitable distance for
his conveniently observing her, and for taking off his
hat. She always treated him like a boy, which he
liked.

The usual salutations passed.

"I don't know where my people are," said
Lady Ambermere majestically. "Have you seen my
motor?"

"Yes, dear lady; it's in—er—at your own arms,"
said Georgie brightly. "Happy motor!"

If Lady Ambermere unbent to anybody, she unbent
to Georgie. He was of quite good family, because his
mother had been a Bartlett, and a second cousin of
her deceased husband. Sometimes when she talked
to Georgie she said "we," implying thereby his
connection with the aristocracy; this gratified
Georgie nearly as much as did her treatment of him as
being quite a boy still. It was to him as a boy still
that she answered.

"Well, the happy motor, you little rascal, must
come to my arms instead of being at them," she said,
with the quick wit for which Riseholme pronounced

her famous. " Fancy being able to see my motor at that distance. Young eyes ! "

It was really young spectacles, but Georgie did not mind that. In fact he would not have corrected the mistake for the world.

" Shall I run across and fetch it for you ? " he asked.

" In a minute. Whistle on your fingers like a vulgar street-boy," said Lady Ambermere. " I'm sure you know how to."

Georgie had not the slightest idea, but with the courage of youth, he presumed (with the prudence of middle-age) that he would not really be called upon to perform so unimaginable a feat, and put two fingers up to his mouth.

" Here goes, then ! " he said, greatly daring. (He knew perfectly well that the dignity of Lady Ambermere would not permit rude, vulgar whistling, of which he was hopelessly incapable, to summon her motor.) She made a feint of stopping her ears with her hands.

" Don't do anything of the kind," she said. " In a minute you shall walk with me across to the Arms, but tell me this first. I have just been to say to our good Mrs. Lucas that very likely I will look in at her garden-party on Friday, if I have nothing else to do. But who is this wonderful creature she is expecting ? Is he an Indian conjuror ? If so, I should like to see him, because when Ambermere was in Madras I remember one coming to the Residency who had cobras and that sort of thing. I told Mrs. Lucas I didn't like snakes, and she said there shouldn't be any. In fact, it was all rather mysterious, and she didn't at present know if he was coming or not. I only said ' No snakes ! I insist on no snakes.' "

Georgie relieved her mind about the chance of

there being snakes, and gave a short *précis* of the ascertained habits of the Guru, laying special stress on his high caste.

" Yes, some of those Brahmins are of very decent family," admitted Lady Ambermere. " I was always against lumping all dark-skinned people together and calling them niggers. When we were at Maαras I was famed for my discrimination."

They were walking across the green as Lady Ambermere gave vent to these liberal sentiments, and Georgie even without the need of his spectacles could see Peppino, who had spied Lady Ambermere from the door of the market-gardener's, hurrying down the street, in order to get a word with her before " her people " drove her back to The Hall.

" I came in to Riseholme to-day to get rooms at the Arms for Olga Bracely," she observed.

" The prima-donna ? " asked Georgie, breathless with excitement.

" Yes ; she is coming to stay at the Arms for two nights with Mr. Shuttleworth."

" Surely——" began Georgie.

" No ; it is all right ; he is her husband ; they were married last week," said Lady Ambermere. " I should have thought that Shuttleworth was a good enough name, as the Shuttleworths are cousins of the late lord, but she prefers to call herself Miss Bracely. I don't dispute her right to call herself what she pleases : far from it, though who the Bracelys were, I have never been able to discover. But when Charlie Shuttleworth wrote to me, saying that he and his wife were intending to stay here for a couple of days, and proposing to come over to The Hall to see me, I thought I would just look in at the Arms myself, and see that they were promised proper accommodation.

They will dine with me to-morrow. I have a few people staying, and no doubt Miss Bracely will sing afterwards. My Broadwood was always considered a remarkably fine instrument. It was very proper of Charlie Shuttleworth to say that he would be in the neighbourhood, and I daresay she is a very decent sort of woman."

They had come to the motor by this time—the rich, the noble coach, as Mr. Pepys would have described it—and there was poor Miss Lyall hung with parcels, and wearing a faint sycophantic smile. This miserable spinster, of age so obvious as to be called uncertain, was Lady Ambermere's companion, and shared with her the glories of The Hall, which had been left to Lady Ambermere for life. She was provided with food and lodging and the use of the cart like a hip-bath, when Lady Ambermere had errands for her to do in Riseholme, so what could a woman want more? In return for these bounties, her only duty was to devote herself body and mind to her patroness, to read the paper aloud, to set Lady Ambermere's patterns for needlework, to carry the little Chinese dog under her arm, and wash him once a week, to accompany Lady Ambermere to church, and never to have a fire in her bedroom. She had a melancholy, wistful little face ; her head was inclined with a backward slope on her neck, and her mouth was invariably a little open showing long front teeth, so that she looked rather like a roast hare sent up to table with its head on. Georgie always had a joke ready for Miss Lyall, of the sort that made her say : " Oh, Mr. Pillson ! " and caused her to blush. She thought him remarkably pleasant.

Georgie had his joke ready on this occasion.

" Why, here's Miss Lyall ! " he said. " And what

has Miss Lyall been doing while Ladyship and I
have been talking? Better not ask, perhaps."

" Oh, Mr. Pillson! " said Miss Lyall, as punctually
as a cuckoo-clock when the hands point to the hour.

Lady Ambermere put half her weight on to the step
of the motor, causing it to creak and sway.

" Call on the Shuttleworths, Georgie," she said.
" Say I told you to. Home! "

Miss Lyall effaced herself on the front seat of the
motor, like a mouse hiding in a corner, after Lady
Ambermere had got in, and the footman mounted
the box. At that moment Peppino, with his bag of
bulbs, squeezed his way, a little out of breath, between
two cabs by the side of the motor. He was just
too late, and the motor moved off. It was very
improbable that Lady Ambermere saw him at all.

Georgie felt very much like a dog with a bone
in his mouth, who only wants to get away from all
the other dogs, and discuss it quietly. It is safe to
say that never in twenty-four hours had so many
exciting things happened to him. He had ordered
a *toupet*, he had been looked on with favour by a Guru,
all Riseholme knew that he had had quite a long
conversation with Lady Ambermere, and nobody in
Riseholme, except himself, knew that Olga Bracely
was going to spend two nights here. Well he remembered her marvellous appearance last year at Covent
Garden in the part of Brünnhilde. He had gone to
town for a drastic but rejuvenating visit to his dentist,
and the " tarsomeness " of being betwixt and between
had been quite forgotten by him when he saw her awake
to Siegfried's kiss on the mountain-top. " *Das ist
keine Mann*," Siegfried had said, and, to be sure, that
was very clever of him, for she looked like some slim,
beardless boy, and not in the least like those great

fat fraus at Baireuth, whom nobody could have mistaken for a man as they bulged and heaved even before the strings of the breastplate were cut by his sword. And then she sat up and hailed the sun, and Georgie felt for a moment that he had quite taken the wrong turn in life when he settled to spend his life in this boyish, maidenly manner with his embroidery and his china-dusting at Riseholme. He ought to have been Siegfried. . . . He had bought a photograph of her in her cuirass and helmet, and often looked at it when he was not too busy with something else. He had even championed his goddess against Lucia, when she pronounced that Wagner was totally lacking in knowledge of dramatic effects. To be sure, she had never seen any Wagner opera, but she had heard the overture to *Tristan* performed at the Queen's Hall, and if that was Wagner, well——

Already, though Lady Ambermere's motor had not yet completely vanished up the street, Riseholme was gently closing in round him, in order to discover by discreet questions (as in the game of Clumps) what he and she had been talking about. There was Colonel Boucher with his two snorting bull-dogs closing in from one side, and Mrs. Weston in her bath-chair being wheeled relentlessly towards him from another, and the two Misses Antrobus sitting playfully on the stocks on the third, and Peppino at close range on the fourth. Everyone knew, too, that he did not lunch till half-past one, and there was really no reason why he should not stop and chat as usual. But with the eye of the true general, he saw that he could most easily break the surrounding cordon by going off in the direction of Colonel Boucher, because Colonel Boucher always said : " Haw, hum," before he descended into

coherent speech, and thus Georgie could forestall
him with " Good-morning, Colonel," before he got to
business. He did not like passing close to those
slobbering bull-dogs, but something had to be done.
. . . Next moment he was clear, and saw that the
other spies were still converging on each other, and
following out his original scheme, he walked briskly
down towards Lucia's house, to listen for any familiar
noises out of Mozart's trio. There they were, and
the soft pedal was down just as he expected, so, that
business being off his mind, he continued his walk for a
few hundred yards more, meaning to make a short
circuit through fields, cross the bridge over the happy
stream that flowed into the Avon, and regain his house
by the door at the bottom of the garden. Then he
would sit and think . . . the Guru, Olga Bracely. . . .
What if he asked Olga Bracely and her husband to
dine, and persuaded Mrs. Quantock to let the Guru
come ? That would be three men and one woman,
and Hermy and Ursy would make all square. Six
for dinner was the utmost that Foljambe permitted.

He had come to the stile that led into the fields,
and sat there for a moment. Lucia's tentative melo-
dies were still faintly audible, but even while he sat
there they stopped, and he guessed that she was looking
out of the window. She was too great to take part
in the morning spying that went on round about the
green, but she often saw a good deal from her window.
He wondered what Mrs. Quantock was meaning to do :
apparently she had not promised the Guru for the garden-party, or else Lady Ambermere would not have said
that Lucia did not know whether he was coming or not.
Perhaps Mrs. Quantock was going to run him herself,
and grant him neither to the Queen nor Georgie. . . .
That was sheer Bolshevism, and at this giddy moment,

Georgie felt that he had the making of a Bolshevist too. Lucia's yoke was heavy sometimes, and he daringly wondered what would happen if he asked Olga Bracely to dinner, without mentioning to Lucia that she would be here on the afternoon of the garden-party. Georgie was a Bartlett on his mother's side, and he played the piano better than Lucia, and he had twenty-four hours' leisure every day, which he could devote to being King of Riseholme. . . . His nature flared up, burning with a red revolutionary flame, that was fed by his secret knowledge about Olga Bracely. Why should Lucia rule everyone with her rod of iron ? Why, and again, why ?

Suddenly he heard his name called in the familiar alto, and there was Lucia in Shakespeare's garden.

" Georgino ! Georgino mio ! " she cried. " *Gino !* "

Out of mere habit, Georgie got down from his stile, and tripped up the road towards her. The manly seething of his soul's insurrection rebuked him, but unfortunately his legs and his voice surrendered.

" *Amica!* " he answered. " Here's Gino ! " (" And why do I say it in Italian ? " he vainly asked himself.)

" Geordie, come and have ickle talk," she said, relapsing into baby-speech. " Me want 'oo wise man to advise ickle Lucia."

" What 'oo want ? " asked Georgie, now quite quelled for the moment.

" Lots-things. Here's pwetty flower for buttonholie. Now tell me about black man. Him no snakes have ? Why Mrs. Quantock say she thinks he no come to poo' Lucia's party-garden ? "

" Oh, did she ? " asked Georgie, relapsing into the vernacular.

" Yes, oh, and by the way, there's a parcel come which I think must be the Mozart trio. Will you come

over to-morrow morning and read it with me ? Yes ?
Half-past eleven, then. But never mind that."

She fixed him with her beady, birdy eye.

" Daisy asked me to ask the Guru," she said, " and
so to oblige poor Daisy I did. And now she says she
doesn't know if he'll come. What does that mean ?
Is it possible that she wants to keep him to herself ?
She has done that sort of thing before, you know."

This probably represented Lucia's statement of the
sad case about the Scotch attorney, and Georgie,
taking it as such, felt rather embarrassed. Also that
bird-like eye seemed to gimlet its way into him, and
divine the secret disloyalty that he had been con-
templating. If she had continued to bore into him,
he might not only have confessed to the gloomiest
suspicions about Mrs. Quantock, but have let go of his
secret about Olga Bracely also, and suggested the
possibility of her and her husband being brought
to the garden-party. But the eye at this moment
unscrewed itself from his again and travelled up the
road.

" There's the Guru ! " she said. " Now we will
see ! "

Georgie, faint with emotion, peered out between the
forms of the peacock and the pine-apple on the yew
hedge, and saw what followed. Lucia went straight
up to the Guru, bowed and smiled and clearly introduced herself. In another moment he was showing
his white teeth and salaaming, and together they
walked back to The Hurst, where Georgie palpitated
behind the yew hedge. Together they entered, and
Lucia's eye wore its benignest aspect.

" I want to introduce to you, Guru," she said,
without a stumble, " a great friend of mine. This
is Mr. Pillson, Guru. Guru, Mr. Pillson. The Guru

is coming to tiffin with me, Georgie. Cannot I persuade you to stop ? "

" Delighted ! " said Georgie. " We met before in a sort of way, didn't we ? "

" Yes indeed. So pleased," said the Guru.

" Let us go in," said Lucia. " It is close on lunch-time."

Georgie followed, after a great many bowings and politenesses from the Guru. He was not sure if he had the makings of a Bolshevik.

CHAPTER V

ONE of Lucia's greatnesses lay in the fact that when
she found anybody out in some act of atrocious meanness, she never indulged in any idle threats of revenge :
it was sufficient that she knew, and would take suitable
steps on the earliest occasion. Consequently when
it appeared, from the artless conversation of the Guru
at lunch, that the perfidious Mrs. Quantock had not
even asked him whether he would like to go to Lucia's
garden-party or not (pending her own decision as to
what she was meaning to do with him), Lucia received
the information with the utmost good-humour, merely
saying : " No doubt dear Mrs. Quantock forgot to
tell you," and did not announce acts of reprisal, such
as striking Daisy off the list of her habitual guests
for a week or two, just to give her a lesson. She
even, before they sat down to lunch, telephoned over
to that thwarted woman to say that she had met
the Guru in the street, and had felt that there was
some bond of sympathy between them, and he had come
back with her, and they were just sitting down to tiffin.
She was pleased with the word " tiffin," and also liked
explaining to Daisy what it meant.

Tiffin was a great success, and there was no need for
the Guru to visit the kitchen in order to make something that could be eaten without struggle. He
talked quite freely about his mission here, and Lucia
and Georgie and Peppino, who had come in rather

84

late, for he had been obliged to go back to the market-gardener's about the bulbs, listened entranced.

" Yes, it was when I went to my friend in London who keeps the book-shop," he said, " that I heard there was English lady who wanted Guru, and I knew I was called to her. No luggage, no anything at all : as I am. Such a kind lady, too, and she will get on well, but she will find some of the postures difficult, for she is what you call globe, round."

" Was that postures when I saw her standing on one leg in the garden ? " asked Georgie, " and when she sat down and tried to hold her toes ? "

" Yes, indeed, quite so, and difficult for globe. But she has white soul."

He looked round with a smile.

" I see many white souls here," he said. " It is happy place, when there are white souls, for to those I am sent."

This was sufficient : in another minute Lucia, Georgie and Peppino were all accepted as pupils, and presently they went out into the garden, where the Guru sat on the ground in a most complicated attitude, which was obviously quite out of reach of Mrs. Quantock.

" One foot on one thigh, other foot on other thigh," he explained. " And the head and back straight : it is good to meditate so."

Lucia tried to imagine meditating so, but felt that any meditation so would certainly be on the subject of broken bones.

" Shall I be able to do that ? " she asked. " And what will be the effect ? "

" You will be light and active, dear lady, and ah— here is other dear lady come to join us."

Mrs. Quantock had certainly made one of her

diplomatic errors on this occasion, She had acquiesced on the telephone in her Guru going to lunch with Lucia, but about the middle of her lunch she had been unable to resist the desire to know what was happening at The Hurst. She could not bear the thought that Lucia and her Guru were together now, and her own note saying that it was uncertain whether the Guru would come to the garden-party or not filled her with the most uneasy apprehensions. She would sooner have acquiesced in her Guru going to fifty garden-parties—all was public, and she could keep an eye and a control on him—rather than that Lucia should have " enticed him in "—that was her phrase—to lunch like this. The only consolation was that her own lunch had been practically inedible, and Robert had languished lamentably for the Guru to return and save his stomach. She had left him glowering over a little mud and water, called coffee. Robert, at any rate, would welcome the return of the Guru.

She waddled across the lawn to where this harmonious party was sitting, and at that moment Lucia began to feel vindictive. The calm of victory, which had permeated her when she brought the Guru in to lunch, without any bother at all, was troubled and broken up, and darling Daisy's note containing the outrageous falsity that the Guru would not for certain accept an invitation which had never been permitted to reach him at all, assumed a more sinister aspect. Clearly Daisy had intended to keep him to herself, and had made a hostile invasion.

" Guru, dear, you naughty thing," said Mrs. Quantock playfully, after the usual salutations had passed. " Why did you not tell *chela* you would not be home for tiffin ? "

The Guru had unwound his legs, and stood up.

" But, see, beloved lady," he said, " how pleasant we all are ! Take not too much thought, when it is only white souls who are together."

Mrs. Quantock patted his shoulder.

" It is all good and kind, Om," she said. " Send out my message of love. There ! "

It was necessary to descend from these high altitudes, and Lucia proceeded to do so, as in a parachute that dropped swiftly at first, and then floated in still air.

" And we're making such a lovely plan, dear Daisy," she said. " The Guru is going to teach us all. Classes ! Aren't you ? "

He held his hands up to his head, palms outwards, and closed his eyes.

" I seem to feel call," he said. " I am sent. Surely the Guides tell me there is a sending of me. What you call classes ? Yes ? I teach : you learn. We all learn. . . . I leave all to you. I will walk a little way off to arbour, and meditate, and then when you have arranged, you will tell Guru, who is your servant. Salaam ! Om ! "

With the Guru in her own house, and with every intention to annex him, it was no wonder that Lucia took the part of chairman in this meeting that was to settle the details of the esoteric brotherhood now actually being formed in Riseholme. Had not Mrs. Quantock been present, Lucia, in revenge for her perfidious conduct about the garden-party invitation, would probably have left her out of the classes altogether, but with her sitting firm and square in a basket-chair, that creaked querulously as she moved, she could not be completely ignored. But Lucia took the lead throughout, and suggested straight away that the smoking-parlour would be the most convenient place to hold the classes in.

" I should not think of invading your house, dear Daisy," she said, " and here is the smoking-parlour, which no one ever sits in, so quiet and peaceful. Yes. Shall we consider that settled then ? "

She turned briskly to Mrs. Quantock.

" And now, where shall the Guru stay ? " she said. " It would be too bad, dear Daisy, if we are all to profit by his classes, that you should have all the trouble and expense of entertaining him, for in your sweet little house he must be a great inconvenience, and I think you said that your husband had given up his dressing-room to him."

Mrs. Quantock made a desperate effort to retain her property.

" No inconvenience at all," she said. " Quite the contrary, in fact, dear. It is delightful having him, and Robert regards him as a most desirable inmate."

Lucia pressed her hand feelingly.

" You and your husband are too unselfish," she said. " Often have I said, ' Daisy and dear Mr. Robert are the most unselfish people I know,' haven't I, Georgino ? But we can't permit you to be so crowded. Your only spare-room, you know, *and* your husband's dressing-room. Georgie, I know you agree with me : we must not permit dear Daisy to be so unselfish."

The bird-like eye produced its compelling effect on Georgie. So short a time ago he had indulged in revolutionary ideas, and had contemplated having the Guru and Olga Bracely to dinner, without even asking Lucia : now the faint stirrings of revolt faded like snow in summer. He knew quite well what Lucia's next proposition would be : he knew, too, that he would agree to it.

" No, that would never do," he said. " It is
simply trespassing on Mrs. Quantock's good nature,
if she is to board and lodge the Guru while he
teaches all of us. I wish I could take him in, but
with Hermy and Ursy coming to-night, I have as little
room as Mrs. Quantock."

" He shall come here," said Lucia brightly, as if she
had just that moment thought of it. " There are
' Hamlet ' and ' Othello ' vacant "—all her rooms were
named after Shakespearian plays—" and it will not
be the least inconvenient. Will it, Peppino ? I
shall really like having him here. Shall we consider
that settled then ? "

Daisy made a perfectly futile effort to send forth
a message of love to all quarters of the compass.
Bitterly she repented of having ever mentioned her
Guru to Lucia : it had never occurred to her that
she would annex him like this. While she was
cudgelling her brains as to how she could arrest this
powerful offensive, Lucia went sublimely on,

" Then there is the question of what we shall pay
him," she said. " Dear Daisy tells us that he scarcely
knows what money is, but I, for one, could never
dream of profiting by his wisdom if I was to pay
nothing for it. The labourer is worthy of his hire,
and so I suppose the teacher is. What if we pay him
five shillings each a lesson : that will make a pound
a lesson ? Dear me ! I shall be busy this August.
Now how many classes shall we ask him to give us ?
I should say six to begin with, if everybody agrees.
One every day for the next week except Sunday.
That is what you all wish ? Yes ? Then shall we
consider that settled ? "

Mrs. Quantock, still impotently rebelling, resorted to
the most dire weapon in her armoury, namely sarcasm.

" Perhaps, darling Lucia," she said, " it would be well to ask my Guru if he has anything to say to your settlings. England is a free country still, even if you happen to have come from India ! "

Lucia had a deadlier weapon than sarcasm, which was the apparent unconsciousness of there having been any. For it is no use plunging a dagger into your enemy's heart if it produces no effect whatever on him. She clapped her hands together, and gave her peal of silvery laughter.

" What a good idea ! " she said. " Then you would like me to go and tell him what we propose ? Just as you like. I will trot away, shall I, and see if he agrees ? Don't think of stirring, dear Daisy : I know how you feel the heat. Sit quiet in the shade. As you know, I am a real salamander, the sun is never *troppo caldo* for me."

She tripped off to where the Guru was sitting in that wonderful position. She had read the article in the Encyclopædia about Yoga right through again this morning, and had quite made up her mind, as, indeed, her proceedings had just shown, that Yoga was, to put it irreverently, to be her August stunt. He was still so deep in meditation that he could only look dreamily in her direction as she approached, but then, with a long sigh, he got up.

" This is beautiful place," he said. " It is full of sweet influences, and I have had high talk with Guides."

Lucia felt thrilled.

" Oh, do tell me what they said to you ! " she exclaimed.

" They told me to follow where I was led : they said they would settle everything for me in wisdom and love."

This was most encouraging, for decidedly Lucia had been settling for him, and the opinion of the Guides was thus a direct personal testimonial. Any faint twitchings of conscience (they were of the very faintest) that she had grabbed dear Daisy's property were once and for ever quieted, and she proceeded confidently to unfold the settlements of wisdom and love, which met with the Guru's entire approval. He shut his eyes a moment and breathed deeply.

" They give peace and blessing," he said. " It is they who ordered that it should be so. Om ! "

He seemed to sink into profound depths of meditation, and Lucia hurried back to the group she had left.

" It is all too wonderful," she said. " The Guides have told him that they were settling everything for him in wisdom and love, so we may be sure we were right in our plans. How lovely to think that we have been guided by them ! Dear Daisy, how wonderful he is ! I will send across for his things, shall I ? and I will have ' Hamlet ' and ' Othello ' made ready for him ! "

Bitter though it was to part with her Guru, it was impious to rebel against the ordinances of the Guides, but there was a trace of human resentment in Daisy's answer.

" Things ! " she exclaimed. " He hasn't got a thing in the world. Every possession chains us down to earth. You will soon come to that, darling Lucia."

It occurred to Georgie that the Guru had certainly got a bottle of brandy, but there was no use in introducing a topic that might lead to discord, and, indeed, even as Lucia went indoors to see about " Hamlet " and " Othello ", the Guru himself, having emerged from meditation, joined them, and sat down by Mrs. Quantock.

"Beloved lady," he said, "all is peace and happiness. The Guides have spoken to me so lovingly of you, and they say it is best your Guru should come here. Perhaps I shall return to your kind house. They smiled when I asked that. But just now they send me here: there is more need of me here, for already you have so much light."

Certainly the Guides were very tactful people, for nothing would have soothed Mrs. Quantock so effectually as a message of that kind, which she would certainly report to Lucia when she returned from seeing about "Hamlet" and "Othello".

"Oh, do they say I have much light already, Guru dear?" she asked. "That is nice of them."

"Surely they said it, and now I shall go back to your house, and leave sweet thoughts there for you. And shall I send sweet thoughts to the house of the kind gentleman next door?"

Georgie eagerly welcomed this proposition, for with Hermy and Ursy coming that evening he felt that he would have plenty of use for sweet thoughts. He even forbore to complete in his own mind the conjecture that was forming itself there, namely that though the Guru would be leaving sweet thoughts for Mrs. Quantock, he would probably be taking away the brandy bottle for himself. But Georgie knew that he was only too apt to indulge in secret cynicisms, and perhaps there was no brandy to take away by this time . . . and, lo and behold, he was being cynical again.

The sun was still hot when, half an hour afterwards, he got into the cab which he had ordered to take him to the station to meet Hermy and Ursy, and

he put up his umbrella with its white linen cover to
shield him from it. He did not take the motor, because
either Hermy or Ursy would have insisted on driving
it, and he did not choose to trust himself in their charge.
In all the years that he had lived at Riseholme, he
never remembered even in winter, when social events—
" work " he called it—were most numerous, so exciting
and varied a week. There were Hermy and Ursy
coming this evening, and Olga Bracely and her
husband (Olga Bracely and Mr. Shuttleworth sounded
vaguely improper : Georgie rather liked that) coming
to-morrow, and Lucia's garden-party the day after,
and every day there was to be a lesson from the Guru,
so that God alone knew when Georgie would have a
moment to himself for his embroidery or to practise
the Mozart trio. But with his hair chestnut-coloured
to the very roots, and his shining nails, and his comfortable boots, he felt extremely young and fit for
anything. Soon, under the influence of the new
creed with its postures and breathings, he would feel
younger and more vigorous yet.

But he wished that it had been he who had found
this pamphlet on Eastern philosophies which had
led Mrs. Quantock to make the inquiries that had
resulted in the epiphany of the Guru. Of course
when once Lucia had heard about it, she was certain
to constitute herself head and leader of the movement,
and it was really remarkable how completely she had
done that. In that meeting in the garden just now
she had just sailed through Mrs. Quantock, as calmly
as a steamer cuts through the waters of the sea, throwing her off from her penetrating bows like a spent wave.
But, baffled though she was for the moment, Georgie
had been aware that Mrs. Quantock seethed with
revolutionary ideas : she deeply resented this

confiscation of what was certainly her property, though she was impotent to stop it, and Georgie knew just what she felt. It was all very well to say that Lucia's schemes were entirely in accord with the purposes of the Guides. That might be so, but Mrs. Quantock would not cease to think that she had been robbed. . . .

Yet nothing mattered if all the class found themselves getting young and active and loving and excellent under this tuition. It was that notion which had taken such entire command of them all, and for his part Georgie did not really care who owned the Guru, so to speak, if only he got the benefits of his teaching. For social purposes Lucia had annexed him, and doubtless with him in the house she would get little instructions and hints that would not count as a lesson, but, after all, Georgie had still got Olga Bracely to himself, for he had not breathed a word of her advent to Lucia. He felt rather like one who, when revolutionary ideas are in the air, had concealed a revolver in his pocket. He did not formulate to himself precisely what he was going to do with it, but it gave him a sense of power to know it was there.

The train came in, but he looked in vain for his sisters. They had distinctly said they were arriving by it, but in a couple of minutes it was perfectly clear that they had done nothing of the kind, for the only person who got out was Mrs. Weston's cook, who, as all the world knew, went into Brinton every Wednesday to buy fish. At the rear of the train, however, was an immense quantity of luggage being taken out, which could not all be Mrs. Weston's fish, and, indeed, even at this distance there was something familiar to Georgie about a very large green hold-all which was dumped there. Perhaps Hermy and Ursy had travelled in the van, because " it was such a lark," or for some other tomboy reason, and he went down the platform to investigate. There were bags of golf-clubs, and a dog, and portmanteaux, and, even as the conviction dawned on him that he had seen some of these objects before, the guard, to whom Georgie always gave half a crown when he travelled by this train, presented him with a note scrawled in pencil. It ran :

" DEAREST GEORGIE,

" It was such a lovely day that when we got to Paddington Ursy and I decided to bicycle down instead, for a lark. So we sent our things on, and we may arrive to-night, but probably to-morrow. Take care of Tiptree : and give him plenty of jam. He loves it.

" Yours,

" HERMY.

" P.S.—Tipsipoozie doesn't really bite : it's only his fun."

Georgie crumpled up this odious epistle, and became aware that Tipsipoozie, a lean Irish terrier, was regarding him with peculiar disfavour, and showing all his teeth, probably in fun. In pursuance of this humorous idea, he then darted towards Georgie, and would have been extremely funny if he had not been handicapped by the bag of golf-clubs to which he was tethered. As it was he pursued him down the platform towing the clubs after him till he got entangled in them and fell down.

Georgie hated dogs at any time, though he had
never hated one so much as Tipsipoozie, and the
problems of life became more complicated than ever.
Certainly he was not going to drive back with Tipsipoozie in his cab, and it became necessary to hire
another for that abominable hound and the rest of the
luggage. And what on earth was to happen when he
arrived home if Tipsipoozie did not drop his fun and
become serious ? Foljambe, it is true, liked dogs,
so perhaps dogs liked her. . . . " But it is most
tarsome of Hermy ! " thought Georgie bitterly.
" I wonder what the Guru would do."

There ensued a very trying ten minutes, in which the
station-master, the porters, Georgie and Mrs. Weston's
maid all called Tipsipoozie a good dog, as he lay on
the ground snapping at the golf-clubs. Eventually a
valiant porter picked up the bag of clubs, and by
holding them out in front of him at the extreme
length of his arms in the manner of a fishing-rod,
with Tipsipoozie on a short chain at the other end of
the bag, like a savage fish, cursing and swearing,
managed to propel him into the cab, and there was
another half-crown gone. Georgie thereupon got into
his cab and sped homewards, in order to arrive there
first and consult with Foljambe. Foljambe usually
thought of something.

Foljambe came out at the noise of the arriving
wheels, and Georgie explained the absence of his
sisters and the advent of an atrocious dog.

" He's very fierce," he said " but he likes jam."

Foljambe gave that superior smile, which sometimes
Georgie resented. Now he hailed it as if it was " an
angel-face's smile."

" I'll see to him, sir," she said. " I've brought up
your tea ! "

" But you'll take care, Foljambe, won't you? " he asked.

" I expect he'd better take care," returned this intrepid woman.

Georgie, as he often said, trusted Foljambe completely, which must explain why he went into his drawing-room, shut the door, and looked out of the window when the cab arrived. She opened the door, put her arms inside, and next moment emerged again with Tipsipoozie on the end of the chain, making extravagant exhibitions of delight. Then, to Georgie's horror, the drawing-room door opened, and in came Tipsipoozie without any chain at all.

Rapidly sending a message of love in all directions like an S.O.S. call, Georgie put a small chair in front of him to shield his legs. Tipsipoozie evidently thought it was a game, and hid behind the sofa to rush out again from ambush.

" Just got snappy being tied to those golf-clubs! " remarked Foljambe.

But Georgie, as he put some jam into his saucer, could not help wondering whether the message of love had not done it.

He dined alone, for Hermy and Ursy did not appear, and had a great polishing of his knick-knacks afterwards, while waiting for them. No one ever felt anxious at the non-arrival of those sisters, for they always turned up from their otter-hunting or their golf sooner or later, chiefly later, in the highest spirits at the larks they had had, with amazingly dirty hands and prodigious appetites. But when twelve o'clock struck he decided to give up all idea of their appearance that night, and having given Tipsipoozie some more jam and a comfortable bed in the woodshed, went upstairs to his room. Though he knew it was still

possible that he might be roused by wild " Cooees ! "
and showers of gravel at his window, and have to
come down and minister to their gross appetites, the
prospect seemed improbable, and he soon went to
sleep.

Georgie awoke with a start some hours later, wondering what had disturbed him.   There was no gravel
rattling at his window, no violent ringing of bicycle-
bells, nor loud genial shouts outraging the decorous
calm of Riseholme, but certainly he had heard something. Next moment, the repeated noise sent his
heart leaping into his throat, for quite distinctly he
heard a muffled sound in the room below, which
he instantly diagnosed with fatal certainty as
burglars.

The first emotion that mingled itself with his sheer
terror was a passionate regret that Hermy and Ursy
had not come. They would have thought it tremendous larks, and would have invented some wonderful offensive with fire-irons and golf-clubs and dumb-
bells. Even Tipsipoozie, the lately abhorred, would
have been a succour in this crisis, and why, oh why,
had not Georgie had him to sleep in his bedroom
instead of making him cosy in the woodshed ?   He
would have let Tipsipoozie sleep on his lovely blue
quilt for the remainder of his days if only Tipsipoozie
could have been with him now, ready to have fun
with the burglars below. As it was, the servants were
in the attics at the top of the house, Dickie slept out,
and Georgie was all alone, with the prospect of having
to defend his property at risk of his life.   Even at
this moment, as he sat up in bed, blanched with terror,
these miscreants might be putting his treasures into
their pockets. The thought of the Fabergé cigarette-
case, and the Louis XVI. snuff-box, and the Queen

Anne toy-porringer which he had inherited all these years, made even life seem cheap, for life would be intolerable without them, and he sprang out of bed, groped for his slippers, since until he had made a plan it was wiser not to show a light, and shuffled stealthily towards the door.

CHAPTER VI

THE door-handle felt icy to fingers already frozen with fright, but he stood firmly grasping it, ready to turn it noiselessly when he had quite made up his mind what to do. The first expedient that suggested itself, with an overpowering sweetness of relief, was that of locking his door, going back to bed again, and pretending that he had heard nothing. But apart from the sheer cowardice of that, which he did not mind so much, as nobody else would ever know his guilt and he could live it down quietly, the thought of the burglars going off quite unmolested with his property was intolerable. Even if he could not summon up enough courage to go downstairs with his life and a poker in his hand, he must at least give them a good fright. They had frightened him, and so he would frighten them. They should not have it all their own way, and if he decided not to attack them (or him) single-handed, he could at least thump on the floor, or call out " Burglars ! " at the top of his voice, or shout " Charles ! Henry ! Thomas ! " as if summoning a bevy of stalwart footmen. The objection to this course however, would be that Foljambe or somebody else might hear him, and in this case, if he did not then go downstairs to mortal combat, the knowledge of his cowardice would be the property of others beside himself. . . . And all the time he hesitated, they were probably filling their pockets with his dearest possessions.

He tried to send out a message of love, but he was totally unable to do so.

Then the little clock on his mantel-piece struck two, which was a miserable hour, sundered so far from dawn.

Though he had lived through years of agony since he got out of bed, the actual passage of time, as he stood frozen to his door-handle, was but the duration of a few brief seconds, and then, making a tremendous call on his courage, he felt his way to his fireplace, and picked up, the poker. The tongs and shovel rattled treacherously, and he hoped that had not been heard, for the essence of his plan (though he had yet no idea what that plan was) must be silence till some awful surprise broke upon the burglars. If only he could summon the police, he could come rushing downstairs with his poker, as the professional supporters of the law gained an entrance to his house, but unfortunately the telephone was downstairs, and he could not reasonably hope to carry on a conversation with the police-station without being overheard by the burglars.

He opened his door with so masterly a movement that there was no sound, either from the hinges or from the handle as he turned it, and peered out. The hall below was dark, but a long pencil of light came from the drawing-room, which showed where the reckless brutes must be, and there, too, alas! was his case of treasures. Then suddenly he heard the sound of a voice, speaking very low, and another voice answered it. At that George's heart sank, for this proved that there must be at least two burglars, and the odds against him were desperate. After that came a low, cruel laugh, and the unmistakable sound of the rattle of knives and forks, and the explosive

uncorking of a bottle. At that his heart sank even
lower yet, for he had read that cool habitual burglars
always had supper before they got to work, and therefore he was about to deal with a gang of professionals.
Also that explosive uncorking clearly indicated champagne, and he knew that they were feasting on his
best. And how wicked of them to take their un-
hallowed meal in his drawing-room, for there was no
proper table there, and they would be making a
dreadful mess over everything.

A current of cool night air swept up the stairs, and
Georgie saw the panel of light from the open drawing-
room door diminish in width, and presently the door
shut with a soft thud, leaving him in the dark. At
that his desperation seemed pressed and concentrated
into a moment of fictitious courage, for he unerringly
reasoned that they had left the drawing-room window
open, and that perhaps in a few moments now they
would have finished their meal and with bulging
pockets would step forth unchallenged into the night.
Why had he never had bells put on his shutters like
Mrs. Weston, who lived in nightly terror of burglars ?
But it was too late to think of that now, for it was
impossible to ask them to step out till he had put
bells up, and then, when he was ready, begin again.

He could not let them go, gorged with his champagne and laden with his treasures, without reprisals
of some sort, and keeping his thoughts steadily away
from revolvers and clubs and sandbags, walked straight
downstairs, threw open the drawing-room door, and
with his poker grasped in his shaking hand, cried out
in a faint thin voice :

" If you move I shall fire ! "

There was a moment of dead silence, and a little
dazzled with the light, he saw what faced him.

At opposite ends of his Chippendale sofa sat Hermy and Ursy. Hermy had her mouth open and held a bun in her dirty hands. Ursy had her mouth shut and her cheeks were bulging. Between them was a ham and a loaf of bread, and a pot of marmalade and a Stilton cheese, and on the floor was the bottle of champagne, and two brimming bubbling tea-cups full of wine. The cork and the wire and the tinfoil, they had, with some show of decency, thrown into the fireplace.

Hermy put down her bun, and gave a great shout of laughter : Ursy's mouth was disgustingly full and she exploded. Then they lay back against the arms of the sofa and howled.

Georgie was very much vexed.

" Upon my word, Hermy ! " he said, and then found it was not nearly a strong enough expression. And in a moment of ungovernable irritation he said :

" Damn it all ! "

Hermy showed signs of recovery first, and, as Georgie came back after shutting the window, could find her voice, while Ursy collected small fragments of ham and bread which she had partially chewed.

" Lord ! What a lark ! " she said. " Georgie, it's *the* most ripping lark !

Ursy pointed to the poker.

" He'll fire if we move," she cried, " or poke the fire, was it ? "

" Ask another ! " screamed Hermy. " O dear, he thought we were burglars, and came down with a poker, brave boy ! It's positively the limit. Have a drink, Georgie."

Suddenly her eyes grew round and awestruck, and pointing with her finger to Georgie's shoulder, she went off into another yell of laughter.

" Ursy! His hair ! " she said, and buried her face in a sofa-cusion.

Naturally Georgie had not put his hair in order when he came downstairs, for nobody thinks about things like that when he is going to encounter burglars single-handed, and there was his bald pate, and his long tresses hanging down one side.

It was most annoying, but when an inevitable annoyance has absolutely occurred, the only possible thing for a decent person to do, is to take it as lightly as possible. Georgie rose gallantly to the occasion, gave a little squeal and ran from the room.

" Down again presently," he called out, and had a heavy fall on the stairs as he went up to his bed-room. There he had a short argument with himself. It was possible to slam his door, go to bed, and be very polite in the morning. But that would never do : Hermy and Ursy would have a joke against him for ever. It was really much better to share in the joke, identifying himself with it. So he brushed his hair in the orthodox fashion, put on a very smart dressing-gown, and came tripping downstairs again.

" My dears, what fun ! " he said. " Let's all have supper. But let's move into the dining-room, where there's a table, and I'll get another bottle of wine, and some glasses, and we'll bring Tipsipoozie in. You naughty girls, fancy arriving at a time like this ! I suppose your plan was to go very quietly to bed, and come down to breakfast in the morning, and give me a fine surprise. Tell me all about it now."

So presently Tipsipoozie was having his marmalade, which did just as well as jam, and they were all cutting slices off the ham and stuffing them in split buns.

" Yes, we thought we might as well do it all in one go " said Hermy, " and it's a hundred and twenty

miles if it's a yard.   And then it was so late when we
got here, we thought we wouldn't disturb you, specially
as the drawing-room window wasn't bolted."

"Bicycles outside," said Ursy, "they'll just have
to be out at grass till morning.   Oh, Tipsi-ipsi-poozie-
woozy, how is you ?   Hope he behaved like the good
little Tiptree that he is, Georgie ? "

"Oh, yes, we made great friends," said Georgie
sketchily.   "He was wee bit upset at the station,
but then he had good tea with his Uncle Georgie and
played hide-and-seek."

Rather rashly, Georgie "made a face" at Tiptree,
the sort of face which amuses children.   But it didn't
amuse Tiptree, who made another face, in which
teeth played a prominent part.

"Fool-dog," said Hermy, carelessly smacking him
across the nose.   "Always hit him if he shows his
teeth, Georgie.   Pass the fizz."

"Well, so we got through the drawing-room window," continued Ursy, "and Golly, we were hungry.
So we foraged, and there we were !   Jolly plucky of
you, Georgie, to come down and beard us."

"Real sport," said Hermy.   "And how's old Fol-
de-rol-de-ray ?   Why didn't she come down and fight
us too ?

Georgie guessed that Hermy was making a humorous
allusion to Foljambe, who was the one person in
Riseholme whom his two sisters seemed to hold in
respect.   Ursy had once set a booby-trap for Georgie,
but the mixed biscuits and Brazil nuts had descended
on Foljambe instead.   On that occasion Foljambe,
girt about in impenetrable calm, had behaved as
if nothing had happened, and trod on biscuits and
Brazil nuts without a smile, as if there was nothing
whatever crumbling and exploding beneath her feet.

That had somehow quelled the two, who, as soon as she left the room again, swept up the mess and put the uninjured Brazil nuts back into the dessert dish. . . . It would never do if Foljambe lost her prestige and was alluded to by some outrageously slangy name.

" If you mean Foljambe," said Georgie icily, " it was because I didn't think it worth while to disturb her."

In spite of their ride, the indefatigable sisters were up early next morning, and the first thing Georgie saw out of his bathroom window was the pair of them practising lofting shots over the ducking-pond till breakfast was ready. He had given a short account of last night's adventures to Foljambe when she called him, omitting the episode about his hair, and her disapproval was strongly indicated by her silence then and the studied contempt of her manner to the sisters when they came in to breakfast.

" Hullo, Foljambe," said Hermy. " We had a rare lark last night."

" So I understand, miss," said Foljambe.

" Got in through the drawing-room window," said Hermy, hoping to make her smile.

" Indeed, miss," said Foljambe. " Have you any orders for the car, sir ? "

" Oh, Georgie, may we run over to the links this morning ? " asked Hermy. " Mayn't Dickie-bird take us there ? "

She glanced at Foljambe to see whether this brilliant wit afforded her any amusement. Apparently it didn't.

" Tell Dickie to be round at half-past ten," said Georgie.

" Yes, sir."

" Hurrah ! " said Ursy. " Come too, Foljambe, and we'll have a three-ball match."

" No, thank you, miss," said Foljambe, and sailed from the room, looking down her nose.

" Golly, what an iceberg ! " said Hermy when the door was quite shut.

Georgie was not sorry to have the morning to himself, for he wanted to have a little quiet practice at the Mozart trio before he went over to Lucia's at half-past eleven, the hour when they had arranged to run through it for the first time. He would also have leisure to do a few breathing exercises before the first Yoga-class, which was to take place in Lucia's smoking-parlour at half-past twelve. That would make a pretty busy morning, and, as for the afternoon, there would be sure to be some callers, since the arrival of his sisters had been expected, and after that he had to go to the " Ambermere Arms " for his visit to Olga Bracely. . . . And what was he to do about her with regard to Lucia ? Already he had been guilty of dis-loyalty, for Lady Ambermere had warned him of the prima-donna's arrival yesterday, and he had not instantly communicated that really great piece of news to Lucia. Should he make such amends as were in his power for that omission, or, greatly daring, should he keep her to himself, as Mrs. Quantock so fervently wished that she had done with regard to the Guru ? After the adventure of last night, he felt he ought to be able to look any situation in the face ; but he found himself utterly unable to conceive himself manly and erect before the bird-like eyes of the Queen if she found out that Olga Bracely had been at Rise-holme for the day of her garden-party, and that Georgie, knowing it and having gone to see her, had not informed the Court of that fact.

The spirit of Bolshevism, the desire to throw off

all authority and act independently, which had
assailed him yesterday, returned now with redoubled
force. If he had been perfectly certain that he would
not be found out, there is no doubt he would have
kept it from her, and yet, after all, what was the glory
of going to see Olga Bracely (and perhaps even entertaining her here), if all Riseholme did not turn green
with jealousy ? Moreover, there was every chance
of being found out, for Lady Ambermere would be at
the garden-party to-morrow, and she would be sure to
wonder why Lucia had not asked Olga. Then it
would come out that Lucia didn't know of that eminent
presence, and Lady Ambermere would be astonished
that Georgie had not told her. Thus he would be in
the situation which his imagination was unable to
face, although he had thrown the drawing-room door
open in the middle of the night and announced that
he would fire with his poker.

No : he would have to tell Lucia, when he went to
read the Mozart trio with her for the first time, and
very likely she would call on Olga Bracely herself,
though nobody had asked her to, and take all the wind
out of Georgie's sails. Sickening though that would
be, he could not face the alternative, and he opened
his copy of the Mozart trio with a sigh. Lucia *did*
push and shove, and have everything her own way.
Anyhow, he would *not* tell her that Olga and her
husband were dining at The Hall to-night ; he would
not even tell her that her husband's name was
Shuttleworth, and Lucia might make a dreadful
mistake, and ask Mr. and Mrs. Bracely. That would
be jam for Georgie, and he could easily imagine
himself saying to Lucia : " My dear, I thought
you must have known that she had married Mr.
Shuttleworth and kept her maiden name ! How

awkward for you ! They are so touchy about that sort of thing."

Georgie heard the tinkle of the treble part of the Mozart trio (Lucia always took the treble, because it had more tune in it, though she pretended that she had not Georgie's firm touch, which made the bass effective) as he let himself into Shakespeare's garden a few minutes before the appointed time. Lucia must have seen him from the window, for the subdued noise of the piano ceased even before he had got as far as Perdita's garden round the sundial, and she opened the door to him. The far-away look was in her eyes, and the black undulations of hair had encroached a little on her forehead ; but, after all, others besides Lucia had trouble with their hair, and Georgie only sympathized.

" *Georgino mio !* " she said. "It is all being so wonderful. There seems a new atmosphere about the house since my Guru came. Something holy and peaceful : do you not notice it ? "

" Delicious ! " said Georgie, inhaling the pot-pourri. " What is he doing now ? "

" Meditating, and preparing for our class. I do hope dear Daisy will not bring in discordant elements."

" Oh, but that's not likely, is it ? " said Georgie. " I thought he said she had so much light."

" Yes, he did. But now he is a little troubled about her, I think. She did not want him to go away from her house, and she sent over here for some silk pyjamas belonging to her husband, which the Guru thought she had given him. But Robert didn't think so at all. The Guru brought them across yesterday after he had left good thoughts for her in her house. . . . But it was

the Guides who wished him to come here : they told
him so distinctly.   It would have been very wrong of
one not to do as they said."

She gave a great sigh.

" Let us have an hour with Mozart," she said, " and
repel all thoughts of discord.   My Guru says that
music and flowers are good influences for those who
are walkers on the Way.   He says that my love for
both of them which I have had all my life will help
me very much."

For a moment the mundane world obtruded itself
into the calm peace.

" Any news in particular ? " she asked.   " I saw
you drive back from the station yesterday afternoon—
for I happened to be looking out of the window in a
little moment of leisure—he says I work too hard, by
the way—and your sisters were not with you.   And
yet there were two cabs, and a quantity of luggage.
Did they not come ? "

Georgie gave a respectably accurate account of all
that had happened, omitting the fact of his terror
when first he awoke, for that was not really a happening, and had had no effect on his subsequent proceedings.   He also omitted the adventure about his
hair, for that, too, was extraneous, and said what
fun they had all had over their supper at half-past
two this morning.

" I think you were marvellously brave, *Georgino*,"
said she, " and most good-natured.   You must have
been sending out love, and so were full of it yourself,
and that casts out fear."

She spread the music open.

" Anything else ? " she asked.

Georgie took his seat, and put his rings on the
candle-bracket.

" Oh, yes," he said, " Olga Bracely, the prima-
donna, you know, and her husband are arriving at the
' Ambermere Arms ' this afternoon for a couple of
days."

The old fire kindled.

" No ! " exclaimed Lucia. " Then they'll be here
for my party to-morrow. Fancy, if she would come
and sing to us ! I shall certainly leave cards to-day,
and write later in the evening, asking her."

" I have been asked to go and see her," said
Georgie.

The music-rest fell down with a loud slap, but
Lucia paid no attention.

" Let us go together, then," she said. " Who asked
you to call on her ? "

" Lady Ambermere," said he.

" When she was in here yesterday ? She never
mentioned it to me. But she would certainly think it
very odd of me not to call on friends of hers, and be
polite to them. What time shall we go ? "

Georgie made up his mind that wild horses should
not drag from him the fact that Olga's husband's
name was Shuttleworth, for here was Lucia grabbing
at his discovery just as she had grabbed at Daisy's
discovery, who was now " her Guru." She should
call him Mr. Bracely.

" Somewhere about six, do you think ? " said he,
inwardly raging.

He looked up, and distinctly saw that sharp, foxy
expression cross Lucia's face, which, from long knowledge of her, he knew to betoken that she had thought
of some new plan. But she did not choose to reveal
it, and re-erected the music-rest.

" That will do beautifully," she said. " And now
for our heavenly Mozart. You must be patient with

me, *Georgino*, for you know how badly I read. *Caro !*
How difficult it looks ! I am frightened ! Lucia
never saw such a dwefful thing to read ! ''

And it had been these very bars which Georgie had
heard through the open window just now.

" Georgie's is much more dwefful ! '' he said, remembering the double sharp that came in the second bar.
" Georgie fwightened, too, at reading it. O-o-h ! ''
and he gave a little scream. " *Cattivo* Mozart, to write
anything so dwefful diffy ! ''

It was quite clear at the class this morning that
though the pupils were quite interested in the abstract
messages of love which they were to shoot out in all
directions, and in the atmosphere of peace with which
they were to surround themselves, the branch of the
subject which thrilled them to the marrow was the
breathing exercises and contortions which, if per-
severed in, would give them youth and activity, fault-
less digestions and indefatigable energy. They all sat
on the floor, and stopped up alternate nostrils, and
held their breath till Mrs. Quantock got purple in the
face, and Georgie and Lucia red, and expelled their
breath again, either with sudden puffs that set the
rushes on the floor quivering, or with long, quiet
exhalations. Then there were certain postures to be
learned, in one of which, entailing the bending of the
body forward, two of Georgie's trouser-buttons gave way
with a sharp snap, and he felt the corresponding member
of his braces, thus violently released, spring up to his
shoulder. Various other embarrassing noises issued
from Lucia and Daisy that sounded like the bursting
of strings or tapes, but everybody pretended to hear
nothing at all, or covered up the report of those
explosions with coughings and clearings of the throat.

But apart from these discordancies, everything was fairly harmonious. Indeed, so far from Daisy introducing discords, she wore a fixed smile, which it would have been purely cynical to call superior, when Lucia asked some amazingly simple question with regard to Om. She sighed, too, at intervals, but these sighs were expression of nothing but patience and resignation, till Lucia's ignorance of the most elementary doctrines was enlightened ; and though she rather pointedly looked in any direction but hers, and appeared completely unaware of her presence, she had not, after all, come here to look at Lucia, but to listen to her own (whatever Lucia might say) Guru.

At the end Lucia, with her far-away look, emerged, you might say, in a dazed condition from the fastnesses of Tibet, where they had been in communion with the Guides, whose wisdom the Guru interpreted to them.

" I feel such a difference already," she said dreamily. " I feel as if I could never be hasty or worried any more at all. Don't you experience that, dear Daisy ? "

" Yes, dear," said she. " I went through all that at my first lesson. Didn't I, Guru dear ? "

" I felt it, too," said Georgie, unwilling not to share in those benefits, and surreptitiously tightening his trouser-strap to compensate for the loss of buttons. " And am I to do that swaying exercise before every meal ? "

" Yes, Georgie," said Lucia, saving her Guru the trouble of answering. " Five times to the right and five times to the left, and then five times backwards and forwards. I felt so young and light just now when we did it that I thought I was rising into the air. Didn't you, Daisy ? "

Daisy smiled kindly.

" No, dear ; that is levitation," she said, " and comes a very long way on."

She turned briskly towards her Guru.

" Will you tell them about that time when you levitated at the Marble Arch ? " she said. " Or will you keep that for when Mrs. Lucas gets rather further on ? You must be patient, dear Lucia ; we all have to go through the early stages before we get to that."

Mrs. Quantock spoke as if she was in the habit of levitating herself, and it was but reasonable, in spite of the love that was swirling about them all, that Lucia should protest against such an attitude. Humility, after all, was the first essential to progress on the Way.

" Yes, dear," she said. " We will tread those early stages together, and encourage each other."

Georgie went home, feeling also unusually light and hungry, for he had paid special attention to the exercise that enabled him to have his liver and digestive organs in complete control ; but that did not prevent him from devoting his mind to arriving at that which had made Lucia look so sharp and foxy during their conversation about Olga Bracely. He felt sure that she was meaning to steal a march on him, that she was planning to draw first blood with the prima-donna, and, as likely as not, claim her for her own, with the same odious greed as she was already exhibiting with regard to the Guru. All these years Georgie had been her faithful servant and coadjutor ; now for the first time was the spirit of independence beginning to seethe within him. The scales were falling from his eyes, and just as he turned into shelter of his mulberry-tree he put on his spectacles for a swift glance at the village green, to see how Riseholme was getting on without him to assist at the morning parliament. His absence and Mrs. Quantock's would be sure to evoke comment, and since the Yoga-classes were always to take place at half-past twelve the fact that they would never be there would soon rise to the level of a first-class mystery. It would, of course, begin to leak out that they and Lucia were having a course of Eastern philosophy that made its pupils young and light and energetic, and there was a sensation !

Like all great discoveries, the solution of Lucia's foxy look broke on him with the suddenness of a lightning-flash, and since it had been settled that she should call for him at six, he stationed himself in the window of his bathroom, which commanded a perfect view of the village green and the entrance to the " Ambermere Arms," at five. He had brought up with him a pair of opera-glasses, with the intention of taking them to bits, so he had informed Foljambe, and washing their lenses, but he did not at once proceed about this, merely holding them ready for use. Hermy and Ursy had gone back to their golf again after lunch, and so callers would be told that they were all out. Thus he could wash the lenses, when he chose to do so, uninterrupted.

The minutes passed on pleasantly enough, for there was plenty going on. The two Misses Antrobus frisked about the green, jumping over the stocks in their playful way, and running round the duck-pond in the eternal hope of attracting Coloner Boucher's attention to their pretty nimble movements. For many years past they had tried to gain Georgie's serious attention, without any result, and lately they had turned to Colonel Boucher. There was Mrs. Antrobus there, too, with her ham-like face and her ear-trumpet, and Mrs. Weston was being pushed round and round the asphalt path below the elms in her bath-chair. She hated going slow, and her gardener and his boy took turns with her during her hour's carriage-exercise, and propelled her, amid streams of perspiration, at a steady four miles an hour. As she passed Mrs. Antrobus, she shouted something at her, and Mrs. Antrobus returned her reply when next she came round.

Suddenly all these interesting objects vanished completely from Georgie's ken, for his dark suspicions were confirmed, and there was Lucia, in her Hitum hat and her Hitum gown, making her gracious way across the green. She had distinctly been wearing " Scrub " this morning at the class, so she must have changed after lunch, which was an unheard-of thing to do for a mere stroll on the green. Georgie knew well that this was no mere stroll : she was on her way to pay a call of the most formal and magnificent kind. She did not deviate a hair-breadth from her straight course to the door of the " Arms," she just waggled her hand to Mrs. Antrobus, blew a kiss to her sprightly daughters, made a gracious bow to Colonel Boucher, who stood up and took his hat off, and went on with the inexorability of the march of destiny, or of Fate knocking at the door in the immortal Fifth Symphony. And in her hand she carried a note. Through his glasses Georgie could see it quite plainly, and it was not a little folded-up half-sheet, such as she commonly used, but a square thick envelope. She disappeared into the " Arms," and

Georgie began thinking feverishly. A great deal depended on how long she stopped there.

A few little happenings beguiled the period of waiting. Mrs. Weston desisted from her wild career, and came to anchor on the path just opposite the door into the "Arms," while the gardener's boy sank exhausted on to the grass. It was quite easy to guess that she proposed to have a chat with Lucia when she came out. Similarly the Misses Antrobus, who had paid no attention to her at all before, ceased from their pretty gambollings, and ran up to talk to her, so they wanted a word too. Colonel Boucher, a little less obviously, began throwing sticks into the ducking-pond for his bulldogs (for Lucia would be obliged to pass the ducking-pond), and Mrs. Antrobus examined the stocks very carefully, as if she had never seen them before.

And then, before a couple of minutes had elapsed, Lucia came out. She had no longer the note in her hand, and Georgie began taking his opera-glasses to bits, in order to wash the lenses. For the present they had served their purpose. "She has left a note on Olga Bracely," said Georgie quite aloud, so powerful was the current of his thoughts. Then as a corollary came the further proposition which might be considered as proved : "But she has not seen her."

The justice of this conclusion was soon proved, for Lucia had hardly disengaged herself from the group of her subjects, and traversed the green on her way back to her house, when a motor passed Georgie's bathroom window, closely followed by a second. Both drew up at the entrance to the "Ambermere Arms." With the speed of a practised optician, Georgie put his opera-glass together again, and after looking through the wrong end of it in his agitation, was in time to see a man—valet-like—get out of the second car, and hold the carriage-door open for the occupants of the first. A woman got out first, tall and boyish in figure, who stood there unwinding her motor-veil. Then she turned round again, and with a thump of his heart that surprised Georgie with its violence, he beheld the well-remembered features of his Brünnhilde.

Swiftly he passed into his bedroom next door, and arrayed himself in his summer Hitums: a fresh (almost pearly) suit of white duck, a mauve tie with an amethyst pin in it, socks, tightly braced up, of precisely the same colour as the tie, so that an ima-ginative beholder might have conjectured that on this warm day the end of his tie had melted and run down his legs, and buckskin shoes with tall slim heels: a straw hat completed this pretty Hitum. He had meant to wear it for the first time at Lucia's party to-morrow, but now, after her meanness, she deserved to be punished. All Riseholme should see it before she did.

The group round Mrs. Weston's chair was still engaged in conversation when Georgie came up, and he casually let slip what a bore it was to pay calls on such a lovely day; but he had promised to visit Miss Olga Bracely, who had just arrived. So there was another nasty one for Lucia, since now all Rise-holme would know of her actual arrival before she did.

"And who, Mr. Georgie," asked Mrs. Antrobus, presenting her trumpet to him in the manner in which an elephant presents its trunk to receive a bun,—" who was that with her ? "

" Oh, her husband, Mr. Shuttleworth," said Georgie.

" They have just been married, and are on their honeymoon."

And if that was not another staggerer for Lucia, it is " diffy," as Georgie would say, to know what a staggerer is. For Lucia would be last of all to know that this was not Mr. Bracely.

" And will they be at Mrs. Lucas's party to-morrow ? " asked Mrs. Weston.

" Oh, does she know them ? " asked Georgie.

" Haw ! hum ! by Jove ! " began Colonel Boucher. " Very handsome woman. Envy you, my boy. Pity it's their honeymoon. Haw ! "

Mrs. Antrobus's trumpet was turned in his direction at this moment, and she heard these sprightly remarks.

" Naughty ! " she said, and Georgie, the envied, passed on into the inn.

He sent in his card, on which he had thought it prudent to write, " From Lady Ambermere," and was presently led through into the garden behind the building. There she was, tall and lovely and welcoming, and held out a most cordial hand.

" How kind of you to come and see us," she said. " Georgie, this is Mr. Pillson. My husband."

" How do you do, Mr. Shuttleworth ? " said Georgie, to show he knew, though his own Christian name had given him quite a start. For the moment he had almost thought she was speaking to him.

" And so Lady Ambermere asked you to come and see us ? " Olga went on. " I think that was much kinder of her than to ask us to dinner. I hate going out to dinner in the country almost as much as I hate not going out to dinner in town. Besides, with that great hook nose of hers, I'm always afraid that in an absent moment I might scratch her on the head

and say 'Pretty Polly.' Is she a great friend of
yours, Mr. Pillson ? I hope so, because everyone
likes his best friends being laughed at."

Up till that moment Georgie was prepared to indicate that Lady Ambermere was the hand and he the
glove. But evidently that would not impress Olga in
the least, and he laughed in a most irreverent manner
instead.

" Don't let us go," she went on. " Georgie, can't
you send a telegram saying that we have just
made a subsequent engagement, and then we'll
ask Mr. Pillson to show us round this utterly adorable
place and dine with us afterwards ? That would be
so much nicer. Fancy living here ! Oh, and do tell
me something, Mr. Pillson. I found a note when I
arrived half an hour ago from Mrs. Lucas, asking me
and Mr. Bracely to go to a garden-party to-morrow.
She said she didn't even hope that I should remember
her, but would we come. Who is she ? Really, I
don't think she can remember me very well, if
she thinks I am Mrs. Bracely. Georgie says
I must have been married before, and that I
have caused him to commit bigamy. That's
pleasant conversation for a honeymoon, isn't it ?
Who is she ? "

" Oh, she's quite an old friend of mine," said
Georgie, " though I never knew she had met you
before. I'm devoted to her."

" Extremely proper. But now tell me this, and
look straight in my face, so that I shall know if you're
speaking the truth. Should I enjoy myself more
wandering about this heavenly place than at her
garden-party ? "

Georgie felt that poor Lucia was really punished
enough by this time.

" You will give her a great deal of pleasure if you go——" he began.

" Ah, that's not fair : it is hitting below the belt to appeal to unselfish motives. I have come here simply to enjoy myself. Go on ; eyes front."

The candour and friendliness of that beautiful face gave Georgie an impulse of courage. Besides, though no doubt in fun, she had already suggested that it would be much nicer to wander about with him and dine together than spend the evening among the splendours of The Hall.

" I've got a suggestion," he said. " Will you come and lunch with me first, and we'll stroll about, and then you can go to the garden-party, and if you don't like it I'll take you away again."

" Done ! " she said. " Now don't you try to get out of it, because my husband is a witness. Georgie, give me a cigarette."

In a moment Riseholme-Georgie had his cigarette-case open.

" Do take one of mine," he said. " I'm Georgie, too."

" You don't say so ! Let's send it to the Psychical Research, or whoever those people are who collect coincidences and say it's spooks. And a match, please, one of you Georgies. Oh, how I should like never to see the inside of an opera-house again. Why mayn't I grow on the walls of a garden like this, or, better still, why shouldn't I have a house and garden of my own here, and sing on the village green, and ask for halfpennies ? Tell me what happens here ! I've always lived in towns since the time a hook-nosed Hebrew, rather like Lady Ambermere took me out of the gutter."

" My dear ! " said Mr. Shuttleworth.

" Well, out of an orphan-school at Brixton, and I
would much prefer the gutter. That's all about my
early life just now, because I am keeping it for my
memoirs, which I shall write when my voice becomes
a little more like a steam-whistle. But don't tell
Lady Ambermere, for she would have a fit, but say you
happen to know that I belong to the Surrey Bracelys.
So I do : Brixton is on the Surrey side. Oh, my dear,
look at the sun ! It's behaving like the best sort of
Claude. *Heile Sonne !* "

" I heard you do that last May," said Georgie.

" Then you heard a most second-rate performance,"
said she. " But really being unlaced by that Thing,
that great fat profligate Peruvian, was almost too
much for me. And the duet ! But it was very
polite of you to come, and we'll do better next time.
Siegfried ! Brünnhilde ! Siegfried ! Miaou ! Miaou !
Bring on the next lot of cats ! Darling Georgie, wasn't
it awful ? And you had proposed to me only the
day before ! "

" I was absolutely enchanted," said Riseholme-
Georgie.

" Yes, but then you didn't have that Thing breathing
beer into your innocent face."

Georgie rose : the first call on a stranger in Riseholme was never supposed to last more than half an
hour, however much you were enjoying it, and never
less, however bored you might be, and he felt sure he
had already exceeded this.

" I must be off," he said. " Too delightful to think
that you and Mr. Shuttleworth will come to lunch with
me to-morrow. Half-past one, shall we say ? "

" Excellent ! But where do you live ? "

" Just across the green. Shall I call for you ? " he
asked.

"Certainly not. Why should you have that
bother?" she said. "Ah, let me come with you to
the inn door, and perhaps you will show me from
there."

She passed through the hall with him, and they
stood together in the sight of all Riseholme, that
strolled about the green at this as at most other
hours. Instantly all faces turned round in their
direction, like so many sunflowers following the sun,
while Georgie pointed out his particular mulberry-
tree. When everybody had had a good look, he
raised his hat.

"*A domani*, then," she said. "So many
thanks."

And quite distinctly she kissed her hand to him as
he turned away. . . .

"So she talks Italian, too," thought Georgie, as
he dropped little crumbs of information to his friends
on his way to his house. "*Domani*—yes, that means
to-morrow. Oh, yes: lunch!"

It is hardly necessary to add that on the table in
his hall there was one of Lucia's commoner kinds of
note, merely a half-sheet folded together in her own
manner. Georgie felt that it was scarcely worth while
to read it, for he felt quite sure that it contained some
excuse for not coming to his house at six in order to
call on Mr. and Mrs. Bracely. But he gave a glance
at it before he rolled it up in a ball for Tipsipoozie to
play with, and found its contents to be precisely what
he expected, the excuse being that she had not done
her practising. But the postscript was interesting,
for it told him that she had asked Foljambe to give
her messenger his copy of *Siegfried*. . . .

Georgie strolled down past The Hurst before dinner.
Mozart was silent now, but there came out of the open

windows the most amazing hash of sound, which he could just recognize as being the piano arrangement of the duet between Brünnhilde and Siegfried in the last act. He would have been dull indeed if he had not instantly guessed what *that* signified.

CHAPTER VII

A FRESH thrill went through an atmosphere already
super-saturated with excitement, when next morning
all Lucia's friends who had been bidden to her garden-
party (Titum) were rung up on the telephone, and
informed that the party was Hitum. That caused
a good deal of extra work, because the Titum robes
had to be put away again, and the Hitums aired
and brushed and valeted. But it was well worth
it, for Riseholme had not the slightest difficulty in
conjecturing that Olga Bracely was to be among the
guests. For a cultured and artistic centre the
presence of a star that blazed so royally in the very
zenith of the firmament of Art absolutely demanded
the Hitum, which the presence of poor Lady
Ambermere (though she would not have liked that at
all) had been powerless to bring out of their cupboards. And these delightful anticipations concentrated themselves with one rose-coloured point of joy,
when no less than two independent observers, without collusion, saw the piano-tuner either entering
or leaving The Hurst, while a third, an ear-witness,
unmistakably heard the tuning of the piano actually
going on. It was thus practically certain that Olga
Bracely was going to sing. It was further known
that something was going on between her and Georgie,
for she had been heard by Miss Antrobus to ask for

Georgie's number at the telephone in the "Ambermere Arms." Etiquette forbade her actually to
listen to what passed, but she could not help hearing
Olga laugh at something (presumably) that Georgie
said. He himself took no part in the green-parlia-
ment that morning, but had been seen to dash into
the fruiterer's and out again, before he went in a
great hurry to The Hurst, shortly after twelve-thirty.
Classes on Eastern philosophy under the tuition of
Mrs. Quantock's Indian were already beginning to
be hinted at, but to-day, in the breathless excitement
about the prima-donna, nobody cared about that :
they might all have been taking lessons in cannibalism.
Finally, about one o'clock, one of the motors in which
the party had arrived yesterday drew up at the
door of the "Ambermere Arms," and presently Mr.
Bracely—no, dear, Mr. Shuttleworth—got in and drove
off alone. That was very odd conduct in a lately-
married bridegroom, and it was hoped that there had
been no quarrel.

Olga had, of course, been given no directions as
to Hitum and Titum, and when she walked across
to Georgie's house shortly after half-past one only
Mrs. Weston, who was going back home to lunch at
top speed, was aware that she was dressed in a very
simple dark blue morning frock, that would almost
have passed for Scrub. It is true that it was exceed-
ingly well cut, and had not the look of having been
rolled up in a ball and hastily ironed out again, that
usually distinguished Scrub, and she also wore a string
of particularly fine pearls round her neck, the sort
of ornament that in Riseholme would only be seen in
an evening Hitum, even if anybody in Riseholme
had owned such things. Lucia, not long ago, had
expressed the opinion that "jewels were vulgar

except at night," and for her part she wore none at all, preferring one Greek cameo of uncertain authenticity.

Georgie received her alone, for Hermy and Ursy were not yet back from their golf.

"It is good of you to let me come without my husband," she said. "His excuse is toothache, and he has driven into Brinton——"

"I'm very sorry," said Georgie.

"You needn't be, for now I'll tell you his real reason. He thought that if he lunched with you he would have to come on to the garden-party, and that he was absolutely determined not to do. You were the thin end of the wedge, in fact. My dear, what a delicious house! All panelled, with that lovely garden behind. And croquet—— May we play croquet after lunch? I always try to cheat, and if I'm found out I lose my temper. Georgie won't play with me, so I play with my maid."

"This Georgie will," said he.

"How nice of him. And do you know what we did this morning, before the toothache didn't begin? We went all over that house three doors away, which is being done up. It belongs to the proprietor of the 'Ambermere Arms.' And—oh, I wonder if you can keep a secret?"

"Yes," said Georgie. He probably had never kept one yet, but there was no reason why he shouldn't begin now.

"Well, I'm absolutely determined to buy it, only I daren't tell my husband until I've done it. He has an odd nature. When a thing is done, settled, and there's no help for it, he finds it adorable, but he also finds fatal objections to doing it at all, if he is consulted about it before it is done. So, not a word!

I shall buy it, make the garden, furnish it, down to the minutest detail, and engage the servants, and then he'll give it me for a birthday present. I had to tell somebody or I should have burst."

Georgie nearly swooned with fervour and admiration.

"But what a perfect plan!" he said. "You really like our little Riseholme?"

"It's not a question of liking : it's a mere detail of not being able to do without it. I don't like breathing, but I should die if I didn't. I want some delicious, hole-in-the-corner, lazy backwater sort of place, where nothing ever happens, and nobody ever does anything. I've been observing all the morning, and your habits are adorable. Nothing ever happens here, and that will precisely suit me, when I get away from my work."

Georgie was nearer swooning than ever at this. He could hardly believe his ears when she talked of Riseholme being a lazy backwater, and almost thought she must have been speaking of London, where, as Lucia had acutely observed, people sat in the Park all morning and talked of each other's affairs, and spent the afternoon at picture galleries, and danced all night. There was a flippant, lazy existence.

But she was far too much absorbed in her project to notice his stupefaction.

"But if you breathe a word," she said, "everything will be spoilt. It has to burst on Georgie—— Oh, and there's another mulberry-tree in your garden, as well as the one in front. It's too much!"

Her eyes followed Foljambe out of the door.

"And I know your parlour-maid is called Paravicini or Grosvenor," she said.

"No, she is Foljambe," said Georgie.

She laughed.

" I knew I was right," she said. " It's practically the same thing. Oh, and last night ! I never had such an awful evening. Why didn't you warn me, and my husband should have had toothache then instead of this morning."

" What happened ? " asked he.

" But the woman's insane, that Ambermere parrot, I mean. Georgie and I were ten minutes late, and she had a jet tiara on, and why did she ask us to dine at a quarter to eight, if she meant a quarter to eight, instead of saying half-past seven ? They were actually going in to dinner when we came, a mournful procession of three moth-eaten men and three whiskered women. Upon which the procession broke up, as if we had been the Riot Act, and was arranged again as a funeral procession, and Georgie with Lady Ambermere was the hearse. We dined in the family vault, and talked about Lady Ambermere's pug. She talked about you, too, and said you were of county family, and that Mrs. Lucas was a very decent sort of woman, and that she herself was going to look in on her garden-party to-day. Then she looked at my pearls, and asked if they were genuine. So I looked at her teeth, and there was no need to ask about them."

" Don't miss out a moment," said Georgie greedily.

" Whenever Lady Ambermere spoke, everybody else was silent. I didn't grasp that at first, for no one had explained the rules. So she stopped in the middle of a sentence, and waited till I had finished. Then she went on again, precisely where she had left off. No rebukes, mind you, no scoldings, but I knew. . . . Then, when we came into the drawing-room, the whiskered ladies and I, there was a little woman like a mouse sitting there, and nobody introduced her.

So naturally I wanted to talk to her. Upon which
the great parrot said, ' Will you kindly fetch my wool-
work, Miss Lyall ? ' and Miss Lyall took a sack out
of the corner, and inside was the sacred carpet. And
then I waited for some coffee and cigarettes, and I
waited and I waited, and I am waiting still. The
Parrot said that coffee always kept her awake, and
that was why. And then Georgie came in with the
others, and I could see by his face that he hadn't
had a cigarette either. It was then half-past nine.
And then each man sat down between two women,
and Pug sat in the middle and looked for fleas. Then
Lady Ambermere got up, and came across the charmed
circle to me. She said, ' I hope you have brought
your music, Mrs. Shuttleworth. Kindly open the
piano, Miss Lyall. It was always considered a
remarkably fine instrument ! ' "

Olga waved the fork on which was impaled a piece
of the pine-apple which Georgie had purchased that
morning at the fruiterer's.

" The stupendous cheek ! " she said. " I thought
it must be a joke, and laughed with the greatest
politeness. But it wasn't. You'll hardly believe
it, but it wasn't ! One of the whiskered ones said,
' That will be a great treat,' and another put on the
face that everyone wears at concerts. And I was so
stunned that I sang, and Lady Ambermere beat
time, and Pug barked."

She pointed a finger at Georgie.

" Never till the Day of Judgment," she said,
" when Lady Ambermere gnashes her beautiful teeth
for ever and ever, will I set foot in that house again.
Nor she in my house. I will set fire to it sooner.
There ! My dear, what a good lunch you have given
me. May we play croquet at once ? "

Lucia's garden-parties were scheduled from five to
seven, and half an hour before the earliest guest
might be expected, she was casting an eagle-eye over
the preparations, which to-day were on a very sump-
tuous scale. The bowls were laid out in the bowling-
alley, not because anybody in Hitum dresses was
the least likely to risk the stooping down and the
strong movements that the game entailed, but because
bowls were Elizabethan. Between the alley and
the lawn nearer to the house was a large marquee,
where the commoner crowd—though no crowd could
be really common in Riseholme—would refresh itself.
But even where none are common there may still be
degrees in rarity, and by the side of this general
refreshment room was a smaller tent, carpeted with
Oriental rugs, and having inside it some half-dozen
chairs, and two seats which can only be described
as thrones, for Lucia's Guru, though throne-worthy,
would very kindly sit in one of his most interesting
attitudes on the floor. This tent was designed only
for high converse, and common guests (if they were
good) would be led into it and introduced to the great
Presences, while for the refreshment of the Presences,
in intervals of audience, a more elaborate meal, with
peaches and four sorts of sandwiches, was laid in the
smoking-parlour. Then those guests for whom
audiences were not provided, could have the felicity
of seeing the great ones pass across the lawn on their
excursion for food, and possibly trip over the croquet
hoops, which had been left up to give an air of naturalness to the lawn. In the smoking-parlour an Elzevir
or two were left negligently open, as if Mr. and Mrs.
Lucas had been reading the works of Persius and
Juvenal when the first guests arrived. In the music-
room, finally, which was not usually used on these

occasions, there were fresh flowers : the piano was
open, and if you had not seen the Elzevirs in the
smoking-parlour, it would have been reasonable for
the early guests, if they penetrated there, to imagine
that Mrs. Lucas had been running over the last act of
Siegfried a minute before.

In this visit of final inspection Lucia was accompanied by her Guru, for he was part of the domestic
dramatis personæ, and she wanted him to be " discovered" in the special tent. She pointed out the
site of his proposed " discovery " to him.

" Probably the first person I shall bring in here,"
she said, " will be Lady Ambermere, for she is noted
for her punctuality. She is so anxious to see you,
and would it not be exciting if you found you had
met before ? Her husband was Governor of Madras,
and she spent many years in India."

" Madras, gracious lady ? " asked the Guru. " I,
too, know Madras : there are many dark spirits in
Madras. And she was at English Residency ? "

" Yes. She says Mr. Kipling knows nothing about
India. You and she will have much to talk about.
I wish I could sit on the floor, too, and listen to what
you say to each other."

" It will be great treat," said the Guru. " I love
all who love my wonderful country."

Suddenly he stopped, and put his hands up to his
head, palms outwards.

" There are wonderful vibrations to-day," he said.
" All day I feel that some word is on way from the
Guides, some great message of light."

" Oh, wouldn't it be wonderful if it came to you
in the middle of my garden-party ? " said Lucia
enthusiastically.

" Ah, gracious lady, the great word comes not so.

It comes always in solitude and quiet. Gracious lady knows that as well as Guru."

Pure Guruism and social pre-eminence struggled together in Lucia. Guruism told her that she ought to be ecstatic at the idea of a great message coming, and should instantly smile on his desire for solitude and quiet, while social pre-eminence whispered to her that she had already dangled the presence of a high-caste mystic from Benares before the eyes of Lady Ambermere, who only came from Madras. On the other hand, Olga Bracely was to be an even more resplendent guest than either Lady Ambermere or the Guru: surely Olga Bracely was enough to set this particular garden-party on the giddiest of pinnacles. And an awful consequence lurked as a possibility if she attempted to force her Guru to remain, and that was that conceivably he might choose to go back to the pit whence he was digged, namely, the house of poor Daisy Quantock. The thought was intolerable, for with him in her house she had seen herself as Dispenser of Eastern Mysteries and Mistress of Omism to Riseholme. In fact, the Guru was her August stunt; it would never do to lose him before the end of July, and rage to see all Riseholme making pilgrimage to Daisy. There was a thin-lipped firmness, too, about him at this moment: she felt that under provocation he might easily defy or desert her. She felt she had to yield, and so decided to do so in the most complete manner.

"Ah, yes," she said. "I know how true that is. Dear Guru, go up to 'Hamlet': no one will disturb you there. But if the message comes through before Lady Ambermere goes away, promise me you will come out to us."

He went to the house, where the front door was

already open to admit Lady Ambermere, who was
telling "her people" when to come back for her,
and fled with the heels of his slippers tapping on the
oak stairs up to "Hamlet." Softly he shut out the
dark spirits from Madras, and made himself even
more secure by turning the key in his door. It would
never do to appear as a high-caste Brahmin from
Benares before anyone who knew India and its races
at all, for he might not correspond with her recollections of such gentlemen.

Lady Ambermere's arrival was soon followed by
that of other guests, and instead of going into the
special tent reserved for the Presences, she took up a
commanding position on the middle of the lawn, where
she could examine everybody through her tortoise-
shell-handled lorgnette. She kept Peppino by her,
who darted forward to shake hands with his wife's
guests, and then darted back again to listen to her.
Poor Miss Lyall stood behind her chair, and from
time to time, as ordered, gave her a cape, or put up
her parasol, adjusted her footstool for her, or took
up Pug or put him down, as her patroness required.
Most of the time Lady Ambermere kept up a majestic
monologue.

"You have a pretty little garden here, Mr. Lucas,"
she said, "though perhaps inconveniently small.
Your croquet lawn does not look to me the full size,
and then there is no tennis-court. But I think you
have a little strip of grass somewhere, which you use
for bowls, have you not? Presently I will walk
round with you and see your domain. Put Pug down
again, please, Miss Lyall, and let him run about.
See, he wants to play with one of those croquet balls;
put it in motion for him, and he will run with it.
Bless me, who is that coming up the path at such a

tremendous speed in a bath-chair? Oh, I see, it is
Mrs. Weston. She should not go as fast as that. If
Pug was to stray on to the path he would be run over.
Better pick up Pug again, Miss Lyall, till she has gone
by. And here is Colonel Boucher. If he had brought
his bulldogs I should have asked him to take them
away again. I should like a cup of tea, Miss Lyall,
with plenty of milk in it, and not too strong. You
know how I like my tea. And a biscuit or something
for Pug, with a little cream in a saucer or anything
that's handy."

" Won't you come into the smoking-parlour, and
have tea there, Lady Ambermere? " asked Peppino.

" The smoking-parlour? " asked she. " How very
strange to lay tea in a smoking-room."

Peppino explained that nobody had in all prob-
ability used the smoking-parlour to smoke in for
five or six years.

" Oh, if that is so, I will come," said she. " Better
bring Pug along, too, Miss Lyall. There is a croquet-
hoop. I am glad I saw it, or I should have stumbled
over it perhaps. Oh, this is the smoking-parlour, is
it? Why do you have rushes on the floor? Put Pug
in a chair, Miss Lyall, or he may prick his paws.
Books, too, I see. That one lying open is an old one.
It is Latin poetry. The library at The Hall is very
famous for its classical literature. The first Viscount
collected it, and it numbers many thousands of
volumes."

" Indeed, it is the most wonderful library," said
Peppino. " I can never tear myself away from it
when I am at The Hall."

" I do not wonder. I am a great student myself,
and often spend a morning there, do I not, Miss
Lyall? You should have some new glass put in

your windows, Mr. Lucas.   On a dark day it must
be very difficult to see here.   By the way, your good
wife told me that there was a very remarkable Indian,
who would be at her party, a Brahmin from Benares,
she said.   I should like to have a talk with him while
I am having my tea.   Kindly prepare a peach for
me, Miss Lyall."

Peppino had heard about the retirement of the
Guru, in consequence of a message from the Guides
being expected, and proceeded to explain this to
Lady Ambermere, who did not take the slightest
notice, as she was looking at the peaches through her
lorgnette.

"That one nearest me looks eatable," she said.
"And then I do not see Miss Olga Bracely, though
I distinctly told her I should be here this afternoon,
and she said Mrs. Lucas had asked her.   I hope to
hear her sing again this afternoon.   She sang to us
yesterday evening at The Hall, and very creditably
indeed.   Her husband, Mr. Shuttleworth, is a cousin
of the late Lord's."

Lucia had come into the smoking-parlour during
this speech, and heard those fatal words.   At the
moment she would gladly have recalled her invitation
to Olga Bracely altogether, sooner than have alluded
therein to Mr. Bracely.   But that was one of the
irremediable things of life, and since it was no use
wasting regret on that, she was only the more eager
for Olga to come, whatever her husband's name was.
She braced herself up to the situation.

"Peppino, are you looking after Lady Ambermere ?" she said.   "Dear Lady Ambermere, I hope
they are all taking care of you."

"A very decent peach," said Lady Ambermere.
"The south wall of my garden is covered with them,

and they are always of a peculiarly delicious flavour.
The Hall is famed for its peaches. I understood that
Miss Bracely was going to be here, Mrs. Lucas. I
cannot imagine what makes her so late. I was always
famed for my punctuality myself. I have finished
my tea ! "

The lawn outside was now growing thick with people,
all in their Hitums, and Lady Ambermere, as she
emerged from the smoking-parlour again, viewed the
scene with marked disfavour. The two Misses
Antrobus had just arrived, and slipped up to their
hostess with pretty cries :

" We are dreadfully late," said the eldest, " but it
was all Piggy's fault."

" No, Goosie, it was yours," said the other. " How
can you be so naughty as to say it was mine ? Dear
Mrs. Lucas, what a lovely party it's being, and may
we go and play bowls ? "

Lady Ambermere regarded their retreating backs,
as they raced off with arms intertwined, to the
bowling-green. " And who are those young ladies ? "
she asked. " And why Piggy and Goosie ? Miss Lyall,
do not let Pug go to the bowls. They are very heavy."

Elsewhere Mrs. Antrobus was slowly advancing
from group to group, with her trumpet violently
engaged in receiving refreshment. But conversation
was not quite so vivacious as usual, for there was an
attitude of intense expectation about, with regard
to the appearance of Miss Bracely, that made talk
rather jerky and unconsecutive. Then also it had
gone about that the mysterious Indian, who had been
seen now and then during the last week, was actually
staying with Mrs. Lucas, and why was he not here ?
More unconjecturable yet, though not so thrillingly
interesting, was the absence of Mr. Georgie. What

could have happened to him that he was not flitting
about on his mistress's errands and being the life
and soul of the party? It was in vain that Mrs.
Antrobus plodded on her methodical course, seeking
answers to all those riddles, and that Mrs. Weston, in
her swifter progression, dashed about in her bath-
chair from group to group, wherever people seemed
to be talking in an animated manner. She could
learn nothing, and Mrs. Antrobus could learn nothing ;
in fact, the only information to be had on the subject
was what Mrs. Weston herself supplied. She had a
very high-coloured, handsome face, and an extremely
impressive manner, as if she was imparting information of the very highest importance. She naturally
spoke in a loud, clear voice, so that she had not got
to raise it much even when she addressed Mrs.
Antrobus. Her wealth of discursive detail was absolutely unrivalled, and she was quite the best observer
in Riseholme.

" The last I saw of Miss Bracely," she said, exactly
as if she had been told to describe something on oath
in the witness-box, " was a little after half-past one
to-day. It must have been after half-past, because
when I got home it was close on a quarter to two, and
I wasn't a hundred yards from my house when I saw
her. As soon as I saw her I said to my gardener-
boy, Henry Luton, who was pushing me—he's the
son of old Mrs. Luton, who kept the fish shop, and
when she died last year I began to get my fish from
Brinton, for I didn't fancy the look of the new person
who took on the business, and Henry went to live with
his aunt. That was his father's sister, not his mother's,
for Mrs. Luton never had a sister, and no brothers,
either. Well, I said to Henry, ' You can go a bit
slower, Henry : as we're late, we're late, and a minute

or two more doesn't make any difference.' 'No, ma'am,' said Henry, touching his cap, so we went slower. Miss Bracely was just opposite the ducking-pond then, and presently she came out between the elms. She had just an ordinary morning frock on ; it was dark blue, about the same shade as your cape, Mrs. Antrobus, or perhaps a little darker, for the sunshine brightened it up. Quite simple it was, nothing grand. And she looked at the watch on her wrist, and she seemed to me to walk a little quicker after that, as if she was a bit late, just as I was. But slower than I was going, I could not go, for I was crawling along, and before she got off the grass I had come to the corner of Church Lane, and though I turned my head round sharp, like that, as we turned into it, so as to catch the last of her, she hadn't more than stepped off the grass on to the road, before the laurestinus at the corner of Colonel Boucher's garden—no, of the Vicar's garden—hid her from me. And if you ask me——" Mrs. Weston stopped for a moment, nodding her head up and down, to emphasize the importance of what she had said, and to raise the expectations of Mrs. Antrobus to the highest pitch as to what was coming.

"And if you ask me where I think she was going, and what she was going to do," she said, " I believe she was going out to lunch, and that she was going to one of those houses there, just across the road, for she made a bee-line across the green towards them. Well, there are three houses there : there's Mrs. Quantock's, and it couldn't have been that, else Mrs. Quantock would have had some news of her, and Colonel Boucher's, and it couldn't have been that, for the Colonel would have had news of her, and we all know whose the third house just there is."

Mrs. Antrobus had not completely followed this powerful reasoning.

"But Colonel Boucher and Mrs. Quantock are both here, eh ? " said she.

Mrs. Weston raised her voice a little.

"That's what I'm saying," she announced, "but who isn't here whom we should expect to see, and where's his house ? "

It was generally felt that Mrs. Weston had hit the nail on the head. What that nail precisely was, no one knew, because so far she had not explained why either Olga Bracely or Georgie were absentees. But now came the climax, bang on the top of the nail, a shrewd, straight stroke.

"So there she was, having her lunch with Mr. Georgie," said Mrs. Weston, now introducing his name for the first time, with the highest dramatic art, " and they would be seeing round his house afterwards. And then when it was time to come here, Mr. Georgie would have remembered that the party was Hitum, not Titum, and there was Miss Bracely not in Hitum at all, nor even Titum, in my opinion, but Scrub. No doubt she said to him, ' Is it a very grand sort of party, Mr. Pillson ? ' and he couldn't do other than reply, for we all received notice that it was Hitum—mine came about twelve—he couldn't do other than reply, ' Yes, Miss Bracely, it is.' ' Good gracious me,' she would say, ' and I've only got this old rag on. I must go back to the "Ambermere Arms," and tell my maid '—for she brought a maid in that second motor—' and tell my maid to put me out something tidy.' ' But that will be a great bother for you,' he would say, or something of that sort, for I don't pretend to know what he actually did say, and she would reply, ' Oh, Mr. Pill-

son, but I must put on something tidy, and it would
be so kind of you, if you would wait for me while
I do that, and let us go together.' That's what *she*
said."

Mrs. Weston made a sign to her gardener to proceed, wishing to leave the stage at the moment of
climax.

"And that's why they're both late," she said, and
was whirled away in the direction of the bowling-
green.

The minutes went on, and still nobody appeared
who could possibly have accounted for the three-lined
whip of Hitum, but by degrees Lucia, who had
utterly failed to decoy Lady Ambermere into the
place of thrones, began to notice a certain thinning
on her lawns. Her guests, it would seem, were not
in process of dispersal, for it was a long way off
seven o'clock yet, and also none would be so ill-
mannered as to leave without shaking hands and saying
what a delicious afternoon they had spent. But certainly the lawns grew emptier, and she was utterly
unable to explain this extraordinary phenomenon,
until she happened to go close to the windows of
her music-room. Then, looking in, she saw that not
only was every chair there occupied, but people were
standing about in expectant groups. For a moment
her heart beat high. . . . Could Olga have arrived,
and by some mistake have gone straight in there?
It was a dreamlike possibility, but it burst like a ray
of sunshine on the party that was rapidly becoming a
nightmare to her—for everyone, not Lady Ambermere alone, was audibly wondering when the Guru
was coming, and when Miss Bracely was going to
sing.

At the moment, as she paused, a window in the

music-room was opened, and Piggy's odious head looked out.

"Oh, Mrs. Lucas," she said, "Goosie and I have got beautiful seats, and Mamma is quite close to the piano, where she will hear excellently. Has she promised to sing *Siegfried*? Is Mr. Georgie going to play for her? It's *the* most delicious surprise; how could you be so sly and clever as not to tell anybody?"

Lucia cloaked her rage under the most playful manner, as she ran into the music-room through the hall.

"You naughty things!" she said. "Do all come into the garden! It's a garden-party, and I couldn't guess where you had all gone. What's all this about singing and playing? I know nothing of it!" She herded the incredulous crowd out into the garden again, all in their Hitums, every one of them, only to meet Lady Ambermere, with Pug and Miss Lyall, coming in.

"Better be going, Miss Lyall," she said. "Kindly run out and find my people. Oh, here's Mrs. Lucas. Been very pleasant indeed, thank you. Good-bye. Your charming garden. Yes."

"Oh, but it's very early," said Lucia. "It's hardly six yet."

"Indeed!" said Lady Ambermere. "Been so charming," and she marched out after Miss Lyall into Shakespeare's garden.

It was soon terribly evident that other people were sharing Lady Ambermere's conclusion about the delights of the afternoon, and the necessity of getting home. Colonel Boucher had to take his bulldogs for a run, and walk off the excitement of the party; Piggy and Goosie explained to their mother that nobody was going to sing, and by silvery laughter tried to drown her just indignation, and presently Lucia had the agony of seeing Mrs. Quantock seated on one of the thrones that had been designed for much worthier ends, and Peppino sitting on the other, while a few guests drifted about the lawn with the anæmic purposelessness of autumn leaves. What with the Guru presumably meditating upstairs still, and with Olga Bracely most conspicuously absent, she had hardly nervous energy left to wonder what could have become of Georgie. Never in all the years of his ministry had he failed to be at her elbow through the entire duration of her garden-parties, flying about on her errands like a tripping Hermes, and herding her flocks if she wanted them in one part of the garden rather than another, like a sagacious sheep-dog, and coming back to heel again ready for further tasks. But to-day Georgie was mysteriously away, for he had neither applied for leave nor given any explanation, however improbable, of his absence. He at least would have prevented Lady Ambermere, the only corner-stone of the party, from going away in what must be called a huff, and have continued to tell Lucia how marvellous she was, and what a beautiful party they were having. With the prospect of two other much more magnificent corner-stones, Lucia had not provided any further entertainment for her guests : there was not the conjuror from Brinton, nor the three young ladies who played banjo-trios, nor even the mild performing doves which cooed so prettily and walked up their mistress's outstretched fingers according to order, if they felt disposed. There was nothing to justify Hitums ; there was scarcely even sufficient to warrant Titums. Scrub was written all over the desert's dusty face !

It was about half-past six when the miracles began,
and without warning the Guru walked out into the
garden. Probably he had watched the departure of
the great motor, with its chauffeur and footman, and
Miss Lyall and Lady Ambermere and Pug, and with
his intuitive sagacity had conjectured that the danger
from Madras was over. He wore his new red slippers,
a wonderful turban and an ecstatic smile. Lucia
and Daisy met him with cries of joy, and the remaining
guests, those drifting autumn leaves, were swept up,
as it were, by some compelling broom and clustered
in a heap in front of him. There had been a Great
Message, a Word of Might, full of Love and Peace.
Never had there been such a Word. . . .

And then, even before they had all felt the full
thrill of that, once more the door from the house
opened, and out came Olga Bracely and Georgie.
It is true that she had still her blue morning frock,
which Mrs. Weston had designated as Scrub, but it
was a perfectly new Scrub, and if it had been completely covered with Paris labels, they would not
have made its *provenance* one whit clearer.

" Dear Mrs. Lucas," she said, " Mr. Georgie and I
are terribly late, and it was quite my fault. There
was a game of croquet that wouldn't come to an end,
and my life has been guided by only one principle, and
that is to finish a game of croquet whatever happens.
I missed six trains once by finishing a game of croquet.
And Mr. Georgie was so unkind : he wouldn't give
me a cup of tea, or let me change my frock, but dragged
me off to see you. And I won ! "

The autumn leaves turned green and vigorous again,
and while Georgie went to get refreshment for his
conqueror, they were all introduced. She allowed
herself to be taken with the utmost docility—how

unlike Somebody—into the tent with the thrones : she confessed to having stood on tiptoe and looked into Mrs. Quantock's garden, and wanted to see it so much from the other side of the wall. And this garden, too—might she go and wander all over this garden when she had finished the most delicious peach that the world held ? She was so glad she had not had tea with Mr. Georgie : he would never have given her such a good peach. . . .

Now the disappointed and departed guests in their Hitums lingering on the village green a little, and being rather sarcastic about the utter failure of Lucia's party, could hardly help seeing Georgie and Olga emerge from his house and proceed swiftly in the direction of The Hurst, and Mrs. Antrobus, who retained marvellous eyesight as compensation for her defective hearing, saw them go in, and simultaneously thought that she had left her parasol at The Hurst. Next moment she was walking thoughtfully away in that direction. Mrs. Weston had been the next to realize what had happened, and though she had to go round by the road in her bath-chair, she passed Mrs. Antrobus a hundred yards from the house, her pretext for going back being that Lucia had promised to lend her the book by Antonio Caporelli (or was it Caporetto ?)

So once more the door into the garden opened, and out shot Mrs. Weston. Olga by this time had made her tour of the garden, and might she see the house ? She might. There was a pretty music-room. . . . At this stage, just as Mrs. Weston was poured out into the garden, as with flood-gates being opened, the crowd that had gone away and now returned, came surging into Shakespeare's garden, and never had the mermaid's tail, behind which was secreted the electric bell, experienced such feverish usage. Pressure after pressure invoked

its aid, and the pretexts for readmission were soon not
made at all, or simply disregarded by the parlour-
maid. Colonel Boucher might have left a bulldog,
or Mrs. Antrobus an ear-trumpet, or Miss Antrobus
(Piggie) a shoe-lace, or the other Miss Antrobus
(Goosie) a shoe-horn : but in brisk succession the
guests who had been so sarcastic about the party on
the village green jostled each other in order to revisit
the scenes of their irony. Miss Olga Bracely had been
known to enter the portals, and as many of them who
entered after her found a Guru as well.

Olga was in the music-room, whither the crowd in
the hall followed her. People were introduced to her,
and sank down into the nearest chairs : Mrs. Antrobus
took up her old place by the keyboard of the piano.
Everybody seemed to be expecting something, and
by degrees the import of their longing was borne in
upon Olga. They waited, and waited, and waited,
much as she had waited for a cigarette the evening
before. She looked at the piano, and there was a
comfortable murmur from her audience. She looked
at Lucia, who gave a great gasp, and said nothing at
all. She was the only person present who was standing now, except her hostess, and Mrs. Weston's gardener, who had wheeled his mistress's chair into an
admirable position for hearing. She was not too well
pleased, but after all . . .

" Would you like me to sing ? " she asked Lucia.
" Yes ? Ah, there's the copy of *Siegfried*. Do you
play ? "

Lucia could not smile any more than she was smiling
already.

" Is it very diffy ? " she asked. " Could I read it,
Georgie ? Shall I try ? "

She slid into the music-stool.

" Me to begin ? " she asked, finding that Olga had
opened the book at the Salutation of Brünnhilde, which
Lucia had practised so diligently all the morning.

She got no answer. Olga, standing by her, had
assumed a perfectly different aspect. For her gaiety,
her lightness, was substituted an air of intense concentrated seriousness, which Lucia did not understand
at all. She was looking straight in front of her, gathering herself in, and paying not the smallest attention to
Lucia or anybody else.

" One, two," said Lucia. " Three. Now," and she
plunged wildly into a sea of demi-semi-quavers.

Olga had just opened her mouth, but shut it again.

" No," she said. " Once more," and she whistled
the *motif*.

" Oh ! it's so diffy ! " said Lucia, beginning again.
" Georgie ! Turn over ! "

Georgie turned over, and Lucia, counting audibly
to herself, made an incomparable mess all over the
piano.

Olga turned to her accompanist.

" Shall I try ? " she said.

She sat down at the piano, and made some sort of
sketch of the accompaniment, simplifying, and yet
retaining the essence. And then she sang. . . .

CHAPTER VIII

THROUGHOUT August Guruism reigned supreme over the cultured life of Riseholme, and the priestess and dispenser of its mysteries was Lucia. Never before had she ruled from so elate a pinnacle, nor wielded so secure a supremacy. None had access to the Guru but through her : all his classes were held in the smoking-parlour, and he meditated only in " Hamlet," or in the sequestered arbour at the end of the laburnum walk. Once he had meditated on the village green, but Lucia did not approve of that, and had led him, still rapt, home by the hand.

The classes had swelled prodigiously, for practically all Riseholmists now were at some stage of instruction, with the exception of Hermy and Ursy, who pronounced the whole thing " piffle," and, as gentle chaff for Georgie, sometimes stood on one leg in the middle of the lawn and held their breath. Then Hermy would say, " One, two, three ! " and they shouted " Om ! " at the tops of their discordant voices. Now that the Guru was practically interned in The Hurst, they had actually never set eyes on him, for they had not chosen to come to the Hitum garden-party, preferring to have a second round of golf, and meeting Lucia next day had been distinctly irreverent on the subject of Eastern philosophy. Since then she had not been aware of their existence.

Lucia now received instruction from the Guru in a class all by herself, so prodigious was her advance in Yoga, for she could hold her breath much longer than anybody else, and had mastered six postures, while the next class consisted of the other original members, namely, Daisy Quantock, Georgie and Peppino. They had got on very well too, but Lucia had quite shot away from them, and now, if the Guru had other urgent spiritual claims on him, she gave instruction to a less advanced class herself. For this purpose she habited herself in a peculiarly becoming dress of white linen, which reached to her feet and had full, flowing sleeves, like a surplice. The girdle of it was a silver cord with long tassels, and it had mother-of-pearl buttons and a hood at the back, lined with white satin, which came over her head. Below its hem as she sat and taught in a really rather advanced posture, showed the toes of her white morocco slippers, and she called it her " Teacher's Robe." The class which she taught consisted of Colonel Boucher, Piggy Antrobus and Mrs. Weston : sometimes the Colonel brought his bulldogs with him, who lay and snorted precisely as if they were doing breathing exercises too. A general air of joyful mystery and spiritual endeavour blew balmily round them all, and without any doubt the exercises and the deep breathing were extremely good for them.

One evening towards the end of the month Georgie was sitting in his garden, for the half-hour before dressing-time, thinking how very busy he was, and yet how extraordinarily young and well he felt. Usually this month, when Hermy and Ursy were with him was very fatiguing, and in ordinary years he would have driven away with Foljambe and Dickie on the day after their departure, and had a quiet week by the seaside. But now, though his sisters were going away to-morrow morning, he had no intention of taking a well-earned rest, in spite of the fact that not only had he been their host all this time, but had done an amazing quantity of other things as well. There had been the daily classes to begin with, which entailed much work in the way of meditation and exercises, as well as the actual learning, and also he had had another job which might easily have taxed his energies to the utmost any other year. For Olga Bracely had definitely bought that house without which she had felt that life was not worth living, and Georgie all this month had at her request been exercising a semi-independent supervision over its decoration and furnishing. She had ordered the general scheme herself and had sent down from London the greater part of the furniture, but Georgie was commissioned to report on any likely pieces of old stuff that he could find, and if expedition was necessary to act on his own responsibility and buy them. But, above all, secrecy was still necessary till the house was so complete that her Georgie might be told, and by the end of the month Riseholme generally was in a state of prostration caused by the violent and feverish curiosity as to who had taken the house. Georgie had gone so far as to confess that he knew, but the most frantic appeals as to the owner's identity had fallen on obdurate, if not deaf, ears. Not the smallest hint would he give on the subject, and though those incessant visits to the house, those searchings for furniture, the bestowal of it in suitable places, the superintendence of the making of the garden, the interviewings of paper-hangers, plumbers, upholsterers, painters, carpenters, and so forth, occupied a great deal of time, the delicious mystery about it all, and the fact that he was doing it for so adorable a creature, rendered his exertions a positive refreshment. Another thing which, in conjunction with this and his youth-giving studies, made him feel younger than ever, was the discreet arrival and perfect success of his *toupet*. No longer was there any need to fear the dislocation of his espaliered locks. He felt so secure and undetectable in that regard that he had taken to wearing no hat, and was soon about to say that his hair was growing more thickly than ever in consequence. But it was not quite time for that yet : it would be inartistic to suggest that just a couple of weeks of hatlessness had produced so marked a result.

As he sat at ease after the labours of the day he pondered how the coming of Olga Bracely to Riseholme would affect the economy of the place. It was impossible to think of her, with her beauty, her charm, her fame, her personality, as taking any second place in its life. Unless she was really meaning to use Riseholme as a retreat, to take no part in its life at all, it was hard to see what part she would take, except the first part. One who by her arrival at Lucia's ever-memorable party, had converted it in a moment from the most dull of Scrubs (in a psychical sense) to the Hitumest gathering ever known, could not lay aside her distinction and pre-eminence. Never had Lucia " scored " so amazingly as over Olga's late appearance, which had the effect of bringing back all her departed guests with the compulsion of a magnet over iron-filings, and sending up the whole party like a rocket into the zenith of social success. All Riseholme knew that Olga had come (after playing croquet with Georgie the entire afternoon) and had given them, free, gratis, and for nothing, such a treat as only the wealthiest could obtain with the most

staggering fees. Lady Ambermere, driving back
to the Hall with Pug and poor Miss Lyall, was the
only person who had not shared in that, and she
knew all about it next day, for Georgie had driven
out on purpose to tell her, and met Lucia coming away.
How, then, would the advent of Olga affect Riseholme's
social policies generally, and how would it affect Lucia
in particular ?   And what would Lucia say when
she knew on whose behalf Georgie was so busy with
plumbers and painters, and buying so many of the
choicest treasures in the " Ambermere Arms " ?

Frankly, he could not answer these conundrums :
they presupposed inconceivable situations, which yet,
though inconceivable, were shortly coming to pass,
for Olga's advent might be expected before October,
that season of tea-parties that ushered in the multi-
farious gaieties of the winter.   Would Olga form part
of the moonlit circle to whom Lucia played the first
movement of the Moonlight Sonata, and give a long
sigh at the end, like all the rest of them ?   And would
Lucia, when they had all recovered a little from the
invariable emotion, go to her and say : " Olga *mia*,
just a little bit out of the *Valkyrie ?* It would be so
pleasant." Somehow Georgie, with all his imagination, could not picture such a scene.   And would Olga
take the part of second citizenness, or something of
the sort, when Lucia played Portia ? Would Olga
join the elementary class of Yoga, and be instructed
by Lucia in her Teacher's Robe ? Would she sing
treble in the Christmas Carols, while Lucia beat time,
and said, in syllables dictated by the rhythm :
" Trebles a little flat ! My poor ears ! " ? Georgie
could not imagine any of these things, and yet, unless
Olga took no part in the social life of Riseholme at all
(and that was equally inconceivable), what was the

alternative ? True, she had said that she was coming
here because it was so ideally lazy a backwater, but
Georgie did not take that seriously. She would soon
see what Riseholme was when its life poured down in
spate, whirling her punt along with it. And, finally,
what would happen to him when Olga was set as a
shining star in this firmament ? Already he revolved
about her, he was aware, like some eager, delighted
little moon, drawn away from the orbit where it had
circled so contentedly by the more potent planet.
And the measure of his detachment from that old orbit
might be judged precisely by the fact that the process
of detachment which was already taking place was
marked by no sense of the pull of opposing forces at
all. The great new star sailing into the heavens had
just picked him up by force of its superior power of
attraction, even as by its momentary conjunction
with Lucia at the garden-party it had raised her to a
magnitude she had never possessed before. That
magnitude was still hers, and no doubt would be
until the great star appeared again. Then, without
effort its shining must surely eclipse every other
illumination, just as without effort it must surely
attract all the little moons to itself. Or would Lucia
manage somehow or other, either by sheer force of will,
by desperate and hostile endeavour, or, on the other
hand, by some supreme tact and cleverness, to harness
the great star to her own chariot ? He thought the
desperate and hostile endeavour was more in keeping
with Lucia's methods, and this quiet evening hour
represented itself to him as the lull before the storm.

The actual quiet of the moment was suddenly broken
into. His front-door banged, and the house was
filled with running footsteps and screams of laughter.
But it was not uncommon for Hermy and Ursy to make

this sort of entrance, and at the moment Georgie had not the slightest idea of how much further-reaching was the disturbance of the tranquillity. He but drew a couple of long breaths, said " Om " once or twice, and was quite prepared to find his deeper calm unshattered.

Hermy and Ursy ran down the steps into the garden where he sat, still yelling with laughter, and Georgie's imagination went no further than to suppose that one of them had laid a stymie for the other at their golf, or driven a ball out of bounds, or done some other of those things that appeared to make the game so diverting to them.

" Georgie, you'll never guess ! " cried Hermy. " The Guru, the Om—— "

" —Of high caste and extraordinary sanctity—— " cried Ursy.

" The Brahmin from Benares—— " shrieked Hermy.

" The Great Teacher ! Who do you think he is ? " said Ursy.

" We'd never seen him before—— "

" But we recognized him at once—— "

" He recognized us, too, and didn't he run ?—— "

" Into The Hurst, and shut the door—— "

Georgie's deeper calm suddenly quivered like a jelly.

" My dears, you needn't howl so, or talk quite so loud," he said. " All Riseholme will hear you. Tell me without shouting who it was you thought you recognized."

" There's no thinking about it," said Hermy. " It was one of the cooks from the Calcutta Restaurant in Bedford Street—— "

" Where we often have lunch," said Ursy. " He makes the most delicious curries."

" Especially when he's a little tipsy," said Hermy.

" And is about as much a Brahmin as I am."

" And always said he came from Madras."

" We always tip him to make the curry himself, so he isn't quite ignorant about money."

" O Lord ! " said Hermy, wiping her eyes. " If it isn't the limit ! "

" And to think of Mrs. Lucas and Colonel Boucher, and you and Mrs. Quantock, and Piggy and all the rest of them, sitting round a cook," said Ursy, " and drinking in his wisdom. Mr. Quantock was on the right tack after all when he wanted to engage him."

Georgie, with a fallen heart, had first to satisfy himself that this was not one of his sisters' jokes, and then tried to raise his fallen heart by remembering that the Guru had often spoken of the dignity of simple manual work, but somehow it was a blow, if Hermy and Ursy were right, to know that this was a tipsy contriver of curry. There was nothing in the simple manual office of curry-making that could possibly tarnish sanctity, but the amazing tissue of falsehoods with which the Guru had modestly masked his innocent calling was not so markedly in the spirit of the Guides, as retailed by him. It was of the first importance, however, to be assured that his sisters had not at present communicated their upsetting discovery to anybody but himself, and after that to get their promise that they would not do so.

This was not quite so easy, for Hermy and Ursy had projected a round of visits after dinner to every member of the classes, with the exception of Lucia, who should wake up next morning to find herself the only illusioned person in the place.

" She wouldn't like that, you know," said Hermy, with brisk malice. " We thought it would serve her

out for never asking us to her house again after her
foolish old garden-party."

" My dear, you never wanted to go," said Georgie.

" I know we didn't, but we rather wanted to tell
her we didn't want to go. She wasn't nice. Oh, I
don't think we can give up telling everybody. He
has made such sillies of you all. I think he's a real
sport."

" So do I," said Ursy. " We shall soon have him
back at his curry-oven again. What a laugh we shall
have with him."

They subsided for just as long as it took Foljambe
to come out of the house, inform them that it was a
quarter of an hour to dressing-time, and return again,
and they all rose obediently.

" Well, we'll talk about it at dinner-time," said
Georgie diplomatically. " And I'll just go down to
the cellar first to see if I can find something you like."

" Good old Georgie," said Hermy. " But if you're
going to bribe us, you must bribe us well ! "

" We'll see," said he.

Georgie was quite right to be careful over his Veuve
Clicquot, especially since it was a bottle of that admirable beverage that Hermy and Ursy had looted from
his cellar on the night of their burglarious entry. He
remembered that well, though he had—chiefly from
the desire to keep things pleasant about his house—
joined in " the fun," and had even produced another
half-bottle. But to-night, even more than ever, there
was need for the abolition of all petty economies, for
the situation would be absolutely intolerable if Hermy
and Ursy spread about Riseholme the fact that the
innocent circle of Yoga philosophers had sat at the
feet of no Gamaliel at all, but at those of a curry-
cook from some low restaurant. Indeed, he brought

up a second bottle to-night, with a view, if Hermy
and Ursy were not softened by the first, of ad-
ministering that also. They would then hardly be in
a condition to be taken seriously, if they still insisted
on making a house-to-house visit in Riseholme and
tearing the veil from off the features of the Guru.
Georgie was far too upright of purpose to dream of
making his sisters drunk, but he was willing to make
great sacrifices in order to render them kind. What
the inner circle would do about this cook he had no
idea, and must talk to Lucia about it, before the
advanced class to-morrow morning. But anything
was better than letting Hermy and Ursy loose on Riseholme with their rude laughter and discreditable
exposures. This evening safely over, he could discuss
with Lucia what was to be done, for Hermy and Ursy
would have vanished at cock-crow as they were going
in for some golf-competition at a safe distance. Lucia
might recommend doing nothing at all, and wish to
continue the enlightening studies as if nothing had
happened. But Georgie felt that the romance would
have evaporated from the classes as regards himself.
Or again they might have to get rid of the Guru somehow. He only felt quite sure that Lucia would agree
with him that Daisy Quantock must not be told. She
with her thwarted ambitions of being the prime dispenser of Guruism to Riseholme might easily " turn
nasty," and let it be widely known that she and Robert
had seen through that fraud long ago, and had considered whether they should not offer the Guru the
situation of cook in their household, for which he was
so much better qualified. She might even add that
his leanings towards her pretty housemaid had alone
dissuaded her.

The evening went off with a success more brilliant

than Georgie had anticipated, and it was quite un-
necessary to open the second bottle of Veuve Clicquot.
Hermy and Ursy, perhaps under the influence of the
first, perhaps from innate good-nature, perhaps because
they were starting so very early next morning, and
wanted to be driven into Brinton, instead of taking a
slower and earlier train at Riseholme, readily gave up
their project of informing the whole of Riseholme of
their discovery, and went to bed as soon as they had
rooked their brother of eleven shillings at Cut-throat
Bridge. They continued to say, " I'll play the Guru,"
whenever they had to play a knave, but Georgie found
it quite easy to laugh at that, so long as the humour
of it did not spread. He even said, " I'll Guru you,
then," when he took a trick with the Knave of
Trumps. . . .

The agitation and uncertainty caused him not to
sleep very well, and in addition there was a good deal
of disturbance in the house, for his sisters had still
all their packing in front of them when they went to
bed, and the doze that preceded sleep was often broken
by the sound of the banging of luggage, the crash of
golf-clubs, and steps on the stairs as they made ready
for their departure. But after a while these disturbances ceased, and it was out of a deep sleep that he
awoke with the sense that some noise had roused
him. Apparently they had not finished yet, for
there was surely some faint stir of movement somewhere. Anyhow, they respected his legitimate desire
for quiet, for the noise, whatever it was, was extremely
stealthy and subdued. He thought of his absurd
alarm about burglars on the night of their arrival, and
smiled at the notion. His *toupet* was in a drawer close
to his bed, but he had no substantial impulse to put it
on and make sure that the noise was not anything

else than his sisters' preparations for their early start. For himself, he had everything packed and corded long before dinner if he was to start next day, except just a suit-case that would hold the apparatus of immediate necessities, but then dear Hermy and Ursy were so ramshackle in their ways. Some time he would have bells put on all the shutters, as he had determined to do a month ago, and then no sort of noise would disturb him any more. . . .

The Yoga-class next morning was (unusually) to assemble at ten, since Peppino, who would not miss it for anything, was going to have a day's fishing in the happy stream that flowed into the Avon, and he wanted to be off by eleven. Peppino had made great progress lately, and had certain curious dizzy symptoms when he meditated which were highly satisfactory.

Georgie breakfasted with his sisters at eight (they had enticed the motor out of him to convey them to Brinton), and when they were gone, Foljambe informed him that the housemaid had a sore throat and had not " done " the drawing-room. Foljambe herself would " do " it when she had cleaned the young ladies' rooms (there was a hint of scorn in this) upstairs, and so Georgie sat in the window-seat of the dining-room and thought how pleasant peace and quietness were. But just when it was time to start for The Hurst, in order to talk over the disclosures of the night before with Lucia before the class, and perhaps to frame some secretive policy which would obviate further exposure, he remembered that he had left his cigarette-case in the drawing-room (the pretty straw one with a little turquoise in the corner), and went to find it. The window was open, so apparently Foljambe *had* just come in to let fresh air into the atmosphere which Hermy and Ursy had so uninterruptedly contaminated last night with their " fags," as they can them, but his cigarette-case was not on the table where he thought he had left it. He looked round, and then stood rooted to the spot.

His glass-case of treasures was not only open but empty. Gone was the Louis XVI. snuff-box, gone was the miniature by Karl Huth, gone the piece of Bow china, and gone the Fabergé cigarette-case. Only the Queen Anne toy-porringer was there, and in the absence of the others, it looked to him, as no doubt it had looked to the burglar, indescribably insignificant.

Georgie gave a little low, wailing cry, but did not tear his hair, for obvious reasons. Then he rang the bell three times in swift succession, which was the signal to Foljambe that even if she was in her bath she must come at once. In she came, with one of Hermy's horrid woollen jerseys, that had been left behind, in her hand.

" Yes, sir, what is it ? " she asked, in an agitated manner, for never could she remember Georgie having rung the bell three times, except once when a fish-bone had stuck in his throat, and once again when a note had announced to him that Piggy was going to call and hoped to find him alone.

For answer Georgie pointed to the rifled treasure-case.

" Gone ! Burgled ! " he said. " Oh, my God ! "

At that supreme moment the telephone-bell sounded.

" See what it is," he said to Foljambe, and put the Queen Anne toy-porringer in his pocket.

She came hurrying back.

" Mrs. Lucas wants you to come round at once," she said.

" I can't," said Georgie. " I must stop here and send for the police. Nothing must be moved," and he hastily replaced the toy-porringer on the exact circle of pressed velvet where it had stood before.

" Yes, sir," said Foljambe, but in another moment she returned.

" She would be very much obliged if you would come at once," she said. " There's been a robbery in her house."

" Well, tell her there's been one in mine," said Georgie irritably. Then good-nature mixed with furious curiosity came to his aid.

" Wait here then, Foljambe, on this very spot," he said, " and see that nobody touches anything. I shall probably ring up the police from The Hurst. Admit them."

In his agitation he put on his hat, instead of going bare-headed, and was received by Lucia, who had clearly been looking out of the music-room window, at the door. She wore her Teacher's Robe.

" Georgie," she said, quite forgetting to speak Italian in her greeting, " someone broke into Philip's safe last night, and took a hundred pounds in bank-notes. He had put them there only yesterday, in order to pay in cash for that cob. And my Roman pearls."

Georgie felt a certain pride of achievement.

" I've been burgled, too," he said. " My Louis XVI. snuff-box is worth more than that, and there's the piece of Bow china, and the cigarette-case, and the Karl Huth as well."

" My dear ! Come inside," said she. " It's a gang. And I was feeling so peaceful and exalted. It will make a terrible atmosphere in the house. My Guru will be profoundly affected. An atmosphere where

thieves have been will stifle him. He has often told
me how he cannot stop in a house where there have
been wicked emotions at play. I must keep it from
him. I cannot lose him."

Lucia had sank down on a spacious Elizabethan
settee in the hall. The humorous spider mocked
them from the window, the humorous stone-fruit from
the plate beside the pot-pourri bowl. Even as she
repeated "I cannot lose him" again, a tremendous
rap came on the front-door, and Georgie, at a sign
from his queen, admitted Mrs. Quantock.

"Robert and I have been burgled," she said.
"Four silver spoons—thank God, most of our things
are plated !—eight silver forks and a Georgian tankard.
I could have spared all but the last."

A faint sigh of relief escaped Lucia. If the foul
atmosphere of thieves permeated Daisy's house, too,
there was no great danger that her Guru would go
back there. She instantly became sublime.

"Peace !" she said. "Let us have our class
first, for it is ten already, and not let any thought of
revenge or evil spoil that for us. If I sent for the
police now I could not concentrate. I will not
tell my Guru what has happened to any of us, but
for poor Peppino's sake I will ask him to give us
rather a short lesson. I feel completely calm. Om !"

Vague nightmare images began to take shape in
Georgie's mind, unworthy suspicions based on his
sisters' information the evening before. But with
Foljambe keeping guard over the Queen Anne porringer, there was nothing more to fear, and he followed
Lucia, her silver cord with tassels gently swinging
as she moved, to the smoking-parlour, where Peppino
was already sitting on the floor, and breathing in a
rather more agitated manner than was usual with the

advanced class. There were fresh flowers on the table, and the scented morning breeze blew in from the garden. According to custom, they all sat down and waited, getting calmer and more peaceful every moment. Soon there would be the tapping of slippered heels on the walk of broken paving-stones outside, and for the time they would forget these disturbances. But they were all rather glad that Lucia was to ask her Guru to give them a shorter lesson than usual.

They waited. Presently the hands of the Cromwellian timepiece, which was the nearest approach to an Elizabethan clock that Lucia had been able at present to obtain, pointed to a quarter-past ten.

" My Guru is a little late," said she.

Five minutes afterwards Peppino sneezed. Two minutes after that Daisy spoke, using irony.

" Would it not be well to see what has happened to your Guru, dear ? " she asked. " Have you seen your Guru this morning ? "

" No, dear," said Lucia, not opening her eyes, for she was concentrating ; " he always meditates before a class."

" So do I," said Daisy ; " but I have meditated long enough."

" Hush ! " said Lucia. " He is coming."

That proved to be a false alarm, for it was nothing but Lucia's Persian cat, who had a quarrel with some dead laurel leaves. Lucia rose.

" I don't like to interrupt him," she said, " but time is getting on."

She left the smoking-parlour with the slow, supple walk that she adopted when she wore her Teacher's Robe. Before many seconds had passed, she came back more quickly and with less suppleness.

" His door is locked," she said, " and yet there's no key in it."

" Did you look through the keyhole, Lucia *mia* ? " asked Mrs. Quantock, with irrepressible irony.

Naturally Lucia disregarded this.

" I knocked," she said, " and there was no reply. I said : " Master, we are waiting,' and he didn't answer."

Suddenly Georgie spoke, as with the report of a cork flying out of a bottle.

" My sisters told me last night that he was the curry-cook at the Calcutta Restaurant," he said. " They recognized him, and they thought he recognized them. He comes from Madras, and is no more a Brahmin than Foljambe is."

Peppino bounced to his feet.

" What ? " he cried. " Let's get a poker and break in the door ! I believe he's gone ; I believe he's the burglar. Ring for the police ! "

" Curry-cook, is he ? " said Daisy. " Robert and I were right after all. We knew what your Guru was best fitted for, dear Lucia, but then, of course, you always knew best, and you and he have been fooling us all finely. But you didn't fool me. I knew when you took him away from me what sort of a bargain you had made. Guru indeed ! He's the same class as Mrs. Eddy, and I saw through her fast enough. And now what are we to do ? For my part, I shall just get home and ring up for the police, and say that the Indian who has been living with you all these weeks has stolen my spoons and forks and my Georgian tankard. Guru indeed ! Burglaroo, I call him ! There ! "

Her passion, like Hyperion's, had lifted her upon her feet, and she stood there defying the whole of the advanced class, short and stout and wholly ridiculous, but with some revolutionary menace about her. She was not exactly " terrible as an army with banners," but she was terrible as an elderly lady with a long-standing grievance which had been accentuated by the loss of a Georgian tankard, and that was terrible enough to make Lucia adopt a conciliatory attitude. Bitterly she repented having stolen Daisy's Guru at all, if the suspicions now thickening in the air proved to be true, but, after all, they were not proved yet. The Guru might still walk in from the arbour in the laburnum-alley which they had not yet searched, or he might be levitating with his door-key in his pocket. It was not probable but it was possible, and at this crisis possibilities were things that must be clung to, for otherwise you would simply have to submerge, like those U-boats. They searched all the garden, but found no trace of the curry-cook ; they made guarded inquiries of the servants as to whether he had been seen, but nothing whatever could be learned about him. So when Peppino took a ponderous hammer and a stout chisel from his tool-chest, and led the way upstairs, they all knew that the decisive moment had come. Perhaps the Guru might be meditating (for, indeed, it was likely that he had a good deal to meditate about), but perhaps—— Peppino called to him in his most sonorous tones, and said that he would be obliged to break his lock if no answer came, and presently the house resounded with knockings as terrible as those in *Macbeth*, and much louder. Then suddenly the lock gave, and the door was open.

The room was empty, and, as they had all conjectured by now, the bed was unslept in. They opened the drawers of the wardrobe, and they were as empty as the room. Finally Peppino unlocked the door of a large cupboard that stood in the corner, and with a clinking and crashing of glass there poured out a cataract of empty brandy bottles. Emptiness: that was the key-note of the whole scene, and blank consternation its effect.

"My brandy!" said Mrs. Quantock, in a strangled voice. "There are fourteen or fifteen bottles. That accounts for the glazed look in his eyes which you, dear Lucia, thought was concentration. I call it distillation."

"Did he take it from your cellar?" asked Lucia, too shattered to feel resentment, but still capable of intense curiosity.

"No; he had a standing order from me to order any little things he might want from my tradesmen. I wish I had my bills sent in every week."

"Yes, dear," said Lucia.

Georgie's eye sought hers.

"I saw him buy the first bottle," he said. "I remember telling you about it. It was at Rush's."

Peppino gathered up his hammer and chisel.

"Well, it's no use sitting here and thinking of old times," he observed. "I shall ring up the police-station, and put the whole matter into their hands, as far as I am concerned. They'll soon lay hands on him, and he can do his postures in prison for the next few years."

"But we don't know that it was he who committed all these burglaries yet," said Lucia.

No one felt it was worth answering this, for the others had all tried and convicted him already.

"I shall do the same," said Georgie.

"My tankard!" said Mrs. Quantock.

Lucia got up.

"Peppino *mio*," she said, "and you, Georgie, and

QUEEN LUCIA 167

you, Daisy, I want you, before you do anything at all,
to listen to me for five minutes. Just consider this.
What sort of figure shall we all cut if we put the matter
into the hands of the police? They will probably
catch him, and it will all come out that we have
been the dupes of a curry-cook. Think what we have
all been doing for this last month; think of our classes,
our exercises, our—everything. We have been made
fools of, but, for my part, I simply couldn't bear that
everybody should know I had been made a fool of.
Anything but that. What's a hundred pounds com-
pared to that, or a tankard——"

" My Louis XVI. snuff-box, which I inherited, was
worth at least that without the other things," said
Georgie, still with a secret satisfaction in being the
greatest sufferer.

" And it was my hundred pounds, not yours,
carissima," said Peppino. But it was clear that Lucia's
words were working within him like leaven.

" I'll go halves with you," she said. " I'll give you
a cheque for fifty pounds."

" And who would like to go halves in my tankard? "
said Daisy, with bitter irony. " I want my tankard ! "

Georgie said nothing, but his mind was extremely
busy. There was Olga soon coming to Riseholme,
and it would be awful if she found it ringing with the
tale of the Guru, and glancing across to Peppino, he
saw a thoughtful and sympathetic look in his eyes,
that seemed to indicate that his mind was working
on parallel lines. Certainly Lucia had given them all
something to meditate upon. He tried to imagine the
whole story being shouted into Mrs. Antrobus's ear-
trumpet on the village green, and could not endure the
idea. He tried to imagine Mrs. Weston ever ceasing

to talk about it, and could not picture her silence.
No doubt they had all been taken in, too, but here in
this empty bedroom were the original dupes, the silly
bleating bell-wethers.

After Mrs. Quantock's inquiry a dead silence fell.

"What do you propose, then?" asked Peppino,
showing signs of surrender.

Lucia exerted her utmost wiles.

"*Caro!*" she said, "I want 'oo to propose. Daisy
and me two silly women; we want 'oo and Georgie
to tell us what to do. But if Lucia must speak,
I fink——" She paused a moment, and observing
strong disgust at her playfulness on Mrs. Quantock's
face, reverted to ordinary English again.

"I should do something of this sort," she said. "I
should let it be known that dear Daisy's Guru had
left us quite suddenly, and that he had had a call
somewhere else. His work here was done; he had
established our classes, and set all our feet upon the
Way. He always said that something of the sort
might happen to him——"

"I believe he had planned it all along," said Georgie.
"He knew the thing couldn't last for ever, and when
my sisters recognized him, he concluded it was time
to bolt."

"With all the available property he could lay hands
on," said Mrs. Quantock.

Lucia fingered her tassels.

"Now about the burglaries," she said. "It won't
do to let it be known that three burglaries were committed in one night, and that simultaneously Daisy's
Guru was called away——"

"My Guru, indeed!" said Mrs. Quantock, fizzing
with indignation at the repetition of this insult.

"That might give rise to suspicion," continued

Lucia, calmly disregarding the interruption, " and we must stop the news from spreading. Now with regard to our burglary . . . let me think a moment."

She had got such complete control of them all now that no one spoke.

" I have it," she said. " Only Boaler knows, for Peppino told her not to say a word till the police had been sent for. You must tell her, *carissimo*, that you have found the hundred pounds. That settles that. Now you, Georgie."

" Foljambe knows," said Georgie.

" Then tell her not to say a word about it. Put some more things out in your lovely treasure-case ; more heirlooms, no one will notice. And you, Daisy ? "

" Robert is away," said she, quite meekly, for she had been thinking things over. " My maid knows."

" And when he comes back, will he notice the loss of the tankard ? Did you often use it ? "

" About once in ten years."

" Chance it then," said Lucia. " Just tell your maid to say nothing about it."

She became deliciously modest again.

" There ! " she said. " That's just a little rough idea of mine, and now Peppino and Georgie will put their wise heads together, and tell us what to do."

That was easily done : they repeated what she had said, and she corrected them if they went wrong. Then once again she stood fingering the tassels of her Teacher's Robe.

" About our studies," she said. " I, for one, should be very sorry to drop them altogether, because they made such a wonderful difference to me, and I think you all felt the same. Look at Georgie now : he looks ten years younger than he did a month ago, and as for Daisy, I wish I could trip about as she does.

And it wouldn't do, would it, to drop everything just because Dai—the Guru had been called away ? It would look as if we weren't really interested in what he taught us, as if it was only the novelty of having a —a Brahmin among us that had attracted us."

Lucia smiled benignly at them all.

" Perhaps we shall find, by and by, that we can't progress much all by ourselves," she said, " and it will all drop quietly. But don't let us drop it with a bang. I shall certainly take my elementary class as usual this afternoon."

She paused.

" In my Robe, just as usual," she said.

CHAPTER IX

THE fish for which Mrs. Weston sent to Brinton
every week, since she did not like the look of the
successor to Tommy Luton's mother, was steaming
disregarded on the dish, while with fork and fish-slice
in her hand, as aids to gesticulation, she was recounting
to Colonel Boucher the complete steps that had led
up to her remarkable discovery.

" It was the day of Mrs. Lucas's garden-party," she
said, " when first I began to have my ideas, and
you may be sure I kept them to myself, for I'm not
one to speak before I'm pretty sure, but now if the
Prime Minister came to me on his bended knee and said
it wasn't so, I shouldn't believe him. Well, as you
may remember, we all went back to Mrs. Lucas's party
again about half-past six, and it was an umbrella that
one had left behind, and a book that another wanted to
borrow, and what not; for me it was a book all about
Venice, and I'm sure most interesting, but I haven't had
time to glance at it yet, and there was Miss Bracely
just come ! "

Mrs. Weston had to pause a moment, for her maid
Elizabeth Luton (cousin of Tommy) jogged her elbow
with the dish-cover in a manner that could not fail to
remind her that Colonel Boucher was still waiting for
his piece of brill. As she carved it for him, he rapidly
ran over in his mind what seemed to be the main points

so far, for as yet there was no clue whatever as to the
purpose of this preliminary matter.   He guessed either
the Guru or Miss Bracely.   He received his piece of
brill, and Mrs. Weston laid down her carving im-
plements again.

"You'd better help yourself, ma'am," said Elizabeth discreetly.

"So I had, and I'll give you a piece of advice too,
Elizabeth, and that is to give the Colonel a glass of
wine.   Burgundy !   I was only wondering this afternoon when it began to turn chilly, if there was a bottle
or two of the old Burgundy left, which Mr. Weston
used to be so fond of, and there was.   He bought it
on the very spot where it was made, and he said there
wasn't a headache in it, not if you drank it all night.
He never did, for a couple of glasses and one more
was all he ever took, so I don't know how he knew
about drinking it all night, but he was a very fine
judge of wine.   So I said to Elizabeth, ' A bottle of
the old Burgundy, Elizabeth.'   Well !   On   that
evening I stopped behind a bit, to have another look
at the Guru, and get my book, and when I came up
the street again, what should I see but Miss Bracely
walking in to the little front garden at Old Place.
It was getting dark, I know, and my eyes aren't like
Mrs. Antrobus's, but I saw her plain enough.   And
if it wasn't the next day, it was the day after that,
that they began mending the roof, and since then,
there have been plumbers and painters and upholsterers and furniture vans at the door day and night."

"Haw, hum," said the Colonel, "then do you mean
that it's Miss Bracely who has taken it ? "

Mrs. Weston nodded her head up and down.

"I shall ask you what you think when I've told
you all," she said.   "Well !   There came a day, and

if to-day's Friday, it would be last Thursday fortnight, and if to-day's Thursday, for I got mixed about
it this morning, and then I never get it straight till
next day, but if to-day's Thursday, then it would be
last Wednesday fortnight, when the Guru went away
very suddenly, and I'm sure I wasn't very sorry,
because those breathings made me feel very giddy, and
yet I didn't like to be out of it all. The two sisters of
Mr. Georgie went away the same day, and I've often
wondered whether there was any connection between
the two events, for it was odd their happening together
like that, and I'm not sure we've heard the last of it
yet."

Colonel Boucher began to wonder whether this was
not going to be about the Guru after all, and helped
himself to half a partridge. This had the effect of
diverting Mrs. Weston altogether.

" No," she said, " I insist on your taking a whole
bird. They are quite small, and I was disappointed
when I saw them plucked, but a bit of cold ham and
a savoury is the rest of your dinner. Mary asked me
if I wouldn't have an apple tart as well, but I said
' No : the Colonel never touches sweets, but he'll
have a partridge, a whole partridge,' I said, ' and he
won't complain of his dinner.' Well ! On the day
that they all went away, whatever the explanation of
that was, I was sitting in my chair opposite the ' Arms '
when out came the landlord followed by two men
carrying the settle that stood on the right of the fireplace in the hall. So I said : ' Well, landlord, who has
ordered that handsome piece ? ' for handsome it was,
with its carved arms. And he said : ' Good morning,
ma'am '—no, ' Good afternoon, ma'am,' it would be—
It's for Miss——' And then he stopped dead and
corrected himself : ' It's for Mr. Pillson.' "

Mrs. Weston rapidly took a great quantity of mouthfuls of partridge. As soon as possible she went on.

"So perhaps you can tell me where it is now, if it was for Mr. Georgie," she said. "I was there only two days ago, and it wasn't in his hall, or in his dining-room or in his drawing-room, for though there are changes there, that settle isn't one of them. It's his treasure-case that's so altered. The snuff-box is gone, and the cigarette case, and the piece of Bow china, and instead there's a rat-tail spoon which he used to have on his dinner-table, and made a great fuss with, and a bit of Worcester china that used to stand on the mantelpiece, and a different cigarette case, and a bead-bag. I don't know where that came from, but if he inherited it, he didn't inherit much that time. I priced it at five shillings. But there's no settle in the treasure-case or out of it, and if you want to know where that settle is, it's in Old Place, because I saw it there myself, when the door was open as I passed. He bought it—Mr. Georgie—on behalf of Miss Bracely, unless you suppose that Mr. Georgie is going to live in Old Place one day and his own house the next. No : it's Miss Bracely who is going to live at Old Place, and that explains the landlord saying ' Miss ' and then stopping. For some reason, and I daresay that won't puzzle me long, now I can give my mind to it, she's making a secret about it, and only Mr. Georgie and the landlord of the ' Arms ' know. Of course, he had to, for Old Place is his, and I wish I had bought it myself now, for he got it for an old song."

"Well, by Jove, you have pieced it together finely," said Colonel Boucher.

"Wait a bit," said Mrs. Weston, rising to her climax. "This very day, when Mary, that's my cook,

was coming back from Brinton with that bit of brill
we've been eating, for they hadn't got an ounce of
turbot, which I wanted, a luggage-train was standing
at Riseholme station, and they had just taken out of
it a case that could have held nothing but a grand
piano. And if that's not enough for you, Colonel,
there were two big dress-baskets as well, which I
think must have contained linen, for they were corded,
and it took two men to move each of them, Mary
said, and there's nothing so heavy as linen properly
packed, unless it's plate, and there printed on them
in black—no, it would be white, because the dress-
baskets were black—were two initials, O. B. And
if you can point to another O. B. in Riseholme I shall
think I've lost my memory."

At this moment of supreme climax, the telephone-
bell rang in the hall, shrill through the noise of cracking
walnuts, and in came Elizabeth with the news that Mr.
Georgie wanted to know if he might come in for half-
an-hour and chat. If it had been Olga Bracely herself,
she could hardly have been more welcome; virtue
(the virtue of observation and inference) was receiving
its immediate reward.

"Delighted: say I'm delighted, Elizabeth," said Mrs.
Weston, "and now, Colonel, why should you sit
all alone here, and I all alone in the drawing-room.
Bring your decanter and your glass with you, and you
shall spare me half a glass for myself, and if you can't
guess what one of the first questions that I shall ask
Mr. Georgie is, well——"

Georgie made haste to avail himself of this hospitality, for he was bursting with the most important
news that had been his since the night of the burglaries,
and the edge of that had been taken off it by the fact
that the only two people who had ever heard about

it, had been burgled too. But to-day he had received
permission to let it be known that Olga was coming
to Old Place, for Mr. Shuttleworth had been informed
of the purchase and furnishing of the house, and had,
as expected, presented his wife with it, a really magnificent gift. So now Riseholme might know, too,
and Georgie, as eager as Hermes, if not quite so swift,
tripped across to Mrs. Weston's on his delightful
errand. It was, too, of the nature of just such a punitive expedition as Georgie thoroughly enjoyed, for Lucia
all this week had been rather haughty and cold with
him, on account of his firm refusal to tell her who the
purchaser of Old Place was. He had admitted that
he knew, but had said that he was under promise not
to reveal that, until permitted, and Lucia had been
haughty in consequence. She had, in fact, been
so haughty that when Georgie rang her up just now,
before ringing Mrs. Weston up, to ask if he might
spend his *après-diner* there, fully intending to tell
her the great news, she had replied through her parlour-maid that she was very busy at her piano. Very
well : if she preferred the second and third movements
of the Moonlight Sonata, which she had seriously
taken in hand, to Georgie's company, why, he would
offer himself and his great news elsewhere. But
he determined not to bring it out at once : that sort
of thing must be kept till he said it was time to go
away. Then he would bring it out, and depart in the
blaze of success.

He had brought a pretty piece of embroidery with
him to occupy himself with, for his work had fallen
into sad arrears during August, and he settled himself comfortably down close to the light, so that, at
the cost of very little eye-strain, he need not put on
his spectacles.

" Any news ? " he asked, according to the invariable formula.

Mrs, Weston caught the Colonel's eye. She was not purposing to bring out her tremendous interrogation just yet.

" Poor Mrs. Antrobus. Toothache ! " she said. " I was in the chemist's this morning, and who should come in but Miss Piggy, and she wanted a drop of laudanum and had to say what it was for, and even then she had to sign a paper. Very unpleasant, I call it, to be obliged to let a chemist know that your mother has a toothache. But there it was, tell him she had to, or go away without any laudanum. I don't know whether Mr. Doubleday wasn't asking more than he should, just out of inquisitiveness, for I don't see what business it is of his. I know what I should have done if I had been Miss Piggy. I should have said : ' Oh, Mr. Doubleday, I want it to make laudanum tartlets ; we are all so fond of laudanum tartlets.' Something sharp and sarcastic like that, to show him his place. But I expect it did Mrs. Antrobus good, for there she was on the green in the afternoon, and her face wasn't swollen, for I had a good look at her. Oh, and there was something I wanted to ask you, Mr. Georgie, and I had it on the tip of my tongue a moment ago. We talked about it at dinner, the Colonel and I, while we were eating our bit of part-ridge, and I thought ' Mr. Georgie will be sure to be able to tell us,' and if you didn't ring up on the tele-phone immediately afterwards. That seemed quite providential, but what's the use of that, if I can't remember what it was that I wanted to ask you ? "

This seemed a good opening for his startling news, but Georgie rejected it, as it was too early yet.

" I wonder what it could have been," he said.

" Well, it will come back to me presently, and
here's our coffee, and I see Elizabeth hasn't forgotten
to bring a drop of something good for you two gentlemen.   And I don't say that I won't join you, if Elizabeth will bring another glass.   What with a glass of
Burgundy at my dinner, and a drop of brandy now,
I shall be quite tipsy, unless I take care.   The Guru
now, Mr. Georgie,—no, that's not what I wanted to
ask you about—but has there been any news of the
Guru ? "

For a moment in this juxtaposition of the topics of
brandy and Guru, Georgie was afraid that something
might have leaked out about the contents of the
cupboard in " Hamlet ".   But it was evidently a chance
combination, for Mrs. Weston went straight on without
waiting for any answer.

" What a day that was," she said, " when he and
Miss Olga Bracely were both at Mrs. Lucas's garden-
party !   Ah, now I've got it ;   now I know what I
wanted to ask.   When will Miss Olga Bracely come
to live at Old Place ?   Quite soon now, I suppose ! "

If Georgie had not put down his embroidery with
great expedition, he would undoubtedly have pricked
his finger.

" But how on earth did you know she was coming
at all ? " he said.   " I was just going to tell you that
she was coming, as a great bit of news.   How tarsome !   It's spoiled all my pleasure."

" Haw, hum, not a very gallant speech, when you're
talking to Mrs. Weston," said the Colonel, who hated
Georgie's embroidery.

Luckily the pleasure in the punitive part of the
expedition remained and Georgie recovered himself.
He had some news, too : he could answer Mrs. Weston's
question.

" But it was to have been such a secret until the whole thing was ready," he said. " I knew all along : I have known since the day of the garden-party. No one knew but me, not even her husband."

He was well rewarded for the recovery of his temper. Mrs. Weston put down her glass of something good untasted.

" What ? " she said. " Is she going to live here alone in hiding from him ? Have they quarrelled so soon ? "

Georgie had to disappoint her about this, and gave the authentic version

" And she's coming next week, Monday probably," he said.

They were all now extremely happy, for Mrs. Weston felt convinced that nobody else had put two and two together with the same brilliant result as herself, and Georgie was in the even superior position of having known the result without having to do any addition at all, and Colonel Boucher enjoyed the first-fruits of it all. When they parted, having thoroughly discussed it, the chief preoccupation of each of them was as to among how many people they could be the first to spread the tidings. Mrs. Weston could tell Elizabeth that night, and Colonel Boucher his bull-dogs, but the first blood was really drawn by Georgie, who, seeing a light in Mrs. Quantock's drawing-room when he returned, dropped in for a moment and scored a right and left by telling Robert, who let him in, before going upstairs, and Mrs. Quantock when he got there. It was impossible to do any more that night.

Lucia was always very busy of a morning in polishing the sword and shield of Art, in order to present herself daily to her subjects in shining armour, and keep a little ahead of them all in culture, and thus did not as a rule take part in the parliaments on the green. Moreover, Georgie usually dropped in before lunch, and her casual interrogation "Any news?" as they sat down to the piano, elicited from him, as in a neat little jug, the cream of the morning's milkings. To-day she was attired in her Teacher's Robe, for the elementary class, though not always now in full conclave, gathered at her house on Tuesdays and Thursdays. There had been signs of late that the interest of her pupils was on the wane, for Colonel Boucher had not appeared for two meetings, nor had Mrs. Weston come to the last, but it was part of Lucia's policy to let Guruism die a natural death without herself facilitating its happy release, and she meant to be ready for her class at the appointed times as long as anybody turned up.

Besides, the Teacher's Robe was singularly becoming, and she often wore it when there was no question of teaching at all.

But to-day, though she would not have been surprised at no arrival of pupils, she was still in consultation with her cook over the commissariat of the day, when a succession of tinklings from the mermaid's tail announced that a full meeting was assembling. Her maid, in fact, had announced to her without pause, except to go to the door and back, though it still wanted a few minutes to eleven, that Colonel Boucher, Mrs. Weston, Mrs. Antrobus and Piggy were all assembled in the smoking-parlour. Even as she passed through the hall on her way there, Georgie came hurrying across Shakespeare's garden, his figure distorted through the wavy glass of the windows, and she opened the door to him herself.

"Georgino *mio*," she said, "'oo not angry with

Lucia for saying she was busy last night ? And now I'm just going to take my Yoga-class. They all came rather early and I haven't seen any of them yet. Any news ? "

Georgie heaved a sigh : all Riseholme knew by this time, and he was going to score one more by telling Lucia.

" My dear, haven't you heard yet ? " he asked. " I was going to tell you last night."

" The tenant of Old Place ? " asked Lucia unerringly.

" Yes. Guess ! " said Georgie tantalizingly. This was his last revelation, and he wanted to spin it out.

Lucia decided on a great stroke, involving risks but magnificent if it came off. In a flash she guessed why all the Yoga-class had come so super-punctually : each of them she felt convinced wanted to have the joy of telling her, after everybody else knew, who the new tenant was. On the top of this bitterness was the added acrimony of Georgie, whose clear duty it was to have informed her the moment he knew, wanting to make the same revelation. She had already had her own suspicions, for she had not forgotten the fact that Olga Bracely and Georgie had played croquet all afternoon when they should have been at her garden-party, and she determined to risk all for the sake of spoiling Georgie's pleasure in telling her.

She gave her silvery laugh, that started, so she had ascertained, on A flat above the treble clef.

" Georgino, did all my questions as to who it was really take you in ? " she asked. " Just as if I hadn't known all along ! Why, Miss Olga Bracely, of course ! "

Georgie's fallen face showed her . how completely she had spoiled his pleasure, and how right she was.

" Who told you ? " he asked.

She rattled her tassels.

" Little bird ! " she said. " I must run away to my class, or they will scold me."

Once again, before they settled down to high philosophies, Lucia had the pleasure of disappointing the ambitions of her class to surprise, inform and astonish her.

" Good morning to you all," she said, " and before we settle down, I'll give you a little bit of news now that I'm allowed to. Dear Miss Olga Bracely, whom I think you all met here, is coming to live at Old Place. Will she not be a great addition to our musical parties. Now, please."

But this splendid bravado was but a scintillation on a hard and highly polished surface, and had Georgie been able to penetrate into Lucia's heart he would have found complete healing for his recent severe mortification. He did not really believe that Lucia had known all along, like himself, who the new tenant was, for her inquiries had seemed to be pointed with the most piercing curiosity, but after all, Lucia (when she did not forget her part) was a fine actress, and perhaps all the time he thought he had been punishing her, she had been fooling him. And, in any case, he certainly had not had the joy of telling her : whether she had guessed or really knew, she had told him, and there was no getting over it. He went back straight home and drew a caricature of her.

But if Georgie was sitting with a clouded brow, Lucia was troubled by nothing less than a raging tornado of agitated thought. Though Olga would undoubtedly be a great addition to the musical talent of Riseholme, would she fall into line, and, for instance, " bring her music " and sing after dinner when Lucia

asked her ? As regards music, it was possible that
she might be almost too great an addition, and
cause the rest of the gifted amateurs to sink
into comparative insignificance. At present Lucia
was high-priestess at every altar of Art, and she
could not think with equanimity of seeing anybody
in charge of the ritual at any. Again, to so eminent
an opera-singer there must be conceded a certain
dramatic knowledge, and, indeed, Georgie had often
spoken to Lucia of that superb moment when Brünnhilde woke and hailed the sun. Must Lucia give up
the direction of dramatic art as well as of music ? . . .

Point by point pricked themselves out of the
general gloom, and hoisted danger signals ; then
suddenly the whole was in blaze together. What if
Olga took the lead, not in this particular only or in
that, but attempted to constitute herself supreme in
the affairs of Riseholme ? It was all very well for her
to be a brilliant bird of passage just for a couple of
days, and drop, so to speak, " a moulted feather,
an eagle's feather," on Lucia's party, thereby causing
it to shine out from all previous festivities, making
it the Hitumest affair that had ever happened, but
it was a totally different matter to contemplate her
permanent residence here. It seemed feasible that
then she might keep her feathers to line her own eyrie.
She thought of Belshazzar's feast, and the writing of
doom on the wall which she was Daniel enough to
interpret herself. " Thy kingdom is divided," it
said, " and given to the Bracelys or the Shuttleworths."

She rallied her forces. If Olga meant to show herself
that sort of woman, she should soon know with whom
she had to deal. Not but what Lucia would give
her the chance first of behaving with suitable loyalty

and obedience—she would even condescend to co-operate with her so long as it was perfectly clear that she aimed at no supremacy. But there was only one lawgiver in Riseholme, one court of appeal, one dispenser of destiny.

Her own firmness of soul calmed and invigorated her, and changing her Teacher's Robe for a walking dress, she went up the road that led by Old Place, to see what could be observed of the interior from outside.

CHAPTER X

ONE morning about the middle of October, Lucia was seated at breakfast, frowning over a note which she had just received. It began without any formality, and was written in pencil.

"Do look in about half-past nine on Saturday, and be silly for an hour or two. We'll play games and dance, shall we? Bring your husband, of course, and don't bother to reply.

"O. B."

"An invitation," she said icily, as she passed it to her husband. "Rather short notice."

"We're not doing anything, are we?" he asked.

Peppino was a little imperceptive sometimes.

"No, it wasn't that I meant," she said. "But there's a little more informality about it than one would expect."

"Probably it's an informal party," said he.

"It certainly seems most informal. I am not accustomed to be asked quite like that."

Peppino began to be aware of the true nature of the situation.

"I see what you mean, *cara*," he said, "so don't let us go. She will take the hint perhaps."

Lucia thought this over for a moment, and found that she rather wanted to go. But a certain resentment that had been slowly accumulating in her mind for some days past began to leak out, before she consented to overlook Olga's informality.

"It is a fortnight since I called on her," she said, "and she has not even returned the call. I daresay they behave like that in London in certain circles, but I don't know that London is any better for it."

"She has been away twice since she came," said Peppino. "She has hardly been here for a couple of days together yet."

"I may be wrong," said Lucia. "No doubt I am wrong. But I should have thought that she might have spared half-an-hour out of those days in returning my call. However, she thought not."

Peppino suddenly recollected a thrilling piece of news which, most unaccountably, he had forgotten to tell Lucia.

"Dear me, something slipped my memory!" he said. "I met Mrs. Weston yesterday afternoon, who told me that Miss Bracely had seen her in her bath-chair and had taken the handles from Tommy Luton, and pushed her twice round the green, positively running."

"That does not seem to me of very prime importance," said Lucia, though she was thrilled to the marrow. "I do not wonder it slipped your memory, *caro.*"

"*Carissima*, wait a minute. That is not all. She told Mrs. Weston that she would have returned her call, but that she hadn't got any calling-cards."

"Impossible!" cried Lucia. "They could have printed them at 'Ye Olde Booke Shop' in a couple of hours."

"That may be so; indeed, if you say so, it is," said Peppino. "Anyhow, she said she hadn't got any calling-cards, and I don't see why she should lie about it."

"No, it is not the confession one would be likely to make," said she, "if it was not true. Or even if it was," she added.

"Anyhow, it explains why she has not been here," said Peppino. "She would naturally like to do everything in order, when she called on you, *carissima*. It would have been embarrassing if you were out, and she could not hand in her cards."

"And about Mr. Shuttleworth?" asked she in an absent voice, as if she had no real interest in her question.

"He has not been seen yet at all, as far as I can gather."

"Then shall we have no host, if we drop in to-morrow night?"

"Let us go and see, *cara*," said he gaily.

Apart from this matter of her call not being returned, Lucia had not as yet had any reason to suspect Olga of revolutionary designs on the throne. She had done odd things—pushing Mrs. Weston's chair round the green was one of them, smoking a cigarette as she came back from church on Sunday was another—but these she set down to the Bohemianisms and want of polish which might be expected from her upbringing, if you could call an orphan school at Brixton an upbringing at all. This terrific fact Georgie had let slip in his stern determination to know twice as much about Olga as anybody else, and Lucia had treasured it. She had in this last fortnight labelled Olga as "rather common," retaining, however, a certain respect for her professional career, given that that professional career was to be thrown down as a carpet for her own feet. But, after all, if Olga was a bit

Bohemian in her way of life, as exhibited by the absence of calling-cards, Lucia was perfectly ready
to overlook that, confident in the refining influence
of Riseholme, and to go to the informal party next
day, if she felt so disposed, for no direct answer was
asked for.

There was a considerable illumination in the windows
of Old Place when she and Peppino set out after dinner
next night to go to the " silly " party, kindly over-
looking the informality and the absence of a return-
visit to her call.   It had been a sloppy day of rain, and
as was natural, Lucia carried some very smart indoor
shoes in a paper-parcel, and Peppino had his Russian
goloshes on. These were immense snow-boots, in
which his evening-shoes were completely encased,
but Lucia preferred not to disfigure her feet to that
extent, and was shod in neat walking-boots which she
could exchange for her smart satin footwear in the
cloak-room. The resumption of walking-boots when
the evening was over was rather a feature among the
ladies, and was called " the cobbler's at-home."
The two started rather late, for it was fitting that
Lucia should be the last to arrive. They had come to
the door of Old Place, and Peppino was fumbling in
the dark for the bell, when Lucia gave a little cry of
agony and put her hands over her ears, just as if she had
been seized with a double earache of peculiar intensity.

" Gramophone," she said faintly.

There could be no doubt about that. From the
window close at hand came out the excruciating strains
of a very lusty instrument, and the record was that
of a vulgar " catchy " waltz-tune, taken down
from a brass-band. All Riseholme knew what her
opinion about gramophones was : to the lover of
Beethoven they were like indecent or profane lan-

guage loudly used in a public place. Only one of those hellish instruments, so far as was known, had ever come to Riseholme, and that was introduced by the misguided Robert Quantock. Once he had turned it on in her presence, but the look of agony which crossed her face was such that he had to stop it immediately.

Then the door was opened, and the abominable noise poured out in increased volume.

Lucia paused for a moment in indecision. Would it be the great, the magnificent thing to go home without coming in, trusting to Peppino to let it be widely known what had turned her back from the door? There was a good deal to be said for that, for it would be living up to her own high and immutable standards. On the other hand she particularly wanted to see what standard of entertaining Olga was initiating. The " silly evening " was quite a new type of party, for since Lucia had directed and controlled the social side of things there had been no " silly evenings " of any kind in Riseholme, and it might be a good thing to ensure the failure of this (in case she did not like it) by setting the example of a bored and frosty face. But if she went in, the gramophone must be stopped. She would sit and wince, and Peppino must explain her feeling about gramophones. That would be a suitable exhibition of authority. Or she might tell Olga. . . .

Lucia put on her satin shoes, leaving her boots till the hour for " the cobbler's at-home " came, and composing her face to a suitable wince, was led by a footman on tiptoe to the door of the big music room which Georgie had spoken of.

" If you'll please to slip in very quietly, ma'am," he said.

The room was full of people ; all Riseholme was
there, and since there were not nearly enough chairs
(Lucia saw *that* at once), a large number were sitting
on the floor on cushions. At the far end of the room
was a slightly raised daïs, to the corner of which the
grand piano had been pushed, on the top of which,
with its braying trumpet pointing straight at Lucia,
was an immense gramophone. On the daïs was
Olga, dancing. She was dressed in some white, soft
fabric, shimmering with silver, which left her beautiful arms bare to the shoulder. It was cut squarely
and simply about the neck, and hung in straight
lines down to just above her ankles. She held in her
hands some long shimmering scarf of brilliant red,
that floated and undulated as she moved, as if inspired
by some life of its own that it drew out of her slim,
superb vitality. From the cloud of shifting crimson,
with the slow billows of silver moving rhythmically
round her body, that beautiful face looked out, seriously
smiling and brimming with life. . . .

Lucia had hardly entered when, with a final bray,
the gramophone came to the end of its record, and
Olga swept a great curtsey, threw down her scarf, and
stepped off the daïs. Georgie was sitting on the floor
close to it, and jumped up, leading the applause. For
a moment, though several heads had been turned at
Lucia's entrance, nobody took the slightest notice of
her ; indeed, the first apparently to recognize her presence was her hostess, who just kissed her hand to her,
and then continued talking to Georgie. Then Olga
threaded her way through the besprinkled floor, and
came up to her.

" How wise you were to miss that very poor performance," she said. " But Mr. Georgie insisted that
I should make a fool of myself."

"Indeed, I am sorry not to have been here for it,"
said Lucia in her most stately manner. "It seemed to
me very far from being a poor performance, very far
indeed. *Caro mio*, you remember Miss Bracely?"

"*Si, si; molto bene*," said Peppino, shaking hands.

"Ah, and you talk Italian!" said Olga. "*Che
bella lingua!* I wish I knew it."

"You have a very good pronunciation," said Lucia.

"*Grazie tante!* You know everyone here, of course.
Now what shall we do next? Clumps or charades, or
what? Ah, there are some cigarettes. Won't you
have one?"

Lucia gave a little scream of dismay.

"A cigarette for me? That would be a very odd
thing," she said. Then relenting, as she remembered
that Olga must be excused for her ignorance, she added,
"You see I never smoke. Never!"

"Oh, you should learn," said Olga. "Now let's
play clumps. Does everyone know clumps? If they
don't, they will find out. Or shall we dance? There's
the gramophone to dance to."

Lucia put up her hands in playful petition.

"Oh, please, no gramophone!" she said.

"Oh, don't you like it?" said Olga. "It's so
horrible that I adore it, as I adore dreadful creatures in
an aquarium. But I think we won't dance till after
supper. We'll have supper extremely soon, partly
because I am dying of famine, and partly because
people are sillier afterwards. But just one game of
clumps first. Let's see: there are enough for four
clumps. Please make four clumps everybody, and—
and will you and two more go out with Mr. Georgie,
Mrs. Lucas? We will be as quick as we can, and we
won't think of anything that will make Mr. Georgie
blush. Oh, there he is! He heard!"

Olga's intense enjoyment of her own party was rapidly galvanizing everybody into a much keener gaiety than was at all usual in Riseholme, where as a rule the hostess was somewhat anxious and watchful, fearing that her guests were not amusing themselves, or that the sandwiches would give out. There was a sit-down supper when the clumps were over (Mrs. Quantock had been the first to guess Beethoven's little toe on his right foot, which made Lucia wince), and there were not enough men and maids to wait, so people foraged for themselves, and Olga paraded up and down the room with a bottle of champagne in one hand and a dish of lobster salad in the other. She sat for a minute or two first at one table, and then at another, and asked silly riddles, and sent to the kitchen for a ham, and put out all the electric light by mistake, when she meant to turn on some more. Then when supper was over they all took more seats back into the music-room and played musical chairs, at the end of which Mrs. Quantock was left in with herself, and it was believed that she said " Damn," when Mrs. Quantock won. Georgie was in charge of the gramophone, which supplied deadly music, quite forgetting that this was agony to Lucia, and not even being aware when she made a sign to Peppino, and went away, having a " cobbler's at-home " all to herself. Nobody noticed when Saturday ended and Sunday began, for Georgie and Colonel Boucher were cock-fighting on the floor, Georgie screaming out " How tarsome ! " when he was upset, and Colonel Boucher, very red in the face, saying, " Haw, hum ! Never thought I should romp again like this. By Jove, most amusing ! " Georgie was the last to leave, and did not notice till he was half-way home that he had a ham-frill adorning his shirt-front. He hoped that it had

been Olga who put it there, when he had to walk blind-
fold across the room and try to keep in a straight line.

Riseholme got up rather late next morning and had
to hurry over its breakfast in order to be in time for
church. There was a slight feeling of reaction abroad,
a sense of having been young and amused, and of
waking now to the fact of church-bells and middle-
age. Colonel Boucher singing the bass of " A few more
years shall roll," felt his mind instinctively wandering
to the cock-fight the evening before, and depressedly
recollecting that a considerable number of years had
rolled already. Mrs. Weston, with her bath-chair
in the ,aisle and Tommy Luton to hand her hymn-
book and prayer-book as she required, looked sideways at Mrs. Quantock, and thought how strange it
was that Daisy so few hours ago had been racing round
a solitary chair with Georgie's finger on the gramophone; while Georgie, singing tenor by Colonel
Boucher's ample side, saw with keen annoyance that
there was a stain of tarnish of silver on his forefinger,
accounted for by the fact that after breakfast he had
been cleaning the frame that held the photograph of
Olga Bracely, and had been astonished to hear the
church-bells beginning. Another conducement to
depression on his part was the fact that he was lunching
with Lucia, and he could not imagine what Lucia's
attitude would be towards the party last night. She
had come to church rather late with Peppino, having
no use for the General Confession, and sang with
stony fervour. She wore her usual church-face,
from which nothing whatever could be gathered. A
great many stealthy glances right and left from everybody failed to reveal the presence of their hostess of
last night. Georgie, in particular, was sorry for
this : he would have liked her to show that capacity

for respectable seriousness which her presence at
church that morning would have implied; while
Lucia, in particular, was glad of this, for it confirmed
her view that Miss Bracely was not, nor could ever
be, a true Riseholmeite. She had thought as much
last night, and had said so to Peppino. She purposed
to say the same to Georgie to-day.

Then came a stupefying surprise, as Mr. Rumbold
walked from his stall to the pulpit for the sermon.
Generally he gave out the number of the short anthem
which accompanied this manœuvre, but to-day he
made no such announcement. A discreet curtain
hid the organist from the congregation, which veiled
his gymnastics with the stops, and his antic dancing
on the pedals, and now when Mr. Rumbold moved
from his stall, there came from the organ the short
introduction to Bach's *Du mein gläubiges Herz*, which
even Lucia had allowed to be nearly " equal " to
Beethoven. And then came the voice. . . . The
reaction after the romp last night went out like a
snuffed candle at this divine singing, which was charged
with the joyfulness of some heavenly child. It grew
low and soft, it rang out again, it lingered and tarried,
it quickened into the ultimate triumph. No singing
could have been simpler, but that simplicity could
only have sprung from the highest art. But now the
art was wholly unconscious; it was part of the singer,
who but praised God as the thrushes do. She who
had made gaiety last night, made worship this
morning.

As they sat down for the discourse, Colonel Boucher
discreetly whispered to Georgie: " By Jove ! " And
Georgie rather more audibly answered " Adorable."
Mrs. Weston drew half-a-crown from her purse instead
of her usual shilling, to be ready for the offertory,

and Mrs. Quantock wondered if she was too old to learn to sing. . . .

Georgie found Lucia very full of talk that day at luncheon and markedly more Italian than usual. Indeed, she put down an Italian grammar when he entered the drawing-room, and covered it up with the essays of Antonio Caporelli. This possibly had some connection with the fact that she had encouraged Olga last night with regard to her pronunciation.

"*Ben arrivato, Georgio,*" she said. "*Ho finito il libro di Antonio Caporelli questo momento. E magnifico!*"

Georgie thought she had finished it long ago, but perhaps he was mistaken. The sentence flew off Lucia's tongue as if it was perched there all quite ready.

"*Sono un poco fatigata dopo il*—dear me, how rusty I am getting in Italian, for I can't remember the word," she went on. "Anyhow, I am a little tired after last night. A delightful little party, was it not? It was clever of Miss Bracely to get so many people together at so short a notice. Once in a way that sort of romp is very well."

"I enjoyed it quite enormously," said Georgie.

"I saw you did, *cattivo ragazzo*," said she. "You quite forgot about your poor Lucia and her horror of that dreadful gramophone. I had to exert all the calmness that Yoga has given me not to scream. But you were naughty with the gramophone over those musical chairs—unmusical chairs, as I said to Peppino, didn't I, *caro?*—taking it off and putting it on again so suddenly. Each time I thought it was the end. *E pronto la colazione. Andiamo!*"

Presently they were seated : the menu, an unusual

thing in itself at lunch, was written in Italian, the scribe being clearly Lucia.

" I shall want a lot of Georgino's *tempo* this week," she said, " for Peppino and I have quite settled we must give a little after-dinner party next Saturday, and I want you to help me to arrange some impromptu tableaux. Everything impromptu must just be sketched out first, and I daresay Miss Bracely worked a great deal at her dance last night, and I wish I had seen more of it. She was a little awkward in the management of her draperies, I thought, but I daresay she does not know much about dancing. Still it was very graceful and effective for an amateur, and she carried it off very well ! "

" Oh, but she is not quite an amateur," said Georgie. " She has played in *Salome.*"

Lucia pursed her lips.

" Indeed, I am sorry she played in that," she said. " With her undoubtedly great gifts I should have thought she might have found a worthier object. Naturally I have not heard it : I should be very much ashamed to be seen there. But about our tableaux now. Peppino thought we might open with the execution of Mary Queen of Scots. It is a dreadful thing that I have lost my Roman pearls. He would be the executioner, and you the priest. Then I should like to have the awakening of Brünnhilde."

" That would be lovely," said Georgie, " Have you asked Miss Olga if she will ? "

" *Georgino mio*, you don't quite understand," said Lucia. " This party is to be for Miss Bracely. I was her guest last night in spite of the gramophone, and, indeed, I hope she will find nothing in my house that jars on her as much as her gramophone jarred on me. I had a dreadful nightmare last night—didn't

I, Peppino ?—in consequence. About the Brünnhilde
tableau. I thought Peppino would be Siegfried, and
perhaps you could learn just fifteen or twenty bars
of the music and play it while the curtain was up.
You can play the same over again if it is encored. Then
how about King Cophetua and the beggar-maid.
I should be with my back to the audience, and should
not turn round at all : it would be quite your tableau. We will just sketch them out, as I said, and
have a grouping or two to make sure we don't get in
each other's way, and I will see that there are some
dresses of some kind, which we can just throw on.
The tableaux with a little music, serious music, would
be quite sufficient to keep everybody interested."

By this time Georgie had got a tolerable inkling of
the import of all this. There was not at present to
be war ; there was to be magnificent Medicean rivalry,
artist gloriously competing with artist in splendour.
To confirm his view, Lucia went on with gathering
animation.

" I do not purpose to have games, romps shall I
call them ? " she said, " for as far as I know Riseholme—and perhaps I know it a little better than dear
Miss Bracely—Riseholme does not care for that sort
of thing. It is not quite in our line : we may be right
or wrong, I am sure I do not know, but as a matter of
fact, we *don't* care for that sort of thing. Dear Miss
Bracely did her very best last night : I am sure she
was prompted only by the most hospitable motives, but
how should she know ? The supper too. Peppino
counted nineteen empty champagne-bottles——"

" Eighteen, *carissima*," said Peppino.

" I think you told me nineteen, *caro*, but it makes
very little difference. Eighteen empty champagne-
bottles standing on the sideboard, and no end to the

caviare sandwiches which were left over. It was all
too much, though there were not nearly enough
chairs, and, indeed, I never got one at all except just
at supper."

Lucia leaned forward over the table, with her hands
clasped.

"There was display about it, *Georgino*, and you
know how I hate display," she said. "Shakespeare was content with the most modest scenery
for his masterpieces, and it would be a great mistake
if we allowed ourselves to be carried away by mere
wasteful opulence. In all the years I have lived here,
and contributed in my humble way to the life of
the place, I have heard no complaints about my
suppers or teas, nor about the quality of entertainment
which I offer my guests when they are so good as to
say ' *Si*,' to *le mie invitazione*.' Art is not advanced
by romping, and we are able to enjoy ourselves without
two hundred caviare sandwiches being left over.
And such wasteful cutting of the ham! I had to slice
the chunk she gave me over and over again before
I could eat it."

Georgie felt he could not quite let this pass.

"Well, I had an excellent supper," he said, "and
I enjoyed it very much. Besides, I saw Peppino
tucking in like anything. Ask him what he thought
of it."

Lucia gave her silvery laugh.

"*Georgino*, you are a boy," she said artfully, "and
' tuck in,' as you so vulgarly call it, without thinking.
I'm saying nothing against the supper, but I'm sure
that Peppino and Colonel Boucher would have felt
better this morning if they had been wiser last night.
But that's not the real point. I want to show Miss
Bracely, and I'm sure she will be grateful for it, the

sort of entertainment that has contented us at Rise-holme for so long. I will frame it on her lines : I will ask all and sundry to drop in with just a few hours' notice, as she did. Everything shall be good, and there shall be about it all something that I seemed to miss last night. There was a little bit—how shall I say it—a little bit of the footlights about it all. And the footlights didn't seem to me to have been extin-guished at church-time this morning. Her singing of that very fine aria was theatrical ; I can't call it less than theatrical."

She fixed Georgie with her black beady eye, and smoothed her undulated hair.

" Theatrical," she said again. " Now let us have our coffee in the music-room. Shall Lucia play little bit of Beethoven to take away nasty taste of gramophone ? She no likey gramophone at all. Nebber ! "

Georgie now began to feel himself able to sympathize with that surfeited swain who thought how happy he could be with either, were t'other dear charmer away. Certainly he had been very happy with Lucia all these years, before t'other dear charmer alighted in Riseholme, and now he felt that should Lucia decide, as she had often so nearly decided, to spend the winter on the Riviera, Riseholme would still be a very pleasant place of residence. He had never been quite sure how seriously she had contemplated a winter on the Riviera, for the mere mention of it had always been enough to make him protest that Riseholme could not possibly exist without her, but to-day, as he sat and heard (rather than listened to) a series of slow movements, with a brief and hazardous at-tempt at the scherzo of the " Moonlight," he felt that if any talk of the Riviera came up, he would not

be quite so insistent as to the impossibility of Riseholme continuing to exist without her. He could,
for instance, have existed perfectly well this Sunday
afternoon if Lucia had been even at Timbuctoo or
the Antipodes, for as he went away last night, Olga
had thrown a casual intimation to him that she would
be at home for lunch, if he had nothing better to do,
and cared to drop in. Certainly he had nothing better
to do, but he had something worse to do. . . .

Peppino was sitting in the window-seat, with eyes
closed, because he listened to music better so, and
with head that nodded occasionally, presumably for
the same reason. But the cessation of the slow movement naturally made him cease to listen, and he stirred
and gave the sigh with which Riseholme always
acknowledged the end of a slow movement. Georgie
sighed too, and Lucia sighed; they all sighed, and
then Lucia began again. So Peppino closed his eyes
again, and Georgie continued his mental analysis
of the situation.

At present, so he concluded, Lucia did not mean
war. She meant, as by some great armed demon-
stration, to exhibit the Riseholme spirit in its full
panoply, and thus crush into dazzled submission
any potential rivalry. She meant also to exert an
educational influence, for she allowed that Olga had
great gifts, and she meant to train and refine those
gifts, so that they might, when exercised under benign
but autocratic supervision, conduce to the strength
and splendour of Riseholme. Naturally she must be
loyally and ably assisted, and Georgie realized that
the tableau of King Cophetua (his tableau as she
had said) partook of the nature of a bribe, or, if that
word was invidious, of a raising of his pay. It was
equally certain that this prolonged recital of slow move-

ment was intended to produce in his mind a vivid
consciousness of the contrast between the romp last
night and the present tranquil hour, and it did not
fail in this respect.

Lucia shut the piano-lid, and almost before they had
given their sighs, spoke.

" I think I will have a little dinner-party first,"
she said. " I will ask Lady Ambermere. That will
make us four with you, Georgie, and Miss Bracely
and Mr. Shuttleworth will make six. The rest I shall
ask to come in at nine, for I know Lady Ambermere
does not like late hours. And now shall we talk over
our tableaux ? "

So even Lucia's mind had not been wholly absorbed
in Beethoven, though Georgie, as usual, told her she
had never played so divinely.

CHAPTER XI

THE manœuvres of the next week became so breath-lessly complicated that by Wednesday Georgie was almost thinking of going away to the seaside with Foljambe and Dicky in sheer despair, and in after years he could not without great mental effort succeed in straightening it all out. . . . That Sunday evening Lucia sent an invitation to Lady Ambermere for " dinner and tableaux," to which Lady Ambermere's " people " replied by telephone on Monday afternoon that her ladyship was sorry to be unable. Lucia, therefore, gave the idea of a dinner-party up, and reverted to her original scheme of an evening party got up on the spur of the moment, like Olga's. The rehearsals for these impromptu tableaux meantime went forward behind closed doors, and Georgie wrestled with twenty bars of the music of the " Awakening of Brünnhilde." Lucia intended to ask nobody until Friday evening, and Olga should see what sort of party Riseholme could raise at a moment's notice.

Early on Tuesday morning the devil entered into Daisy Quantock, probably by means of subconscious telepathy, and she proceeded to go round the green at the morning parliament, and ask everybody to come in for a good romp on Saturday evening, and they all accepted. Georgie, Lucia and Olga were absentees, and so, making a house-to-house visitation, she went first to Georgie. He with secret knowledge of the

tableaux (indeed he was stitching himself a robe to
be worn by King Cophetua at the time), hastily bundled
it under the table and regretted that he was already
engaged. This was rather mysterious, but he might
have planned, for all Mrs. Quantock knew, an evening
when he would be " busy indoors," and since those
evenings were never to be pried upon, she asked no
questions, but went off to Lucia's, to give her invitation there. There again she was met with a
similarly mysterious refusal. Lucia so much regretted
that she and Peppino were unable to come, and she
hoped Daisy would have a lovely party. Even as
she spoke, she heard her telephone bell ringing, and
hurried off to find that Georgie, faithful lieutenant,
was acquainting her with the fact that Mrs. Quantock
was planning a party for Saturday : he did not know
how far she had got. At that moment she had got
just half-way to Old Place, walking at unusual speed.
Lucia grasped the situation with amazing quickness,
and cutting off Georgie with a snap, and abandoning
all idea of an impromptu party, rang up Olga. She
would secure her, anyhow. . . .

The telephone was in the hall, and Olga, with her
hat on, was just preparing to go out, when the bell
sounded. The words of grateful acceptance were
on her very lips, when her front-door bell rang too,
rang long and was repeated with only half a minute's
pause, and there was Mrs. Quantock on the doorstep
with her invitation for Saturday night. Olga. was
obliged to refuse, but promised to look in if she was
not very late in getting away from Mrs. Lucas's.
Another romp would be lovely.

Already the evils of decentralization and over-
lapping were becoming manifest. Lucia rang up
house after house, only to find that its inhabitants

were already engaged. She had got Olga and Georgie, and could begin the good work of education and the crushing of rivalry, not by force but by pure and refined example, but Mrs. Quantock had got everybody else. In the old days this could never have happened, for everything revolved round one central body. Now with the appearance of this other great star, all the known laws of gravity and attraction were upset.

Georgie, again summoned to the telephone, recommended an appeal to Mrs. Quantock's better nature, which Lucia rejected, doubting whether she had one.

" But what about the tableaux ? " asked Georgie. " We three can't very well do tableaux for Miss Olga to look at."

Then Lucia showed herself truly great.

" The merit of the tableaux does not consist in the number of the audience," she said.

She paused a moment.

" Have you got the Cophetua robe all right ? " she asked.

" Oh, it'll do," said Georgie dejectedly.

On Tuesday afternoon Olga rang up Lucia again to say that her husband was arriving that day, so might she bring him on Saturday ? To this Lucia cordially assented, but she felt that a husband and wife sitting together and looking at another husband and wife doing tableaux would be an unusual entertainment, and not characteristic of Riseholme's best. She began to waver about the tableaux, and to consider dinner instead. She also wondered whether after all she had been wronging dear Daisy, and whether she had a better nature after all. Perhaps Georgie might ascertain.

Georgie was roused from a little nap by the telephone, for he had fallen asleep over King Cophetua's robe. Lucia explained the situation and delicately suggested that it would be so easy for him to " pop in " to dear Daisy's, and be very diplomatic. There was nobody like Georgie for tact. So with a heavy yawn he popped in.

" You've come about this business on Saturday," said Daisy unerringly. " *Haven't* you ? "

Georgie remembered his character for tact.

" How wonderful of you to guess that ! " he said. " I thought I might see if we couldn't arrange something if we put our heads together. It's such a pity to split up. We—I mean Lucia has got Miss Olga and her husband coming, and——"

" And I've got everybody else," said Daisy brightly. " And Miss Bracely is coming over here, if she gets away early. Probably with such a small party she will."

" Oh, I shouldn't count on that," said he. " We are having some tableaux, and they always take longer than you think. Dear me, I shouldn't have said that, as they were to be impromptu, but you know how thorough Lucia is : she is taking a great deal of trouble about them."

" I hadn't heard about that," said Mrs. Quantock. She thought a moment.

" Well, I don't want to spoil Lucia's evening," she said, " for I'm sure nothing could be so ridiculous as three people doing tableaux for two others. And on the other hand, I don't want her to spoil mine, for what's to prevent her going on with tableaux till church-time, if she wishes to keep Miss Bracely away from my house ? I'm sure, after the way she behaved about my Guru—well, never mind that. How

would it be, if we had the tableaux first at Lucia's
and then came on here ? If Lucia cares to suggest
that to me, and my guests consent, I don't mind
doing that."

By six o'clock on Tuesday evening, therefore, all
the telephone bells of Riseholme were merrily ringing
again. Mrs. Quantock stipulated that Lucia's party
should end at 10.45 precisely, if it didn't end before,
and that everyone should then be free to flock across
to her house. She proposed a romp that should
even outshine Olga's, and was deep in the study of
a manual of " Round Games," which included " Hunt
the Slipper." . . .

Georgie and Peppino took turns at the telephone,
ringing up all Mrs. Quantock's guests, and informing
them of the double pleasure which awaited them on
Saturday. Since Georgie had let out the secret of
the impromptu tableaux to Mrs. Quantock there was
no reason why the rest of Riseholme should not learn
of this first-hand from The Hurst, instead of second-
hand (with promises not to repeat it) from Mrs. Quantock. It appeared that she had a better nature than
Lucia credited her with, but to expect her not to tell
everybody about the tableaux would be putting
virtue to an unfair strain.

" So that's all settled," said Georgie, as he returned
with the last acceptance, " and how fortunately it has
happened after all. But what a day it has been.
Nothing but telephoning from morning till night.
If we go on like this the company will pay a dividend
this year, and return us some of our own pennies."

Lucia had got a quantity of pearl beads, and was
stringing them for the tableau of Mary Queen of Scots.
" Now that everyone knows," she said, " we might

allow ourselves a little more elaboration in our preparations. There is an Elizabethan axe at the Ambermere Arms, which I might borrow. Then about the
Brünnhilde tableau. It is dawn, is it not? We might
have the stage quite dark when the curtain goes up,
and turn up a lamp very slowly behind the scene,
so that it shines on my face. A lamp being turned
up very slowly is wonderfully effective. It produces
a perfect illusion. Could you manage that with
one hand from the piano, Georgino?"

"I'm quite sure I couldn't," said he.

"Well, then, Peppino must do it before he comes
on. We will have movement in this tableau. I
think that will be quite a new idea. Peppino shall
come in—just two steps—when he has turned the
lamp up, and he will take off my shield and armour——"

"But the music will never last out," cried Georgie.
"I shall have to start earlier."

"Yes, perhaps that would be better," said Lucia
calmly. "That real piece of chain-armour, too;
I am glad I remembered Peppino had that. Marshall
is cleaning it now, and it will give a far finer effect
than the tawdry stuff they use in opera. Then I sit
up very slowly, and wave first my right arm and then
my left, and then both. I should like to practise that
now on the sofa."

Lucia had just lain down, when the telephone
sounded again, and Georgie got up.

"That's to announce a dividend," he said, and
tripped into the hall.

"Is that Mrs. Lucas's?" said a voice he knew.

"Yes, Miss Olga," he said, "and this is me."

"Oh, Mr. Georgie, how fortunate," she said. "You
can give my message now to Mrs. Lucas, can't you?
I'm a perfect fool, you know, and horribly forgetful."

" What's the matter ? " asked Georgie.

" It's about Saturday. I've just remembered that Georgie and I—not you, you know—are going away for the week-end. Will you tell Mrs. Lucas how sorry I am ? "

Georgie went back to the music-room, where Lucia had just got both her arms waving. But at the sight of his face, she dropped them.

" Well, what is it ? " she said.

Georgie gave the message, and she got off the sofa.

" I am sorry that Miss Bracely will not see our tableaux," she said, " but as she was not acting in them I do not know that it makes much difference."

A deadly flatness, although Olga's absence made no difference, descended on the three. Lucia did not resume her arm-work, for after all these years her acting might be supposed to be good enough for Riseholme without further practice, and nothing more was heard of the borrowing of the axe from the Ambermere Arms. But having begun to thread her pearl-beads, she finished them ; Georgie, however, cared no longer whether the gold border of King Cophetua's mantle went quite round the back or not, and having tacked on the piece he was working at, rolled it up. It was just going to be an ordinary party, after all. His cup was empty.

But Lucia's was not yet quite full, for at this moment Miss Lyall's pony hip-bath stopped at the gate, and a small stable-boy presented a note, which required an answer. In spite of all Lucia's self-control, the immediate answer it got was a flush of heightened colour.

" Mere impertinence ! " she said. " I will read it aloud.

" DEAR MRS. LUCAS,

" I was in Riseholme this morning, and learn from Mrs. Weston that Miss Bracely will be at your house on Saturday night. So I shall be enchanted to come to dinner after all. You must know I make a rule of not going out in the evening, except for some special reason, but it would be a great pleasure to hear her sing again. I wonder if you would have dinner at 7.30, instead of 8, as I do not like being out very late."

There was a short pause.

" *Caro*," said Lucia, " perhaps you would kindly tell Miss Lyall that I do not expect Miss Bracely on Saturday, and that therefore I do not expect Lady Ambermere either. A verbal message will be quite sufficient."

" My dear——" he began.

" I will do it myself, then," she said.

It was as Georgie walked home after the delivery of this fell message, that he wanted to fly away and be at rest with Foljambe and Dickie. He had been frantically excited ever since Sunday at the idea of doing tableaux before Olga, and to-day in especial had been a mere feverish hash of telephoning and sewing, all ending in nothing at all, for neither tableaux nor romps seemed to hold the least attraction for him now that Olga was not going to be there. And then all at once it dawned on him that he must be in love with Olga, for why else should her presence or absence make such an astounding difference to him. He stopped dead opposite Mrs. Quantock's mulberry tree.

" More misery ! More unhappiness ! " he said to himself.

Really if life at Riseholme was to become a series
of agitated days ending in devastating discoveries,
the sooner he went away with Foljambe and Dickie
the better. He did not quite know what it was like
to be in love, for the nearest he had previously ever
got to it was when he saw Olga awake on the mountain-top, and felt that he had missed his vocation in
not being Siegfried, but from that he guessed. This
time, too, it was about Olga, not as framed in
the romance of legend and song, but as she herself
appeared at Riseholme, taking, as she did now, an
ecstatic interest in the affairs of the place. So short
a time ago, when she contemplated coming here first,
she had spoken of it as a lazy backwater. Now she
knew better than that, for she could listen to Mrs.
Weston for longer than anybody else, and yet ask
for more histories when even she had run dry. And
yet Lucia seemed hardly to interest her at all. Georgie
wondered why that was.

He raised his eyes as he muttered these desolated
syllables, and there was Olga, just letting herself out
of the front garden of Old Place. Georgie's first impulse was to affect not to see her, and turn into his
bachelor home, but she had certainly seen him, and
made so shrill and piercing a whistle on her fingers,
that, pretend as he would not to have seen her, it was
ludicrous to appear not to have heard her. She
beckoned to him.

" Georgie, the most awful thing has happened,"
she said, as they came within speaking distance.
" Oh, I called you Georgie by mistake then. When
one once does that, one must go on doing it on purpose."

" Guess ! " she said in the best Riseholme manner.

" You can come to Lucia's party after all," said he.

" No, I can't. Well, you'll never guess because
you move in such high circles, so I'll tell you. Mrs.
Weston's Elizabeth is going to be married to Colonel
Boucher's Atkinson. I don't know his Christian
name, nor her surname, but they're the ones ! "

" You don't say so ! " said Georgie, stung for a
moment out of his own troubles. " But will they
both leave ? What will either of the others do ?
Mrs. Weston can't have a manservant, and how on
earth is she to get on without Elizabeth ? Besides——"

A faint blush mounted to his cheek.

" I know. You meant babies," said Olga ruthlessly.
" Didn't you ? "

" Yes," said Georgie.

" Then why not say so ? You and I were babies
once, though no one is old enough to remember that,
and we shouldn't have liked our parents' friends to have
been ashamed to mention us. Georgie, you are a
prude."

" No, I'm not," said Georgie, remembering he was
probably in love with a married woman.

" It doesn't matter whether you are or not. Now
there's only one thing that can happen to the others.
They must marry each other, too. Then Atkinson can
continue to be Colonel Boucher's man, and Elizabeth
Mrs. Boucher's parlour-maid, unless she is busy with
what made you blush. Then they can get help in ; you
will lend them Foljambe, for instance. It's time you
began to be of some good in your wicked selfish life.
So that's settled. It only remains for us to make them
marry each other."

" Aren't you getting on rather fast ? " asked Georgie.

" I'm not getting on at all at present. I'm only
talking. Come into my house instantly, and we'll
drink vermouth. Vermouth always makes me brilliant,

unless it makes me idiotic, but we'll hope for the best.
I was just coming to find you."

Presently they were seated in Olga's music-room,
with a bottle of vermouth between them.

" Now drink fair, Georgie," she said, " and as you
drink tell me all about the young couple's emotional
history."

" Atkinson and Elizabeth ? " asked Georgie.

" No, my dear ; Colonel Boucher and Mrs. Weston.
They have an emotional history. I am sure you all
thought they were going to marry each other once.
And they constantly dine together *tête-à-tête*. Now
that's a very good start. Are you sure he hasn't got
a wife and family in Egypt, or she a husband and
family somewhere else ? I don't want to rake up
family skeletons."

" I've never heard of them," said Georgie.

" Then we'll take them as non-existent. You certainly would have heard of them if there were any,
and very likely if there weren't. And they both like
eating, drinking and the latest intelligence. Don't
they ? "

" Yes. But——"

" But what ? What more do you and they want ?
Isn't that a better start for married life than many
people get ? "

" But aren't they rather old ? " asked Georgie.

" Not much older than you and me, and if it wasn't
that I've got my own Georgie, I would soon have
somebody else's. Do you know whom I mean ? "

" No ! " said Georgie firmly. Though all this
came at the end of a most harrowing day, it and the
vermouth exhilarated him.

" Then I'll tell you just what Mrs. Weston told me.
' He's always been devoted to her,' she said, ' and he

has never looked at anybody else. There was Piggy
Antrobus—' Now do you know whom I mean? "
Georgie suddenly giggled.
" Yes," he said.
" Then don't talk about yourself so much, my dear,
and let us get to the point. Now this afternoon I
dropped in to see Mrs. Weston, and as she was telling
me about the tragedy, she said by accident (just as I
called you Georgie just now by accident), 'And I
don't know what Jacob will do without Atkinson.'
Now is or is not Colonel Boucher's name Jacob?
There you are, then! That's one side of the question.
She called him Jacob by accident, and so she'll call
him Jacob on purpose before very long."

Olga nodded her head up and down in precise
reproduction of Mrs. Weston.

" I'd hardly got out of the house," she said in precise imitation of Mrs. Weston's voice, " before I met
Colonel Boucher. It would have been about three
o'clock—no, it couldn't have been three, because I
had got back home and was standing in the hall when
it struck three, and my clock's a shade fast if anything.
Well, Colonel Boucher said to me : ' Haw, hum,
quite a domestic crisis, by Jove ! ' And so I pretended
I didn't know, and he told me all about it. So I said :
' Well, it *is* a domestic crisis, and you'll lose Atkinson.'
' Haw, hum,' said he, ' and poor Jane—I should say
Mrs. Weston—will lose Elizabeth.' There ! "

She got up and lit a cigarette.

" Oh, Georgie, do you grasp the inwardness of
that ! " she said. " Their dear old hearts were laid
bare by the trouble that had come upon them, and each
of them spoke of the other as each felt of the other.
Probably neither of them had said Jacob or Jane in
the whole course of their lives. But the angel of the

Lord descended and troubled the waters. If you think that's profane, have some more vermouth. It's making me brilliant, though you wouldn't have thought it. Now listen !"

She sat down again close to him, her face brimming with a humorous enthusiasm. Humour in Riseholme was apt to be a little unkind: if you mentioned the absurdities of your friends there was just a speck of malice in your wit. But with her there was none of that. She imitated Mrs. Weston with the most ruthless fidelity, and yet it was kindly to the bottom. She liked her for talking in that emphatic voice and being so particular as to what time it was.

" Now, first of all, you are coming to dine with me to-night," she said.

" Oh, I'm afraid that to-night——" began Georgie, shrinking from any further complications. He really must have a quiet evening and go to bed very early.

" What are you afraid of to-night ? " she asked. " You're only going to wash your hair. You can do that to-morrow. So you and I, that's two, and Mrs. Weston and Colonel Jacob, that's four, which is enough, and I don't believe there's anything to eat in the house. But there's something to drink, which is my point. Not for you and me, mind ; we've got to keep our heads and be clever. Don't have any more vermouth. But Jane and Jacob are going to have quantities of champagne. Not tipsy, you understand, but at their best, and unguardedly appreciative of each other and us. And when they go away they will exchange a word or two at Mrs. Weston's door, and she will ask him in. And then they'll settle to marry each other. And when they wake up to-morrow morning they will both wonder how they could possibly, and faintly ask themselves what everybody else will say.

And then they'll thank God and Olga and Georgie
that they did, and live happily for an extraordinary
number of years. My dear, how infinitely happier
they will be together than they are being now. Funny
old dears ! Each at its own fireside, saying that it's
too old, bless them ! And you and I will sing 'The
Voice that breathed o'er Eden,' and in the middle our
angel-voices will crack, and we will sob into our handkerchief, and the Voice will be left breathing deeply
all by itself like the Guru. Why did you never tell me
about the Guru ? Mrs. Weston's a better friend to us
than you are, and I must ring for my cook—no, I'll
telephone first to Jacob and Jane and see what there
is to eat afterwards. Then you will sit here quietly,
and I will tell you what your part is."

During dinner, according to Olga's plan of campaign,
the conversation was to be general, because she hated
to have two conversations going on when only four
people were present, for she found that she always
wanted to join in the other one. This was the main
principle she inculcated on Georgie, stamping it on
his memory by a simile of peculiar vividness. " Imagine there is an Elizabethan spittoon in the middle
of the table," she said, " and keep on firmly spitting
into it. I want you when there's any pause to spit
about two things : one, how dreadfully unhappy
both Jacob and Jane will be without their paragons ;
the other, how pleasant is conversation and companionship. I shall be chaffing *you*, mind, all the
time, and saying *you* must get married. After dinner
I shall probably stroll in the garden with Jacob.
Don't come. Keep him after dinner for some little
while, for there's my opportunity of talking to Jane,
and give him at least three glasses of port. Gracious,
it's time to dress, and the Lord prosper us."

Georgie found himself the last to arrive, when he
got back to Olga's, and all three of them shook hands
rather as people shake hands before a funeral. They
went in to dinner at once, and Olga instantly began.

"How many years did you say your admirable Atkinson had been with you?" she asked Colonel
Boucher.

"Twenty, getting on for twenty-one," said he.
"Great nuisance: 'pon my word it's more than a
nuisance."

Georgie had a bright idea.

"But what's a nuisance, Colonel?" he asked.

"Eh, haven't you heard? I thought it would
have been all over the place by now. Atkinson's
going to be married."

"No!" said Georgie. "Whom to?"

Mrs. Weston could not bear not to announce this
herself.

"To my Elizabeth," she said. "Elizabeth came
to me this morning. 'May I speak to you a minute,
ma'am?' she said. I thought nothing more than
that perhaps she had broken a teacup. 'Yes,'
said I quite cheerfully, 'and what have you come to
tell me?'"

It was getting almost too tragic, and Olga broke in:
"Let's try to forget all about it for an hour or two,"
she said. "It was nice of you all to take pity on me,
and come and have dinner, otherwise I should have been
quite alone. If there's one thing I cannot bear, it's
being alone in the evening. And to think that anybody chooses to be alone when he needn't! Look
at that wretch there "—she pointed to Georgie—
"who lives all by himself instead of marrying. Liking
to be alone is the worst habit I know: much worse
than drink."

" Now do leave me alone," said Georgie.

" I won't, my dear, and when dinner is over Mrs.
Weston and I are going to put our heads together,
and when you come out we shall announce to you the
name of your bride. I should put a tax of twenty
shillings in the pound on all bachelors : they should
all marry or starve ! "

Suddenly she turned to Colonel Boucher.

" Oh, Colonel," she said, " what have I been saying ?
How dreadfully stupid of me not to remember that
you were a bachelor too. But I wouldn't have you
starve for anything. Have some more fish instantly
to show you forgive me. Georgie, change the subject—
you're always talking about yourself."

Georgie turned with admirable docility to Mrs.
Weston.

" It's too miserable for you," he said. " How will
you get on without Elizabeth ? How long has she
been with you ? "

Mrs. Weston went straight back to where she had
left off.

" So I said, ' What have you come to tell me ? '
quite cheerfully, thinking it was a teacup. And
she said, ' I'm going to be married, ma'am ! ' and she
blushed so prettily that you'd have thought she was
a girl of twenty, though she was seventeen when she
came to me—no, she was just eighteen—and that's
fifteen years ago, and that makes her thirty-three.
' Well, Elizabeth,' I said, ' you haven't told me yet
who it is, but whether it's the Archbishop of Canter-
bury or the Prince of Wales—for I felt I had to make
a little joke like that—I hope you'll make him as
happy as you've made me all these years ! ' "

" You old darling," said Olga ; " I should have gone
into hysterics and forbade the banns."

" No, Miss Bracely, you wouldn't," said Mrs. Weston, " you'd have been just as thankful as me that she'd got a good husband to take care of and to be taken care of by. So then Elizabeth said : ' Lor, ma'am, it's none of they—not them great folks. It's the Colonel's Atkinson.' You ask the Colonel for Atkinson's character and then you'd be just as thankful as I was."

" The Colonel's Atkinson is a slow coach, just like Georgie," said Olga. " They've been living side by side all these years, and why couldn't the man make up his mind before ? The only redeeming circumstance is that he has done it now. Our poor Georgie now——"

" Now you're going to be rude to Colonel Boucher again," said Georgie. " Colonel, we've been asked here to be insulted."

Colonel Boucher had nothing stronger than a mild tolerance for Georgie and rather enjoyed snubbing him.

" Well, if you call a glass of wine and a dinner like this an insult," he said, " 'pon my word I don't know what you'd call a compliment."

" I know what I call a compliment," said Olga, " and that's your all coming to dine with me at such short notice. About Georgie's approaching nuptials now——"

" You're too tarsome," said he. " If you go on like that I shan't ask you to the wedding. Let's talk about Elizabeth's. When are they going to get married, Mrs. Weston ? "

" That's what I said to Elizabeth. ' Get an almanack, Elizabeth,' I said, ' so that you won't choose a Sunday. Don't say the 20th of next month without looking it out. But if the 20th isn't a Sunday, or a Friday mind, for though I don't believe in such things, still you never know—' There was Mrs. Antrobus now," said Mrs. Weston, suddenly putting in a footnote to her speech to Elizabeth, " it was on a Friday she married, and within a year she got as deaf as you see her now. Then Mr. Weston's uncle—his uncle by marriage, I should say—his was another Friday marriage, and they missed their train when going off on their honeymoon and had to stay all night where they were without a sponge or a toothbrush between them, for all their luggage was in the train being whirled away to Torquay. ' So make it the 20th, Elizabeth,' I said, ' if it isn't a Friday or a Sunday, and I shall have time to look round me, and so will the Colonel, though I don't expect that either of us will find your equals ! And don't cry, Elizabeth,' I said, for she was getting quite watery, ' for if you cry about a marriage, what'll be left for a funeral ? ' "

" Ha ! upon my word, I call that splendid of you," said the Colonel. " I told Atkinson I wished I had never set eyes on him, before I wished him joy."

Olga got up.

" Look after Colonel Boucher, Georgie," she said, " and ring for anything you want. What a moon ! Isn't it heavenly ? How Atkinson and Elizabeth must be enjoying it ! "

The two men spent a half-hour of only moderately enjoyable conversation, for Georgie kept the grind-stone of the misery of his lot without Atkinson and the pleasures of companionship firmly to the Colonel's nose. It was no use for him to attempt to change the subject to the approaching tableaux, to a vague rumour that Piggy had fallen face-down-wards in the ducking-pond, that Mrs. Quantock and her husband had turned a table this afternoon with remarkable results, for it had tapped out that his

name was Robert and hers Daisy. Whichever way
he turned, Georgie herded him back on to the stony
path that he had been bidden to take, with the result
that when Georgie finally permitted him to go into
the music-room he was athirst for the more genial
companionship of the ladies. Olga got up as they
entered.

"Georgie's so lazy," she said, "that it's no use
asking him. But do let you and me have a turn up
and down my garden, Colonel. There's a divine moon,
and it's quite warm."

They stepped out into the windless night.

"Fancy its being October," she said. "I don't
believe there is any winter in Riseholme, nor autumn
either for that matter. You are all so young, so
deliciously young. Look at Georgie in there : he's
like a boy still, and as for Mrs. Weston, she's twenty-
five : not a day older."

"Yes, wonderful woman," said he. "Always
agreeable and lively. Handsome too : I consider
Mrs. Weston a very handsome woman. Hasn't
altered an atom since I knew her."

"That's the wonderful thing about you all," said
she. "You are all just as brisk and young as you
were ten years ago. It's ridiculous. As for you, I'm
not sure that you're not the most ridiculous of the lot.
I feel as if I had been having dinner with three delightful
cousins a little younger—not much, but just a little
—than myself. Gracious ! How you all made me
romp the other night here. What a pace you go,
Colonel ! What's your walking like if you call this a
stroll ? "

Colonel Boucher moderated his pace. He thought
Olga had been walking so quickly.

"I'm sure I'm very sorry," he said. "Certainly

Riseholme is a healthy bracing place. Perhaps
we do keep our youth pretty well. God bless me,
but the days go by without one's noticing them.
To think that I came here with Atkinson close on ten
years ago."

This did very well for Olga : she swiftly switched
off on to it.

" It's quite horrid for you losing your servants,"
she said. " Servants do become friends, don't they,
especially to anyone living alone ? Georgie and
Foljambe now ! But I shouldn't be a bit surprised
if Foljambe had a mistress before very long."

" No, really ? I thought you were just chaffing
him at dinner. Georgie marrying, is he ? His wife'll
take some of his needlework off his hands. May I
—ah—may I inquire the lady's name ? "

Olga decided to play a great card. She had just
found it, so to speak, in her hand, and it was most
tempting. She stopped.

" But can't you guess ? " she said. " Surely I'm
not absolutely on the wrong tack ? "

" Ah, Miss Antrobus," said he. " The one I think
they call Piggy. No, I should say there was nothing
in that."

" Oh, that had never occurred to me," said she. " I
daresay I'm quite wrong. I only judged from what
I thought I noticed in poor Georgie. I daresay it's
only what he should have done ten years ago, and
there's but a little ember left. Let us talk about
something else, though we won't go in quite yet,
shall we ? "

She felt quite safe in her apparent reluctance to
tell him ; the Riseholme gluttony for news made it
imperative for him to ask more.

" Really, I must be very dull," he said. " I daresay

an eye new to this place sees more. Who is it, Miss Bracely ? "

She laughed.

" Ah, how bad a man is at observing a man ! " she said. " Didn't you see him at dinner ? He hardly took his eyes off her."

She had a great and glorious reward. Colonel Boucher's face grew absolutely blank in the moonlight with sheer astonishment.

" Well, you surprise me ! " he said. " Surely a fine woman, though lame, wouldn't look at a needle-woman—well, leave it at that."

He stamped his feet, and put his hands in his pockets.

" It's growing a bit chilly," he said. " You'll be catching cold, Miss Bracely, and what will your husband say if he finds out I've been strolling about with you out of doors after dinner ? "

" Yes, we'll go in," she said. " It is chilly. How thoughtful you are for one."

Georgie, little knowing the cat's-paw that had been made of him, found himself being detached from Mrs. Weston by the Colonel, and this suited him very well, for presently Olga said she would sing, unless anybody minded, and called on him to accompany her. She stood just behind him, leaning over him sometimes with a hand on his shoulder, and sang those ruthless simple English songs appropriate to the matter in hand. She sang, " I attempt from Love's Sickness to fly," and " Sally in Our Alley " and " Come, live with me," and sometimes beneath the rustle of leaves turned over she whispered to him. " Georgie, I'm cleverer than anybody ever was, and I shall die in the night," she said once. Again more enigmatically she said, " I've been a cad, but I'll tell you about it when they're gone. Stop behind." And then some

whisky came in, and she insisted on the " young people "
having some of that ; finally she saw them off at the
door, and came running back to Georgie.

" I've been a cad," she said, " because I hinted
that you were in love with Mrs. Weston. My dear,
it was simply perfect ! I believe it to have been
the last straw, and if you don't forgive me you needn't.
Wasn't it clever ? He simply couldn't stand that,
for it came on the top of your all being so young."

" Well, really——" said Georgie.

" I know. And I must be a cad again. I'm going
up to my bedroom—you may come too if you like—
because it commands a view of Church Road. I
shouldn't sleep a wink unless I knew that he had gone
in with her. It'll be precisely like Faust and Mar-
guerite going into the house, and you and I are
Mephistopheles and Martha. Come, quick ! "

From the dark of her window they watched Mrs.
Weston's bath-chair being pushed up the lit road.

" It's the Colonel pushing it," whispered Olga,
squeezing him into a corner of the window. " Look !
There's Tommy Luton on the path. Now they've
stopped at her gate. . . . I can't bear the sus-
pense. . . . Oh, Georgie, they've gone in ! And
Atkinson will stop, and so will Elizabeth, and you've
promised to lend them Foljambe. Which house will
they live at, do you think ? Aren't you happy ? "

CHAPTER XII

THE miserable Lucia started a run of extreme bad luck about this time, of which the adventure or misadventure of the Guru seemed to be the first instance ; or perhaps the news of her want of recognition of the August moon, which Georgie had so carefully saluted, may have arrived at that satellite by October. For she had simply " cut " the August moon. . . .

There was the fiasco about Olga coming to the tableaux, which was the cause of her sending that very tart reply, *via* Miss Lyall, to Lady Ambermere's impertinence, and the very next morning Lady Ambermere, coming again into Riseholme, perhaps for that very purpose, had behaved as Lucia had behaved to the moon, and cut her. That was irritating, but the counter-irritant to it had been that Lady Ambermere had then gone to Olga's, and been told that she was not at home, though she was very audibly practising in her music-room at the time. Upon which Lady Ambermere had said " Home " to her people, and got in with such unconcern of the material world that she sat down on Pug.

Mrs. Quantock had heard both " Home " and Pug, and eagerly told Lucia, who was a hundred yards away, about it. She also told her about the engagement of Atkinson and Elizabeth, which was all she knew about events in those houses. On which Lucia, with a kind smile, had said, " Dear Daisy, what

224

slaves some people are to their servants. I'm sure
Mrs. Weston and Colonel Boucher will be quite
miserable, poor things. Now I must run home.
How I wish I could stop and chat on the green ! "
And she gave her silvery laugh, for she felt much
better now that she knew Olga had said she was
out to Lady Ambermere, when she was so audibly in.

Then came a further piece of bad luck. Lucia
had not gone more than a hundred yards past Georgie's
house when he came out in a tremendous hurry.
He rapidly measured the distance between himself
and Lucia, and himself and Mrs. Quantock, and made
a bee-line for Mrs. Quantock, since she was the nearest.
Olga had just telephoned to him. . . .

" Good-morning," he said breathlessly, determined
to cap anything she said. " Any news ? "

" Yes, indeed," she said. " Haven't you heard ? "
Georgie had one moment of heart-sink.

" What ? " he said.

" Atkinson and Eliz——" she began.

' Oh, that," said he. " And talking of them,
of course you've heard the rest ? *Haven't* you ?
Why Mrs. Weston and Colonel Boucher are going
to follow their example, unless they set it themselves
and get married first."

" No ! " said Mrs. Quantock in the loudest possible
Riseholme voice of surprise.

" Oh, yes. I really knew it last night. I was
dining at Old Place and they were there. Olga
and I both settled there would be something to tell
in the morning. Shall we stroll on the green a few
minutes ? "

Georgie had a lovely time. He hurried from person
to person, leaving Mrs. Quantock to pick up a few
further gleanings. Everyone was there except Lucia,

and she, but for the accident of her being rather farther
off than Mrs. Quantock, would have been the first
to know.

When this was finished he sat to enjoy the warm
comforting glow of envy that surrounded him. Nowa-
days the meeting-place on the green had insensibly
transferred itself to just opposite Old Place, and it
was extremely interesting to hear Olga practising as
she always did in the morning. Interesting though
it was, Riseholme had at first been a little disappointed
about it, for everyone had thought that she would
sing Brünnhilde's part or Salome's part through every
day, or some trifle of that kind. Instead she would
perform an upwards scale in gradual *crescendo*, and on
the highest, most magnificent note would sing at
the top of her voice "Yawning York!" Then
starting soft again she would descend in *crescendo* to
a superb low note and enunciate "Love's lilies
lonely." Then, after a dozen repetitions of this, she
would start at full voice, and just whisper that York
was yawning, and do the same with Love's lilies.
But you never could tell : on some mornings there would
be long trills and leapings on to high notes, or long
notes and leapings into trills, and occasionally she
sang a real song. That was worth waiting for, and
Georgie did not hesitate to let drop that she had sung
four last night to his accompaniment. And hardly had
he repeated that for the third time when she appeared
at her window, and before all Riseholme called out
" Georgie ! " with a trill at the end, like a bird shaking
its wings. Before all Riseholme ! So in he went.
Had Lucia known that, it would quite have wiped the
gilt off Lady Ambermere's being refused admittance.
In point of fact it did wipe the gilt off, when, about an
hour afterwards, Georgie went to lunch, because he

told her. And if there had been any gilt left about anywhere, that would have vanished too when, in answer to some rather damaging remark she made about poor Daisy's interests in the love-affairs of other people's servants, she learned that it was the love-affairs of their superiors about which all Riseholme had been talking for at least an hour by now.

Again the tableaux on Saturday were unlucky, for in the Brünnhilde scene Peppino, in his agitation, turned the lamp that was to be a sunrise completely out, and Brünnhilde had to hail the midnight instead, or at any rate a very obscure twilight. Georgie, it is true, with wonderful presence of mind turned on an electric light when he had finished playing, but it was more like a flash of lightning. The tableaux were over well before 10.45, and though Lucia, in answer to the usual pressings, said she would " see about " doing them again, she felt that Mrs. Weston and Colonel Boucher, who made their first public appearance as the happy pair, attracted more than their proper share of attention. The only consolation was that the romps that followed at poor Daisy's were a complete fiasco. It was in vain, too, at supper that she went from table to table, and helped people to lobster salad and champagne, and had not enough chairs, and generally imitated all that had apparently made Olga's party so supreme a success. But on this occasion the recipe for the dish and not the dish itself was served up, and the hunting of the slipper produced no exhilaration in the chase. . . .

But far more subversive events followed. Olga came back next week, and immediately after Lucia received a card for an evening " At home," with " Music " in the bottom left-hand corner. It happened to be wet that afternoon, and seeing Olga's

shut motor coming from the station with four men
inside, she leaped to the conclusion that these were
four musicians for the music. A second motor
followed with luggage, and she quite distinctly saw
the unmistakable shape of a 'cello against the window.
After that no more guessing was necessary, for it was
clear that poor Olga had hired the awful string-quartet
from Brinton that played in the lounge of the Royal
Hotel after dinner. The Brinton string-quartet! She
had heard them once at a distance, and that was
enough! Lucia shuddered as she thought of those
doleful fiddlers. It was indeed strange that Olga,
with all the opportunities she had had for hearing
good music, should hire the Brinton string-quartet,
but, after all, that was entirely of a piece with her
views about the gramophone. Perhaps the gramophone would have its share in this musical evening.
But she had said she would go: it would be very
unkind to Olga to stop away now, for Olga must
know by this time her passion for music, so she went.
She sincerely hoped that she would not be conducted
to the seat of honour, and have to say a few encouraging words to the string-quartet afterwards. Once
again she came rather late, for the music had begun.
It had only just begun, for she recognized—who should
recognize if not she?—the early bars in a Beethoven
quartet. She laid her hand on Peppino's arm.

" Brinton : Beethoven," she said limply.

She slipped into a chair next to Daisy Quantock,
and sat in her well-known position when listening
to music, with her head forward, her chin resting on
her hand, and the far-away look in her eyes. Nothing,
of course, could wholly take away the splendour
of that glorious composition, and she was pleased
that there was no applause between the movements,

for she had rather expected that Olga would clap
and interrupt the unity of it all. Occasionally, too,
she was agreeably surprised by the Brinton string-
quartet : they seemed to have some inklings, though
not many. Once she winced very much when a
string broke.

Olga (she was rather a restless hostess) came up
to her when it was over.

" So glad you could come ! she said. " Aren't
they divine ? "

Lucia gave her most indulgent smile.

" Perfect music ! Glorious ! " she said. " And they
really played it very creditably. But I am a little spoiled,
you know, for the last time I heard that it was performed
by the Spanish Quartet. I know one ought never
to compare, but have you ever heard the Spanish
Quartet, Miss Bracely ? "

Olga looked at her in surprise.

" But they are the Spanish Quartet ! " she said,
pointing to the players.

Lucia had raised her voice rather as she spoke, for
when she spoke on music she spoke for everybody to
hear. And a great many people undoubtedly did
hear, among whom, of course, was Daisy Quantock.
She gave one shrill squeal of laughter, like a slate-
pencil, and from that moment granted plenary abso-
lution to *poor dear* Lucia for all her greed and
grabbing with regard to the Guru.

But instantly all Olga's good nature awoke : unwittingly (for her remark that this *was* the Spanish
Quartet had been a mere surprised exclamation)
she had made a guest of hers uncomfortable, and
must at once do all she could to remedy that.

" It's a shocking room for echoes, this," she said.
" Do all of you come up a little nearer, and you will

be able to hear the playing so much better. You lose all shade, all fineness here. I came here on purpose to ask you to move up, Mrs. Lucas: there are half a dozen chairs unoccupied near the platform."

It was a kindly intention that prompted the speech, but for all practical purposes quite barren, for so many people had heard Lucia's remarks, and Peppino had already alluded to the Brinton quartet. In that fell moment the Bolshevists laid bony fingers on the sceptre of her musical autocracy.

Staggering from those blows, she had to undergo an even shrewder stroke yet. Already in the intelligence department she had been sadly behind-hand in news, her tableaux party had been anything but a success. This one little remark of Olga's had shaken her musically, but at any rate up till this moment she had shown herself mistress of the Italian tongue, while to strengthen that she was being very diligent with her dictionary, grammar and Dante's *Paradiso*. Then as from a bolt out of a clear sky that temple was completely demolished in the most tragic fashion.

A few days after the evening of the Spanish-Brinton Quartet, Olga received a letter from Signor Cortese, the great Italian composer, to herald the completion of his opera *Lucretia*. Might he come down to Riseholme for a couple of nights, and, figuratively, lay it at her feet, in the hope that she would raise it up, and usher it into the world? All the time he had been writing it, as she knew, he had thought of her in the name part, and he would come down to-day, to-morrow, at a moment's notice by day or night, to submit it to her. Olga was delighted and sent an effusive telegram of many sheets, full of congratulation and welcome, for she wanted above

all things to " create " the part. So would Signor
Cortese come down that very day ?

She ran upstairs with the news to her husband.

" My dear, *Lucretia* is finished," she said, " and
that angel offers it me. Now what are we to do
about dinner to-night ? Jacob and Jane are coming,
and neither you nor they, I suppose, speak one word
of Italian, and you know what mine is, firm and
intelligible and operatic, but not conversational. What
are we to do ? He hates talking English. . . . Oh, I
know ! If I can only get Mrs. Lucas. They always
talk Italian, I believe, at home. I wonder if she can
come. She's musical too, and I shall ask her husband,
I think : that'll be a man over, but it will be another
Italiano."

Olga wrote at once to Lucia, mentioning that Cortese
was staying with them, but, quite naturally, saying
nothing about the usefulness of Peppino and her being
able to engage the musician in his own tongue, for
that she took for granted. An eager affirmative (such
a great pleasure) came back to her. For the rest of
the day, Lucia and Peppino made up neat little sentences to let off to the dazzled Cortese, at the last
moment, to show that they could have talked Italian
all the time had there been any occasion for doing so.

Mrs. Weston and Colonel Boucher had already
arrived when Lucia and her husband entered, and
Lucia had quite a shock to see on what intimate terms
they were with their hostess. They actually called
each other Olga and Jacob and Jane, which was most
surprising and almost painful. Lucia (perhaps because
she had not known about it soon enough) had been a
little satirical about the engagement, rather as if it
was a slight on her that Jacob had not been content
with celibacy and Jane with her friendship, but she

was sure she wished them both " nothing but well."
Indeed, the moment she had got over the shock of seeing
them so intimate with Olga, she could not have been
surpassed in cordiality.

" We see but little of our old friends now," she
said archly to Olga, " but we must excuse their desire
for solitude in this first glow of their happiness. Peppino
and I remember that sweet time, oh, ever so long ago."
This might have been tact, or it might have been
cat. That Peppino and she sympathized and remembered their beautiful time was tact, that it was so
long ago was cat. Altogether it might be described
as a cat showing tact. There was, too, a slight air of
patronage about it, and if there was one thing Mrs.
Weston would not, could not and did not even intend
to stand, it was that. Besides, it had reached her
ears that Mrs. Lucas had said something about there
being no difficulty in finding bridesmaids younger
than the bride.

" Fancy ! How clever of you to remember so long
ago," she said. " But then you have the most
marvellous memory, dear, and keep it wonderfully ! "
Olga intervened.

" How kind of you and Mr. Lucas to come at such
short notice," she said. " Cortese hates talking English,
so I shall put him between you and me, and you'll
talk to him all the time, won't you ? And you won't
laugh at me, will you, when I join in with my atrocious
attempts ? And I shall buttress myself on the other
side with your husband, who will firmly talk across
me to him."

Lucia had to say something. A further exposure
was at hand, quite inevitable. It was no use for her
and Peppino to recollect a previous engagement. . . .

" Oh, my Italian is terribly rusty," she said, know-

ing that Mrs. Weston's eye was on her. . . . Why had
she not sent Mrs. Weston a handsome wedding-
present that morning ?

" Rusty ? We will ask Cortese about that when
you've had a good talk to him. Ah, here he is ! "

Cortese came into the room, florid and loquacious,
pouring out a stream of apology for his lateness to
Olga, none of which was the least intelligible to Lucia.
She guessed what he was saying, and next moment
Olga, who apparently understood him perfectly, and
told him with enviable fluency that he was not late
at all, was introducing him to her, and explaining
that " *la Signora* " (Lucia understood this) and her
husband talked Italian. She did not need to reply
to some torrent of words from him addressed to
her, for he was taken on and introduced to Mrs. Weston
and the Colonel. But he instantly whirled round to
her again, and asked her something. Not knowing in the least what he said, she replied.

" *Si ; tante grazie.* "

He looked puzzled for a moment, and then repeated
his question in English.

" In what deestrict of Italy 'ave you voyaged most ? "

Lucia understood that : so did Mrs. Weston, and
Lucia pulled herself together.

" *In Roma !* " she said. " *Che bella città ! Adoro
Roma, ed il mio marito. Non e vero, Peppino ?* "

Peppino cordially assented : the familiar ring of this
firm intelligible Italian restored his confidence, and
he asked Cortese whether he was not very fond of
music. . . .

Dinner seemed interminable to Lucia. She kept a
watchful eye on Cortese, and if she saw he was about
to speak to her, she turned hastily to Colonel Boucher,
who sat on her other side, and asked him something

about his *cari cani*, which she translated to him. While he answered she made up another sentence in Italian about the blue sky or Venice, and very meanly said her husband had been there, hoping to direct the torrent of Italian eloquence on him. But she knew that, as talker of Italian, neither she nor Peppino had a rag of reputation left them, and she dismally regretted that they had not chosen French, of which they both knew about as much, instead of Italian, for the vehicle of their linguistic distinction.

Olga meantime continued to understand all that Cortese said, and to reply to it with odious fluency, and at the last, Cortese having said something to her which made her laugh, he turned to Lucia.

" I 'ave said to Meesis Shottlewort' . . ." and he proceeded to explain his joke in English.

" *Molto bene*," said Lucia, with a dying flicker. " *Molto divertente. Non è vero, Peppino.*"

" *Si, si*," said Peppino miserably.

And then the final disgrace came, though it was something of a relief to have it over. Cortese, in excellent spirits with his dinner and his wine and the prospect of Olga taking the part of Lucretia, turned beamingly to Lucia again.

" Now we all spick English," he said. " This is one very pleasant evening. I enjoy me very much. *Ecco!* "

Just once more Lucia shot up into flame.

" *Parlate Inglese molto bene*," she said, and except when Cortese spoke to Olga, there was no more Italian that night.

Even the unique excitement of hearing Olga " try over " the great scene in the last act could not quite absorb Lucia's attention after this awful fiasco, and though she sat leaning forward with her chin in her hand, and the far-away look in her eyes, her mind was furiously busy as to how to make anything whatever out of so bad a job. Everyone present knew that her Italian, as a vehicle for conversation, had suffered a complete breakdown, and it was no longer any real use, when Olga did not quite catch the rhythm of a passage, to murmur "*Uno, due, tre,*" unconsciously to herself : she might just as well have said "One, two, three," for any effect it had on Mrs. Weston. The story would be all over Riseholme next day, and she felt sure that Mrs. Weston, that excellent observer and superb reporter, had not failed to take it all in, and would not fail to do justice to it. Blow after blow had been rained upon her palace door : it was little wonder that the whole building was aquiver. She had thought of starting a Dante class this winter, for printed Italian, if you had a dictionary and a translation in order to prepare for the class, could be easily interpreted : it was the spoken word which you had to understand without any preparation at all, not in the least knowing what was coming, that had presented such unsurmountable difficulties. And yet who, when the story of this evening was known, would seek instruction from a teacher of that sort ? Would Mrs. Weston come to her Dante class ? Would she ? Would she ? No, she would not. Assigning reasons.

Lucia lay long awake that night, tossing and turning in her bed in " Midsummer-Night's Dream," and reviewing the full array of those unlucky affairs. As she eyed them, black shapes against the glow of her firelight, it struck her that the same malevolent influence inspired them all. For what had caused the failure and flatness of her tableaux (omitting the unfortunate incident about the lamp) but the absence of Olga ?

Who was it who had occasioned her unfortunate remark
about the Spanish Quartet but Olga, whose clear duty
it had been, when she sent the invitation for the
musical party, to state (so that there could be no
mistake about it) that those eminent performers were
to entrance them ? Who could have guessed that she
would have gone to the staggering expense of having
them down from London ? The Brinton Quartet was the
utmost that any sane imagination could have pictured,
and Lucia's extremely sane imagination had pictured
just that, with such extreme vividness that it had
never occurred to her that it could be anybody else.
Certainly Olga should have put " Spanish Quartet "
in the bottom left-hand corner instead of " Music,"
and then Lucia would have known all about it, and
have been speechless with emotion when they had
finished the Beethoven, and wiped her eyes, and pulled
herself together again. It really looked as if Olga
had laid a trap for her. . . . Even more like a trap
were the horrid events of this evening. Trap was
not at all too strong a word for them. To ask her to
the house, and then suddenly spring upon her the fact
that she was expected to talk Italian . . . was that
an open, an honourable proceeding ? What if Lucia
had actually told Olga (she seemed to recollect it)
that she and Peppino often talked Italian at home ?
That was no reason why she should be expected, off-
hand like that, to talk Italian anywhere else. She
should have been told what was expected of her, so
as to give her a chance of having a previous engagement. Lucia hated underhand ways, and they were
particularly odious in one whom she had been willing
to educate and refine up to the highest standards of
Riseholme. Indeed it looked as if Olga's nature was
actually incapable of receiving cultivation. She went

on her own rough independent lines, giving a romp
one night, and not coming to the tableaux on another,
and getting the Spanish Quartet without consultation
on a third, and springing this dreadful Pentecostal
party on them all. Olga clearly meant mischief: she
wanted to set herself up as leader of art and culture
in Riseholme. Her conduct admitted of no other
explanation.

Lucia's benevolent scheme of educating and refining vanished like morning mists, and through her
drooping eyelids the firelight seemed strangely red.
She had been too kind, too encouraging: now she
must collect her forces round her, and be stern. As
she dozed off to sleep, she reminded herself to ask
Georgie to lunch next day. He and Peppino and she
must have a serious talk. She had seen Georgie
comparatively little just lately, and she drowsily and
uneasily wondered how that was.

Georgie by this time had quite got over the desolation
of the moment when standing in the road opposite
Mrs. Quantock's mulberry-tree he had given vent to
that bitter cry of " More misery! more unhappiness! "
His nerves, on that occasion, had been worn to fiddle-
strings with all the fuss and fiasco of planning the
tableaux, and this fancying himself in love had been the
last straw. But the fact that he had been Olga's chosen
confidant in her wonderful scheme of causing Mrs.
Weston and the Colonel to get engaged, and the distinction of being singled out by Olga for this friendly
intimacy, had proved a great tonic. It was quite
clear that the existence of Mr. Shuttleworth constituted a hopeless bar to the fruition of his passion,
and, if he was completely honest with himself, he was
aware that he did not really hate Mr. Shuttleworth

for standing in his path. Georgie was gentle in all
his ways, and his manner of falling in love was very
gentle, too. He admired Olga immensely, he found
her stimulating and amusing, and since it was
out of the question really to be her lover, he would
have enjoyed next best to that being her brother,
and such little pangs of jealousy as he might experience
from time to time were rather in the nature of small
electric shocks voluntarily received. He was devoted
to her with a warmth that his supposed devotion to
Lucia had never kindled in him ; he even went so far
as to dream about her in an agitated though respect-
ful manner. Without being conscious of any un-
reality about his sentiments, he really wanted to
dress up as a lover rather than to be one, for he
could form no notion at present of what it felt like
to be absorbed in anyone else. Life was so full as
it was : there really was no room for anything else,
especially if that something else must be of the quality
which rendered everything else colourless. This state
of mind, this quality of emotion was wholly pleasur-
able and quite exciting, and instead of crying out
" More misery ! more unhappiness ! " he could now,
as he passed the mulberry, say to himself " More
pleasures ! More happiness ! "

Yet as he ran down the road to lunch with Lucia,
he was conscious that she was likely to stand, an
angel perhaps, but certainly one with a flaming
sword, between him and all the interests of the new
life which was undoubtedly beginning to bubble in
Riseholme, and to which Georgie found it so pleasant
to take his little mug and have it filled with exhilarat-
ing liquid. And if Lucia proved to be standing in
his path, forbidding his approach, he too was armed
for combat with a revolutionary weapon, consist-

ing of a rolled-up copy of some of Debussy's morsels
for the piano. Olga had lent it him a few days ago,
and he had been very busy over *Poissons d'or*. He
was further armed by the complete knowledge of
the Italian débâcle last night, which, from his knowledge of Lucia, he judged must constitute a crisis.
Something would have to happen. . . . Several times
lately, Olga had, so to speak, run full-tilt into Lucia,
and had passed on, leaving a staggering form behind
her. And in each case, so Georgie clearly perceived,
Olga had not intended to butt into or stagger anybody. Each time she had knocked Lucia down purely
by accident, but if these accidents occurred with such
awful frequency, it was to be expected that Lucia
would find another name for them : they would have
to be re-christened. With all his Riseholme appetite
for complications and events, Georgie foresaw that he
was not likely to go empty away from this lunch.
In addition, there were other topics of extraordinary
interest, for really there had been very odd
experiences at Mrs. Quantock's last night, when
the Italian débâcle was going on a little way up the
road. But he was not going to bring that out at once.

Lucia hailed him with her most cordial manner, and
with a superb effrontery began to talk Italian just
as usual, though she must have guessed that
Georgie knew all about last night.

" *Ben arrivato, amico mio*," she said. " Why, it
must be three days since we met. " *Che ha fatto il
signorino ?* And what have you got there ? "

Georgie having escaped being caught over Italian,
had made up his mind not to talk any more ever.

" Oh, these. Some little things by Debussy," he said.
" I want to play one of them to you afterwards. I've
just been glancing through it."

" *Bene, molto bene !* " said she. " Come in to lunch. But I can't promise to like it, Georgino. Isn't Debussy the man who always makes me want to howl like a dog at the sound of the gong, and wonder when it is going to begin. Where did you get them from ? "

" Olga lent me them," said Georgie negligently. He really did call her Olga to her face now, by request.

Lucia's bugles began to sound.

" Yes, I should think Miss Bracely would admire that sort of music," she said. " I suppose I am too old-fashioned, though I will not condemn your little pieces of Debussy before I have heard them. Old-fashioned ! Yes ! I was certainly too old-fashioned for the music she gave us last night. *Dio mio !* "

" Oh, didn't you enjoy it ? " asked he.

Lucia sat down, without waiting for Peppino.

" Poor Miss Bracely ! " she said. " It was very kind of her in intention to ask me, but she would have been kinder to have asked Mrs. Antrobus instead, and told her not to bring her ear-trumpet. To hear that lovely voice—for I do her justice, and there are lovely notes in her voice, *lovely*—to hear that voice shrieking and screaming away, in what she called the great scene, was simply pitiful. There was no melody, and above all there was no form. A musical composition is like an architectural building : it must be built up and constructed. How often have I said that ! You must have colour, and you must have line, otherwise I cannot concede you the right to say you have music."

Lucia finished her egg in a hurry, and put her elbows on the table.

" I hope I am not hide-bound and limited," she said, " and I think you will acknowledge, Georgie, that I

am not. Even in the divinest music of all, I am not
blind to defects, if there are defects. The Moonlight
Sonata, for instance. You have often heard me say
that the two last movements do not approach the first
in perfection of form. And if I am permitted to
criticize Beethoven, I hope I may be allowed to suggest
that Mr. Cortese has not produced an opera which
will render *Fidelio* ridiculous. But really I am chiefly
sorry for Miss Bracely. I should have thought it
worth her while to render herself not unworthy to
interpret *Fidelio*, whatever time and trouble that
cost her, rather than to seek notoriety by helping to
foist on to the world a fresh combination of engine-
whistles and grunts. *Non è vero*, Peppino? How late
you are."

Lucia had not determined on this declaration of
war without anxious consideration. But it was quite
obvious to her that the enemy was daily gaining
strength, and therefore the sooner she came to
open hostilities the better, for it was equally obvious
to her mind that Olga was a pretender to the throne
she had occupied for so long. It was time to mobilize,
and she had first to state her views and her plan of
campaign to the chief of her staff.

" No, we did not quite like our evening, Peppino and
I, did we, *caro?*" she went on. " And Mr. Cortese!
His appearance! He is like a huge hair-dresser.
His touch on the piano: if you can imagine a wild
bull butting at the keys, you will have some idea of
it. And above all, his Italian! I gathered that he
was a Neapolitan, and we all know what Neapolitan dialect is like. Tuscans and Romans, who between them,
I believe—*lingua Toscana in bocca Romana*, remember—know how to speak their own tongue, find Neapoli-
tans totally unintelligible. For myself, and I speak

for *mio sposo* as well, I do not want to understand what
Romans do not understand. *La bella lingua* is
sufficient for me."

" I hear that Olga could understand him quite well,"
said Georgie, betraying his complete knowledge of all
that had happened.

" That may be so," said Lucia. " I hope she understood his English too, and his music. He had not
an ' h ' when he spoke English, and I have not the
slightest doubt in my own mind that his Italian was
equally illiterate. It does not matter : I do not see
that Mr. Cortese's linguistic accomplishments concern
us. But his music does, if poor Miss Bracely, with
her lovely notes, is going to study it and appear as
Lucretia. I am sorry if that is so. Any news ? "

Really it was rather magnificent, and it was war as
well : of that there could not be the slightest doubt.
All Riseholme by this time knew that Lucia and
Peppino had not been able to understand a word of what
Cortese had said, and here was the answer to the
backbiting suggestion, vividly put forward by Mrs.
Weston on the green that morning, that the explana-
tion was that Lucia and Peppino did not know Italian.
They could not reasonably be expected to know Nea-
politan dialect : the language of Dante satisfied their
humble needs. They found it difficult to understand
Cortese when he spoke English, but that did not imply
that they did not know English. Dante's tongue and
Shakespeare's tongue sufficed them. . . .

" And what were the words of the libretto like ? "
asked Georgie. " The piece that Olga sang."

Lucia fixed him with her beady eye, ready and eager
to show how delighted she was to bestow approbation
wherever it was deserved.

" Wonderful ! " she said. " I felt, and so did

Peppino, that the words were as utterly wasted on that
formless music as was poor Miss Bracely's voice.
How did it go, Peppino ?   Let me think ! "

Lucia raised her head again with the far-away look.

" *Amore misterio !* " she said.   " *Amore profondo !
Amore profondo del vasto mar.*   Ah, there was our poor
bella lingua again.   I wonder who wrote the libretto."

" Mr. Cortese wrote the libretto," said Georgie.
" Olga told me so."

Lucia did not hestitate for a moment, but gave her
silvery laugh.

" Oh, dear me, no," she said.   " If you had heard
him talk you would know he could not have done so.
Well, have we not had enough of Mr. Cortese and his
works ?   Any news ?   What did you do last night
when Peppino and I were in our *purgatorio* ? "

Georgie was almost equally glad to get off the subject of Italian.   The less said in or of Italian the
better.   Who wanted rows in Riseholme ?

" I was dining with Mrs. Quantock," he said.   " She
had a very interesting Russian woman staying with
her, Princess Popoffski."

Lucia laughed again.

" Dear Daisy ! " she said.   " Tell me about the
Russian Princess.   Was she a Guru ?   Dear me, how
easily some people are taken in !   The Guru !   Well,
we were all in the same boat there.   We took the
Guru at poor Daisy's valuation, and I still believe
he had very remarkable gifts, curry-cook or not.
But Princess Popoffski now——"

" We had a séance," said Georgie.

" Indeed !   And Princess Popoffski was the medium ? "

Georgie grew a little dignified.

" It is no use adopting that tone, *cara*," he said,
relapsing into Italian.   " You were not there : you

were having your purgatory at Olga's. And Mr.
Cortese did write the libretto. It was very remarkable. We touched hands all round the table : there
was no possibility of fraud."

Lucia's views on psychic phenomena were clearly
known to Riseholme ; those who produced them were
fraudulent, those who were taken in by them were
dupes. Consequently there was irony in the baby-
talk of her reply :

" Me dood ! " she said. " Me vewy dood, and me
listen carefully. Tell Lucia ! "

Georgie recounted the experiences. The table had
rocked and tapped out names. The table had whirled
round, though it was a very heavy table. Georgie
had been told that he had two sisters, one of whose
names, if translated from the Latin, meant a bear.

" How did the table know that ? " he asked.
" Ursa, a bear, you know ; Ursula, a little bear. And
then, while we were sitting there, the Princess went
into a trance. She said there was a beautiful spirit
present, who blessed us all. She called Mrs. Quantock
Margherita, which as you may know is the Italian for
Daisy——"

Lucia smiled.

" Thank you for explaining, *Georgino*," she said.

There was no mistaking the irony of that, and
Georgie thought he would be ironical too.

" I didn't know if you knew," he said. " I thought
it might be Neapolitan dialect."

" Pray go on ! " said Lucia, breathing through her
nose.

" And she said I was Georgino," said Georgie,
" but that there was another Georgino not far off.
That was odd, because Olga's house, with Mr. Shuttleworth, was so close. . . . And then the Princess went

into very deep trance, and the spirit that was there took possession of her."

" And who was that ? " asked Lucia.

" His name was Amadeo. She spoke in Amadeo's voice—indeed, it was Amadeo who was speaking. He was a Florentine and knew Dante quite well. He materialized : I saw him."

A bright and glorious vision flashed upon Lucia. The Dante class might not (even though it was clearly understood that Cortese spoke unintelligible Neapolitan) be a complete success if the only attraction was that she herself taught Dante ; but it would be quite a different proposition if Princess Popoffski, controlled by Amadeo, Dante's friend, was present. They might read a Canto first, and then hold a séance of which Amadeo—via Princess Popoffski—would take charge. While this was simmering in her mind, it was important to drop all irony and be extremely sympathetic.

" Georgino ! How wonderful ! " she said. " As you know, I am sceptical by nature, and want all evidence carefully sifted. I daresay I am too critical, and that is a fault. Peppino is very critical too ; I have caught it from him. But fancy getting in touch with a friend of Dante's ! What would one not give ? Tell me : what is this Princess like ? Is she the sort of person one could ask to dinner ? "

Georgie was still sore over the irony to which he had been treated. He had, moreover, the solid fact behind him that Daisy Quantock (Margherita) had declared that in no circumstances would she permit Lucia to annex her Princess. She had forgiven Lucia for annexing the Guru (and considering that she had only annexed a curry-cook, it was not so difficult), but she was quite determined to run her Princess herself.

" Yes, you might ask her," he said. If irony was going about, there was no reason why he should not have a share.

Lucia bounced from her seat as if it had been a spring cushion.

" We will have a little party," she said. " We three, and dear Daisy and her husband and the Princess. I think that will be enough : psychics hate a crowd, because it disturbs the influences. I do **not** say I believe in her power yet, but I am quite open-minded : I should like to be convinced. That's my attitude ! Let me see ! We are doing nothing to-morrow. Let us have our little dinner to-morrow. I will send a line to dear Daisy at once, and say how enormously your account of the séance has interested me. I should like dear Daisy to have something to console her for that terrible fiasco about her Guru. And then, Georgino *mio*, I will listen to your Debussy. Do not expect anything : if it seems to me formless, I shall say so. But if it seems to me promising, I shall be equally frank. Perhaps it is great : I cannot tell you about that till I have heard it. Let me write my note first."

That was soon done, and Lucia, having sent it by hand, came into the music-room and drew down the blinds over the window, through which the November sun was streaming. Very little art, as she had once said, would " stand " daylight : only Shakespeare and Dante and Beethoven, and perhaps Bach, could compete with the sun.

Georgie, for his part, would have liked rather more light, but, after all, Debussy wrote such very odd chords and sequences that it was not necessary to wear his spectacles. Lucia sat in a high chair near the piano, with her chin in her hand, tremendously alert.

Georgie took off his rings and laid them on the candle-bracket, and ran his hands nimbly over the piano.

"*Poissons d'or*," he said. "Goldfish!"

"Yes; *Pesci d' oro*," said Lucia, explaining it to Peppino.

Lucia's face changed as the elusive music proceeded. The far-away look died away and became puzzled: her chin came out of her hand, and the hand it came out of covered her eyes. Before Georgie had got to the end, the answer to her note came, and she sat with it in her hand, which, released from covering her eyes, tried to beat time. On the last note she got up with a regretful sigh.

"It is finished?" she asked. "And yet I feel inclined to say 'When is it going to begin?' I haven't been fed: I haven't drunk in anything. Yes, I warned you I should be quite candid. And there's my verdict. I am sorry. Me vewy sowwy! But you played it, I am sure, beautifully, Georgino: you were a *buono avvocato*: you said all that could be said for your client. Shall I open this note before we discuss it more fully? Give Georgie a cigarette, Peppino! I am sure he deserves one after all those accidentals."

She pulled up the blind again in order to read her note, and as she read her face clouded.

"Ah! I am sorry for that," she said. "Peppino, the Princess does not go out in the evening; they always have a séance there. I daresay Daisy means to ask us some evening soon. We will keep an evening or two open. It is a long time since I have seen dear Daisy; I will pop in this afternoon."

CHAPTER XIII

SPIRITUALISM, and all things pertaining to it, swept over Riseholme like the amazing growth of some tropical forest, germinating in the most unlikely soil, and rearing into huge fantastic growths. In the centre of this wonderful jungle was a temple, so to speak, and that temple was the house of Mrs. Quantock. . . .

A strange Providence was the origin of it all. Mrs. Quantock, a week before, had the toothache, and, being no longer in the fold of Christian Science, found that it was no good at all to tell herself that it was a false claim. False claim it might be, but it was so plausible a one that it quite deceived her, and she went up to London to have its falsity demonstrated by a dentist. Since the collapse of Yoga, and the flight of the curry-cook, she had embarked on no mystical adventure, and she starved for some new fad. Thus when her first visit to the dentist was over (the tooth required three treatments) and she went to a vegetarian restaurant to see if there was anything enlightening to be got out of that, she was delighted to find herself sitting at a very small table with a very communicative lady who ate cabbages in perfectly incredible quantities. She had a round pale face, like the moon behind thin clouds, enormous eyebrows that almost met over the nose, a strange, slow voice, of husky tone, and a pronunciation quite as foreign as Signor Cortese's. She wore some very

curious rings, with large engraved amethysts and
turquoises in them, and, as in the first moments of
their conversation she had volunteered the information
that vegetarianism was the only possible diet for any
who cultivated their psychical powers, Mrs. Quantock
asked her if those finger-ornaments had any mystical
signification. They had : one was Gnostic, one was
Rosicrucian, and the other was Cabalistic. . . . It is
easy to picture Mrs. Quantock's delight : adventure
had met her with smiling mouth and mysterious eyes.
In the course of an animated conversation of half
an hour, this lady explained that if Mrs. Quantock
was, like her, a searcher after psychical mysteries,
and cared to come to her flat at half-past four that
afternoon, she would try to help her. She added,
with some little diffidence, that the fee for a séance
was a guinea, and, as she left, took a card out of a case
encrusted with glowing rubies, and gave it her. That
was the Princess Popoffski.

Now here was a curious thing. For the last few
evenings at Riseholme Mrs. Quantock had been ex-
perimenting with a table, and finding that it creaked
and tilted and tapped in the most encouraging way
when she and Robert laid their hands on it, and that
something—whatever it was that moved the table—
had indicated by raps that her name was Daisy and
his Robert, as well as giving them other information
which could not so easily be verified, Robert had
grown quite excited about it, and was vexed that the
séance was interrupted by his wife's expedition to
London. But now how providential that was. She
had walked straight from the hands of the dentist
into the arms of Princess Popoffski.

It was barely half-past four when Mrs. Quantock
arrived at the Princess's flat, in a quiet side-street off

Charing Cross Road. A small, dapper little gentleman received her, who explained that he was the Princess's secretary, and conducted her through several small rooms into the presence of the Sibyl. These rooms, so Mrs. Quantock thrillingly noticed, were dimly lit by oil lamps that stood in front of shrines containing images of the great spiritual guides from Moses down to Madame Blavatski ; a smell of incense hung about ; there were vases of flowers on the tables, and strange caskets set with winking stones. In the last of these rooms the Princess was seated, and for the moment Mrs. Quantock hardly recognized her, for she wore a blue robe, which left her massive arms bare, and upon them writhed serpent-shaped bracelets of many coils. She fixed her eyes on Mrs. Quantock, as if she had never seen her before, and made no sign of recognition.

"The Princess has been meditating," said the secretary in a hoarse whisper. "She'll come to herself presently."

For a moment meditation unpleasantly reminded Mrs. Quantock of the Guru, but nothing could have been less like that ill-starred curry-cook than this majestic creature. Eventually she gave a great sigh and came out of her meditation.

"Ah, it is my friend," she said. "Do you know that you have a purple halo ? "

This was very gratifying, especially when it was explained that only the most elect had purple halos, and soon other elect souls assembled for the séance. In the centre of the table was placed a musical box and a violin, and hardly had the circle been made, and the lights turned down, when the most extraordinary things began to happen. A perfect storm of tappings issued from the table, which violently pitched and rocked, and presently there came peals of laughter in a high

voice, and those who had been before said that it was
Pocky. He was a dear naughty boy, so Mrs. Quantock's neighbour explained to her, so full of fun, and
when on earth, had been a Hungarian violinist. Still
invisible, Pocky wished them all much laughter and
joy, and then suddenly said : " 'Ullo ! 'ullo, 'ere's
a new friend. I like her." And Mrs. Quantock's
neighbour, with a touch of envy in her voice, told
her that Pocky clearly meant her. Then Pocky said
that they had been having heavenly music on the
other side that day, and that if the new friend would
say " Please," he would play them some of it.

So Mrs. Quantock, trembling with emotion, said
" Please, Pocky," and instantly he began to play on
the violin the spirit-tune which he had just been
playing on the other side. After that, the violin
clattered back on to the middle of the table again, and
Pocky, blowing showers of kisses to them all, went
away amid peals of happy laughter.

Silence fell, and then a deep bass voice said, " I
am coming, Amadeo ! " and out of the middle of the
table appeared a faint luminousness. It grew upwards and began to take form. Swathes of white
muslin shaped themselves in the dimness, and then
appeared a white face in the topmost folds of the
muslin, with a Roman nose and a melancholy expression. He was not gay like Pocky, but he was intensely
impressive, and spoke some lines in Italian when asked
to repeat a piece of Dante. Mrs. Quantock knew
they were Italian, because she recognized *notte* and
uno and *caro*, familiar words on Lucia's lips.

The séance came to an end, and Mrs. Quantock
having placed a guinea with the utmost alacrity in a
sort of offertory-plate which the Princess's secretary
negligently but prominently put down on a table in

one of the other rooms, waited to arrange for another
séance. But most unfortunately the Princess was
leaving town next day on a much needed holiday, for
she had been giving three séances a day for the last
two months and required rest.

" Yes, we're off to-morrow, the Princess and I,"
said he, " for a week at the Royal Hotel at Brinton.
Pleasant bracing air, always sets her up. But after
that she'll be back in town. Do you know that part
of the country ? "

Daisy could hardly believe her ears.

" Brinton ? " she said. " I live close to Brinton."

The whole scheme flashed complete upon her, even
as Athene sprang full-grown from the brain of Zeus.

" Do you think that she might be induced to spend
a few days with me at Riseholme ? " she said. " My
husband and I are so much interested in psychical
things. You would be our guest, too, I hope. If
she rested for a few days at Brinton first ? If she came
on to me afterwards ? And then if she was thoroughly
rested, perhaps she would give us a séance or two.
I don't know——"

Mrs. Quantock felt a great diffidence in speaking of
guineas in the same sentence with Princesses, and had
to make another start.

" If she was thoroughly rested," she said, " and if
a little circle perhaps of four, at the usual price, would
be worth her while. Just after dinner, you know,
and nothing else to do all day but rest. There are
pretty drives, and beautiful air. All very quiet, and
I think I may say more comfortable than the hotel.
It would be such a pleasure."

Mrs. Quantock heard the clinking of bracelets from
the room where the Princess was still reposing, and
there she stood in the door, looking unspeakably

majestic, but very gracious. So Mrs. Quantock put
her proposition before her, the secretary coming to
the rescue on the subject of the usual fees, and when,
two days afterwards, she returned to Riseholme, it
was to get ready the spare room and Robert's room
next it for these thrilling visitors, whose first séance
Georgie and Piggy had attended, on the evening of
the Italian débâcle. . . .

The Quantocks had taken a high and magnificent
line about the " usual fees " for the séances, an
expensive line, but then Roumanian oils had been
extremely prosperous lately. No mention whatever of these fees was made to their guests, no offertory-plate was put in a prominent position in the hall.
There was no fumbling for change on the discreet
pressure of coins into the secretary's hand ; the entire
cost was borne by Roumanian oils. The Princess and
Mrs. Quantock, apparently, were old friends ; they
spoke to each other at dinner as " dear friend," and
the Princess declared in the most gratifying way
that they had been most intimate in a previous incarnation, without any allusion to the fact that in this
incarnation they had met for the first time last week
at a vegetarian restaurant. She was kind enough,
it was left to be understood, to give a little séance
after dinner at the house of her " dear friend."

Now the Princess was to stay three nights, and,
therefore, as soon as Mrs. Quantock had made sure of
that, she proceeded to fill up each of the séances
without asking Lucia to any of them. It was not that
she had not fully forgiven her for her odious grabbing
of the Guru, for she had done that on the night of
the Spanish Quartet ; it was rather that she meant
to make sure that there would, by no possibility, be

anything to forgive concerning her conduct with regard to the Princess. She could not grab her (and so call Daisy's power of forgiveness into play again), if she never came near her, and Daisy meant to take proper precautions that she should not come near her. Accordingly Georgie and Piggy were asked to the first séance (if it did not go very well, it would not particularly matter with them), Olga and Mr. Shuttleworth were bidden to the second, and Lady Ambermere, with Georgie again, to the third. This—quite apart from the immense interest of psychic phenomena— was deadly work, for it would be bitter, indeed, to Lucia to know, as she most undoubtedly would, that Lady Ambermere, who had cut her so firmly, was dining and coming to the séance, and that Georgie would be dining twice and coming to two séances. Daisy, it must again be repeated, had quite forgiven Lucia about the Guru, but Lucia must take the consequences of what she had done. . . .

It was after the first séance that the frenzy for spiritualism seized Riseholme. The Princess, with great good-nature and further fees, gave some further exhibitions of her psychical powers in addition to the evening séances, and even as Georgie the next afternoon was receiving Lucia's cruel verdict about Debussy, the Sibyl was looking at the hands of Colonel Boucher and Mrs. Weston, and unerringly probing into their past, and lifting the corner of the veil, giving them bright glimpses into the future. She knew that the two were engaged, for that she had learned from Mrs. Quantock in her morning's drive, and did not attempt to conceal the fact ; but how could it be accounted for that, looking impressively from the one to the other, she said that a woman no longer young but tall, and with fair hair, had crossed their lives and had been connected

with one of them for years past ? It was impossible
to describe Elizabeth more accurately than that, and
Mrs. Weston, in high excitement, confessed that her
maid, who had been with her for fifteen years, entirely
corresponded with what the Princess had seen in her
hand. After that it took only a moment's further
scrutiny for the Princess to discover that Elizabeth
was going to be happy too. . . . Then she found that
there was a man connected with Elizabeth, and
Colonel Boucher's hand, to which she transferred her
gaze, trembled with delighted anticipation. She
seemed to see a man there ; she was not quite sure,
but was there a man who perhaps had been known
to him for a long time ? There was. And then by
degrees the affairs of Elizabeth and Atkinson were
unerringly unravelled. It was little wonder that the
Colonel pushed Mrs. Weston's bath-chair with record
speed to " Ye Signe of Ye Daffodile," and by the
greatest good luck obtained a copy of the " Palmist's
Manual."

At another of these informal séances, attended by
Goosie and Mrs. Antrobus, even stranger things had
happened, for the Princess's hand, as they held a
little preliminary conversation, began to tremble
and twitch even more strongly than Colonel Boucher's,
and Mrs. Quantock hastily supplied her with a pencil
and a quantity of sheets of foolscap paper, for this
trembling and twitching implied that Raschia, an
ancient Egyptian priestess, was longing to employ
the Princess on automatic writing. After a few wild
scrawls and plunges with the pencil, the Princess,
though she still continued to talk to them, covered
sheet after sheet with large flowing handwriting. This,
when it was finished and the Princess sank back
in her chair, proved to be the most wonderful spiritual

discourse, describing the happiness and harmony which pervaded the whole universe, and was only temporarily obscured by the mists of materiality. These mists were wholly withdrawn from the vision of those who had passed over. They lived in the midst of song and flowers and light and love. . . . Towards the end there was a less intelligible passage about fire from the clouds. It was rendered completely intelligible the very next day when there was a thunderstorm—surely an unusual occurrence in November. If that had not happened, Mrs. Quantock's interpretation of it as referring to Zeppelins would have been found equally satisfactory. It was no wonder after that, that Mrs. Antrobus, Piggy and Goosie spent long evenings with pencils and paper, for the Princess said that most people had the gift of automatic writing, if they would only take pains and patience to develop it. Everybody had his own particular guide, and it was the very next day that Piggy obtained a script clearly signed Annabel. Nicostratus and Jamifleg followed very soon after for Mrs. Antrobus and Goosie, and so there was no jealousy.

But the crown and apex of these manifestations were undoubtedly the three regular séances which took place before the three select circles after dinner. Musical boxes resounded, violins gave forth ravishing airs, the sitters were touched by unseen fingers when everybody's hands were touching all round the table, and from the middle of it materializations swathed in muslin were built up. Pocky came, visible to the eye, and played spirit music; Amadeo, melancholy and impressive, recited Dante, and Cardinal Newman, not visible to the eye but audible to the ear, joined in singing " Lead, kindly Light," which the secretary

requested them to sing, and blessed them at the conclusion. Lady Ambermere was so much impressed
and so nervous of driving home alone, that she insisted
on Georgie's going back to the Hall with her, and
consigning her to Pug or Miss Lyall, and for the three
days of the Princess's visit there was practically no
subject discussed at the parliaments on the green
except the latest manifestations. Olga sent to town
for a crystal, and Georgie for a planchette, and Riseholme temporarily became a spiritualistic republic, with
the Princess as priestess and Mrs. Quantock as president.

Lucia, all this time, was almost insane with pique
and jealousy, for she sat in vain waiting for an
invitation to a séance, and would, long before the
three days were over, have welcomed with enthusiasm
a place at one of the inferior and informal exhibitions.
Since she could not procure the Princess for dinner,
she asked Daisy to bring her to lunch or tea, or at any
hour day or night which was convenient. She made
Peppino hang about opposite Daisy's house, with
orders to drop his stick, or let his hat blow off, if he
saw even the secretary coming out of the gate, so as
possibly to enter into conversation with him, while
she positively forced herself one morning into Daisy's
hall, and cried " Margherita " in silvery tones. On this
occasion Margherita came out of the drawing-room
with a most determined expression on her face, and
shut the door carefully behind her.

" Dearest Lucia," she said, " how nice to see you
What is it ? "

" I just popped in for a chat," said she. " I haven't
set eyes on you since the evening of the Spanish
Quartet."

" No ! So long ago as that, is it ? Well, you must
come in again sometime very soon, won't you ? The

day after to-morrow I shall be much less busy. Promise to look in then."

" You have a visitor with you, have you not ? "
asked Lucia desperately.

" Yes ! Two indeed, dear friends of mine. But I am
afraid you would not like them. I know your opinion
about anything connected with Spiritualism, and—
isn't it silly of us ?—we've been dabbling in that."

" Oh, but how interesting ! " said Lucia. " I—I
am always ready to learn, and alter my opinions if
I am wrong."

Mrs. Quantock did not move from in front of the
drawing-room door.

" Yes ? " she said. " Then we will have a great
talk about it when you come to see me the day after
to-morrow. But I know I shall find you hard to
convince."

She kissed the tips of her fingers in a manner so hopelessly final that there was nothing to do but go away.

Then, with poor generalship, Lucia altered her
tactics, and went up to the village green, where Piggy
was telling Georgie about the script signed Annabel.
This was repeated again for Lucia's benefit.

" Wasn't it too lovely ? " said Piggy. " So Annabel's
my guide, and she writes a hand quite unlike mine."

Lucia gave a little scream, and put her fingers to her
ears.

" Gracious me ! " she said. " What has come over
Riseholme ? Wherever I go I hear nothing but talk
of séances, and spirits, and automatic writing. Such
a pack of nonsense, my dear Piggy. I wonder at a
sensible girl like you."

Mrs. Weston, propelled by the Colonel, whirled up
in her bath-chair.

" The ' Palmist's Manual ' is too wonderful," she

said, "and Jacob and I sat up over it till I don't know
what hour. There's a break in his line of life, just at
the right place, when he was so ill in Egypt, which is
most remarkable, and when Tommy Luton brought
round my bath-chair this morning—I had it at the
garden-door, because the gravel's just laid at my
front-door, and the wheels sink so far into it—'Tommy,'
I said, 'let me look at your hand a moment,' and there,
on his line of fate, was that little cross that means a
bereavement. It came just right, didn't it, Jacob?
when he was thirteen, for he's fourteen this year, and
Mrs. Luton died just a year ago. Of course, I didn't
tell Tommy that, for I only told him to wash his hands,
but it was most curious. And has your planchette
come yet, Mr. Georgie? I shall be most curious to
see what it writes, so if you've got an evening free
any night soon just come round for a bit of dinner, and
we'll make an evening of it, with table-turning and
planchette and palmistry. Now tell me all about
the séance the first night. I wish I could have been
present at a real séance, but of course Mrs. Quantock
can't find room for everybody, and I'm sure it was
most kind of her to let the Colonel and me come in
yesterday afternoon. We were thrilled with it, and
who knows but that the Princess didn't write the
'Palmist's Manual,' for on the title-page it says it's
by 'P.,' and that might be Popoffski as easily as not,
or perhaps Princess."

This allusion to there not being room for everybody
was agony to Lucia. She laughed in her most silvery
manner.

"Or perhaps Peppino," she said. "I must ask
mio caro if he wrote it. Or does it stand for Pillson?
Georgino, are you the author of the 'Palmist's
Manual?' *Ecco!* I believe it was you."

This was not quite wise, for no one detested irony more than Mrs. Weston, or was sharper to detect it. Lucia should never have been ironical just then, nor, indeed, have dropped into Italian.

" No ! " she said, " I'm sure it was neither *il Signor Peppino* nor *il Signor Pillson* who wrote it. I believe it was the *Principessa*. So *ecco!* And did we not have a delicious evening at Miss Bracely's the other night ? Such lovely singing, and so interesting to know that Signor Cortese made it all up. And those lovely words, for though I didn't understand much of them, they sounded so exquisite. And fancy Miss Bracely talking Italian so beautifully when we none of us knew she talked it at all."

Mrs. Weston's amiable face was crimson with suppressed emotion, of which these few words were only the most insignificant leakage, and a very awkward pause succeeded, which was luckily broken by everybody beginning to talk again very fast and brightly. Then Mrs. Weston's bath-chair scudded away, Piggy slipped across to the stocks where Goosie was sitting with a large sheet of foolscap, in case her hand twitched for automatic script, and Lucia turned to Georgie, who alone was left.

" Poor Daisy ! " she said. " I dropped in just now, and really I found her very odd and strange. What with her -crazes for Christian Science, and Uric Acid and Gurus and Mediums, one wonders if she is quite sane. So sad ! I should be dreadfully sorry if she had some mental collapse : that sort of thing is always so painful. But I know of a first-rate place for rest-cures : I think it would be wise if I just casually dropped the name of it to Mr. Robert, in case. And this last craze seems so terribly infectious. Fancy Mrs. Weston studying palmistry ! It is too comical

but I hope I did not hurt her feelings by suggesting
that Peppino and you wrote the Manual. It is dangerous to make little jokes to poor Mrs. Weston."

Georgie quite agreed with that, but did not think it
necessary to say in what sense he agreed with it.
Every day now Lucia was pouring floods of light on a
quite new side of her character, which had been un-
developed, like the print from some photographic plate
lying in the dark, so long as she was undisputed mistress
of Riseholme. But, so it struck him now, since the
advent of Olga she had shown a critical, ironical
standpoint, which previously she had reserved for
Londoners. At every turn she had to criticize and
condemn where once she would only have praised.
So few months ago, there had been that marvellous
Hitum garden-party, when Olga had sung, long
after Lady Ambermere had gone away. That was her
garden-party ; the splendour and success of it had been
hers, and no one had been allowed to forget that until
Olga came back again. But the moment that happened, and she began to sing on her own account
(which after all, so Georgie thought, she had a perfect
right to do), the whole aspect of affairs was changed.
She romped, and Riseholme did not like romps : she
sang in church, and that was theatrical : she gave a
party with the Spanish Quartet, and Brinton was
publicly credited by Lucia with the performance.
Then on the top had come Mrs. Quantock and her
Princess, and, lo ! it would be kind to remember the
name of an establishment for rest-cures, in the hope
of saving poor Daisy's sanity. Then again Colonel
Boucher and Mrs. Weston were intending to get
married, and consulted a Palmist's Manual, so they,
too, helped to develop the print that had lain so long
in the dark.

" Poor thing ! " said Lucia, " it is dreadful to have
no sense of humour, and I'm sure I hope that Colonel
Boucher will thoroughly understand that she has none
before he speaks the fatal words. But then he has
none either, and I have often noticed that two people
without any sense of humour find each other most
witty and amusing. A sense of humour, I expect, is
not a very common gift ; Miss Bracely has none at
all, for I do not call romping humour. And as for
poor Daisy, what can rival her solemnity in sitting
night after night round a table with some one who may
or may not be a Russian princess—Russia, of course,
is a very large place, and one does not know how many
princesses there may be there—and thrilling over a
pot of luminous paint, or a false nose, and calling it
Amadeo, the friend of Dante ? "

This was too much for Georgie.

" But you asked Mrs. Quantock and the Princess to
dine with you," he said, " and hoped there would be a
séance afterwards. You wouldn't have done that if
you thought it was only a false nose and a pot of
luminous paint."

" I may have been impulsive," said Lucia, speaking
very rapidly. " I daresay I am impulsive, and if
my impulses lie in the direction of extending such
poor hospitality as I can offer to my friends, and their
friends, I am not ashamed of them. Far otherwise. But when I see and observe the awful effects
of this so-called spiritualism on people whom I should
have thought sensible and well-balanced—I do not
include poor dear Daisy among them—then I am only
thankful that my impulses did not happen to lead me
into countenancing such piffle, as your sister so truly
observed about poor Daisy's Guru."

They had come opposite Georgie's house, and suddenly his drawing-room window was thrown open. Olga's head looked out.

"Don't have a fit, Georgie, to find me here," she said. "Good morning, Mrs. Lucas : you were behind the mulberry, and I didn't see you. But something's happened to my kitchen range, and I can't have lunch at home. Do give me some. I've brought my crystal, and we'll gaze and gaze. I can see nothing at present except my own nose and the window. Are you psychical, Mrs. Lucas ? "

This was the last straw : all Lucia's grievances flocked together like swallows for their flight, and on the top came this open annexation of Georgie. There was Olga, sitting in his window, all unasked, and demanding lunch, with her silly, ridiculous crystal in her hand, wondering if Lucia was psychical.

The silver laugh was a little shrill. It started a full tone above its normal pitch.

"No, dear Miss Bracely," she said. "I am afraid I am much too commonplace and matter-of-fact to care about such things. It is a great loss, I know, and deprives me of the pleasant society of Russian princesses. But we are all made differently : that is very lucky. I must get home, Georgie."

It certainly seemed very lucky that everyone was not precisely like Lucia at that moment, or there would have been quarrelling.

She walked quickly off, and Georgie entered his house. Lucia had really been remarkably rude, and, if allusion was made to it, he was ready to confess that she seemed a little worried. Friendship would allow that, and candour demanded it. But no allusion of any sort was made. There was a certain flush on Olga's face, and she explained that she had been sitting over the fire.

The Princess's visit came to an end next day, and all the world knew that she was going back to London by the 11.0 a.m. express. Lady Ambermere was quite aware of it, and drove in with Pug and Miss Lyall, meaning to give her a lift to the station, leaving Mrs. Quantock, if she wanted to see her guest off, to follow in the fly which no doubt had been ordered. But Daisy had no intention of permitting this sort of thing, and drove calmly along with her dear friend in Georgie's motor, leaving the baffled Lady Ambermere to follow or not as she liked. She did like, though not much, and found herself on the platform among a perfect crowd of Riseholmites who had strolled down to the station on this lovely morning to see if parcels had come. Lady Ambermere took very little notice of them, but managed that Pug should give his paw to the Princess as she took her seat, and waved her hand to Mrs. Quantock's dear friend, as the train slid out of the station.

" The late lord had some Russian relations," she said majestically. " How did you get to know her ? "

" I met her at Tsarkoe Selo," was on the tip of Mrs. Quantock's tongue, but she was afraid that Lady Ambermere might not understand, and ask her when she had been there. It was grievous work making jokes to Lady Ambermere. . . .

The train sped on to London, and the Princess opened the envelope which her hostess had given her, and found that *that* was all right. Her hostess had also provided her with an admirable lunch, which her secretary took out of a Gladstone bag. When that was finished, she wanted her cigarettes, and as she looked for these, and even after she had found them she continued to search for something else. There was the musical box there, and some curious pieces of elastic, and the violin was in its case, and there was a white mask. But she still continued to search. . . .

About the same time as she gave up the search, Mrs. Quantock wandered upstairs to the Princess's room. A less highly vitalized nature than hers would have been in a stupor of content, but she was more in a frenzy of content than a stupor. How fine that frenzy was may be judged from the fact that perhaps the smallest ingredient in it was her utter defeat of Lucia. She cared comparatively little for that glorious achievement, and she was not sure that when her dear friend came back again, as she had arranged to do on her next holiday, that she would not ask Lucia to come to a séance. Indeed she had little but pity for the vanquished, so great were the spoils. Never had Riseholme risen to such a pitch of enthusiasm, and with good cause had it done so now, for of all the wonderful and exciting things that had ever happened there these séances were the most delirious. And, better even than the excitement of Riseholme, was the cause of its excitement, for spiritualism and the truth of inexplicable psychic phenomena had flashed upon them all. Tableaux, romps, Yoga, the Moonlight Sonata, Shakespeare, Christian Science, Olga herself, Uric Acid, Elizabethan furniture, the engagement of Colonel Boucher and Mrs. Weston, all these tremendous interests had paled like fire in the sunlight before the revelation that had now dawned. By practice and patience, by zealous concentration on crystals and palms, by the waiting for automatic script to develop, you attained to the highest mysteries, and could evoke Cardinal Newman, or Pocky. . . .

There was the bed in which the Sibyl had slept: there was the fresh vase of flowers, difficult to procure in November, but still attainable, which she loved to have standing near her. There was the chest of drawers in which she had put her clothes, and Mrs. Quantock pulled them open one by one, finding fresh emanations and vibrations everywhere. The lowest one stuck a little, and she had to use force to it.

The smile was struck from her face, as it flew open. Inside it were billows of the finest possible muslin. Fold after fold of it she drew out, and with it there came a pair of false eyebrows. She recognized them at once as being Amadeo's. The muslin belonged to Pocky as well.

She needed but a moment's concentrated thought, and in swift succession rejected two courses of action that suggested themselves. The first was to use the muslin herself: it would help in summer garments for years. The chief reason against that was that she was a little old for muslin. The second course was to send the whole paraphernalia back to her dear friend, with or without comment. But that would be tantamount to a direct accusation of fraud. Never any more, if she did that, could she dispense her dear friend to Riseholme like an expensive drug. She would not so utterly burn her boats. There remained only one judicious course of action, and she got to work.

It had been a cold morning, clear and frosty, and she had caused a good fire to be lit in the Princess's bedroom for her to dress by. It still prospered in the grate, and Mrs. Quantock, having shut the door and locked it, put on to it the false eyebrows, which, as they turned to ash, flew up the chimney. Then she fed it with muslin: yards and yards of muslin she

poured on to it ; never had there been so much muslin,
nor any so exquisitely fine. It went to her heart to
burn it, but this was no time for minor considerations :
every atom of that evidence must be purged by fire.
It was impossible that the Princess should write to her
dear friend and say that she had left some eyebrows
and a hundred yards of finest muslin behind her, for,
knowing what she did, it would be to her interest as
well as Mrs. Quantock's that those properties should
vanish as if they had never been. Up the chimney
in sheets of flame went this delightful fabric : sometimes it roared there, as if it had set the chimney on
fire, and she had to pause, shielding her scorched face,
until the hollow rumbling had died down. But at
last the holocaust was over, and she unlocked the door
again. No one knew but she, and no one should ever
know. The Guru had turned out to be a curry-cook,
but no intruding Hermy had been here this time.
As long as crystals fascinated and automatic writing
flourished, the secret of the muslin and the eyebrows
should repose in one bosom alone. All Riseholme had
been electrified by spiritualism, and, even now, the
séances had been cheap at the price. The only in-
sulated bit of Riseholme was Lucia, and luckily
she had been permitted no lot or part in those
manifestations.

She had hardly got downstairs when Robert came
in from the green, where he had been recounting the
experiences of the last séance.

" Looked as if there was a chimney on fire," he said.
" I wish it was the kitchen chimney. Then, perhaps,
the beef mightn't be so raw as it was yesterday."

Thus is comedy intertwined with tragedy !

CHAPTER XIV

GEORGIE was very busily engaged during the first weeks of December on a water-colour sketch of Olga sitting at her piano and singing. The difficulty of it was such that at times he almost despaired of accomplishing it, for the problem of how to draw her face with her mouth wide open and yet retain the likeness seemed almost insoluble. Often he sat in front of his looking-glass with his mouth open, and diligently drew his own face, in order to arrive at the principles of the changes of line which took place. Certainly the shape of a person's face when his mouth was wide open altered so completely that you would have thought him quite unrecognizable, however skilfully the artist reproduced his elongated countenance, and yet Georgie could easily recognize that face in the glass as his. Forehead, eyes and cheek-bones alone retained their wonted aspect : even the nose seemed to lengthen if you opened your mouth very wide. . . . Then how, again, was he to indicate that she was singing and not yawning or preparing a sneeze ? His most successful sketch at present looked precisely as if she was yawning, and made Georgie's jaws long to yawn too. Perhaps the shape of the mouth in the two positions was really the same, and it was only the sound that led you to suppose that an open-mouthed person was singing. Possibly the piano would supply the necessary suggestion : Olga would not sit down at the piano merely to yawn or sneeze, for she could do that anywhere.

Then a brilliant idea struck him : he would introduce a shaded lamp standing on the piano, and thus her face would be in red shadow. Naturally this entailed fresh problems with regard to light, but light seemed to present less difficulty than likeness. Besides, he could make her dress and the keys of the piano very like indeed. But when he came to painting again he despaired. There must be red shadow on her face, and yellow light on her hands and on her green dress, and presently the whole thing looked not so much like Olga singing by lamplight, as a lobster-salad spread out in the sunlight. The more he painted, the more vividly did the lettuce leaves and the dressing and the lobster emerge from the paper. So he took away the lamp, and shut Olga's mouth, and there she would be at her piano just going to sing.

These artistic agonies had rewards which more than compensated for them, for regularly now he took his drawing-board and his paint-box across to her house, and sat with her while she practised. There were none of love's lilies lone or yawning York now, for she was very busy learning her part in *Lucretia*, spending a solid two hours at it every morning, and Georgie began to perceive what sort of work it implied to produce the spontaneous ease with which Brünnhilde hailed the sun. More astounding, too, was the fact that this mere learning of notes was but the preliminary to what she called " real work." By and by, when she had got through the mere mechanical part of it, she would have to study. . . . Then when her practice was over, she would indulgently sit with her head in profile against a dark background, and Georgie would suck one end of his brush and bite the other,

and wonder whether he would ever produce anything
which he could dare offer her.   By professional poring
on her face, he grew not to admire only but to adore it,
by daily contact with her there began to dawn on him
the April-mind which illuminated it.

"Georgie, I'm going to scold you," she said one
day, as she took up her place against the black panel.
"You're a selfish little brute.   You think of nothing
but your own amusement.   Did that ever strike
you ? "

Georgie gasped with surprise.   Here was he spending the whole of every morning trying to do something
which would be a worthy Christmas present for her,
to say nothing of the hours he had spent with his
mouth open in front of his looking-glass and the cost of
the beautiful frame which he had ordered, and yet he
was supposed to be only thinking about himself.   Of
course, Olga did not know that the picture was to be
hers. . . .

"How horrid you are ! " he said.   "You're always
finding fault with me.   Explain."

"Well, you're neglecting your old friends for your
new one," she said.   "My dear, you should never
drop an old friend.   For instance, when did you last
play duets with Mrs. Lucas ? "

"Oh, not so very long ago," said Georgie.

"Quite long enough, I am sure.   But I don't actually
mean sitting down and thumping the piano with her.
When did you last think about her and make plans for
her and talk baby-language ? "

"Who told you I ever did ? " asked Georgie.

"Gracious !   How can I possibly remember that
sort of thing ?   I should say at a guess that everybody told me.   Now poor Mrs. Lucas is feeling out of
it, and neglected and dethroned.   It's all on my mind

rather, and I'm talking to you about it, because it's largely your fault. Now we're talking quite frankly, so don't fence and say it's mine. I know exactly what you mean, but you are perfectly wrong. Primarily, it's Mrs. Lucas's fault, because she's quite the stupidest woman I ever saw, but it's partly your fault too."

She turned round.

"Come, Georgie, let's have it out," she said. "I'm perfectly powerless to do anything, because she detests me, and you've got to help her and help me, and drop your selfishness. Before I came here, she used to run you all, and give you treats like going to her tableaux and listening to her playing that old Moonlight Sonata, and talking seven words of Italian. And then I came along with no earthly intention except to enjoy my holiday, and she got it into her head that I was trying to run the place instead of her. Isn't that so? Just say 'Yes.'"

"Yes," said Georgie.

"Well, that puts me in an odious position, and a helpless position. I did my best to be nice to her : I went to her house until she ceased to ask me, and asked her here for anything that I thought would amuse her, until she ceased to come. I took no notice of her rudeness, which was remarkable, or of her absurd patronizing airs, which didn't hurt me in the smallest degree. But, Georgie, she would continue to make such a dreadful ass of herself, and think it was my fault. Was it my fault that she didn't know the Spanish Quartet when she heard it, or that she didn't know a word of Italian when she pretended she did, or that the other day (it was the last time I saw her, when you played your Debussy to us at Aunt Jane's) she talked to me about inverted fifths?"

Olga suddenly burst out laughing, and Georgie assumed the Riseholme face of intense curiosity.

" You must tell me all about that," he said, " and I'll tell you the rest which you don't know."

Olga succumbed too, and began to talk in Aunt Jane's voice, for she had adopted her as an aunt.

" Well, it was last Monday week," she said, " or was it Sunday ? No, it couldn't have been Sunday, because I don't have anybody to tea that day, as Elizabeth goes over to Jacob's and spends the afternoon with Atkinson, or the other way about, which doesn't signify, as the point is that Elizabeth should be free. So it was Monday, and Aunt Jane—it's me talking again—had the tea-party at which you played 'Poissons d'Or'. And when it (the goldfish) was finished Mrs. Lucas gave a great sigh, and said ' Poor Georgino ? Wasting his time over that rubbish,' though she knew quite well that I had given it you. And so I said : ' Would you quite call it rubbish, do you think ? ' and she said : ' Quite. Every rule of music is violated. Don't those inverted fifths make you wince, Miss Bracely ? ' "

Olga laughed again, and spoke in her own voice.

" Oh, Georgie, she is an ass," she said. " What she meant, I suppose, was consecutive fifths : you can't invert a fifth. So I said (I really meant it as a joke) : ' Of course there is that, but you must forgive Debussy that for the sake of that wonderful passage of submerged tenths ! ' And she took it quite gravely, and shook her head, and said she was afraid she was a purist. What happened next ? That's all I know."

" Directly afterwards," said Georgie, greedily, " she brought the music to me, and asked me to show her where the passage of submerged tenths came. I didn't know, but I found some tenths, and she

brightened up and said : ' Yes, it is true : those
submerged tenths are very impressive.' Then I suggested that the submerged tenth was not a musical
expression, but referred to the population. On which
she said no more, but when she went away she asked
me to lend her Dalston's Manual of ' Harmony.' I
daresay she is looking for anything about tenths still."

Olga lit a cigarette and became grave again.

" Well, it can't go on," she said. " We can't have the
poor thing feeling angry and out of it. Then there was
Mrs. Quantock absolutely refusing to let her see the
Princess——"

" That was her own fault," said Georgie. " It was
because she was so greedy about the Guru."

" That makes it all the bitterer. And I can't do
anything because she blames me for it all. I would
ask her and her Peppino here every night, and listen
to her dreary tunes all evening, and let her have it
all her own way, if it would do any good. But things
have gone too far : she wouldn't come. It has all
happened without my noticing it. I never added it
all up as it went along, and I hate it."

Georgie thought of the spiritualistic truths.

" If you're an incarnation," he said, in a sudden glow
of admiration, " you're the incarnation of an angel.
How you can forgive her odious manners to you——"

" My dear, shut up," said Olga. " We've got to do
something. Now how would it be if you gave a nice
party on Christmas night, and asked her at once ?
Ask her to help you in getting it up : make it clear
she's going to run it."

" All right. You'll come, won't you ? "

" Certainly I will not. Perhaps I will come in afterwards with Goosie or some one of that sort. Don't
you see it would spoil it all if I was at dinner ? You

must, rather pointedly, leave me out. Give her a nice, expensive, refined Christmas present too. You might give her that picture you're doing of me—no, I suppose she wouldn't like that. But just comfort her and make her feel you can't get on without her. You've been her right hand all these years. Make her give her tableaux again, and oh, I think you must ask me in afterwards. I long to see her and Peppino as Brünnhilde and Siegfried. Just attend to her, Georgie, and buck her up. Promise me you will. And do it as if your heart was in it, otherwise it's no good."

Georgie began packing up his paint-box. This was not the plan he had hoped for on Christmas Day, but if Olga wished this, it had got to be done.

" Well, I'll do my best," he said.

" Thanks ever so much. You're a darling. And how is your planchette getting on ? I've been lazy about my crystal, but I get so tired of my own nose."

" Planchette would write nothing but a few names," said Georgie, omitting the fact that Olga's was the most frequent. " I think I shall drop it."

This was but reasonable, for since Riseholme had some new and absorbing excitement every few weeks, to say nothing of the current excitement of daily life, it followed that even the most thrilling pursuits could not hold the stage for very long. Still, the interest in spiritualism had died down with the rapidity of the seed on stony ground.

" Even Mrs. Quantock seems to have cooled," said Olga. " She and her husband were here last night, but she looked rather bored when I suggested table-turning. I wonder if anything has happened to put her off it ? "

" What do you think could have ? " asked Georgie, with Riseholme alacrity.

" Georgie, do you really believe in the Princess and Pocky ? " she asked.

Georgie looked round to see that there was no one within hearing.

" I did at the time," he said; " at least, I think I did. But it seems less likely now. Who was the Princess, anyway ? Why didn't we ever hear of her before ? I believe Mrs. Quantock met her in the train or something."

" So do I," said Olga. " But not a word. It makes Aunt Jane and Uncle Jacob completely happy to believe in it all. Their lines of life are enormous, and they won't die till they're over a hundred. Now go and see Mrs. Lucas, and if she doesn't ask you to lunch you can come back here."

Georgie put down his picture and painting apparatus at his house, and went on to Lucia's, definitely conscious that though he did not want to have her to dinner on Christmas Day, or to go back to his duets and his A.D.C. duties, there was a spice and savour in so doing that came entirely from the fact that Olga wished him to, that by this service he was pleasing her. In itself it was distasteful, in itself it tended to cut him off from her, if he had to devote his time to Lucia, but he still delighted in doing it. " I believe I am falling in love with her," said Georgie to himself. " She's wonderful ; she's big ; she's——"

At that moment his thoughts were violently diverted, for Robert Quantock came out of his house in a violent hurry, merely scowled at Georgie, and positively trotted across the green in the direction of the newsagent's. Instantly Georgie recollected that he had seen him there already this morning before his visit to Olga, buying a new twopenny paper, in a yellow cover, called *Todd's News*. They had had

a few words of genial conversation, and what could
have happened in the last two hours that made Robert
merely gnash his teeth at Georgie now, and make a
second visit to the paper-shop? It was impossible not
to linger a moment, in order to see what Robert did
when he got to the paper-shop, and with the aid of his
spectacles Georgie perceived that he presently loaded
himself with a whole packet of papers in yellow covers,
presumably *Todd's News*. Flesh and blood could
not resist the cravings of curiosity, and making a
detour, so as to avoid being gnashed at again by
Robert, who was coming rapidly back in his direction, he strolled round to the paper-shop himself, and
asked for a copy of *Todd's News*. Instantly the
bright December morning grew dark with mystery,
for the proprietor told him that Mr. Quantock had
bought every copy he possessed of it. No further
information could be obtained, except that he
had bought a copy of every other daily paper as
well.

Georgie could make nothing whatever of this, and
having observed Robert hurrying into his house
again, went on his own errand to Lucia. Had he seen
what Robert did when he got home, it is doubtful if
he could have avoided breaking into the house and
snatching a copy of *Todd's News* from him. . . .

Robert went to his study, and locked the door. He
drew out from under his blotting-pad the first copy
of *Todd's News*, that he had bought earlier in the
morning, and put it with the rest. Then, with a
furrowed brow, he turned to the police-reports in the
Times, and, after looking at them, laid the paper
down. He did the same to the *Daily Telegraph*, the
Daily Mail, the *Morning Post*, the *Daily Chronicle*.
Finally (this was the last of the daily papers), he

perused the *Daily Mirror*, tore it in shreds, and said
" Damn."

He sat for a while in profound thought, trying to recollect if anybody in Riseholme except Colonel Boucher
took in the *Daily Mirror*. But he felt morally certain
that no one did, and letting himself out of his study,
and again locking the door after him, he went into
the street, and saw at a glance that the Colonel was
employed in whirling Mrs. Weston round the green.
Instead of joining them, he hurried to the Colonel's
house, and, for this was no time for half measures,
fixed Atkinson with his eye, and said he would like
to write a note to Colonel Boucher. He was shown
into his sitting-room, and saw the *Daily Mirror* lying
open on the table. As soon as he was left alone, he
stuffed it into his pocket, told Atkinson he would
speak to the Colonel instead of writing a note, and
intercepted the path of the bath-chair. He was nearly
run over, but stood his ground, and in a perfectly
firm voice asked the Colonel if there was any news
in the morning papers. With the Colonel's decided
negative ringing joyfully in his ears, he went home
again, and locked himself for the second time into his
study.

There is a luxury, when some fell danger has been
averted by promptness and presence of mind, in living
through the moment of that danger again, and Robert
opened *Todd's News* (for that gave the fuller account),
and read over the paragraph in the Police news
headed " Bogus Russian Princess." But now he
gloated over the lines which had made him shudder
before, when he read how Marie Lowenstein, of 15,
Gerald Street, Charing Cross Road, calling herself
Princess Popoffski, had been brought up at the Bow
Street Police Court for fraudulently professing to tell

fortunes and produce materialized spirits at a séance in her flat. Sordid details followed : a detective who had been there seized an Italian apparition by the throat, and turned on the electric light. It was the woman Popoffski's throat that he held, and her secretary, Hezekiah Schwarz, was discovered under the table detaching an electric hammer. A fine was inflicted. . . .

A moment's mental debate was sufficient to determine Robert not to tell his wife. It was true that she had produced Popoffski, but then he had praised and applauded her for that : he, no less than she, had been convinced of Popoffski's integrity, high rank and marvellous psychic powers, and together they had soared to a pinnacle of greatness in the Riseholme world. Besides, poor Daisy would be simply flattened out if she knew that Popoffski was no better than the Guru. He glanced at the tall pile of *Todd's News* and at the grate. . . .

It had been a cold morning, clear and frosty, and a good fire prospered in the grate. Out of each copy of *Todd's News* he tore the page on which were printed the police reports, and fed the fire with them. Page after page he put upon it : never had so much paper been devoted to one grate. Up the chimney they flew in sheets of flame : sometimes he was afraid he had set it on fire, and he had to pause, shielding his scorched face, until the hollow rumbling had died down. With the page from two copies of the *Daily Mirror*, the holocaust was over, and he unlocked the door again. No one in Riseholme knew but he, and no one should ever know. Riseholme had been electrified by spiritualism, and even now the séances had been cheap at the price.

The debris of all these papers he had removed by

the housemaid, and this was hardly done when his
wife came in from the green.

" I thought there was a chimney on fire, Robert,"
she said.   " You would have liked it to be the kitchen-
chimney, as you said the other day."

" Stuff and nonsense, my dear," said he.   " Lunch-
time, isn't it ? "

" Yes.   Ah, there's the post.   None for me, and
two for you."

She looked at him narrowly as he took his letters.
Perhaps their subconscious minds (according to her
dear friend's theory) held communication, but only
the faintest unintelligible ripple of that appeared
on the surface.

" I haven't heard from my Princess since she went
away," she remarked.

Robert gave a slight start : he was a little off his
guard from the reaction after his anxiety.

" Indeed ! " he said.   " Have you written to her ? "
She appeared to try to remember.

" Well, I really don't believe I have," she said.
" That is remiss of me.   I must send her a long
budget one of these days."

This time he looked narrowly at her.   Had she a
secret, he wondered, as well as he ?   What could it
be ? . . .

Georgie found his mission none too easy, and
it was only the thought that it was a labour of love,
or something very like it, that enabled him to persevere.   Even then for the first few minutes he
thought it might prove love's labour lost, so bright
and unreal was Lucia.

He had half crossed Shakespeare's garden, and
had clearly seen her standing at the window of the

music-room, when she stole away from the window, and next moment the strains of some slow movement, played very loud, drowned the bell on the mermaid's tail so completely that he wondered whether it had rung at all. As a matter of fact, Lucia and Peppino were in the midst of a most serious conversation when Georgie came through the gate, which was concerned with deciding what was to be done. A party at The Hurst some time during Christmas week took place as regularly as the festival itself, but this year everything was so unusual. Who was to be asked, in the first place? Certainly not Mrs. Weston, for she had talked Italian to Lucia in a manner impossible to misinterpret, and probably, so said Lucia with great acidity, she would be playing children's games with her *promesso*. It was equally impossible to ask Miss Bracely and her husband, for relations were already severed, on account of the Spanish Quartet and Signor Cortese, and as for the Quantocks, did Peppino expect Lucia to ask Mrs. Quantock again ever? Then there was Georgie, who had become so different and strange, and . . . Well, here was Georgie. Hastily she sat down at the piano, and Peppino closed his eyes for the slow movement.

The opening of the door was lost on Lucia, and Peppino's eyes were closed. Consequently Georgie sat down on the nearest chair, and waited. At the end Peppino sighed, and he sighed too.

" Who is that? " said Lucia sharply. " Why, is it you, Georgie? What a stranger! Aren't you? Any news? "

This was all delivered in the coldest of tones, and Lucia scratched a morsel of wax off E flat.

" I've heard none," said Georgie, in great discomfort. " I just dropped in."

Lucia fixed Peppino with a glance. If she had shouted at the top of her voice she could not have conveyed more unmistakably that she was going to manage this situation.

" Ah, that is very pleasant," she said. " Peppino and I have been so busy lately that we have seen nobody. We are quite country-cousins, and so the town-mouse must spare us a little cheese. How is dear Miss Bracely now ? "

" Very well," said Georgie. " I saw her this morning."

Lucia gave a sigh of relief.

" That is good," she said. " Peppino, do you hear ? Miss Bracely is quite well. Not overtired with practising that new opera ? *Lucy Greecia*, was it ? Oh, how silly I am ! *Lucretia :* that was it, by that extraordinary Neapolitan. Yes. And what next ? Our good Mrs. Weston, now ! Still thinking about her nice young man ? Making orange-flower wreaths, and choosing bridesmaids ? How naughty I am ! Yes. And then dear Daisy ? How is she ? Still entertaining princesses ? I look in the Court Circular every morning to see if Princess Pop—Pop—Popoff, isn't it ?—if Princess Popoff has popped off to see her cousin the Czar again. Dear me ! "

The amount of malice, envy and nearly all uncharitableness which Lucia managed to put into this quite unrehearsed speech was positively amazing. She had not thought it over beforehand for a moment : it came out with the august spontaneity of lightning leaping from a cloud. Not till that moment had Georgie guessed at a tithe of all that Olga had felt so certain about, and a double emotion took hold of him. He was astounded at Lucia, never having conjectured how she must have suffered before she attained to so superb a sourness, and he adored the intuition that had guessed it and was only sorry for it. The outburst was not quite over yet, though Lucia felt distinctly better.

"And you, Georgie," she said, "though I'm sure we are such strangers that I ought to call you Mr. Pillson—what have you been doing ? Playing Miss Bracely's accompaniments, and sewing wedding-dresses all day, and raising spooks all night ? Yes."

Lucia had caught this " Yes " from Lady Amber-mere, having found it peculiarly obnoxious. You laid down a proposition, or asked a question, and then confirmed it yourself.

"And Mr. Cortese," she said, "is he still roaring out his marvellous English and Italian ? Yes. What a full life you lead, Georgie ! I suppose you have no time for your painting now."

This was not a bow drawn at a venture, for she had seen Georgie come out of Old Place with his paint-box and drawing-board, but this direct attack on him did not lessen the power of the "sweet charity" which had sent him here. He blew the bugle to rally all the good-nature of which he was capable.

"No, I've been painting just lately," he said ; "at least, I have been trying to. I'm doing a little sketch of Miss Bracely at her piano, which I want to give her on Christmas Day. But it's so difficult. I wish I had brought it round to ask your advice, but you'd only have screamed with laughter at it. It's a dreadful failure : much worse than those I gave you for your birthdays. Fancy your keeping them still in your lovely music-room. Send them to the pantry, and I'll do something better for your next birthday."

Lucia, try as she might, could not help being rather

touched by this. There they all were: " Golden
Autumn Woodland," " Bleak December," " Yellow
Daffodils " and " Roses of Summer." . . .

" Or have them blacked over by the boot-boy,"
she said. " Take them down, Georgie, and let us
send them to be blacked."

This was much better: there was playfulness
behind the sarcasm now, which peeped out from it.
He made the most of that.

" We'll do that presently," he said. " Just now I
want to engage you and Peppino to dine with me on
Christmas Day. Now don't be tarsome and say
you're engaged. But one can never tell with you."

" A party ? " asked Lucia suspiciously.

" Well, I thought we would have just one of our
old evenings again," said Georgie, feeling himself
remarkably clever. " We'll have the Quantocks,
shan't we, and Colonel and Mrs. Colonel, and you and
Peppino and me, and Mrs. Rumbold. That'll make
eight, which is more than Foljambe likes, but she
must lump it. Mr. Rumbold is always singing
carols all Christmas evening with the choir, and she
will be alone."

" Ah, those carols ! said Lucia, wincing.

" I know : I will provide you with little wads of
cotton-wool. Do come ; we'll have just a party of
eight. I've asked no one else yet : perhaps nobody
will come. I want you and Peppino, and the rest
may come or stop away. Do say you approve."

Lucia could not yield at once. She had to press her
finger to her forehead.

" So kind of you, Georgie," she said, " but I must
think. Are we doing anything on Christmas night,
carissimo ? Where's your engagement-book. Go and
consult it."

This was a grand manœuvre, for hardly had Peppino left the room when she started up with a little scream and ran after him.

"Me so stupid," she cried. "Me put it in smoky-room, and poor *caro* will look for it ever so long. Back in minute, Georgino."

Naturally this was perfectly clear to Georgie. She wanted to have a short private consultation with Peppino, and he waited rather hopefully for their return, for Peppino, he felt sure, was bored with this Achilles-attitude of sitting sulking in the tent. They came back wreathed in smiles, and instantly embarked on the question of what to do after dinner. No romps : certainly not, but why not the tableaux again ?

The question was still under debate when they went in to lunch. It was settled affirmatively during the macaroni, and Lucia said that they all wanted to work her to death, and so get rid of her. They had thought—she and Peppino—of having a little holiday on the Riviera, but anyhow they would put it off till after Christmas. Georgie's mouth was full of crashing toast at the moment, and he could only shake his head. But as soon as the toast could be swallowed, he made the usual reply with great fervour.

Georgie was hardly at all complacent when he walked home afterwards and thought how extremely good-natured he had been, for he could not but feel that this marvellous forbearance was a sort of mistletoe-growth on him, quite foreign really to his nature. Never before had Lucia showed so shrewish and venomous a temper ; he had not thought her capable of it. For the gracious queen, there was substituted a snarling fish-wife, but then as Georgie calmly pursued the pacific mission of comfort to which

Olga had ordained him, how the fish-wife wrinkles
had been smoothed out and the asps divorced from
her tongue! Had his imagination ever pictured
Lucia saying such things to him, it would have supplied
him with no sequel but a complete severance of
relations between them. Instead of that he had
consulted and truckled to her . . . truckled : yes,
he had truckled, and he was astonished at himself.
Why had he truckled ?

And the beautiful mouth and kindly eyes of Olga
supplied the answer. Certainly he must drop in at
once, and tell her the result of the mission. Perhaps
she would reward him by calling him a darling again.
Really he deserved that she should say something
nice to him.

It was a day of surprises for Georgie. He found
Olga at home, and recounted, without losing any of
the substance, the sarcasms of Lucia, and his own
amazing tact and forbearance. He did not comment :
he just narrated the facts in the vivid Riseholme
manner, and waited for his reward.

Olga looked at him a moment in silence.

" Oh, poor Mrs. Lucas ! " she said. " She must
have been miserable to have behaved like that !
I am so sorry. Now what else can you do, Georgie,
to make her feel better ? "

" I think I've done everything that could have been
required of *me*," said Georgie. " It was all I could
do to keep my temper at all. I will give my party
at Christmas, because I promised you I would."

" Oh, but it's ten days to Christmas yet," said
Olga. " Can't you paint her portrait, and give it
her for a present. Oh, I think you could, playing
the Moonlight Sonata."

Georgie felt terribly inclined to be offended and tell

Olga that she was tired of him ; or to be dignified and say he was unusually busy. Never had he shown such forbearance towards downright rudeness as he had shown to Lucia, and though he had done that for Olga's sake, she seemed to be without a single spark of gratitude, but continued to urge her request.

" Do paint a little picture of her," she repeated. " She would love it : and make her young and interesting. Think over it anyhow : perhaps you'll think of something better than that. And now won't you go and secure all your guests for Christmas at once ? "

Georgie turned to leave the room, but just as he got to the door she spoke again.

" I think you're a brick," she said.

Somehow this undemonstrative expression of approval began to glow in Georgie's heart as he walked home. Apparently she took it for granted that he was going to behave with all the perfect tact and good-temper that he had shown. It did not surprise her in the least : she had almost forgotten to indicate that she had noticed it at all. And that, as he thought about it, seemed a far deeper compliment than if she had told him how wonderful he was. She took it for granted, neither more nor less, that he would be kind and pleasant whatever Lucia said. He had not fallen short of her standard. . . .

CHAPTER XV

GEORGIE'S Christmas guests had just taken their
seats at his round table without a cloth, and he hoped
that Foljambe would be quick with the champagne,
because there had been rather a long wait before
dinner, owing to Lucia and Peppino being late, and
conversation had been a little jerky. Lucia, as usual,
had sailed into the room without a word of apology,
for she was accustomed to come last when she went
out to dinner, and on her arrival dinner was always
announced immediately. The few seconds that intervened were employed by her in saying just one kind
word to everybody. To-night, however, the kind
words had not been received with the gratified
responses to which she was accustomed : there was a
different atmosphere abroad, and it was as if she was no
more than one-eighth of the entire party. . . . But it
would never do to hurry Foljambe, who was a little
upset already by the fact of there being eight to
dinner, which was two more than she approved of.

Lucia was on Georgie's right, Mrs. Colonel (as she
had decided to call herself) on his left. Next her was
Peppino, then Mrs. Quantock, then the Colonel, then
Mrs. Rumbold (who resembled a grey suspicious
mouse), and Mr. Quantock completed the circle round
to Lucia again. Everyone had a small bunch of
violets in the napkin, but Lucia had the largest. She
had also a footstool.

" Capital good soup," remarked Mr. Quantock.
" Can't get soup like this at home."

There was dead silence. Why was there never a
silence when Olga was there? wondered Georgie.
It wasn't because she talked : she somehow caused
other people to talk.

" Tommy Luton hasn't got measles," said Mrs.
Weston. " I always said he hadn't, though there
are measles about. He came to work as usual this
morning, and is going to sing in the carols to-
night."

She suddenly stopped.

Georgie gave an imploring glance at Foljambe, and
looked at the champagne glasses. Foljambe took no
notice. Lucia turned to Georgie, with an elbow on
the table between her and Mr. Quantock.

" And what news, Georgie ? " she said. " Peppino
and I have been so busy that we haven't seen
a soul all day. What have you been doing. Any
planchette ? "

She looked brightly at Mrs. Quantock.

" Yes, dear Daisy, I needn't ask you what you've
been doing. Table-turning, I expect. I know how
interested you are in psychical matters. I should
be, too, if only I could be certain that I was not
dealing with fraudulent people."

Georgie felt inclined to give a hollow groan and
sink under the table when this awful polemical rhetoric
began. To his unbounded surprise Mrs. Quantock
answered most cordially.

" You are quite right, dear Lucia," she said.
" Would it not be terrible to find that a medium,
some dear friend perhaps, whom one implicitly trusted,
was exposed as fraudulent ? One sees such exposures
in the paper sometimes. I should be miserable if

I thought I had ever sat with a medium who was not honest. They fine the wretches well though, if they are caught, and they deserve it."

Georgie observed, and could not the least understand, a sudden blank look cross Robert's face. For the moment he looked as if he was dead but had been beautifully stuffed. But Georgie gave but a cursory thought to that, for the amazing supposition dawned on him that Lucia had not been polemical at all, but was burying instead of chopping with the hatchet. It was instantly confirmed, for Lucia took her elbow off the table and turned to Robert.

" You and dear Daisy have been very lucky in your spiritualistic experiences," she said. " I hear on all sides what a charming medium you had. Georgie quite lost his heart to her."

" 'Pon my word, and she was delightful," said Robert. " Of course she was a dear friend of Daisy's, but one has to be very careful when one hears of the dreadful exposures, as my wife said, that occur sometimes. Fancy finding that a medium whom you believed to be perfectly honest had yards and yards of muslin and a false nose or two concealed about her. It would sicken me of the whole business."

A loud pop announced that Foljambe had allowed them all some champagne at last, but Georgie hardly heard it, for glancing up at Daisy Quantock he observed that the same dead and stuffed look had come over her face which he had just now noticed on her husband's countenance. Then they both looked up at each other with a glance that to him bristled with mystery. An agonized questioning, an imploring petition for silence seemed to inspire it : it was as if each had unwittingly made some hopeless *faux pas*. Then they instantly looked away from each other again ; their necks seemed to crack with the rapidity with which they turned them right and left, and they burst into torrents of speech to the grey suspicious mouse and the Colonel respectively.

Georgie was utterly mystified : his Riseholme instinct told him that there was something below all this, but his Riseholme instinct could not supply the faintest clue as to what it was. They both knew something about the Princess, but surely if Daisy had read in the paper that the Princess had been exposed and fined, she would not have touched on so dangerous a subject. Then the curious incident about *Todd's News* irresistibly occurred to him, but that would not fit the case, since it was Robert and not Daisy who had bought that inexplicable number of the yellow print. And then Robert had hinted at the discovery of yards and yards of muslin and a false nose. Why had he done that unless he had discovered them, or unless . . . Georgie's eyes grew round with the excitement of the chase . . . unless Robert had some reason to suspect the integrity of the dear friend, and had said this at pure haphazard. In that case what was Robert's reason for suspicion ? Had *he*, not Daisy, read in the paper of some damaging disclosure, and had Daisy (also having reason to suspect the Princess) alluded to the damaging exposures in the paper by pure haphazard ? Anyhow, they had both looked dead and stuffed when the other alluded to frauds by mediums, and both had said how lucky their experiences had been. Oh !—Georgie almost said it aloud—what if Robert had seen a damaging exposure in *Todd's News,* and therefore bought up every copy that was to be had ? Then, indeed, he would look dead and stuffed when Daisy alluded to damaging exposures in the paper. Had a stray copy escaped him, and did Daisy know ? What did Robert know ? Had they exquisite secrets from each other ?

Lucia was being talked to across him by Mrs. Weston, who had also pinned down the attention of Peppino on the other side of her. At that precise moment the flood of Mrs. Quantock's spate of conversation to the Colonel dried up, and Robert could find nothing more to say to the grey mouse. Georgie in this backwater of his own thoughts was whirled into the current again. But before he sank he caught Mrs. Quantock's eye and put a question that arose from his exciting backwater.

" Have you heard from the Princess lately ? " he asked.

Robert's head went round with the same alacrity with which he had turned it away.

" Oh, yes," said she. " Two days ago, was it, Robert ? "

" I heard yesterday," said Robert.

Mrs. Quantock looked at her husband with an eager, encouraging earnestness.

" So you did ! " she said. " I'm getting jealous. Interesting, dear ? "

" Yes, dear ; haw, haw," said Robert, and again their eyes met. This time Georgie had no doubts at all. They were playing the same game : they smiled and smirked at each other. They had not been playing the same game before. Now they recognized that there was a conspiracy between them. . . . But he was host : his business for the moment was to make his guests comfortable, and not pry into their inmost bosoms. So before Mrs. Weston realized that she had the whole table attending to her, he said :

" I shall get it out of him after dinner. And I'll tell you, Mrs. Quantock."

" Before Atkinson came to the Colonel," said Mrs.
Weston, " and that was five years before Elizabeth
came to me—let me see, was it five or was it four
and a half ?—four and a half we'll say—he had another
servant, whose name was Ahab Crow."

" No ! " said Georgie.

" Yes ! " said Mrs. Weston, hastily finishing her
champagne, for she saw Foljambe coming near.
" Yes, Ahab Crow. He married too, just like Atkinson is going to, and that's an odd coincidence in itself.
I tell the Colonel that if Ahab Crow hadn't married
he would be with him still, and who can say that he'd
have fancied Elizabeth. And if he hadn't, I don't
believe that the Colonel and I would ever have—well,
I'll leave that alone to spare my blushes. But that's
not what I was saying. Whom do you think Ahab
Crow married ? You can have ten guesses each,
and you would never come right, for it can't be a
common   name.   It   was   Miss   Jackdaw.   Crow :
Jackdaw. I never heard anything like that, and if
you ask the Colonel about it, he'll confirm every word
I said. Boucher : Weston—why that's quite commonplace in comparison, and I'm sure that's an event
enough for me."

Lucia gave her silvery laugh.

" Dear Mrs. Weston," she said, " you must really
tell me at once when the happy day will be.   Peppino
and I are thinking of going to the Riviera——"

Georgie broke in.

" You shan't do anything of the kind," he said.
" What's to happen to us ? 'Oo vewy selfish, Lucia ! "

The conversation broke up again into duets and
trios, and Lucia could have a private conversation
with her host. But half an hour ago, so Georgie reflected, they had all been walking round each other

like dogs going on tiptoe with their tails very tightly
curled, and growling gently to themselves, aware that
a hasty snap, or the breach of the smallest observance
of etiquette, might lead to a general quarrel. But
now they all had the reward of their icy politenesses :
there was no more ice, except on their plates, and the
politeness was not a matter of etiquette. At present
they might be considered a republic, but no one knew
what was going to happen after dinner. Not a word
had been said about the tableaux.

Lucia dropped her voice as she spoke to him, and
put in a good deal of Italian for fear she might be
overheard.

" *Non cognosce* anybody ? " she asked. " *I tab-
lini*, I mean. And are we all to sit in the *aula*, while
the *salone* is being got ready ? "

" *Si*," said Georgie. " There's a fire. When you
go out, keep them there. *I domestichi* are making
salone ready."

" *Molto bene.* Then Peppino and you and I just
steal away. *La lampa* is acting beautifully. We
tried it over several times."

" Everybody's tummin'," said Georgie, varying the
cipher.

" Me so *nervosa !* " said Lucia. " Fancy me doing
Brünnhilde before opera-Brünnhilde. Me can't bear
it."

Georgie knew that Lucia had been thrilled and
delighted to know that Olga so much wanted to
come in after dinner and see the tableaux, and he found
it quite easy to induce Lucia to nerve herself up to an
ordeal so passionately desired. Indeed he himself
was hardly less excited at the thought of being King
Cophetua. . . .

At that moment, even as the crackers were being

handed round, the sound of the carol-singers was heard from outside, and Lucia had to wince as " Good King Wenceslas looked out." When the Page and the King sang their speeches, the other voices grew soft, so that the effect was of a solo voice accompanied. When the Page sang, Lucia shuddered.

" That's the small red-haired boy who nearly deafens me in church," she whispered to Georgie. " Don't you hope his voice will crack soon ? "

She said this very discreetly, so as not to hurt Mrs. Rumbold's feelings, for she trained the choir. Everyone knew that the King was Mr. Rumbold, and said " Charming " to each other, after he had sung.

" I liked that boy's voice, too," said Mrs. Weston. " Tommy Luton used to have a lovely voice, but this one's struck me as better trained even than Tommy Luton's. Great credit to you, Mrs. Rumbold."

The grey suspicious mouse suddenly gave a shrill cackle of a laugh, quite inexplicable. Then Georgie guessed.

He got up.

" Now nobody must move," he said, " because we haven't drunk ' Absent friends ' yet. I'm just going out to see that the singers have a bit of supper in the kitchen before they go on."

His trembling legs would scarcely carry him to the door, and he ran out. There were half a dozen little choir-boys, four men, and one tall cloaked woman. . . .

" Divine ! " he said to Olga. " Aunt Jane thought your voice very well-trained. Come in soon, won't you ? "

" Yes : all flourishing ? "

" Swimming," said Georgie. " Lucia hoped your voice would crack soon. But it's all being lovely."

He explained about food in the kitchen, and hurried back to his guests. There was the riddle of the Quantocks to solve : there were the tableaux imminent : there was the little red-haired boy coming in soon. What a Christmas night !

Soon after Georgie's hall began to fill up with guests, and yet not a word was said about tableaux. It grew so full that nobody could have said for certain whether Lucia and Peppino and he were there or not. Olga certainly was ; there was no mistaking that fact. And then Foljambe opened the drawing-room door and sounded a gong. . . .

The lamp behaved perfectly, and an hour later one Brünnhilde was being extremely kind to the other as they sat together.

"If you really want to know my view, dear Miss Bracely," said Lucia, "it's just that. You must *be* Brünnhilde for the time being. Singing, of course, as you say, helps it out : you can express so much by singing. You are so lucky there. I am bound to say I had qualms when Peppino—or was it Georgie ? —suggested we should do Brünnhilde and Siegfried. I said it would be so terribly difficult. Slow : it has to be slow, and to keep gestures slow when you cannot make them mere illustrations of what you say—well, I am sure it is very kind of you to be so flattering about it—but it is difficult to do that."

"And you thought them all out for yourself ? " said Olga. "Marvellous ! "

"Ah, if I had ever seen you do it," said Lucia, "I am sure I should have picked up some hints ! And King Cophetua ! Won't you give me a little word for our dear King Cophetua ? I was so glad, after the strain of Brünnhilde, to have my back to the audience.

Even then there is the difficulty of keeping quite still, but I am sure you know that better than I do, from having done Brünnhilde yourself. Georgie was very much impressed by your performance of it. And Mary Queen of Scots now! The shrinking of the flesh, and the resignation of the spirit! That is what I tried to express. You must come and help me next time I attempt this sort of thing again. That will not be quite soon, I am afraid, for Peppino and I are thinking of going to the Riviera for a little holiday."

" Oh, but how selfish ! " said Olga. " You mustn't do that ! "

Lucia gave the silvery laugh.

" You are all very tiresome about my going to the Riviera," she said. " But I don't promise that I shall give it up yet. We shall see ! Gracious ! How late it is. We must have sat very long over dinner. Why were not you asked to dinner, I wonder ! I shall scold Georgie for not asking you ! Ah, there is dear Mrs. Weston going away. I must say good-night to her. She would think it very strange if I did not. Colonel Boucher too ! Oh, they are coming this way to save us the trouble of moving."

A general move was certainly taking place, not in the direction of the door, but to where Olga and Lucia were sitting.

" It's snowing," said Piggy excitedly to Olga. " Will ou mark my footsteps well, my page ? "

" Piggy, you—you Goosie," said Olga hurriedly. " Goosie, weren't the tableaux lovely ? "

" And the carols," said Goosie. " I adored the carols. I guessed. Did you guess, Mrs. Lucas ? "

Olga resorted to the mean trick of treading on Goosie's foot, and apologizing. That was cowardly,

because it was sure to come out sometime. And
Goosie again trod on dangerous ground by saying
that if the Page had trodden like that, there was no
need for any footsteps to be marked by the King.

It was snowing fast, and Mrs. Weston's wheels left
a deep track, but in spite of that Daisy and Robert
had not gone fifty yards from the door when they
came to a full stop.

" Now what is it ? " said Daisy. " Out with it.
Why did you talk about the discovery of muslin ? "

" I only said that we were fortunate in a medium,
whom, after all, you picked up at a vegetarian restaurant," said he. " I suppose I may indulge in
general conversation. If it comes to that, why did
you talk about exposure in the papers ? "

" Generalconversation," said Mrs. Quantock, all
in one word. " So that's all, is it ? "

" Yes," said Robert. " You may know something,
and——"

" Now don't put it all on me," said Daisy. " If
you want to know what I think, it is that you've
got some secret."

" And if you want to know what I think," he
retorted, " it is that I know you have."

Daisy hesitated a moment : the snow was white
on her shoulder, and she shook her cloak.

" I hate concealment," she said. " I found yards
and yards of muslin and a pair of Amadeo's eyebrows in that woman's bedroom the very day she
went away ! "

" And she was fined last Thursday for holding a
séance, at which a detective was present," said Robert.
" 15, Gerard Street. He seized Amadeo or Cardinal
Newman by the throat, and it was that woman."

She looked hastily round.

"When you thought that the chimney was on fire, I was burning muslin," she said.

"When you thought the chimney was on fire, I was burning every copy of *Todd's News*," said he. "Also a copy of the *Daily Mirror*, which contained the case. It belonged to the Colonel. I stole it."

She put her hand through his arm.

"Let's get home," she said. "We must talk it over. No one knows one word, except you and me?"

"Not one, my dear!" said Robert cordially. "But there are suspicions. Georgie suspects, for instance. He saw me buy all the copies of *Todd's News*; at least he was hanging about. To-night he was clearly on the track of something, though he gave us a very tolerable dinner."

They went into Robert's study: it was cold, but neither felt it, for they glowed with excitement and enterprise.

"That was a wonderful stroke of yours, Robert," said she. "It was masterly: it saved the situation. The *Daily Mirror*, too; how right you were to steal it. An inquisitive paper, I always thought. Yes, Georgie suspects something, but luckily he doesn't know what he suspects."

"That's why we both said we had just heard from that woman," said Robert.

"Of course. You haven't got a copy of *Todd's News*, have you?"

"No; at least I burned every page of the police reports," said he. "It was safer."

"Quite so. I cannot show you Amadeo's eyebrows for the same reason Nor the muslin. Lovely muslin, my dear: yards of it. . . Now what we must do is this: We must continue to be interested in psychical things : we mustn't drop them, or seem to be put off them. I wish now I had taken you into my confidence at the beginning and told you about Amadeo's eyebrows."

" My dear, you acted for the best," said he. " So did I when I didn't tell you about *Todd's News*. Secrecy even from each other was more prudent, until it became impossible. And I think we should be wise to let it be understood that we hear from the Princess now and then. Perhaps in a few months, she might even visit us again. It—it would be humorous to be behind the scenes, so to speak, and observe the credulity of the others."

Daisy broke into a broad grin.

" I will certainly ask dear Lucia to a séance, if we do," she said. " Dear me ! How late it is : there was such a long wait between the tableaux. But we must keep our eye on Georgie, and be careful how we answer his impertinent questions. He is sure to ask some. About asking that woman down again, Robert. It might be foolhardly, for we've had an escape, and shouldn't put our neck into the same noose again. On the other hand, it would disarm suspicion for ever if, after a few months, I asked her to spend a few days of holiday here. You said it was a fine only, not imprisonment ? "

The week was a busy one ; Georgie, in particular, never had a moment to himself. The Hurst, so lately a desert, suddenly began to rejoice with joy and singing, and broke out into all manner of edifying gaieties. Lucia, capricious queen, quite forgot all the vitriolic things she had said to him, and gave him to understand that he was just as high in favour as ever before, and he was as busy with his duties as ever he had been. Whether he would have fallen into his old place so

readily if he had been a free agent was a question that
did not arise, for though it was Lucia who employed
him, it was Olga who drove him there. But he had
his consolation, for Lucia's noble forgiveness of all the
disloyalties against her included Olga's as well, and
out of all the dinners and music parties, and recitations
from Peppino's new book of prose-poems, which was
already in proof, and was read to select audiences from
end to end, there was none to which Olga was not
bidden, and none at which she failed to appear. Lucia
even overlooked the fact that she had sung in the
carols on Christmas night, though she had herself
declared that it was the voice of the red-haired boy
which was so peculiarly painful to her. Georgie's
picture of her (she never knew that Olga had really
commissioned it) hung at the side of the piano in the
music-room, where the print of Beethoven had hung
before, and it gave her the acutest gratification. It
represented her sitting, with eyes cast down at her
piano, and was, indeed, much on the same scheme as
the yet unfinished one of Olga, which had been post-
poned in its favour, but there was no time for Georgie
to think out another position, and his hand was "in"
with regard to the perspective of pianos. So there it
hung, with its title, " The Moonlight Sonata," printed
in gilt letters on its frame, and Lucia, though she continued to say that he had made her far, far too young,
could not but consider that he had caught her expression exactly. . . . .

So Riseholme flocked back to The Hurst, like sheep
that have been astray, for it was certain to find Olga
there, even as it had hurried there, deeply breathing,
to the classes of the Guru. It had to sit through the
prose-poems of Peppino, it had to listen to the old, old
tunes, and sigh at the end, but Olga mingled her

sighs with theirs, and often, after a suitable pause, Lucia would say winningly to Olga :

" One little song, Miss Bracely ?   Just a stanza ? Or am I trespassing too much on your good-nature ? Where is your accompanist ?   I declare I am jealous of him : I shall pop into his place some day ! Georgino, Miss Bracely is going to sing us something. Is not that a treat ?   Sh-sh, please, ladies and gentlemen."

And she rustled to her place, and sat with the farthest-away expression ever seen on mortal face, while she trespassed on Miss Bracely's good-nature.

Then Georgie had his other picture to finish, which he hoped to get ready in time to be a New Year's present, since Olga had insisted on Lucia's being done first. He had certainly secured an admirable likeness of her, and there was in it just all that his stippled, fussy representation of Lucia lacked. " Bleak December," and " Yellow Daffodils," and the rest of the series lacked it too : for once he had done something in the doing of which he had forgotten himself. It was by no means a work of genius, for Georgie was not possessed of one grain of that, and the talent it displayed was by no means of a high order ; but it had something of the naturalness of a flower that grew from the earth which nourished it.

On the last day of the year he was putting a few final touches to it, little high reflected lights on the black keys, little blacknesses of shadow in the moulding of the panel behind her head. He had finished with her altogether, and now she sat in the window-seat, looking out, and playing with the blind-tassel. He had been so much absorbed in his work that he had scarcely noticed that she had been rather unusually silent.

"I've got a piece of news for you," she said at length.

Georgie held his breath as he drew a very thin line of body-colour along the edge of A flat.

"No! What is it?" he said. "Is it about the Princess?"

Olga seemed to hail this as a diversion.

"Ah, let's talk about that for a minute," she said. "What you ought to have done was to order another copy of *Todd's News* at once."

"I know I ought, but I couldn't get one when I thought of it afterwards. That was tarsome. But I feel sure there was something about her in it."

"And you can't get anything out of the Quantocks?"

"No, though I've laid plenty of traps for them. There's an understanding between them now. They both know something. When I lay a trap, they look at each other."

"What sort of traps?"

"Oh, anything. I say suddenly, 'What a bore it is that there are so many frauds among mediums, especially paid ones.' You see, I don't believe for a moment that these séances were held for nothing, though *we* didn't pay for going to them. And then Robert says that he would never trust a paid medium, and she looks at him approvingly, and says, 'Dear Princess!' The other day it was a very good trap. I said suddenly, 'Is it true that the Princess is coming to stay with Lady Ambermere?' It wasn't a lie: I only asked."

"And then?" said Olga.

"Robert gave an awful twitch: not a jump exactly, but a twitch. But she was on the spot and said, 'Ah, that would be nice. I wonder if it's true? The

Princess didn't mention it in her last letter.' And
then he looked at her approvingly. There is something there, no one shall convince me otherwise."

Olga suddenly burst out laughing.

" What's the matter ? " asked Georgie.

" Oh, it's all so delicious ! " she said. " I never
knew before how terribly interesting little things were.
It's all wildly exciting, and there are fifty things going
on just as exciting. Is it all of you who take such a
tremendous interest in them that makes them so
absorbing, or is it that they are absorbing in themselves, and ordinary dull people, not Riseholmites,
don't see how exciting they are ? Tommy Luton's
measles : the Quantocks' secret : Elizabeth's lover !
And to think that I believed I was coming to a backwater."

Georgie held up his picture and half closed his eyes.

" I believe it's finished," he said. " I shall have it
framed, and put it in my drawing-room."

This was a trap, and Olga fell into it.

" Yes, it will look nice there," she said. " Really,
Georgie, it is very clever of you."

He began washing his brushes.

" And what was your news ? " he said.

She got up from her seat.

" I forgot all about it, with talking of the Quantocks' secret," she said. " That just shows you :
I completely forgot. Georgie, I've just accepted an
offer to sing in America, a four months' engagement,
at fifty thousand million pounds a night. A penny
less, and I wouldn't have gone. But I really can't
refuse. It's all been very sudden, but they want to
produce *Lucretia* there before it appears in England.
Then I come back, and sing in London all the summer.
Oh, me ! "

There was dead silence, while Georgie dried his brushes.

" When do you go ? " he asked.

" In about a fortnight."

" Oh ! " said he.

She moved down the room to the piano and shut it without speaking, while he folded the paper round his finished picture.

" Why don't you come too ? " she said at length. " It would do you no end of good, for you would get out of this darling twopenny place, which will all go inside a nutshell.   There are big things in the world —seas, continents, people, movements, emotions.   I told my Georgie I was going to ask you, and he thoroughly approves.   We both like you, you know. Come for a couple of months, anyhow : of course, you'll be our guest, please."

The world at that moment had grown absolutely black to him, and it was by that that he knew who, for him, was the light of it.   He shook his head.

" Why can't you come ? " she said again.

He looked at her straight in the face.

" Because I adore you," he said.

EPILOGUE OR PREFACE

THE glad word went round Riseholme one March morning that the earliest flower in Perdita's garden was in bloom. The day was one of those glories of the English spring-time, with large white clouds blown across wide spaces of blue sky by the south-west wind, and with swift shadows that bowled across the green below them. Parliament was in full conclave that day, and in the elms the rooks were busy.

An awful flatness had succeeded Olga's departure. Riseholme naturally took a good deal of credit for the tremendous success which had attended the production of *Lucretia* in New York, since it so rightly considered that the real cradle of the opera was here, where she had tried it over for the first time. Lucia seemed to remember it better than anybody, for she could recall all sorts of things which no one else had the faintest recollection of : how she had discussed music with Signor Cortese, and how he had asked her where she had her musical training. Such a treat to talk Italian with a Roman—*lingua Toscana in bocca Romana*—and what a wonderful evening it was ! Poor Mrs. Colonel recollected very little of this, but Lucia had long been aware that her memory was going sadly. . . . After *Lucretia*, Olga had appeared in some of her old rôles, notably in the part of Brünnhilde, and Lucia was very reminiscent of that charming party on Christmas Day at dear Georgino's, when they had the tableaux. Dear Olga was so simple and unspoiled : she had come to Lucia afterwards, and asked her to tell her how she had worked out her scheme of gestures in the awakening, and Lucia had been very glad, very glad indeed, to give her a few hints. In fact, Lucia was quite herself : it was only her subjects whom it had been a little hard to stir up. Georgie, in particular, had been very listless and dull, and Lucia, for all her ingenuity, was at a complete loss to find any reason for it.

But to-day the warm inflowing tide of spring seemed to renovate the muddy flats, setting the weeds, that had lain dank and dispirited, afloating again on the return of the water. No one could quite resist the magic of the season, and Georgie, who had intended, out of mere politeness, to go to see the first of Perdita's stupid flowers (having been warned of its epiphany by telephone from The Hurst), found, when he set foot outside his house on that warm, windy morning, that it would be interesting to stroll across the green first and see if there was any news. All the news he had really cared about for the last two months was news from America, of which he had a small packet done up in a pink riband.

After getting rid of Piggy, he went to the newspaper-shop to get his *Times*, which most unaccountably had not arrived, and the sight of *Todd's News*, in its yellow cover, stirred his drowsy interest. Not one atom of light had ever been thrown on that extraordinary occurrence when Ro'ert bought the whole issue, and though Olga never tailed to inquire, he had not been able to give her the slightest additional information. Occasionally he set a languid trap for one of the Quantocks, but they never by any chance fell into it. The whole affair must be classed, with problems like the origin of evil, among the insoluble mysteries of life.

It was possible to get letters by the second post an hour earlier than the house-to-house delivery by calling at the office, and as Georgie was waiting for his *Times*, Mrs. Quantock came hurrying out of the post-office with a small packet in her hands, which she was opening as she walked. She was so much absorbed in this that she did not see Georgie at all, though she passed quite close to him, and soon after shed a registered envelope. At that, the " old familiar glamour " began to steal over him again, and he found himself wondering with intensity what it contained. . . .

She was now some hundred yards in front of him, walking in the direction of The Hurst, and there could be no doubt that she, too, was on her way to see Perdita's first flower. He followed her, going more briskly than she, and began to catch her up. Soon (this time by accident, not in the manner in which, through eagerness, she had untidily thrown the registered envelope away) she dropped a small paper, and Georgie picked it up, meaning to give it her. It had printing on the outer leaf of it, and was clearly a small pamphlet, and he could not possibly help seeing what that printing was, for it was in capital letters :

" INCREASE YOUR HEIGHT "

Georgie quickened his step, and the old familiar glamour brightened round him. As soon as he got within speaking distance, he called to her, and as she turned round, " like a guilty thing surprised," a little box flew out of her hand. As it fell, the lid came off, and there were scattered on the green grass a multitude of red lozenges.

She gave a cry of dismay.

" Oh ! Mr. Georgie, how you startled me ! " she said. " Do help me to pick them up. Do you think

the damp will have hurt them? Any news? I was
so wrapped up in what I was doing that I've spoken
to nobody."

Georgie assisted in the recovery of the red lozenges.

"You dropped this as you walked," he said. "I
picked it up in order to give it you."

"Oh, that is kind, and did you see what it was?"

"I couldn't help seeing the outside," said Georgie.

She looked at him a moment, wondering what was the
most prudent course. If she only thanked him for re-
storing it to her, he would probably tell everybody. . . .

"Well, then I shall let you into the whole secret,"
she said. "It's the most wonderful invention, and
increases your height, whatever your age is, from two
to six inches. Fancy! There are some exercises you
have to do, rather like those Yoga ones, every
morning, and you eat three lozenges a day. Quite
harmless they are, and then you soon begin to shoot
up. It sounds incredible, doesn't it, but there are
so many testimonials that I can't doubt it is genuine.
Here's one of a man who grew six inches. I saw it
advertised in some paper and sent for it. Only a
guinea! What fun when Robert begins to see that
I am taller than he is! But now not a word! Don't
tell dear Lucia, whatever you do. She is half a head
taller than I, and it would be no fun if everybody grew
from two to six inches. You may write for them, and
I'll give you the address, but you must tell nobody."

"Too wonderful!" said Georgie. "I *shall* watch
you. Here we are. Look, there's Perdita's first
flower. What a beauty!"

It was not necessary to press the mermaid's tail,
for Lucia had seen them from the music-room, and
they heard her high heels clacking over the polished
floor of the hall.

" Listen ! There'll soon be more need of them ! "
said Mrs. Quantock. " And I've got something else
to tell you. Lucia may hear that. Ah, dear Lucia,
what a wonderful Perdita-blossom ! "

" Is it not ? " said Lucia, blowing kisses to Georgie
and giving them to Daisy. " That shows spring is
here. *Primavera !* And Peppino's *piccolo libro* comes
out to-day. I should not be a bit surprised if you
each of you found a copy of it arrive before evening.
Glorious ! It's glorious ! "

Surely it was no wonder that Georgie's blood began
to canter along his arteries again. There had been
very pleasant exciting years before now, requiring for
their fuel no more than there was ready at this moment
to heap on the fire. Mrs. Quantock was on tiptoe, so
to speak, to increase her height. Peppino was just
delivered of a third of these vellum volumes with seals
and tapes outside. Mrs. Weston was going to become
Mrs. Colonel at the end of the week, and at the same
hour and church Elizabeth was going to become Mrs.
Atkinson. Had these things no savour, because——

" How is 'oo," said Georgie, with a sudden flush
of the springtime through him. " Me vewy well, sank
'oo, and me so want to read Peppino's bookie-bookie."

" 'Oo come in," said Lucia. " Evewybody come in.
Now, who's got 'ickle bit news ? "

Mrs. Quantock had been walking on her toes all
across the hall, in anticipation of the happy time when
she would be from two to six inches taller. As Mr. Alder-
stout said, in his convincing pamphlet, the world
assumed a totally different aspect when you were even
two inches taller. She was quite sorry to sit down.

" Is next week very full with you, dear Lucia ? "
she asked.

Lucia pressed her finger to her forehead.

"Monday, Tuesday, Wednesday," she began. "No, not Tuesday. I am doing nothing on Tuesday. You want to be the death of me between you. Why?"

"I hope that my dear friend Princess Popoffski will be staying with me," said Mrs. Quantock. "Do get over your prejudice against spiritualism, and give it a chance. Come to a séance on Tuesday. You too, of course, Georgie: I know better than to invite Lucia without you."

Lucia put on the far-away look which she reserved for the masterpieces of music and for Georgie's hopeless devotion.

"Lovely! That will be lovely!" she said. "Most interesting! I shall come with a perfectly open mind."

Georgie scarcely lamented the annihilation of a mystery. He must have invented the mystery, for it all collapsed like a card-house if the Princess was coming back. The séances had been most remarkable too; and he would have to get out his planchette again.

"And what's going to happen on Wednesday?" he asked Lucia. "All I know is that I've not been asked. Me's offended."

"'Ickle surprise," said Lucia. "You're not engaged that evening, are you? Nor you, dear Daisy? That's lovely. Eight o'clock? No, I think a quarter to. That will give us more time. Shan't tell you what it is."

Mrs. Quantock, grasping her lozenges, wondered how much taller she would be by then. As Lucia played to them, she discreetly drew a lozenge out of the box, and put it into her mouth, in order to begin growing at once. It tasted rather bitter, but not unpleasantly so. . . .